# Julia

# Julia

## the story of a life

## Joan Grindley

This is a work of fiction. Names, characters, places and incidents
either are the product of the author's imagination or are used
fictitiously, and any resemblance to any actual persons, living or
dead, events, or locales is entirely coincidental.

This book was printed in the United States of America.

**To order additional copies of this book, contact:**
Xlibris Corporation
1-888-795-4274
www.Xlibris.com
Orders@Xlibris.com

# BOOK I

# Chapter 1

It is March 1903. Cold harsh winds are swirling around the East River trying to make contact with the large gray vessel making its way into New York Harbor. Julia stands at the rail of the *Catalonia* trying to catch her first glimpse of the Statue of Liberty. She pulls her coat collar up higher under her chin and peers into the early morning mist. She can see the Lady in the distance now along with many small boats, much smaller than the *Catalonia*, scurrying back and forth across the gray expanse of water. After living on this huge ship for almost a month, she revels in the sounds of the harbor and the blast of the ships' horns.

"I am here; I am really here," she shouts into the wind. "This is truly America where George and I will make our life."

Julia's words are carried away by the wind and no one on the deck is even the slightest bit aware of the joy emanating from this beautiful young girl of thirteen years. She stares again at the tall Lady of Liberty in the harbor who seems to be beckoning just to her. Julia first heard about this wondrous lady from her parish priest, Fr. Bergard, back in Budapest, and more recently from some of the older passengers here on the ship, and she is not disappointed. Just looking at her, holding the torch so high in her hand, Julia can feel a lump rising in her throat as she again contemplates the reality that she is now, for the first time in her young life, truly free. No more Julia, the orphaned foster child of Anna and Adam Frye, but Mrs. George Pedesch – wife and free woman in this new land. She can feel the excitement among the other passengers as an officer directs them to line up on the deck in preparation for landing and disembarking.

"Please find your assigned areas," he shouts above the din of milling humanity. "Remember that the areas are assigned according to cabin class, so pay close attention to where you belong."

Those in steerage, like Julia and George, are relegated to the lower decks. George grabs Julia's arm and with their valises in the other, attempts to forge a path in front of him and protect Julia at the same time. When they finally reach the lower decks, they feel like cattle jammed together in a pen. As they struggle to find a place to stand with people pushing and shoving all around them, Julia can hear fear in the cry of a baby struggling to get out of its mother's arms. A shiver runs through her and she moves closer to George.

George remains silent and stays close beside his bride, trying to shield her from the mass of people swarming around them. Julia feels his hand resting firmly on her shoulder, and from the corner of her eye she can see George fending off the approaching crowd with the other hand. People are trying to push past them in a wave, all rushing to get to their places on the deck. The noise gets louder and louder as the crowd surges forward. Children are whimpering and mothers are shushing them. Everyone wants to get a better view of the land and be in the first wave of immigrants to leave the *Catalonia*.

"Hurry, George," Julia shouts now to be heard above the noise, "we must get to our assigned places. I want to be one of the first ones to disembark. We're really in America now. Please, let's hurry."

George follows her without a word. He balances his hold on the two valises and forges a path through the throng ahead of them, using the valises like battering rams in an attempt to make their path easier. They reach their assigned deck, but there are so many people in this one area, it is hard to stay together. Another officer is there trying desperately to maintain order. Everyone is so excited at finally reaching land that the crowd can barely contain itself. With George pushing ahead, they work their way into the front row near the rail. Julia relaxes for a moment and then leans against the rail to stabilize herself. George stays close beside her, holding her arm tightly with his free hand. They stop and wait anxiously for the next announcement to come from the officer in charge.

Julia grips the rail and looks out again on the gray water of New York harbor. As they wait, her mind begins to wander into the past.

It seems like many months have passed since they left their home in Budapest. Her wedding day is still like a bad dream to Julia. She recalls very well how Anna Frye was so eager for her wedding to take place that Julia hardly knew what was happening. She can still hear Anna speaking in her head.

"How lucky you are to be getting such a good husband," Anna reminded her. Julia was illegitimate after all, a fact Anna had let slip one day in a fit of rage. Her mother had been of royal blood – a countess Anna later admitted, who had fallen in love with a commoner.

"Your father was no better than my Adam," she had shrieked. "Royals do not marry the likes of us; so here you are, instead of in a dirty orphanage somewhere. You should thank God every night that me and Adam took you in when your mother begged us," she added with satisfaction. "No one else would have you, I reckon – tall, skinny thing that you are."

On the day of the wedding Anna had insisted that Julia put on the only other clean linen shift she owned and then presented her with a bunch of half-dead flowers gathered from the parched soil of the side garden. She then directed Julia to sit on a bench under the huge beech tree that shaded one corner of the yard and wait there until she called her. The tree was a giant copper beach whose arms spread wide toward the sky and had been in this spot for as long as Julia could remember. On rare occasions when she wasn't being forced to wash floors or clean the privy, she would play blind mans bluff with two of Anna's youngest children under this great old tree. It represented comfort to her and always made her feel safe when she was beneath the vast umbrella of its branches.

The priest, a tall, thin, undernourished-looking man, arrived. He appeared very somber in his tall black hat and long black coat. His heavy, wiry beard reached almost to his waist, and he gave the appearance of an aging prophet. Julia eyed him with fear and trembling. She remembered feeling so ashamed and frightened that she could not look him directly in the face. She did not want the priest to suspect that she had never met her husband-to-be and would not even know his name until Anna Frye formally introduced them.

Abruptly, the ship's horn sounds a blast, jolting Julia back to reality. She looks over at her husband, still unable to believe that she is really a married woman at thirteen. Although George is six years older than Julia, he is as unprepared for marriage and the real world as she is, a fact Julia is now fully cognizant of. George had spent the last two years of his life in a seminary outside of Budapest, studying to be a priest. His greedy parents pulled him out when they struck a deal with Anna and Adam Frye. Adam had inherited a small plot of land from his grandfather which was on the border of the land owned by George's father, Lucas Pedesch. Adam's land contained the only natural watering spot for miles around and George's father wanted that piece of land for his own. Adam and Anna wanted to get rid of Julia, who was, in their opinion, becoming more of a liability than a help. They had no real use for the land Lucas wanted, so agreed to sell it to him if he would allow George to marry Julia and take her off their hands. Lucas's greed won out and a deal was struck. He gave his son two tickets on the *Catalonia* as a wedding gift and shipped the newlyweds off to the New World.

Julia feels very awkward and uncomfortable each evening when she must lie down next to George on their bunk in the bowels of the ship.

"He must feel as awkward as I do," she thinks to herself, "but he does not show it or let on in any way that I would notice; and I try to show him my gratitude whenever possible. He is a caring person and his very presence makes me feel secure and cared for – an uncommon feeling for me thus far in my life."

The couple has no privacy because there are so many families crammed into the small compartments. Children overflow into the aisles like kittens fighting for a place at their mother's teats. After wolfing down their meager supper each evening, they are permitted to take a short run on the deck, under the watchful eye of one of the officers. At his command, they are then coaxed back inside and into their bunks by their parents.

Real baths are unheard of, but each child receives a thorough scrubbing on the face, neck and ears every evening. Every mother has a bit of rough cloth put aside and reserved for that purpose. Soap too is at a premium, but a tiny sliver provided at the start of their journey can be made to last for weeks. The water in the pails is used over and over, but the parents are determined that the children shall bring good habits of hygiene with them to their new home. The water buckets for washing are kept just across the aisle from the slop buckets, but no one would ever mistake one for the other. The stench from the latter is so strong sometimes that Julia has to go up on deck just to fill her lungs with fresh air.

Julia tries to keep their buckets separate from the families with children, but sometimes she feels so bad for the mothers with several young children, that she is forced to share what water she and George have. Often when the ship rolls hard at night, some of the buckets tip over and what little water they had for washing is lost. George sees her do this, and smiles to himself. He would do it himself if Julia did not, so it has become a little unspoken secret between them. Sometimes George will sit with a few of the younger ones who understand Hungarian and tell them stories from the small worn Bible he always carries in his pants pocket. His story telling relaxes them and seems to help them settle into sleep after their bath experience.

After all the children are bathed and bedded down, the mothers and fathers cling together in the narrow bunks, hoping to get a bit of rest before the children start clamoring for food again in the morning. Julia thanks God silently that George prefers to spend much of his time up on deck in the evening, talking with the other men from Budapest, because she does not know what to say to him or how to act when they are alone. Julia is aware that she does not know what goes on between men and women when they are married, and is not certain whether George knows either. They are both scared she realizes, but they don't yet know how to help one another.

Whenever Julia hears George enter their compartment, she moves way over to the side of their bunk so he will have enough room to get comfortable. She pretends to be asleep, and he tries hard not to wake her. She tenses as she feels him turn his body toward her and put his hand on her shoulder. His touch is so gentle. She can feel his eyes upon her even though she keeps hers shut tight, and she knows that he is watching her. She feels his hand move across her shoulder and rest behind her neck. It is almost a caress, and Julia waits for what might come next. A few minutes seem like an hour, and then she feels him gently breathing against her back. He is asleep and the warmth of his body penetrates hers. She feels soothed, so closes her eyes against the dark and thus finds sleep.

In the light of day, George doesn't know how to tell Julia that he cares for her, but somehow his unspoken feelings come through. She doesn't know the words to assure him or comfort him, but if by some chance, they have a little bit of privacy, she tries hard to express her feelings.

"I will try very hard to be a good wife and to respect you and care for you as my husband," she tells George.

Then he smiles up at her, takes her face in his strong, sinewy hands, and gently kisses her forehead.

"It pleases me just to look at you, Julia," he responds with lowered head. "I know we were total strangers till the day of our marriage, but I will respect and care for you all the days of my life. I feel blessed that God has seen fit to send you to me. I am very grateful for this blessing, and I will care for you and protect you with my life. I promise you, *Juliashcam.*"

This loving and very personal Hungarian version of Julia's name is the one way George has to show his wife the depth of his affection. Julia feels his love for her, but knows deep down in her heart that she will never be able to return that love, the way she knows he wants her to.

Here they are now in America, their lives forever joined together, for better or for worse, as the priest said on their wedding day. Julia silently vows to work hard and do whatever she can to make their lives secure and safe for their children.

"For we surely will have children," Julia thinks to herself. "This is my dream – to have children and to love and care for them as my mother never loved or cared for me."

The ship's horn sounds again and a voice shouts, "Attention all passengers, the disembarking has begun. When all first and second-class passengers have left the ship, those in steerage may proceed to the gangway. As soon as you are on the dock, you will be directed into the central hall for processing. Please stay in line and refrain from pushing or shoving."

These last words are the hardest to obey. All of the steerage passengers are so anxious to be off this ship that has been their confinement for the past month. When their turn comes, the mass of steerage passengers move almost as one with the crowd down the gangway and into the huge hall at Ellis Island where they will be launched into new lives in a new country.

# Chapter 2

Julia and George enter the great hall at Ellis Island and are immediately overwhelmed by its high ceiling and huge open space. Gigantic windows fill the surrounding walls and some extend upwards into the ceiling. Light streams in from everywhere and gives them the feeling of being under a spotlight in a gigantic theater. In this instance, however, Julia feels like they are part of a huge cast, not merely observers at a performance. There are people everywhere being formed into lines – single lines, double lines, lines just for men and lines only for women. The sound of all these people struggling into lines is almost deafening. Bits and pieces of many languages are swirling about them, and Julia is tempted to cover her ears in an effort to clear her head. Children are crying, old women are groaning, and the din resounds like a huge drum.

Julia and George are herded into a far corner of the huge hall and are pushed into a line with many other immigrants. They are separated almost immediately into groups of men and women. Julia is frightened as George is pushed into a separate line headed for the other side of the room.

As he is pulled away, he tells her, "Do not to be afraid. I will come back for you as soon as they are finished with me, *Juliashcam*."

Julia tries to smile at him, but she is too terrified. She stands firm in her line behind an old lady, dressed all in black and steadying herself with a crooked cane. She mumbles unintelligibly to herself as they move farther and farther toward the front of the line. Julia looks straight ahead, concentrating on the old woman's back. Her shoulders are so bent under the weight of a large pack she has tied to her back that Julia can see easily over her to the rest of the line. After what seems like hours, Julia and the old woman finds themselves at the front of the line. Two men stand facing them. They are separated immediately and, as the old woman shuffles off to the place indicated, Julia waits for her instructions.

"Step forward young woman," the taller man instructs. "I am a doctor and you must submit now to a physical examination. We don't allow any sick people to enter our country."

Julia follows the example of the old woman and walks forward toward the makeshift booth the man indicates. Her hands are shaking and she is sure her heart is going to burst from her chest. She says nothing but obeys his order without raising her eyes from the floor.

"Look up, please," says the man. "I must examine your eyes, ears and mouth."

As Julia raises her eyes to the voice giving orders, she realizes that it belongs to a kindly looking man, not unlike her priest Fr. Bergard. He smiles briefly at her as he examines both her eyes and looks into her ears with a strange-looking instrument.

"Open your mouth, please," he asks in a gentler voice. Julia complies and squeezes her eyes tight as the doctor peers into her open mouth. She opens them abruptly when he begins poking at her with another strange-looking apparatus hanging from around his neck.

"I must listen to your heart and lungs," he confides. "There is nothing to be alarmed about. You appear to be in excellent health."

The doctor pats her shoulder as he speaks. Julia is not certain what he is saying, but gets the distinct impression that she passed the physical examination and is going to be allowed to enter the country. The doctor hands Julia a piece of paper which he stamps with a large rubber stamp and indicates the next line she is to go to. This line is a bit shorter and ends at a long wooden table behind which sits a very stern looking man in uniform who is interrogating each woman in turn. Another man stands behind him whose job it is to translate the questions as each immigrant comes through the line in the event that they do not understand. Most of the immigrants in this line are from Hungary and a few Slavic nations so his help is indispensable.

Julia approaches the front of the line with trepidation. The man in the uniform surveys her briefly and begins the questions at once.

"What country are you from? . . . Do you have relatives here? . . . What kind of work do you do? . . . Any serious illness in the past two months?" – on and on it goes until her brain is numb and she cannot think clearly any more. Then, it is over. She is given another piece of paper with a stamp on it and directed to yet another line.

As Julia looks up she catches sight of the old woman who had been in the first line in front of her. She is being taken from the line by a guard and directed to a room at the other side of the hall. She looks so frail as she hobbles across the huge room that Julia wonders if she will be allowed to stay in America. Someone snaps their fingers and Julia turns. She is at the head of the line now and another man in uniform is beckoning to her to approach the table. Julia walks to where he indicates and yet another man pins a bright red tag on the lapel of her coat and hands her one more piece of paper and an envelope and says, "Welcome to America." Julia is so startled she almost cries out. She looks up to see George rushing toward her from across the room. He has a red tag on his coat too.

They rush toward one another, but before they can embrace, they hear a voice say, "Move on now into the next room and exit by the side doors."

George grabs Julia's hand and begins walking in the direction indicated. When they reach the exit doors George stops and pulls Julia to the side. He gives her a brief hug of reassurance.

"These tags must mean that we have passed all the examinations and are now free to leave the building and continue on our way," he announces proudly.

Julia stands beside her husband and clutches his arm to assure herself that she is no longer alone. Suddenly she realizes that there is a little girl crying loudly next to her.

"Where is my mama? I can't find my brother," she wails. George looks down, smiles, and gently picks up the little girl. He holds her in his arms for a moment and then hoists her up onto his broad shoulders.

In a combination of Hungarian and very broken English George says, "Come little one, look over the heads of the people and see if you can see your mama or your brother."

The little girl stops crying momentarily and cranes her neck in the direction she is facing, straining for a better view. She holds onto George's head with both hands, intent on staying upright. He has to move one of her hands in order to see where he is going.

"Momma, Paulie, here I am. Can't you see me?" she shouts in a language that sounds somewhat familiar to Julia.

"I think it is Czech like Fr. Bergard's housekeeper spoke back in Hungary," she thinks to herself.

Suddenly she sees a woman waving her arms frantically and calling back in what sounds like the same language.

"Rachel, Rachel, here I am. Mama is coming."

The little girl responds immediately and begins to wave back frantically, almost slipping from George's shoulders in her excitement at hearing her mother's voice.

George gently lifts Rachel down from his shoulders and hands her over to her anxious mother.

"God bless you, my son," she cries gratefully, gathering up her little girl and wiping her tears as she heads back into the throng.

George smiles and nods and turns back to Julia. She pats his shoulder, signifying her approval of his actions. He squeezes her hand and leads her through the crowd toward the doorway that appears to lead to the outside.

Finally, after what seems like hours, Julia and George are released into the swarm of humanity outside the great hall. The excitement is rising. Couples are embracing; fathers are tossing their small children up into the air. People are shouting at each other as each person is handed the final papers permitting them entry into this new land of opportunity.

Julia and George pause a moment to catch their breath and survey their surroundings. They are looking out on the water at the edge of the island. A guard announces loudly that ferryboats are moored at a dock on the other side of the island. He indicates with his hand the path they are to take to get there. These ferries, they are told, are ready and waiting to take them to the city known as New York. Fr. Bergard had told Julia that this city is also on an island which is called Manhattan. It is all a bit confusing to Julia and George, but they take a deep breath and head down the path that the guard has indicated. They walk a short way, pushed along by the surging crowd and head for the closest ferry slip.

# Chapter 3

With a little help and some vague directions from one of the kindlier guards at the ferry slip, Julia and George manage to find their way to the Lower East Side.

"Head for Delancey Street," the guard had said. "There you will find some rooms for people like you, just arriving into the country. They might even have a bit of furniture in them too," he added. "They call these buildings Immigrant Shelters, and there is sure to be room for a husband and wife such as yourselves" he concluded with a grin.

It was a very long walk from the ferry slip to Delancey Street. Julia and George wend their way down dirt paths and cobblestone streets filled with people of every nationality they can ever imagine. A silence comes over them as they try to take in their new surroundings. They are both in awe of this strange new city where so many different languages and customs seem to coexist side by side. The smells that assail their nostrils are so unfamiliar, and the kinds of foods they see hanging up outside of the myriad storefronts are overwhelming. Large metal baskets of live shellfish struggling to escape, huge dark red sausages and cloves of garlic and peppers strung on ropes are all swinging in the salty air next to dead chickens, already plucked clean. Huge loaves of bread are arranged in straw baskets, like riotous flowers in a bowl.

"*Gelato, gelato,*" a heavyset man with a large black mustache calls from the corner. He has a small wooden stand set up with paper balloons on strings swinging gaily from the sides. Children come running from every doorway in answer to his call. Julia rushes ahead to see what he is selling. He has paper cups filled with what appears to be creamy colored ice in every color of the rainbow. Remnants of this confection are soon dripping from the chins of every child on the street. George looks at Julia and grins.

"Do you want some colored ice, *Juliashcam*?" he asks. "We have had little to eat or drink today, and this treat might be just the thing to give us some energy. The agent at Ellis Island gave each man two American coins to spend, so it is not like we would be begging. Let me get some for both of us."

George can tell by Julia's smile that she is in total agreement with his idea.

"Actually, George, my throat is so dry that almost anything would be welcome just now, but this colorful and cool looking refreshment is really going to be a treat," Julia announces.

George strides up to the man with the *gelato* and in a shaky voice with a thick accent says, "two please, sir."

"What color, my friend?" the vendor asks.

George turns to Julia questioningly. She points to the one in the man's left hand. George turns back to the man and points to his left hand.

The man smiles and says, "strawberry it is, my friend, and a good choice too."

He hands George two paper cups overflowing with creamy red ice accompanied by two tiny squares of white paper – "to catch the drips," George thinks to himself. George puts out his hand with the two coins.

The man looks at George a bit strangely and then says, "thank you my friend and come back again."

He takes one of the coins and puts two smaller ones in George's big palm. George looks down at his hand. Where once two coins had been, now there were three. He shakes his head from side to side as he returns to where Julia is standing. He hands her a cup of the red ice and then opens his hand for her to inspect the coins.

"I do not understand, *Juliashcam*," he says. "Why did he give me back more coins than I had before?"

"I think that is what they call making change, George." The coins the man gave back to you are probably the value left from the one big coin after you bought the ices. We are going to have to learn about American money and right away too," she adds. "How will we ever be able to buy things in a shop or earn a living here if we don't understand how the money works?"

"You are right, *Juliashcam*, but it will be difficult," says George thoughtfully. "We never handled money in the seminary, so I never even learned much about our Hungarian money while I was there. And now I must learn about American money? How can I do this?" he questions her, looking downcast.

"Never mind, George," responds Julia. "Don't worry about the money. That will be my job," she assures him." Anna never gave me any money on the farm, so this will be a wonderful new learning experience for me. I will learn all there is to know about these American coins, and the paper money too; I will become very smart. Then, when we start to earn a lot of money, I will be able to tell you how much it is."

George smiles and takes the small square of paper that the *gelato* vendor had given him and dabs at her chin. "You look like you are bleeding from the mouth, my dear," he says tenderly and they both laugh.

It is a wonderful moment. We are going to be fine Julia thinks to herself as she runs her tongue over the red ice and walks on down the street with her husband beside her.

They finally manage to find their way, along with several other families who are headed in the same direction. After wandering around like lost children, they look up and see a building with a large sign nailed to the front door. The word on the sign is Shelter. Julia approaches a woman standing on the curb and asks, "is this the Shelter that the man told us about at Ellis Island?"

The woman looks Julia up and down, puts her hands on her ample hips, and says in broken English, "it is that, but you had better hurry inside and stake out a room for yourself 'cause they are goin' mighty fast. This is a prime location here on Delancey Street, you know."

Julia thanks her and inspects the spot where they are standing a bit closer to get her bearings. The green metal sign on the lamppost at the corner says Allen Street, and the sign across the way reads Delancey. I must remember the names of the streets, Julia thinks to herself. The buildings all look alike and are so foreign to me – tall and narrow with steep stairs rising from the road to the front door. They are so different from the low rambling structures I am used to in Budapest. She turns to George.

"We must hurry, George. That woman says the rooms are going fast,"

Julia grabs George's hand and they fairly run up the long dark stairway two flights and secure a room on the third floor. It is only one room, but it has a door and they settle in. Julia sees several other couples who came over with them on the *Catalonia* rushing up the stairs behind them. Julia breathes a sigh of relief when she realizes that no one else has yet claimed this room. It would not be big enough for a family with children, she thinks to herself. That must be why it has not been taken before now.

"This room will be ours, George," Julia exclaims with relief. We will have a place of our own to lay our heads down this night. Thank you God for helping us find a home in New York City."

Julia and George have no furniture of their own, of course, but just as the guard had said, the room came with a bed and a small chest. They are able to get a little bit of light through a small window cut into the common wall of the room adjoining theirs, which happily for those occupants, is on an outside wall with a real window. Daylight is one of the most precious commodities in the Shelter Julia has been told, so they consider themselves very fortunate to have access to any light at all.

"This is a good sign," Julia announces. "Even having an inside window is a blessing."

George nods in agreement. "Yes, it is *Juliashcam*, and maybe this is God's way of telling us we will be all right in this new country. My Director at the Seminary always told me that where there is light, there is hope. And now here we are in our first home and we almost have a real window."

Julia smiles at her husband and he smiles back. It is a good beginning. Some of the inside rooms, they discover later, have no windows at all. The sun never penetrates these stone walls, so some families live their lives in almost perpetual darkness, broken only by the occasional candle or small oil lamp, if they are fortunate enough to be able to afford one.

The slop houses, as the privies are called, are all outside in rows along the rear of the building. If the wind is right, the ugly perfume from these necessaries wafts up and into the building. Maybe it's fortunate, Julia thinks to herself, that we don't have a real window in our room. One of the women who lives on the first floor complains bitterly because the slop houses are only emptied once a month, and the stench is more than she can bear.

George looks for work every day, but it soon becomes apparent that it is not going to be easy for him to earn a living in this neighborhood. Mr. Fineburg, the grocer, wants to hire George to unload the truckloads of produce that arrive daily from the farms outside the city. George is very strong and proves to be a very hard worker. He spends several days there, but his knowledge of English is so poor that he cannot deal with the truck drivers who deliver the produce.

"We can't understand your man and don't know which dock to pull into," one driver grumbles to Mr. Fineburg. "Besides, we expect to be paid as soon as we deliver, and he don't understand our money worth a plug nickel. This ain't no way to run a business."

Mr. Fineburg is a good man and wants to keep George on, but the situation is causing him nothing but aggravation. Finally after only a week he calls George into the back of the store.

"I'm really sorry, George, but I will have to let you go until you can improve your English. I can't afford to have these truck drivers complaining all the time. Maybe in a few months if your English improves, we can try again. I hope you and Julia will understand."

George is discouraged. He knows he should improve his English but seems to have little success in doing so.

"I feel so foolish, *Juliashcam*. No matter how hard I try," he says, "it just comes out all wrong. The more I try, the more uncomfortable and stupid I feel."

When she hears George call her *Juliashcam*, that special Hungarian endearment he reserves just for her, Julia's heart overflows with sympathy for this good and honest man. She tries very hard to encourage him, but the situation with regard to language seems hopeless.

Julia, on the other hand, finds learning this bawdy new language a challenge; and thanks God for her natural facility for learning, especially language. Many of the people in the neighborhood speak another language, but it is quite easy for her to pick up the similarities between them and her native Hungarian. Perhaps it is the Latin that Fr. Bergard taught me in order to read the Mass that makes it easier for me, she thinks to herself. Many of the Latin words translate into some of these other languages. So many of us are from the same area of Eastern Europe too – Czechoslovakia, Romania, Yugoslavia, and Poland. We are all struggling with English and so we try to help one another.

One of Julia's neighbors, Mary Ryan, was from Ireland and already knew a bit of English when she came here. They have become friends, being close to the same age, and Mary has helped her more than anyone else.

"You are a natural," Mary insists. Julia smiles gratefully and is encouraged to try even harder. By carefully listening to Mary and some of the local shopkeepers, she is soon able to speak a few essential words and phrases. "May I have a loaf of bread, please?" is one of her best attempts at English; along with "Where is the streetcar, please?" "Good Day" and "Thank you."

The proprietor of the Shelter and Mr. Fineburg, the grocer,

respond to Julia's smile, which warms her heart. Whenever he sees her, Mr. Krendosh, the proprietor, always says, "Good morning, Julia, and how is the flower of New York City this lovely day?"

Mr. Fineburg also greets her with a smile and never fails to tell her, "You are the prettiest addition to the neighborhood in many a day." This pleases her so much, and she soon feels as though she really belongs somewhere. Her smile will not pay for groceries and other necessities, however, and since George has been unable to find work, Julia is becoming a bit discouraged about their future.

# Chapter 4

Julia begins to survey the neighborhood in earnest. As she walks through the streets, observing the people and the various businesses that have taken hold, it soon becomes apparent that there is very little work for a man who cannot speak the common language of the city and who has no particular skills. It's not that George has to be fluent, she thinks to herself, but he has to at least master a few common words and phrases and learn to handle the currency. His seminary training certainly did not prepare George for a life in the real world.

Even the streetcar conductors have heavy accents, Julia notes; they greet their customers in broken English and a friendly smile. The latter goes a long way thinks Julia, but this is hard for George with strangers he does not know. He's always been wonderful with children, like the little lost girl at Ellis Island, but discourse with his peers is quite another matter. The drivers, Julia has been told, must also take a special test to qualify them to pilot these wonderful conveyances. A bright red streetcar suddenly comes screeching around the corner, as if to punctuate her thoughts. The driver waves a cheery hello to the men and women who are lined up to get into the car.

"Sorry to be late, folks, but I had to get my cable greased," he tells the crowd with a smile in his voice. They push forward and hurry up the steps into the car. Many of the women with children try to get an outside seat so the children can watch the world go by as the streetcar makes its way through the city. It stops every few blocks to let people off and take on new passengers, as long as there is sufficient room to seat them. What an exciting way to travel around the city, Julia thinks to herself.

As she walks on, the smell of freshly baking bread assails her nostrils. Further down the street the crackle of roasting chestnuts can be heard from a pushcart on the corner. Across the street men are unloading large stones from a pushcart in preparation for building a wall around a small park on the corner making a safe haven for the children to play. Most of the men in the neighborhood sell groceries or hardware, or bake bread and pastries, Julia realizes. Some also work with stone or brick, repairing buildings and walls, but all have a skill with which to earn a living. Poor George, Julia realizes, is only skilled in the lessons of the Lord God Almighty. It may serve us well in the hereafter, but it's not much good in the here and now. I won't give up, she admonishes herself; I will find some way for George to earn a living. He must feel useful and the provider for our family or he will be utterly miserable and will not be able to hold his head up with the other men at the Shelter.

Julia soon discovers by talking to her neighbors that she can earn a few pennies here and there by sewing for them – a patch here, a torn pocket there. One day Mrs. Fineburg, the wife of the grocer, stops her on the street.

"I have heard of your handiwork with a needle, Julia; do you think you could make my little girl a dress out of an old discarded one of my sister's?"

Julia is thrilled at the challenge and a chance to earn a little money to buy groceries, so she accepts right away.

"I would be pleased to make a dress for little Rachel," she answers. "When may I come and measure her and see the cloth?"

"You can come this afternoon, Julia, right after the noonday meal," Mrs. Fineburg responds, "and you can get started right away."

"I'll be there, Mrs. Fineburg, and thank you so much." Julia is so excited at the prospect of earning some money that she fairly dances all the way home.

Julia had brought a bit of thread and a few needles and pins with her from Hungary (borrowed from Anna when she wasn't looking), so she had enough with which to begin a small assignment such as this. She might even give me enough money to buy a small sausage to go with our bread she thinks hopefully. George would really like that.

Julia goes to Mrs. Fineburg's flat above the grocery store right after the lunch hour. The grocer's wife welcomes her into the front room which is bright with the afternoon sun and introduces Julia to her daughter, Rachel. Mrs. Fineburg goes into the bedroom and returns with the dress that had belonged to her sister. It is made of soft pink fabric which will be very suitable for a young girl. Julia admires the soft flowing material and assures Mrs. Fineburg that it will make a lovely dress for Rachel. She asks Rachel to stand up so she can take a few measurements with an old tape, also brought from Hungary. Rachel is a bit shy but agrees to Julia's request and turns each time she is asked. It takes Julia only a short time to take all the necessary measurements. When she writes down the last one, she looks up at Rachel and smiles.

"You will look like a princess in your new dress, I promise you," says Julia with confidence and pride.

Rachel smiles back and even turns and gives Julia a hug. Mrs. Fineburg, looking on, is grinning from ear to ear. Julia stands up and thanks Mrs. Fineburg, pats Rachel on the head and heads for the door with the beautiful pink dress tucked under her arm.

"I cannot wait to get home and begin work on Rachel's dress," Julia announces as she leaves the Fineburg's apartment.

Julia works all the rest of the day and halfway through the night to prepare the dress for its first fitting. She stops long enough to make a meager supper for George and then returns to her sewing. The next morning she runs to the grocery store to see Mrs. Fineburg.

"When may I come and give Rachel a fitting?" she inquires. The excitement is evident in her voice and Mrs. Fineburg responds in kind.

"How about right after school, Julia? Rachel will be home by three o'clock and you can come for tea and have her fitting then," says Mrs. Fineburg with satisfaction.

"Oh, yes, that will be just fine," answers Julia. "I'll be there at three o'clock, Mrs. Fineburg."

Julia can barely contain herself until the bewitching hour of three o'clock. George is helping one of their neighbors move some small furniture into their apartment so is unaware of her unabashed state of excitement.

My very first job, she thinks to herself. I hope Mrs. Fineburg will be pleased. This could be the start of a whole new career for me. Three o'clock finally arrives and Julia gathers up the meager tools of her trade and the carefully basted dress for Rachel and heads for the Fineburg's flat. Mrs. Fineburg opens the door and Rachel comes running to give Julia another hug. She eyes the pink dress with interest and Julia hastens to try it on her. Julia takes Rachel's hand and walks with her over to a big mirror in the corner of the bedroom. She watches Rachel's face as she studies herself in the mirror.

"I am a princess, Mama, I am, I am. Come and see," shouts the little girl, excitement rising in her voice.

Rachel's mother comes into the room and gives voice to her own astonishment. "Oh, Julia, it is so beautiful. My Rachel really does look like a princess. You are very talented with the needle, my dear."

Julia smiles with pleasure and begins fitting the dress to the little girl in earnest. "It needs only a few corrections," says Julia. "I should be able to have it ready for you by tomorrow afternoon. I will bring it round after school if that is alright with you, Mrs. Fineburg."

"That will be just fine, my dear, just fine," says Mrs. Fineburg. "Now sit down with us and have a cup of tea. I made some sweet biscuits this morning, and I would like you to taste them and give me your opinion. I am thinking of selling some at the store – a little homemade touch is nice once in a while don't you think?"

"Why thank you, Mrs. Fineburg. I'd be pleased to try one of your biscuits with my tea." Julia did not let on what a treat this was for her. Not only was she having her first cup of tea in America, but her first homemade biscuit as well. She couldn't wait to tell George, but then felt sad as she realized he was not taking part in this treat as well.

As if reading her mind, Mrs. Fineburg said, "please take a biscuit home for your husband to taste also, Julia. It's always good to get a man's opinion as well."

After the pleasantries are over and the tea and biscuits consumed by all, Julia takes her leave and rushes home to tell George of the events of the day. As she approaches the Shelter, she sees George on the front steps, talking to one of his cronies.

"Where have you been, *Juliashcam?*" George inquires and stands up to greet his wife.

"I've been working, George," Julia answers proudly. "I'm making a dress for Mrs. Fineburg's little girl and we had her fitting today. I am going upstairs now to complete the dress I am making for her. By the way, George, Mrs. Fineburg sent home a fresh biscuit for you to taste. She is thinking of selling them at the store. Would you like to eat it here on the steps or shall I bring it upstairs for you to have later?"

"I worked up an appetite helping Mr. Kohl move some furniture, *Juliashcam*, so I think I'll have it now if you don't mind."

Julia smiles and takes a small object wrapped in a napkin out of her pocket and hands it to her husband. "You're in for a treat, my dear," she says as she turns and runs up the steps, anxious to begin work on Rachel's dress.

The next day Mrs. Fineburg is so pleased with the results of Julia's labors that she pays her a whole dollar, and even throws in a bag of day-old beans. Julia is so happy she has to fight the urge to kiss the older woman. Instead she politely poses a question.

"While I am here, Mrs. Fineburg, would you be kind enough to explain to me a little about the American money?"

"I would be more than happy to do that for you Julia. It is always so difficult to grasp the figuring of money in a new country. It took Mr. Fineburg and me awhile to learn it ourselves, but now I think I am an expert. Sit down here with me and we shall begin right now."

Julia spent the remainder of the afternoon with the kindly grocer's wife learning the names of the various coins and paper money and how to make change. When the sun began to set and Julia realized the hour, she thanked Mrs. Fineburg with all her heart for teaching her about money, but most of all for giving her this first job as a seamstress. The news of Julia's talents soon spread throughout the neighborhood and she is launched in her new career as a seamstress, thanks to the kind publicity provided by Mrs. Fineburg.

# Chapter 5

The warm spring days continue to pass in much the same way – George sits on the steps reading the Hungarian newspapers or his beloved Bible with Julia beside him sewing to pay for their next meal. George finds work now and then, but only where his brawn is required and not his brain or his language skills. George still resists learning English but he is not afraid of hard work. While studying in the seminary before he and Julia were married, he was forced to exercise his muscles just as much, if not more, than his brain. Part of studying for the brotherhood apparently, was a dedication to hard physical labor. This training was like a juggernaut in George's brief existence at the seminary.

George is probably an inch shorter than Julia, and even though six years her senior, he has physical strength that never ceases to amaze her. He is somewhat stocky of build and seems to be able to move mountains when the need arises. Julia watched him lift the back of a wagon for Mr. Fineburg last week so that the wheelwright could put a new wheel in its place. She was awestruck at the strength of this quiet man who was her husband. Their neighbors seem to take this strength for granted now as well and often call upon George to help them haul heavy items down stairs or down the block. He responds to all who ask for his help with a smile and a shrug of his broad shoulders. Fortunately, they insist on paying George for his efforts, and he is unable to refuse their generosity.

"Besides," Julia tells him when he balks at accepting the

moncy, "you have more than earned the payment they give you. Who else could they get to do this kind of labor I ask you."

He is happier now that he too is bringing home some money to sustain them and put food on their table.

Julia was always considered tall for her age and able to take care of herself, but she feels especially safe and protected in George's presence. If only he wasn't so very quiet and contemplative, perhaps we could learn to enjoy one another's company more, Julia often thinks to herself. If he is not reading the Hungarian newspaper, she finds his head buried deep in the only book they own, the Bible. Julia sometimes asks him to read to her in his lovely soft, deep voice, but he always declines.

"These lines are for praying, *Juliashcam*, not for telling," he answers.

If only he could speak them in English, what solace he could bring to some of the people here. Even when they talk together, George insists on speaking in Hungarian, and Julia so desperately wants to practice her own English.

"Please speak English, George," she begs, but his answer is always the same.

"It takes too long to get it out, *Juliashcam*, and by the time I say the first two or three words, I have forgotten what I wanted to tell you in the first place."

One afternoon, while in the grocery store, bargaining for a small piece of cold meat for their supper, Julia hears some of the women talking among themselves.

"Have you heard about the great opportunities in the coal mines, Mrs. Fineburg?" asks Mrs. Stroinska. Her husband is one of the men who clean out the privies each month. "I hear tell that the work is hard, but it pays better than anything else our men can find here."

"Oh, I've known about the coal mines for over a week now," chimes in Mrs. Freder, whose husband empties trucks now for the grocer. "We're making plans to go there at the end of the month. Luke has given Mr. Fineburg his notice already I think," she concludes with a smile of satisfaction on her flushed round face.

"Mr. Fineburg and I will be staying," says the grocer's wife. "This is our home now, and we're not going to leave a growing business for any wild goose chase."

"Well, but you and Mr. Fineburg have established yourself in business," counters Mrs. Freder. "I would stay too if I had a good business to run."

Some of the other women join in the conversation, discussing the opportunities being offered by the mining companies south of New York in a place called Pittsburgh, Pennsylvania. Several of their husbands have already decided to pack up and try their luck in the coal mines there. The money is good they say, and although the work is hard, they will be able to save enough money to return to New York in a few years and open up a business too.

What could be so hard about digging coal in a mine, Julia wonders. George is certainly strong enough to do the work and she could teach him just enough English to get by. I could even cook and sew in the mining camp to make extra money. Before you know it, we'll have enough money to return to New York too. I will talk to George tonight and convince him that we should leave here as soon as possible.

George receives her news with little enthusiasm. He resists change almost as much as he does learning English.

"Why do you want to leave here so soon, *Juliashcam*? Haven't you been happy here? We have friends here now and we are settled. I find more work each day, and your sewing makes up the difference," he pleads.

"Oh, George," Julia, cries, "is this all you want from life? Is this why we traveled all the way to America to live in a shelter? Don't you want us to have a home of our own and children to raise?" She begins to cry in earnest. George rises from his chair and takes her gently into his arms. He holds her to him and rocks her from side to side.

"Forgive me, *Juliashcam*," he says softly into her hair. "I didn't know how unhappy you were. Please forgive me for being so selfish."

"It's not that I am so unhappy, George," Julia responds between sobs. "It's just that I want so much more for us than what we have in the shelter. I am willing to work as hard as you and do whatever it takes to make enough money to give us a fresh start in New York. I want us to come back, raise a family, and be proud of our accomplishments. We can do this, George, we can, if we work together. Everyone says that the coal mines pay really good money, and you don't need a special skill or even have to speak much English to do the work. Please think about it. We can be packed and ready to go in a day or two." Julia takes a deep breath after this teary monologue and looks up at her husband with tears still sparkling on her eyelashes.

George sits down and looks up at Julia with tears in his eyes as well and says, "Start packing, *Juliashcam*; you have convinced me as usual. You always seem to know what is best for this family, so I will argue with you no longer. I will work hard and make a good coal miner. You will be proud of me; I promise."

At these words, Julia sits down next to her husband and puts her arms around him. "Oh thank you, George. You won't be sorry! I promise!"

That night is the first time that George and Julia behave as husband and wife. They are both so inexperienced that it is doubtful that they will ever succeed. George sits on the edge of the bed for several minutes and then gets in and lies on his back looking up at the ceiling intently, as if the word of God is written there. Julia, meanwhile, has learned a bit more about marriage and the duties of a wife from some of her more gossipy neighbors. Apparently, George too has received a bit of education from some of his cronies. Urged on by her feelings of gratitude for his agreeing to go to Pennsylvania, Julia snuggles next to him and takes his hand in hers. She waits a few minutes and then rises up on one elbow and brazenly places a kiss on her husband's cheek. This is all the encouragement that the young ex-seminarian needs.

He turns toward his child bride, and the next thing she knows, he is kissing her on the mouth, first tenderly and then with a passion Julia did not suspect he possessed. She returns his kiss, more out of curiosity than passion, but finds the result more than a little pleasurable. Although George's attempts at lovemaking elicit no great consuming passion in Julia, she enjoys the feeling of being loved and caressed by this very strong but gentle man.. With every fiber of her being, Julia tries to return this tenderness and love, and so their marriage is finally consummated.

The very next day Julia hastens to pack up their meager belongings into the two old valises. They say their good-byes to Mr. Krendosh, the Fineburgs, Julia's dear friend, Mary Ryan and a few of their other neighbors. With the few dollars they have managed to put aside, Julia buys two tickets on the afternoon train going from New York to the place they call Pittsburgh. They are embarking once again on another phase of their life together. Julia feels confident that they will succeed, and she thanks God on her knees before she leaves their room in the shelter and they head for the train station.

# Chapter 6

Julia and George have been in the mining camp just outside of Pittsburgh for several weeks now. It is hot and sticky even in the morning when they get up, and Julia feels like she is always soaking wet. Unlike New York, there is seldom a breeze here, perhaps because they are in a valley of sorts, surrounded by mountains and the air just can't seem to get to them. Julia has fashioned a sort-of fan from some large leafy plants she has found at the edge of the woods nearby and uses it to cool her hot face and neck.

George is not finding the work too difficult, but it certainly is hot and dirty. Julia is having trouble keeping him in clean underwear and a change of shirt at least once a week. Water for washing is not very plentiful in the camp. Most of the women make their way down to a small pitiful stream at the edge of the camp and do their laundry there, beating the clothes against the rocks at the water's edge as if willing the dirt to release itself and flow away down stream. Julia has even found a small, secluded cove where she can remove her dress undetected in the heat of the day and take a bath there in the cool water of the stream.

George has learned a few more words of English and can now respond a bit better to the foreman who is a tall, heavy-set, rather gruff man with very little patience.

"Speak up there, Pedesch," he can be heard shouting. "I can't understand a thing you're saying. When in hell are you *immies* gonna learn to speak the language?"

George doesn't talk back to the big man but retreats in silence, vowing to do better the next time they meet. Julia works with him each evening after their meager supper, but the learning comes slowly.

"Why does he call us *immies*, *Juliashcam*?" George asks during one of these sessions.

"I believe it is what is called an abbreviation, George," Julia answers thoughtfully. "It is just short for immigrant which is what we all are – anyone coming here from another country. Please don't pay any attention to him when he says that. Just do your job and everything will be alright."

Julia is beginning to feel a bit squeamish in the mornings lately. "It must be from the drastic change in our diet," she says to no one in particular. We eat a lot more greens and much less meat that we used to."

Bread is still the mainstay of their meals, but it is so coarse that Julia often has trouble swallowing it. George, on the other hand, finds the coarse, dry bread good. It helps fill up that empty cavity he always seems to have in his stomach. He burns up so much energy, Julia thinks, that he needs more nourishment than he usually consumes. She always passes some of her portion of their meal back to George so he won't be hungry when he goes to bed at night. She has little appetite herself lately, especially when she feels nauseous so much of the time. George is so tired when he returns each evening from the mines that he doesn't even notice how much or how little Julia has eaten. He washes up, fills his stomach, and falls into bed exhausted each night.

The only milk available in the camp is from a few goats kept in a small pen for that purpose, and one poor old cow who doesn't even provide enough milk to feed the few children living in the camp. When Julia goes out to the privy early in the morning, she often sees one of the women taking her turn at milking these poor, sad animals. This morning the woman in the pen is rather tall and sturdily built, a match for any goat, Julia thinks, smiling to herself. The woman chases one of the wily goats around the pen until she catches her and then stakes her out on a short lead next to the fence. She draws up a low stool next to the goat and begins milking her at once. As Julia watches, nothing at all comes from the goat's teats. No matter how hard the determined woman pulls on the teats, nothing but a bit of watery liquid drips down. The woman shrugs her shoulders wearily, gets up off the stool, and scans the fenced-in enclosure for a sign of the cow. She spots the animal in the corner of the pen with her back to her, and goes off toward her with the stool in her hand. As the woman approaches, the cow turns and backs herself into the corner, denying the woman access to the rear portion of her scrawny rump. The woman tugs and pulls and finally falls down herself in her effort to get the stubborn cow out of the corner. Several of the other women notice the goings-on and begin to scream with laughter. It is a comical sight, Julia admits to herself, but she does feel sympathy for the poor struggling woman who obviously is in need of some milk for her children. The struggle continues for a few minutes more, and then the poor tired cow gives up and turns herself around once again. She seems to sense that there is no use continuing the struggle. The woman seizes the opportunity. She drops the stool to the ground, shoves a pail under the cow, and begins to haul on the teats with all the strength she can muster. The cow moos loudly in pain, but the woman is not deterred. After a minute or two, a small stream of liquid can be heard hitting the side of the bucket under the cow. The woman smiles with satisfaction and wipes her brow with her free hand. The other women begin to clap in celebration of a job well done. The woman looks up and a huge smile fills her face as she acknowledges the support of her peers.

Julia is able to keep busy by sewing for the miners' wives and earning money for her efforts. She hides it away in an old brown wool sock of George's and sleeps with it under her pillow each night. Even George doesn't know about her secret sock. She is saving to make sure they have a good nest egg when the time comes for them to return to New York.

Things are going along pretty well, and George is working almost every day now. There are so many new men coming in each day though, Julia worries that there will not be enough work for all of them. Word has spread rapidly up north about work being available in the coal mines, and it is bringing in men from all parts of the surrounding states.

Julia is still feeling sick in the mornings, but has convinced herself that it will surely pass. She has made one friend in the camp. Her name is Bertha, and she is a large motherly sort of woman, a few years older than Julia, but with a kind heart and a soft comforting voice. She coils her dark brown hair in a tight bun at the back of her neck and always wears the same coarse blue dress covered with a stiff white apron. Bertha's shoes are the same as those worn by the miners – black and serviceable. She has taken a liking to Julia who enjoys talking with her whenever they can find a little time to socialize, which is not often.

I will talk to Bertha tomorrow, determines Julia, and perhaps she will suggest something that I can do to help control this strange malady of mine.

In the morning as soon as Julia gives George his breakfast and brews a pot of tea, she goes off to find Bertha. She has been living in the camp for almost a year now, Julia knows, so she feels certain Bertha will be able to suggest something to help her. She is more experienced than Julia in the matter of illness and may know what to suggest as a remedy. Julia wanders through the camp looking for her and finally finds her tending the cooking pots outside the main tent.

"Good morning, Bertha, may I speak with you for a minute?" Julia inquires.

"Why of course, Julia," she answers and gets up from her crouched position near the pots. "It will be a pleasant relief to get away from my chores for a few minutes. I just made a fresh pot of coffee; can I pour a cup for you?"

"Oh, no thank you, Bertha," Julia responds. "I'm not feeling too well these days, especially in the morning. Even the smell of the coffee makes my stomach churn."

Julia moves away from the steaming pot and takes a seat on the ground behind the tent. Bertha follows and they sit there in companionable silence for a moment.

"What can be wrong with me, Bertha?" Julia asks worriedly. "I can't keep any food down in the morning any more, and even the evening meal does not tempt me some days."

"There is nothing I can give you for that kind of sickness, Julia," Bertha says with authority. "My mother used to give me dry bread and weak tea to help stop the nausea when I was pregnant," she concluded, looking at Julia with gentle concern.

"What did you say, Bertha? Pregnant? Who, me? You must be mistaken. George and I haven't been, uh, together that way since we came to Pittsburgh. He is always so tired at night, and I am usually not feeling well enough to respond if he weren't. It just can't be; it can't."

It was then that Julia realized with resounding certainty that she had not had her monthly in two months now, and maybe Bertha was indeed correct. She must have gotten pregnant on that last night in New York, just before they left for Pennsylvania. Julia felt the tears start behind her eyes and was ashamed to have her friend see her cry. She turned away from her as if to blow her nose, but Bertha was a wise girl and recognized Julia's anguish at once.

"Oh, Julia, I am so sorry this was not in your plan, but only God decides these things. You know that as well as I do. Come into the tent for a spell, and I'll fix you some soft fresh bread and tea. That will go down much better than the coffee; I promise."

The tent was warm and inviting and just being inside away from the cold and the smells of the camp began to improve Julia's spirits.

"The sickness will pass in another month," Bertha assures her. "You'll feel much better then and will be able to eat again. Remember, Julia, you'll be eating for two – you and the wee *bairn.*" Bertha's Scottish brogue brings a smile to Julia's lips, and the bread and tea soon work their magic in her stomach. She begins to relax.

"It happens to all of us women sooner or later," Bertha announces with a note of certainty in her voice well beyond her years. "I was surprised when I got pregnant too," she adds.

"And where is your baby, Bertha?" Julia asks, and then sucks in her breath as she sees the look on her friend's face. Tears begin to run down the ruddy cheeks, and Julia could have bitten her tongue for asking such an insensitive question.

"The wee *bairn* did not make it into this world, Julia," Bertha answers softly, wiping at the tears making a trail down her cheek. "He died on the way out and we buried him on the hill over there behind the cook tent. I want you to promise me that you'll take care of yourself and then you'll be so happy when the wee one arrives all pink and yowling." Bertha blows her nose hard and goes to hug her friend.

"I am happy, of course, Bertha, Julia interjects. "I do very much want to have a child, but not just yet. In so many ways I still feel like a child myself, but I would never let George or anyone else but you know that. I hoped we could return to New York first with our stake before we started a family."

"*Arrgh*, all will be well, lass. Go home now and rest and get ready to tell your husband the good news," Bertha urges her gently.

"Goodbye, Bertha, I will go now," says Julia, "and I do thank you for being my friend and helping me feel better. At least now I know I'm not dying of some rare disease. Pray for me when I tell George the news. I'm sure it will come as a shock to him too."

Bertha hugs Julia to her and pats her head as if she were a child. Julia waves a farewell and heads back to her tent on the other side of the camp.

When George returns to their tent that night, hot and dirty, Julia notices that there is something different about him. His shoulders are hunched, and the smile he usually greets her with is nowhere in sight.

"There's no easy way to tell you, *Juliashcam*," George begins solemnly, "I was laid off today." Julia draws in her breath in alarm while he continues. "You know that new section of mine we opened just last week; it turned out to be bad luck for us. On my way in this morning, I slipped on a soft shoulder at the entrance we just expanded and let a great metal coal bucket I was carrying drop. The bucket hit the foreman on the ankle and caused him to fall against the shaft. He was so angry when he realized what had happened that he ordered me to be replaced immediately. We have to be out of the camp by sunrise tomorrow," George concludes with his head in his hands and his voice becomes almost inaudible.

Poor George is so contrite that Julia doesn't have the heart to reprimand him for his carelessness. She gives him a kiss on the cheek instead and assures him that she is not provoked and is certain things will be better in the next camp they go to. George takes little solace from this statement, but is grateful at least that his wife is not berating him, as some of the other miners' wives would have.

Julia says nothing about her pregnancy now. This is not the right time Julia decides. Too much has happened already today. George cannot handle much more. She vows to tell him as soon as they are settled in the new camp.

"I'm so very sorry, *Juliashcam*," George says again. "It was stupid and careless of me to drop that bucket. I promise you I will be more vigilant in the future, and an accident like that will never happen again. That foreman has not liked me from the start and this was all the excuse he needed to get rid of me."

"It will be alright, George, you'll see. Now let's get busy getting our things together," Julia urges, pulling out the old valises from the corner of the tent.

They gather up their few meager possessions and pack them into the worn valises and then make their way to the gate. Julia is anxious for them to get on their way before it gets too dark because the next camp is about twenty miles away, but she cannot leave without saying goodbye to her dear friend, Bertha.

"Wait here, George," Julia says. "I will be right back. I must say goodbye to Bertha before we leave. She has been such a good friend to me, I cannot leave without telling her what has happened and where we are going. George nods his head in agreement and puts the valises on the ground next to him.

Julia scans the immediate area and then heads straight for Bertha's tent. She sees the cooking pots hanging over the fire, but Bertha is nowhere in sight. She spies the old woman who was trying to milk the cow the other day. Julia taps her on the shoulder and inquires if she knows where Bertha is.

"I ain't seen her," growls the old woman in response.

"Oh dear," says Julia in obvious distress. "Would you be good enough to give her a message for me? Please tell her that Julia's husband has lost his job, and so they had to leave the camp tonight. Tell her I thank her for everything and I will miss her."

"Well, dearie, I'll try to tell her if I can remember all that," says the old woman. She pauses a moment and then adds, "good luck to you and your husband in the next camp."

Surprised by this last remark, Julia smiles, and thanks her and heads back to where George is waiting for her by their old tent.

George carries both valises and Julia carries their bedding in a bundle over her shoulder. They pass through the iron gate out to the road and begin walking in the direction George indicates.

"It will be a long walk, *Juliashcam*, George says, "do you think we will be able to make it to the next camp before morning?"

"Maybe we will be lucky, George, and get a ride part of the way," Julia answers him. Then, as if by magic, a wagon appears on the road behind them. It is a farmer's wagon filled half full of hay and hauled by two old gray workhorses. As the wagon approaches, the farmer slows the horses to a walk and asks George where they are headed. George looks at Julia questioningly, and she steps forward and answers the farmer in his stead.

"We are going to the next mining camp on this road, sir," says Julia with a smile, heaving the heavy bundle on her shoulder to the other side as she speaks.

"Well now," says the farmer, "that's the direction I'm heading in myself. If you don't mind a little damp hay, you're welcome to climb into the back of the wagon and ride there with me."

"Oh, thank you, sir," says Julia, "we'd be so grateful for the ride. Come George, let's get into the back of the wagon," Julia says in rapid Hungarian.

George follows Julia's command and they settle themselves in between the mounds of hay. The horses whinny slightly and trot on down the road. The ride is uneventful and they arrive at the new camp just at suppertime.

# Chapter 7

The sun is just beginning to set in the western sky as Julia and George enter the gate of the new camp. The smell of meat roasting fills the evening air, and Julia suddenly becomes aware that she is feeling hunger. This is the first time in many weeks she has thought of food in a positive way. This must be a good sign, she tells herself. She turns to George and sees him sniffing the night air as well.

"That food smells awfully good, George, doesn't it," says Julia.

"I didn't realize how hungry I was until we entered the gate and that delicious aroma assailed my nostrils," replied George. "I could eat just about anything right now, *Juliashcam*," he adds, grinning at his own admission.

Just at that moment a tall, broad-shouldered man approaches them from one of the tented areas.

"Good evening and welcome," says the tall man. "I am John Connery, foreman here at the Adam Two Mine. May I be of some assistance to you?"

Julia pulls herself up to her full height next to her husband and looks up at the foreman, a smile forming on her lips. She likes this tall, burly man instantly and so does not hesitate in her response.

"We are Julia and George Pedesch, Mr. Connery, and we are here to find work for my husband, George, in this mining camp if that is possible."

John Connery studies the couple for a moment before

speaking. "Well, my dear," answers the foreman, it seems you've come at a very propitious time. We just happen to be short one scuttler as of this morning. If George wants it, the job is his."

"Oh, my yes, Mr. Connery," Julia answers for George without hesitation, but would you mind telling us just what that is, sir."

John Connery grins and turning his attention to George, who thus far has said not a word, proceeds to explain. "A scuttler, George, is the man who follows behind the coal tram and picks up all the coals that fall off the cart and returns them to the empty bin. It's not much of a job, I admit, but if you handle that alright, as soon as we have an opening for an inside miner, I will give you the first opportunity. You certainly look strong enough to handle mining work. What do you say?"

George looks at Julia hesitantly and speaks to her quickly in Hungarian. Julia nods her head and looks up at John Connery.

"George doesn't yet speak much English, Mr. Connery, but he is working on improving that. He would be more than willing to start out as a scuttler, and you are quite right about his strength. George may not be very tall but he has the strength of a bull. He can do whatever heavy work is necessary in the mine, I assure you."

"Well then," responds John Connery, "it's all set then. Tomorrow you will begin work as a scuttler, but right now let me show you where you will be bunking and then take you down to the cook tent before there is nothing left there for you two to eat. Cook roasted a calf tonight and it is the best meat we have had in some time. You are in for a treat. Most of the families have eaten by now, but there should be enough left to feed you two," he adds with a crooked grin. "Have your fill, and I'll join you there later."

John Connery enters the cook tent before George and Julia finish eating. Their plates are still half laden with dark brown beans, thick with molasses and huge slabs of bread.

"Still eating?" he asks with a smile. "I'd have thought you'd have wolfed it down by now, considering the long way you had to come to get it."

Julia smiles back at him a little embarrassed, and he sits down with his mug of coffee.

"Beans and bread never tasted so good, Mr. Connery, and the meat was so delicious. I can't thank you enough. That is the best meal we have had since arriving in the United States. George has eaten enough for both of us," Julia adds and then immediately regrets her statement. She doesn't want Mr. Connery to think they are eating more than they are worth, especially since George hasn't even started yet. "I don't usually eat much myself, she says," trying to smooth things over.

"Please eat all you want, Julia. George will earn every morsel. I promise you. Mining is not the easiest way to earn a living, my dear," he concludes with a kindly smile. "As soon as there is an opening for a real miner, I will give George a try," he assures them once again.

George nods gratefully, but is silent as usual and offers nothing in the way of conversation. Julia assures John Connery that George is a hard worker and that they are very grateful for this chance and for a place to stay.

"You are entirely welcome, Julia. Now get some rest and I will see you both in the morning."

The big man rises and ambles down the path toward the main part of the camp. Julia and George finish their supper and make their way to the cabin assigned to them to unpack their few belongings and try to get some sleep. Julia suddenly realizes how very tired she is and knows instinctively that it will probably get worse as the weeks and months progress.

I have decided not to tell George about my pregnancy just yet she whispers, as if speaking to the wee baby growing inside her. He is always so protective of me that he will expect me to rest most of the time. I know I have to find work as a seamstress within the camp to increase our meager income, at least until George can be promoted to a regular miner. She falls asleep almost as soon as her head touches the pillow, and when she awakes next morning, George has already left the cabin to begin his day's work.

The next few weeks pass without incident. Julia has succeeded in finding a little work as a seamstress – mending mostly but enough to supplement their small income. Her work is very quick and neat and her reputation with a needle soon spreads throughout the camp. By the time the fifth month comes around, it is beginning to become obvious that Julia is indeed "with child." Her extra aprons can no longer hide the increased size of her belly. The morning sickness has left her by this time, but she is progressively getting tired more easily. It is time to tell George that he is going to be a father in four more months. George is a real miner now and is assigned to a section very deep inside the earth. The very thought of going that far underground terrifies Julia, but she never lets on to George how afraid she really is.

When George returns home this evening, she sits down beside him on the edge of their bed and helps him take off his boots. The light from the moon illumines the dingy surroundings of their room, – a small dresser and a rickety wash stand the only other furnishings. Julia puts her hand on George's big rough one, causing him to turn and look at her questioningly.

"George," she whispers. "I want to tell you something very important."

He looks up at her startled now, expecting the worst, and says, "*Juliashcam*, are you ill? What is wrong, please tell me."

She smiles at the familiar endearment from the old country and answers, "I am with child, George. We are going to have a baby in four more months."

George's mouth drops open and he grabs both her hands in his huge ones and holds her away from him, searching her body for hints of this astounding condition. Then he smiles and holds her close and murmurs into her hair, "you have made me very happy, *Juliashcam*. I am proud to be the father of our child. I will work very hard for us; I promise, and with God's help, we will have a good life in the new country." He wipes his cheek quickly, trying to stem the tide of tears that are beginning to roll down his face.

Julia returns his embrace and smiles up at him in agreement. Somehow the strength of this man permeates her body, and she feels how deeply he cares for her. I must try harder to show George that I care for him too and am so grateful for his love and protection, she thinks to herself. He is the only person, other than Fr. Bergard, the priest from our village in Hungary, who ever genuinely cared if I lived or died. I believe now that God truly did send George to me, and I must work harder at being a good wife.

# Chapter 8

November 1903 arrives in the camp bringing with it bitter cold and howling winds. The icy air seems to penetrate one's very soul. Julia's breath appears to freeze in front of her as it leaves her mouth. She awakens this morning with searing pains in her belly, and knows almost at once that her baby will be born this day. George is not here. He left to go down into the depths of the mine hours ago. Julia gets herself dressed, trying to ignore the terrible pain tearing at her belly and the bone-chilling cold inside their tent. Even the water in the cast iron pot, hanging on the stake over the fire, is frozen. She stumbles outside to look for Mrs. O'Brien, the camp midwife.

"Come in and have coffee with me, Julia," one of the miner's wives calls out to her. "I'm glad to see that you slept a bit later this morning. You will need your strength when that young one makes its entrance into this world."

Julia responds to the invitation with a groan as the pain comes up and grabs her with all of its force. "I don't think I'll have time for coffee," she mutters. "Please help me find Mrs. O'Brien. I think my baby is coming now."

No sooner do these words leave Julia's mouth than the wave of pain comes again, and she slumps to the ground. She doesn't remember much after that except waking up in a strange tent with Mrs. O'Brien staring down at her. Her first realization, after forcing her eyes open, is that she is actually warm. Then she realizes that there are many blankets piled on top of her. She shrinks back into the wonderful comforting warmth that surrounds her. Before Julia can close her eyes again and wallow in this wonderful warmth, a sharp voice rouses her.

"Don't you want to hold your baby?" the voice asks.

Julia tries to sit up a little, but her head begins to spin, and she is forced to lower herself back down onto the cot. She strains her eyes in the darkness of the tent, trying to become more aware of her surroundings. She begins to see shapes and forms and people moving around her.

The squalor of this tent, set aside for the birthing of babies, assaults her senses. The smell of the damp mud floor mingled with her own sweat and blood stings her eyes. Julia shrugs off the sick feeling that threatens to engulf her and answers the woman leaning over her.

"Yes, oh yes, please let me hold my baby."

"Mind you, be gentle with her," a soft female voice whispers beside her ear. "The *bairn* is very small and frail and will need a lot of special care."

As she is speaking, Katie O'Brien places a tiny, slippery form, wrapped in a thin cotton blanket, into Julia's arms; and for the first time she looks down at her daughter, Katya. She and George had agreed early on that this would be their baby's name if it were a girl. The name belonged to George's grandmother, whom he had loved dearly. Mrs. O'Brien is smiling from ear to ear and gently places a kiss on the baby's forehead.

"She's a wee miracle, Julia, though a bit too anxious to be born, I reckon."

"Thank you for coming to me, Mrs. O'Brien. What a comfort it is to have a kind soul like you with me during such a difficult time. I could never have had this baby without you. I will always remember your kindness to me."

Katie O'Brien flushes with pleasure at this high praise. "Remember, Julia, that if it had not been for Mrs. O'Shea coming to get me, the baby might not have made it so easily. You collapsed in front of her tent and she carried you inside herself. She is a strong woman and you have her to thank for getting you inside safely and finding me as quick as she did."

She turns away then and busies herself cleaning up the birthing tent.

"Oh thank you for telling me. Mrs. O'Brien. I have no recollection at all of what happened this morning before Katya was born. I will make a special point of thanking Mrs. O'Shea as soon as I am able to stand on my feet and leave this tent."

Julia remains in the birthing tent for the remainder of the day until the men return from the mine. Katie O'Brien sent word to the foreman, John Connery, to have George come to the birthing tent as soon as he comes up from the tunnel. John Connery assures her that he will send George to her as soon as his feet hit the ground. He also sends his congratulations to Julia on the birth of her first child. The big man has been a good friend to George and Julia and she knows instinctively that his good wishes are most sincere.

When George enters the tent that evening he rushes to Julia's side and smothers her face with kisses. He kneels beside the bed then and stares at her with awe.

"*Juliashcam, Juliashcam*, are you alright? I am so sorry you went through this ordeal without me. You are so brave and strong and I love you so much."

As he stops to catch his breath, George looks down again and sees the tiny baby resting in the crook of Julia's arm. The picture of his wife and first-born child renders him speechless. George slumps to the floor, and then raises himself up on his knees. With bowed head he begins to pray in Hungarian. Only Julia can understand the tender words of thanks he is offering to God for keeping his wife safe and for the gift of this beautiful baby girl. Julia's eyes fill with tears and she turns toward her husband and puts out her arms with the tiny baby encircled therein.

The first time George holds their daughter, the pride in his face brings more tears to Julia's eyes. He holds Katya as if she were going to break at any moment, and keeps rocking her back and forth, all the while humming an old Hungarian lullaby.

"All right, Mr. Pedesch, it's time you took your family home," announces Mrs. O'Brien in her best midwife voice. "If you will take Julia's arm and help her walk to your tent, I will follow right behind you with the baby. We want to get them settled in before the sun goes down."

And so the little family, under the guidance of Mrs. O'Brien, walks across the camp and settles themselves in their tent. George has already fashioned a tiny box to act as a cradle for the new baby when she came, and Julia has sewn a quilt from pieces of rags she collected from the women. Mrs. O'Brien smiles as she lays the baby in the box and takes her leave of the happy couple.

"It is an effort to go to work now, Julia," George tells her their first morning back in their own tent. "I hate being away from our little one, even for a few hours. She is so tiny and helpless, and I love her so much — almost as much as her mother," he adds sheepishly.

Julia's milk has not come in yet, and the milk available from the camp cow is not to Katya's liking. One of the women, realizing the problem, offers to nurse her as she has more than enough milk for Katya and her own baby as well. Even this compassionate gesture does not meet with Katya's approval. Despite all their efforts to keep her fed and warm, it appears that she is just too small and weak to survive in this harsh environment. Julia keeps her wrapped as warm as she can, but the cold November air penetrates through the thin cotton blanket and the homemade quilt. George and Julia keep Katya in bed with them at night, nestled between them for maximum warmth. George tries to hold her so close to him that Julia fears he will smother her.

Even with all their efforts to help her gain strength, Katya survives only a few weeks. They lay her to rest a week before Christmas. The tiny babe dies in George's arms during the night, and when he awakes momentarily to check on her and realizes immediately that she has ceased to breathe, he is inconsolable.

The tears come suddenly and hard, washing his leathery cheeks like a waterfall. Julia can feel her heart breaking as she watches. She is so filled with grief herself that she does not know how to console her poor-grieving husband.

"It is all my fault, *Juliashcam*, that our baby girl came so early. I should not have allowed you to keep working as a seamstress in the camp as well as taking care of me. I should have made you stay in bed and keep off your feet. I could have asked one of the women to cook a little extra for us, and I would have paid her for our share. But I didn't do any of these things, and now our baby, our Katya, is gone. Oh, *Juliashcam*, can you ever forgive me? More importantly, can little Katya ever forgive me?"

George puts his head in his hands and weeps uncontrollably. Forgiving himself is going to be the hardest task of all, Julia thinks.

"It is God's will, George. Please don't blame yourself. Certainly, my doing a bit of sewing to make a few more pennies was not the cause of our daughter's death. Maybe I did not keep her warm enough or force her to drink enough milk. I was her mother after all. I was responsible for her after she was born. Let us stop blaming ourselves and be glad that we had her even for a few weeks. Katya is in God's hands now. She knows we loved her and will always love her. She is warm and fed and at peace now."

George builds a small wooden coffin, using the wood from the little box that Katya slept in when she first came home, and Julia lines it with some pieces of fabric that Katie O'Brien and some of the other women have gathered. There are no more flowers, since the advent of this terrible cold weather, but one of the women picks some rushes and cattails from the nearby pond that have not died from the frost. Julia ties them together with a bit of ribbon saved from a sewing project. George hoists the tiny coffin up onto his shoulders and carries it down to the pond. John Connery grabs a shovel and digs a hole under a huge willow tree. One of the men, whom the miners have dubbed "preacher," says a few words in broken English, and George places the tiny coffin into the ground. John Connery picks up the shovel and begins to fill the small opening with dirt. After a few shovels full, he passes the shovel to George to finish filling the hole. As he drops the last shovel full of earth onto the coffin, George drops to his knees and begins to pray quietly in Hungarian. The crowd disperses, leaving him alone with his grief. John Connery pauses next to the distraught father and pats him gently on the shoulder and then turns and heads up the incline away from the pond.

Julia wants to help George put their daughter to rest in the earth, but is still too weak to wield a shovel. She kneels down on the cold ground and asks God to look after their little girl and to bring peace to her husband George.

It is the first time in her young life that Julia has experienced the real meaning of loss. Unlike her birth mother in Hungary, Julia held her daughter in her arms, smelled her baby skin, kissed her tiny cheeks, and counted her tiny fingers and toes. When she lost Katya, a part of her was lost too. She keeps these thoughts in her heart and struggles to go on the best she can.

After he places Katya in the ground, George displays no further grief. He adopts a brooding silence that no one, including Julia, is able to penetrate. John Connery tries to console him, in the manner of one man to another, but nothing seems to get through the wall he has put around himself. He does his work as he always does, but the heart seems to have gone out of him. Julia has not seen him take his Bible out since the day they placed Katya in the ground. In the past this sacred book was always a part of his daily life and provided him comfort in all things. For the first time in their married life, Julia feels that she must protect her husband, and maybe even from himself. His silent grief has even shut out his creator.

Four weeks after Katya's death, near the end of January, John Connery is ordered by the mine owner to shut down two sections of the main shaft.

"Those veins have gone dry, and they're just not producing

as they should, "the owner grumbles. "We will have to let at least a dozen of the miners go. See to it John; we can't afford to pay men when there is not enough work to go around."

The big Irishman is shattered by this news. He knows how much these families depend on the mine for survival, and many of these men have become his friends. John Connery has been a good friend to George since his arrival and is most sympathetic now in his time of tragedy, but the decision is not his to make. He has to follow orders; and naturally, George is one of the first to go, as he is one of the last to be moved up from scuttler. Sad as Julia is to say goodbye to Katie O'Brien and John Connery, she is almost relieved to leave this camp, because it is a constant reminder of the loss of their poor dear Katya. She could never admit to George that, although she is in mourning too, she is also relieved not to be bringing up a baby in a coal mining camp.

And so they pack up their meager belongings once again in the two old valises and prepare to leave the camp. Julia goes in search of her only friends, Katie O'Brien and Mrs. O'Shea, to say goodbye and thank them once again for all the kindness they have shown her. George and Julia already said their good-byes to John Connery last night with tears and hugs all around. George shook John's hand and expressed his heartfelt thanks to the big man in his very best English.

They leave the next day, heading west for Ohio where they hear that the mines are better operated, and the pay is higher than it is in Pittsburgh. Eventually George ceases his mourning when so many other things require his attention. Just being away from the Pittsburgh mine and all its memories, seem to have brought George back to reality. The first time Julia sees George take the old Bible out of the suitcase, she knows he is learning to deal with his grief. Things will be better for both of them from now on, she feels certain.

Ohio proves to be a bit warmer and is somewhat more comfortable to live in than Pittsburgh was. However, by the time the work slows down there and they are forced to move on to the next camp, Julia is becoming more and more anxious to return to New York. She is still convinced that New York is where they should make their permanent home, and this belief has become a part of her dream. Her "secret sock" is getting heavier and heavier; and each time she tucks it away in the bottom of the old valise, she sees her dream coming closer.

During the next few years, however, George and Julia travel all the way west to Indiana before turning back and heading across the country to their beloved New York. During that time, George works in several mines in West Virginia and western Maryland on their way back east. He also becomes an expert in odd jobs along the way. George, it seems, can fix anything now, from repairing chair legs to simple machines. He still speaks little English, and is still disinclined to increase his knowledge of the language, but he manages to get by. This lack of English does not help him in his quest to support his family, which keeps increasing with each new state they visit. Somehow, with God's help, they do survive and manage to increase their stake too.

During this period of almost five years, Julia gives birth to four more children. Only three of them survive – Irma, now age three and a half, was born in Cleveland, Ohio; Julius, age two, was born in Gary, Indiana, and little Mary, only thirteen months, entered the world in Martinsburg, West Virginia. Their second son, Edward, is born prematurely in Frederick, Maryland, and dies in childbirth. George is devastated once again by Edwards's death, but this time he is able to find solace in prayer and in the presence of the other three children. Irma, Julius, and little Mary all adore their Papa, and he relishes any and all of their childish attentions. The love he receives from his children helps him survive this second loss. Edward's death was also easier to bear, Julia believes, because he never got to hold the baby in his arms. No bond was ever formed between father and son, as had been the case with their dear Katya.

After Katya's death Julia hoped she would have no more

children until they returned to New York, but the good Lord had other ideas. George and Julia re-consummated their marriage on very few occasions, but during every one, Julia managed to conceive another child. And so the little family grew to five.

# Chapter 9

In the spring of 1908 George and Julia arrive back in New York City with their three remaining children. Irma and Julius are strong, hearty youngsters, but Mary is quite thin and frail – a reminder of their dear Katya born in the coal fields of Pennsylvania. They find the city much changed since they first arrived on the *Catalonia* and entered this new land through the portals of Ellis Island.

As she stands there on these familiar streets on a balmy day in June and looks up at the tenement buildings, Julia silently thanks God for bringing them back safely to New York. Delancey Street and Allen Street bear no resemblance whatever to the scene of the old immigrant shelters she recalled from their first arrival in New York. No longer does the aroma of the "slop houses" permeate the air. These new tenements are replete with inside bathrooms, of all things – one on every floor of the building no less. The buildings appear like palaces to George and Julia after the series of mining camps they have been living in. They cannot even compare with their memory of the immigrant shelter they shared with the other passengers arriving on the *Catalonia*. Julia is so excited at the prospect of having a new home with inside plumbing, she can hardly contain herself.

George, on the other hand, seems to take it all in stride, and is only curious about who still lives here that he might know from their old days in the city.

"Do you think anyone will remember us, *Juliashcam?*" he

questions, looking around at the people passing by and searching each one for a familiar face.

"I wouldn't get my hopes up, George," Julia answers. "After all, five years have passed since we lived in this neighborhood. Many of our old friends must have moved on too."

"Maybe some have returned to this part of town just as we did," George retorts hopefully. "I think I'll take a walk down Allen Street and see if I see anyone I know. I'll take Irma and Julius with me if you can manage Mary on your own," he adds.

"Go ahead then," Julia answers, and taking Mary from him and settling the little one on her hip, she prepares to continue walking down Orchard Street. "I intend to find us an apartment before this day is over, George, so look for Mary and me on Orchard Street when you finish your tour of the neighborhood," Julia adds with a grin. Mary whimpers at being shifted yet again but manages a "Bye, Da," before George and the other two children round the corner.

Julia begins walking slowly down Orchard Street, crooning softly to Mary as she strolls along. When she reaches the corner of Orchard and Houston Streets she sees a sign advertising an apartment for rent. Julia knocks on the door of the ground floor apartment and asks if she may look at the apartment for rent. A kindly looking woman appears at the door with a set of keys in her hand.

Eyeing the baby in Julia's arms, she says, "It's a few flights up, miss, but if that's alright with you, then follow me."

Julia nods and shifts Mary to her other side. They begin the climb to the top floor. The apartment has three rooms, a fireplace and, wonder of wonders, an outside window. "On a clear day, we will be able to get a real view of the East River," Julia informs the dozing Mary." It even has a small wood burning stove where I can cook real meals for my family," Julia observes. The landlady points out the other fine points of the apartment and advises Julia that she is very lucky that this apartment is available.

"The tenants who were living here just moved out the day

before yesterday," she announces. The man got a new job across the river in New Jersey working for his uncle and off they went. Otherwise, they would still be here, I assure you," she adds with proud certainty.

Julia smiles thankfully at the woman, and then inquires about the rent.

"That would be $5.50 a month, including the water and light," the landlady informs her. "And if anything goes wrong with the plumbing, my husband will fix it as good as new," she adds proudly.

"Well that seems fair," responds Julia, shifting Mary again to the other hip. "I am quite sure that we will take the apartment. I just want my husband to take a look at it before we make it final," says Julia. "I hope that is agreeable," she adds questioningly.

"Why of course, dearie," the landlady answers. "My name is Mrs. Fine and I'll be right here when you come back with your mister."

When Julia returns to the sidewalk with Mary, she sees George and the children rounding the corner. Irma and Julius come running, anxious to tell her about all the sights and sounds they have encountered on their walk with their papa. George is smiling and can't wait to tell her the news.

"Mr. Fineburg is still here, *Juliashcam*, and he has the most wonderful grocery store you can imagine," announces George. "He gave the children each an apple and a cookie – the ones his wife used to bake when we lived here before. Can you believe it?"

"I am so pleased, George, and now I have news for you too. I have just looked at an apartment on the top floor of this building. I told the landlady that we will be renting it right away. I just want you to see it before I give her the first month's rent in advance. I'm sure you'll like it as much as I do, and we can move in right away."

"If this is where you want to live, Juliashcam, I will agree," George says with conviction. And so saying, he leads the children upstairs to what is to be their new home. They move into the apartment in time for Julia to prepare a pot of soup for dinner on their new stove. She even manages to hang up her little crocheted plaque that says, "Our Happy Home" – a gift from her old friend Bertha, back in Pittsburgh, who made it with her own hands.

"Many of the neighbors are Jewish like our landlady, Mrs. Fine," announces Julia to George at the small round dinner table where they are all gather to eat their evening meal. "There are also a few Irish families living in the building and on the next street, so I am sure there will be a church where we can hear Mass before very long," she adds with a sigh. "I do so miss being inside a real church on Sunday mornings."

To Julia, one of the most amazing things she has seen is the stairway outside the building. Mrs. Fine, the landlady, tells her that this is called a fire escape. If, God forbid, there is a fire in the building, this is how they can escape to safety. What a wonderful country this is – people looking out for each other in case of a fire.

The bathroom on their floor is quite small, but it has a sink and a faucet from which cold water can be drawn whenever they want it. The toilet has a big box above it mounted on the wall with a long chain that you pull each time you use it. Water comes down and cleans out the bowl after every use.

It is like a miracle thinks Julia, but I believe George is afraid of the chain because he goes in there very seldom. He still prefers one of the old outhouses still standing behind the building. He has peace and quiet there he says, but Julia thinks he fears that the water will come down out of the box and drown him.

The front room with the window is their combination kitchen and sitting room. Irma and Julius are in the middle room, and George and Julia use the room in the back with little Mary. Julia still likes to keep her close because she suffers from croup and sometimes gasps for air during the night. Poor little thing, she will never be strong like Irma and Julius.

The tenement building is a wonder in many ways. There is

horsehair wall covering on the walls in the hall, and one side even has a beautiful picture painted in the center. It is a scene of a cottage in the woods with snow falling, and Julia loves to look at it. The ceilings are made of tin and have pretty designs worked into them. They even have one extra wide step before the front door and seven more steps down to the sidewalk. That is where they sit in the evening watching the children play and catching up on the news of the day with their neighbors. As soon as Julia gets Mary to sleep, they bring Irma and Julius down for awhile to mingle with the other children. Julius usually prefers to stay on his father's lap, but Irma joins right in the minute her tiny feet touch the pavement. Sometimes the *gelato* vendor comes by to tempt the children with a treat. Julia remembers well the first time George and she tasted that wonderful cool confection the day that they departed from Ellis Island.

The spring and summer pass happily and relatively uneventfully. The supply of money in the "secret sock" is dwindling, however, and very soon Julia knows she must think of a way for them to get some regular income again. George never seems to question where the next dollar will come from. He just assumes that Julia will take care of it.

Julia falls back on her old skill of sewing and spreads the word among her neighbors that she is available to work as a seamstress. She offers to do repairs and also make some smaller items if they will provide the material. Work begins to come in, and she is just beginning to establish herself when Mary becomes ill. The croup has been getting worse during the warm weather, and their top floor apartment gets very hot during the day. Julia gets little sleep at night because she is up with Mary trying to cool her off and help her to breathe. George sleeps so soundly that he seldom hears the baby cough so Julia handles this night duty all by herself. She does not complain, but one night she sleeps rather soundly for the first time in many days. George is sleeping on the couch in the front room, because two people in the same bed in this heat is almost unbearable.

Julia doesn't know how long Mary has been crying and coughing before she hears her, but when her cries finally awaken her mother, she is gasping for air. Julia rushes to the crib, calling for George as she does so. She puts Mary over her shoulder and pounds on her tiny back with her fist, the way the midwife in Maryland had shown her after little Mary was born. It is no use. Mary's lungs are so full of fluid that she cannot get any air. By the time George comes through the door into the bedroom, their baby daughter has left them.

George sees Julia's tears and senses immediately that Mary has passed on to be with Katya. He picks up the little girl in his arms and holds her close. He begins rocking her gently as he had done with Katya so long ago. As he hums that same Hungarian lullaby, he begins wrapping the tiny body in a clean blanket. Then, with the little girl in his arms, and tears coursing down his face, he leaves the room. Julia follows behind him silently, not willing to break into his grief. He is a man with a purpose, and something tells her not to interfere. He lays Mary gently on the couch while he puts on his jacket and shoes. He picks up the little bundle from the couch and heads for the door.

"Stay here with Irma and Julius," he murmurs. "I will take our Mary down the street to the undertaker."

"But it's five o'clock in the morning, George," Julia stammers between sobs.

"Never mind that, *Juliashcam*," is his answer. "God doesn't sleep and he is waiting for Mary."

With that, he opens the front door and heads down the stairs, hugging the white bundle to his chest. Julia closes the door and returns to the bedroom, trying not to wake Julius and Irma. An hour or so later George returns. Julius and Irma are awake now so Julia goes into their room and sits down on the edge of Irma's bed.

"Come here, Julius, and sit by Mama," Julia says softly. "I have something to tell you."

"What is it Mama, what is it?" both children cry in unison.

"Has something happened to Papa?" asks Irma, noticing that her father is not there with them.

"No, Irma, Papa is fine," Julia answers. "It's little Mary I have to talk to you about. She has left us and gone to be with God. She was just too small and weak to live with us anymore, so God took her to live with him in Heaven."

"But we didn't get a chance to say goodbye to her," wailed Julius with the tears starting to form in his bright blue eyes. "I want to say goodbye to Mary, I do, I do." His voice trailed off as his sister Irma put her chubby arms around him and tried to console him.

"She was really sick, wasn't she, Mama?" Irma asks with a note of sad resignation in her young voice. "I always hear her coughing in the night. It must have made her so very tired. I guess God took pity on her and took her to a special place where she could take a nap whenever she wanted," reasoned the little girl.

"I'm sure that's what happened, Irma," replies her mother. God always looks after children whether they are sick or well. What we have to do now is kneel down and say our good-byes to Mary in a prayer. Just tell her you love her and will remember her every night when you say your prayers. That will make her very happy. Come now, Julius, kneel here next to me and your sister, and we will say our prayer for Mary." Both children knelt down beside their mother and said their good-byes to little Mary and asked God to take extra good care of her.

The funeral took place the next day in a small non-denominational chapel a few blocks from Allen Street. Irma and Julius went with their parents. Mrs. Fineburg, the grocer's wife, came also with one or two other women from the neighborhood. Even Mrs. Fine, their landlady, came to pay her respects. Julia and George were very grateful to everyone for taking time from their busy days to honor their Mary. The funeral director had contacted a priest from an uptown parish because George insisted on a Catholic burial. He was a rather soft-spoken prelate, and the ceremony was brief. They got permission to bury Mary in the tiny cemetery behind the chapel, so that is where they laid her and where the children were able to say their final farewells to their baby sister.

The neighborhood has grown since their arrival almost five years ago, but regretfully, there is still no Catholic Church. There is a beautiful synagogue and the tiny chapel where the few Christians living here can go to and pray as a community and where little Mary was buried just a few months ago. Julia wants more for Irma and Julius. Her strong attachment to her faith is tied to her childhood in Hungary where the only place she can remember being happy was at the rectory with Fr. Bergard, the local priest. Julia remembers back to the times when Anna Frye would send her there to scrub the kitchen floor of the rectory, a job Anna herself hated to do.

"That's all you're fit for – scrubbing floors," she would shout at Julia.

"Yes ma'am," was Julia's only answer on these occasions.

She couldn't wait to get there. The priest, Fr. Bergard, was a kind man who seemed to understand young Julia's state of unhappiness, and tried to make it up to her in so many ways. When she arrived at the rectory, he would greet her warmly.

"Good day, my dear Julia, and have you come to bring me my hug for the day?"

This always made Julia smile, and she would run to him at once, her arms wide in order to hug the girth of this kind and gentle man of God.

Fr. Bergard was so kind to me recalled Julia. He almost made me feel beautiful. I scrubbed those floors with all my might so he would know how much I love to be there with him and his equally kind housekeeper, Maria.

"Come into the kitchen now, Julia," Maria would call at midday. "I have just made some thick nourishing soup. If you are as good a scrubber as Father says you are, I will give you a piece of fruit as well."

Fr. Bergard taught Julia her morning and evening prayers and even read her stories from the big Bible he kept in his paneled library.

"I want you to learn all you can about our Lord, Julia," he would say in his most solemn voice. "Any time you have a question or if you have any trouble at home, please know you can always come to me, and I will help you.

This kindly priest became Julia's best, if not her only friend, and his housekeeper was like the mother she never had. She vowed then and there that she would be the best Catholic she could be and make Fr. Bergard and Maria proud of her.

# Chapter 10

Autumn fills the air and the time has come for little Irma, now four and a half, to begin going to Mass on a regular basis. Julia is determined that Irma will learn about God and the saints in a real church. She begins walking farther and farther from their neighborhood in search of a real house of worship, not just a small chapel like the one up the street from where they live. One day she leaves the children with her neighbor, Kate Ryan, and walks down Houston Street to First Avenue. As she reaches the corner Julia looks up and there at the curb directly in front of her is a big red streetcar.

Julia pauses for an instant and then stuffs her hand into her pocket, searching for the few coins she usually keeps there. Her fingers encircle the two coins nestled at the bottom of her pocket.

"How much?" she says to the conductor as she mounts the steps of the streetcar.

"That will be a nickel, young lady," he answers with a smile.

Julia looks down at her hand. One coin is bigger than the other and for a moment she is not certain which one is the nickel. She proffers her hand to the conductor, and he quickly removes the larger of the two coins from her palm and drops it into the receptacle. Julia nods her thanks and enters the car, taking a seat by an open window.

She is so busy taking in the sights from her seat by the window, that before she knows it, the conductor is shouting, "Last stop – all out for Yorkville."

Yorkville? She hears herself repeat the strange-sounding word. Where in the world am I? She looks up at the sign where the streetcar ends its journey and sees that it says York Avenue, and under it in bright blue letters another sign that proclaims the word Yorkville. Julia steps down from the streetcar and begins to look around her. To her utter delight, she soon discovers many other signs, most of them on storefronts along this new thoroughfare. The signs describe many things familiar to her. Hungarian meats are described on one and pastries on another. Some of the signs just have pictures on them to show their wares, but Julia recognizes them at once from her native land. Julia thinks that some are written in German also. The sights and smells of these tiny establishments are a joy to her senses. It appears that many Hungarian as well as German families have settled here. Best of all, she discovers that there is a beautiful old Hungarian Church just a few blocks from the streetcar station. She enters the church and kneels down, soaking up the beauty of the old stone building. Julia blesses herself with the water from the marble holy water font and begins to pray.

"Thank you, Lord, for bringing me here. This is where George and I belong and where we can raise our children among people from our own country. George will be so pleased when I tell him. He will be as excited as I am to find this wonderful place in New York City."

Julia continues walking through the neighborhood and soon discovers that there is an elementary school here too, only a block from the church. She can make out colorful childish drawings hanging in the windows of the large brick building. She can feel the excitement rising inside her and she rushes further along the street taking in every detail of this new neighborhood. Irma and Julius are going to get a good education; they're not going to grow up ignorant like George and me. As God is my witness, I vow to make this happen. Julia begins canvassing the neighborhood with a vengeance and before long, she finds a building hosting a rather insignificant sign which states that there is an apartment for rent. She takes a deep breath, gathers herself up to her full height, and climbs the stairs. Her English is quite good now and she is sure the landlord will be able to understand her. A rotund, jolly-looking woman opens the door and greets her warmly.

"I am interested in the apartment for rent," Julia blurts out confidently.

"Oh, of course, come right in my dear, and I will show it to you," the woman answers enthusiastically. "You have such lovely blond hair; are you by any chance from the old country – Hungary I mean?" she questions in a warm friendly tone.

"Why yes, from Budapest and my husband too," Julia answers. "We have two children, and my daughter will be ready to go to school next year. I noticed the wonderful elementary school down the street and the beautiful church on the corner, and I knew right away that this is where we should live – if there is an apartment we can afford, of course," Julia went on.

The landlady receives this last pronouncement with a smile and leads Julia up the stairs to the apartment in question. She opens the door proudly and invites Julia to enter.

"The rent is $9.00 a month," she states matter-of-factly – a real bargain in this neighborhood I assure you."

The rent is a bit higher than I anticipated, Julia thinks to herself, but I am confident I can make enough money by sewing to make the payments. The three and a half rooms are large and airy with windows on both ends of the railroad-type flat. It seems like a palace to Julia, and before she stops to think any further, she says, "Yes, I will take this apartment."

"You can move in any time," the landlady informs her, "but you must give me one week's rent in advance as a show of good faith. If it were up to me, I would not insist on this, but my husband is not so lenient. The tenants we had before left in the middle of the night owing us two weeks rent, and now he has become like an old miser – no money, no apartment. I hope you understand," she adds in a kindly voice.

"Of course I do," Julia murmurs, wondering all the while where she is going to come up with the requisite amount of money. "I will be back tomorrow morning with the money, I promise. Meanwhile, please don't rent the apartment to anyone else," Julia pleads.

"Don't worry child, I trust you, and I will look for you tomorrow. My name is Mrs. Ludkin, and what is your name please?"

"Oh, forgive my rudeness," Julia stammers. "My name is Julia Pedesch, and I will indeed be back tomorrow, and thank you, thank you."

All the way home Julia wrestles with how she is going to tell George that they are moving again. Not only that, but where in the world is she going to get the one-week's rent in advance? There is a small amount left in "the sock" but not enough to pay the first week's rent in advance. Her only hope is Kate Ryan, her friend downstairs on the first floor of their building. Kate's father had just died and left her a small legacy she told Julia last week. Kate was thinking of moving uptown too, now that she had a bit of money to call her own. Maybe Kate would give me a small loan, Julia wonders. Once we move, I'm certain I can get lots of work as a seamstress or maybe even something better, and pay her back in a few month's time. With God's help, I know we can find a good steady job for George as well.

Julia gets off the streetcar and runs the last few blocks back to Orchard Street. She is exhilarated by the thought of a better life for her children and her anxiety to talk to Kate Ryan. Julia sees Kate on the front steps of the building, watching her son Brian playing hopscotch with Irma. Little Julius is sitting on the curb petting the Ryan's big tabby cat that is curled in his lap.

"Slow down, Julia girl, you're rushin' like the devil himself is after ya. Are ya alright; is somethin' wrong now?"

"Oh no, Kate, everything is fine – wonderful really. Can I talk to you a minute? I found an apartment, Kate, a wonderful apartment uptown in a place called Yorkville. I have to go back there in the morning, after I talk to George of course. The landlord insists on a week's rent in advance – $2.25 he wants. I have part of it, Kate, but I don't know where to get the rest unless you can find it in your heart to give me a small loan."

"Is it only a few dollars you'll be needin', Julia girl? Now that I'm a rich woman, so to speak, I'd be more than happy to help out my only best friend in all of New York. I know you'd do the same for me if I asked you, wouldn't ya?"

"Oh, Kate, of course I would. Do you mean to say you really will loan me the money I need? Oh, God bless you Kate Ryan; God bless you forever and ever."

Julia rushes over to her friend and gives her such a big hug she almost falls off the stoop. "I'll pay you back, Kate, every penny and with interest too. You'll have it all by the end of the month, I promise."

"Now, Miss Julia, don't be talkin' to me about interest. I don't need to make money on me friends. I'm just as pleased as can be that I can be of some help. "I hate to see you move so far away, Julia girl. Perhaps I'll take a trip uptown meself to this Yorkville place you're so excited about. We might be neighbors again for all you know. Wouldn't that be somethin' now?"

"I can't think of anyone I'd rather have as a neighbor than my best friend, Kate Ryan. When I go back tomorrow, I'll ask Mrs. Ludkin, the landlady, if she knows of any other apartments. If she does, I'll find out where and come and tell you. Oh, Kate, this is all so exciting. I can't wait to tell George and the children."

## Chapter 11

George accepts the news with some misgivings. "If you really want to move again, *Juliashcam,* you know I won't stand in the way. I will miss Mr. Fineburg and some of our neighbors though. I hope this new neighborhood makes you happy, because I don't want to keep moving all over New York City. I do share your joy about having a real church to go to, and I know we must find a school for Irma before she turns five. I'm sure you have made a wise decision for all of us. Let's hope we will all be happy in this Yorkville of yours," he concludes wistfully.

George does not seem to be concerned about the amount of the rent or any of the other details of the move. He knows that Julia will find a way to provide these basic necessities; and of course, he is right. He does assure Julia, however, that he will find work right away and will provide for her and the children if he has to work seven days a week to do it.

To show her gratitude for his enthusiasm and for allowing her to move their family once again, Julia plants a big kiss on George's sunburned cheek. A huge smile covers his face immediately, and seeing this, Julia's heart feels glad. She knows that somehow things will be better for them and prays that George shares her faith in their future.

As it turns out, George only has to work six days a week. Julia wastes no time. The day after they move in to the new apartment, Julia picks up the local newspaper and sees that the City is in dire need of street cleaners. Headlines declare that the new mayor is determined to keep the city streets free of dirt and debris. Within minutes of reading this advertisement, she takes George by the hand and leads him downtown to apply for a position as a street cleaner in New York City. The Supervisor looks at George, and seeing the look of determination on his countenance and his obvious physical qualifications, offers him the job on the spot. Julia responds with her most beguiling smile.

"I will need to get some personal information," the Supervisor tells them.

"I can tell you anything you need to know," Julia assures him. The Supervisor looks over at George, and seeing that he doesn't seem to mind having his wife speak for him, he continues.

"What is your husband's full name and age, and where do you live?" he begins. In a short time Julia provides the Supervisor with all the information required for the employment records. George puts out his hand and manages a creditable 'thank you' before they take their leave and head for home.

Julia is so pleased with the outcome, she can hardly contain herself. George's salary will cover their rent with enough left over for some food. It is the beginning of their dream coming true. After they round the corner, Julia unceremoniously throws herself at George and places a big kiss on his amazed face.

"Oh George, you make me so proud," she exclaims. "I just know this is a good omen of better things to come. We are going to be so happy in our new home, and the children will be happy too. Our dream is starting to come true."

George responds by taking Julia's hand in his and pressing it to his lips. "I love you *Juliashcam*," he stammers. Julia can hear the tears in his voice, but knows that they are tears of happiness. He is such a good man, she thinks to herself; if only I can learn to really love him. I do try, God knows, I try.

Every day Julia packs a tin pail with lunch for her husband – two big chunks of bread, a small tin of sardines (his favorite) and a piece of cheese. She tries to include a piece of fruit too if they can afford it, whatever is in season; and sometimes the grocer gives her a special price if the fruit is just a little soft or has a small bruise. With Irma on one hand and Julius on the other, they deliver the lunch pail to George each day at precisely 11:30 in the morning.

George is permitted one half hour for lunch, and he looks forward to this special visit from his wife and children. Julia can see the pride he feels when he looks at the faces of the other men as they admire his handsome wife and two clean, well-dressed children. Julia tries very hard to always look pretty for George and make him proud of his family. She brushes her hair each morning until it shines and braids Irma's carefully and ties it with a ribbon. Julius is much harder to keep clean and neat as he is always getting into something, but Julia makes him wear his wool knickers and his gray cap on the blond curls when they go to visit Papa at his work. This makes him feel like a big boy he says, but Julia knows he cannot wait to divest himself from the stiff fabric.

Studying Irma intently one evening after dinner, George states simply, "you are a miniature of your mother already, Irma, though smaller in build. Stand up next to your mama; I want to look at you both. You will never be tall and stately like your mama, though just as beautiful. You will be shorter, I think, and take more after me. Julius will be taller, like his mama I think. He even carries himself like you do already, Julia. You have given me two beautiful children, and I am so proud of our family."

Both children rush to give their Papa a hug, and when he thinks Julia is not looking, George drops a tiny hard candy into each small hand. He hoards these from a small stash he purchases from the grocer each time he gets paid. Julia never acknowledges his secret, although she has been well aware of it for some time.

Autumn arrives in all its glory, and the time has come for Irma to begin Kindergarten. Julia has found a neighbor, the sister of their landlady, Mrs. Ludkin, who will watch over Julius in the morning until Irma comes home from school. She has even agreed to keep an eye on both of them if Julia is fortunate enough to find work. She doesn't much like leaving Julius with a comparative stranger, but she has to make certain concessions until she can find work that is more conducive to their schedule.

Irma begins school as if she was born to it and is already singing the praises of her teacher, who spends a good deal of time reading books to her young charges. This delights Irma who has an unflagging curiosity about almost everything.

Irma [pronounced *Eedma* with a long "E" in Hungarian] accosts her mother one afternoon after returning home from school.

"Mama," Irma cries, "I hate my name. Please, please let me change it. One of the girls is my class has the same name as I do, and she is so ugly, Mama. I can't bear to have the same name as someone so ugly. And she's mean too." Irma begins to sob uncontrollably.

"What do you want us to call you, Irma?" Julia asks, trying to maintain a serious expression.

"Emma, I want to be called Emma," she begs. "That is the name of one of the teachers," Irma declares; "and I want to be just like her."

"It is all right with me, Irm – er uh, I mean Emma; but I will have to talk it over with your papa before I can agree."

Julia has some trouble convincing George that it is all right to change their daughter's name at this stage of her life, but as in all else, he finally agrees, in principle anyway. He makes it quite clear at the outset that he will never call either of his children by anything but their given names. Strangely, the name Emma seems to fit their daughter, and this new appellation stays with her the rest of her life.

At this point, Julius, not to be outdone and tired of being teased by his playmates about his rather formidable name, employs the same tactics as his sister, and becomes Jerry. Julia only cares that they are safe, healthy, and happy, and so they keep their new adopted names with her full approval.

Their father's approval is another story altogether. Eventually, George does give in and begins calling his daughter Emma, as if it were her given name. Julius, on the other hand, is a different matter. George cannot bring himself to call their son Jerry no matter how hard he tries. They had named him after George's favorite uncle back in Budapest, and George considers this is a sacred trust. Jerry loves his father very much, and because of this and his gentle temperament, he never complains when George calls him by his given name. No one else is allowed this privilege, however. George continues to call his son by his given name, and never deviates from this ritual during his lifetime.

# Chapter 12

It is autumn of 1910, and Emma is preparing to enter the first grade. Julia sees an advertisement in the classified section of the local newspaper that sounds like it has been written with her in mind.

"Well-to-do family, Upper East Side requires part-time cook/housekeeper for their home."

The address given is on Fifth Avenue, and Julia makes haste to go there the very next day. She takes the streetcar that leaves right from her corner at York Avenue and Seventy ninth Street. It runs straight across to Fifth Avenue. Mrs. Ludkin had casually pointed this out to her one day, and she filed the information away in the back of her head to be kept for future use. That future was now.

Julia enters the streetcar and politely asks the conductor what she should do when the car arrives at Fifth Avenue in order to find the exact address she is looking for. He looks a bit surprised when he hears the numbers she gives him, but tells her to change to the number seven streetcar.

"That will bring you down Fifth Avenue to the sixties, where the address you require is located," he adds with authority.

She also asks the conductor where she should get off, and he informs her that the house she is going to – 840 Fifth Avenue – is between 65th and 66th Streets.

"You won't be able to miss it," he assures her with a knowing grin.

Armed with this precise information, Julia sits back to enjoy the ride. She loves watching all the people as they scurry to work and enjoys looking in the windows of the elegant shops along Fifth Avenue. Before she knows it, she is there.

Her destination, as it turns out, is not a house – it is a mansion! No wonder the conductor said I couldn't miss it, Julia thinks to herself. As she hurries up the walk to the imposing front door, she has a sinking feeling in the pit of her stomach. This is no ordinary family with more money than most, but one of great importance in New York City, Julia reasons. She is certain that her intuition is correct when a stately butler answers the door – after her first knock.

"May I help you, Miss?" he asks in a kind but firm voice.

"Yes, Sir," she responds. "I'm here to apply for the position – the ah – cook position," she stammers.

"Oh, then please go around to the side door, Miss, and ask for Mrs. Umber. She will discuss that position with you."

With that, he waves Julia toward the path on her left and closes the massive front door. She stands staring at the closed door for a moment and then pulls herself up to her full height and follows the path around to the side of the house as she was instructed. Julia knocks once more on another door leading to 840 Fifth Avenue. This time a friendly looking woman answers her knock, and introduces herself as Mrs. Maude Umber.

"I suppose you're here to apply for the position," she says matter-of-factly and ushers Julia inside a huge kitchen. "May I ask your name, my dear?"

"I am Julia Pedesch," she answers, "and I am very pleased to meet you, Mrs. Umber."

Maude Umber closes the door behind her and looks at Julia thoughtfully. "I have been the housekeeper here for more years than I care to count," she informs Julia in a friendly voice, "and it's high time I had some serious help around here."

She smiles so warmly that Julia senses they have established an instant rapport.

"Let's go into the breakfast room where we can be more comfortable" Maude Umber continues, and proceeds down a hallway just off the kitchen.

Julia follows dutifully behind, trying to take in everything around her as they move from one room to another. The kitchen is very large and Julia can see closets filled with magnificent china and unusual serving pieces. An endless array of pots and pans in all sizes and shapes are hanging from the ceiling on hooks attached to a huge metal track, the likes of which Julia has never seen. Several large strange looking machines sit on one of the counters, and she cannot even imagine what wonderful services they might perform. Mrs. Umber strides across the room and indicates a small round table in the corner surrounded by four tall wooden chairs with colorful cushions on them. She gestures toward one of the chairs, and they both sit down at the table.

Maude Umber scrutinizes Julia for a moment and then comments on her "exotic" appearance, as she terms it, and says she especially likes her charming accent.

"What country did you call home, Miss Pedesch?" she inquires.

"It is Mrs. Pedesch, and I am from Hungary, Mrs. Umber, but please call me Julia."

"A married lady you are; and so young! I would never have guessed," added Maude Umber, "and you have a rich heritage in the kitchen, to be sure," she continued, nodding with pleasure. "You would be a pleasant addition to this stodgy old house," she offers with a smile. "I assume you can cook as good as you look," she adds with a grin.

"I certainly hope so," Julia assures her without hesitation. "I can make many of the Hungarian specialties you may have heard of such as stuffed cabbage, chicken *paprikash* with spatzle and *turos gumbotz*, as well as tortes and other wonderful desserts that are staples in my homeland," Julia adds.

"We'll have to introduce your rich Hungarian cooking a little bit at a time," Mrs. Umber warns. "The Colonel has not been exposed to anything but plain meat and potatoes for awhile. He used to be very fond of seasoned food and rich pastries when his wife was in residence, but that has not been for some time now," she adds with a sigh. "I'm sure you can cook plain American food as well, Miss Julia. Am I right?" she went on.

"Oh yes, of course," Julia assures her quickly.

"The Colonel is a lonely man, my dear, and maybe a pretty face and a rich meal will lighten his spirits."

"The Colonel?" Julia interrupts with surprise. "Is the owner of this beautiful home a soldier?"

"Oh no, no my dear Julia," Mrs. Umber answers, laughing out loud. "Forgive me for misleading you. Let me give you a bit of background on this family and the illustrious man you would be working for." Maude Umber sits back in her chair, folds her arms across her ample bosom, and begins.

"The Colonel I speak of is Col. John Jacob Astor IV, son of William Astor and the great-grandson of the famous American fur trader, John Jacob Astor. I'm sure you must have heard the name since you arrived in America." She looked at Julia questioningly.

"I'm afraid not, Mrs. Umber," Julia answers. "My husband George and I have been traveling across the country these past five years, living in mining camps and such. The kind of people we've been meeting would not know about a man as famous and rich as the Colonel. Please go on and tell me all about him and this fine family."

"Well, alright, young woman, I will bring you up to date and give you a bit of a history lesson as well," chided the housekeeper. "After a period of traveling abroad from 1888 to 1891, Col. Astor finally returned to the United States to manage the family fortune from his home here at 840 Fifth Avenue. Many of his close friends call the Colonel "Jack," as you may hear from time to time. At any rate, last year, after several years of marriage, Col. Astor divorced his wife, Ava, and so is presently a bachelor. He lives in this big house all alone now with only his son Vincent for company. Between you and me, Julia, Vincent is not much company; I can tell you. Well, I guess that's enough family history for now, concluded Mrs. Umber. If you ever have any questions that are puzzling you, please don't hesitate to ask. I want you to feel comfortable here while working in the house."

Without drawing a breath, Maude Umber went on. "After hearing all this, my dear, do you think you want the job? If you do, I will hire you on a trial basis for three months," she concluded. That is the way it is done here at the Astor mansion – everyone is hired on a trial basis. I hope you understand and do not take it personally. She looks directly at Julia then and waits for her to speak.

"Yes, oh yes, I do want the job, Mrs. Umber. I'm sure we'll get along just fine, and I'll try to do everything the way you tell me. I am so grateful just to have this chance. I can't thank you enough." Julia pauses and waits for the housekeeper to continue.

"Well now then, it's settled. When can you begin, Julia?"

"How about next Monday morning," Julia answers brightly. "I just have to make a few arrangements for my daughter to be picked up after school, and I will be here by eight o'clock."

"That sounds very satisfactory indeed," says Mrs. Umber with a shrug of her broad, round shoulders, "and if all goes well, you should be able to leave here by one o'clock every day. We might need you to stay longer on a weekend now and then," she adds. "The Colonel is talking about having parties again and putting some life back into this old mansion. Would that be a possibility, do you suppose?"

"I would be glad to work here on an occasional Saturday," Julia responds, "but Sunday is most important for me to spend with my husband and children. I hope that will be all right with you. I want this job very much," Julia continues, "but I need to be home with my family all day on Sundays."

"I totally sympathize, my dear, and I don't think that will present a problem. If a special occasion should arise, I'd let you know well in advance. I think we will get on just fine, you and me; and I look forward to seeing you on Monday morning."

Julia fairly floats out the door, filled with excitement. She hurries up the street to catch the streetcar back up Fifth Avenue and across town to Yorkville. She sees nothing of the ride home; her mind is so full of thoughts of the wonderful mansion she has just visited. She has never seen anything like it before.

I cannot wait to tell George. He will miss not seeing me at lunch time delivering his pail with Jerry, but I am sure I can get Frieda, Mrs. Ludkin's sister, to take over this chore, at least when the weather is good. If it is going to be very cold or rainy or if it snows, I will prepare the lunch pail the night before and George can take it with him in the morning when he leaves for work. The cold air will keep the food fresh, and then Frieda and Jerry will not have to make the trip at all.

After dining tonight on noodles and pot cheese, one of George's favorites, Julia blurts out her news. George appears startled and stands up with a strained look on his face when she says she will be going to Fifth Avenue each morning.

"But that is all the way down on the other side of town, *Juliashcam*," he worries. "Will you be safe traveling all that way by yourself, and what about when the weather is bad?"

"George," she answers, "put your mind at rest. The housekeeper, Mrs. Umber assures me that the streetcars are very safe, and Col. Astor will even pay for me to use it. Each station has a covered waiting area, so if the weather is wet, I can keep perfectly dry. So you see, my husband, there is nothing at all to worry about. I will be traveling in style, like a regular business lady. Aren't you proud of me?"

With that, George stands up and comes toward his wife with his arms open wide. He enfolds her in an embrace and lays kisses in her hair. "Of course I am proud of you *Juliashcam*, you have always been smart and a good wife to me and a mama to our children. Now with both of us working, we can insure a better life for our children. And when you are home in the evenings now you can sew for yourself and us and not for the neighbors anymore. I will miss not seeing you each day bringing me my lunch pail, but that is a small price to pay for our good fortune."

Julia thanks God silently for giving her such a thoughtful and understanding husband and gives George a hug to show her appreciation. She goes to bed dreaming of the mansion on Fifth Avenue. Visions of pots and pans and huge china bowls dance in her head. "A colonel – I, Julia Pedesch, a simple peasant girl, will be working for a real life colonel, and a very rich one at that. I am overwhelmed by my good fortune."

Julia wakes early on Monday eager to return to Fifth Avenue. She is full of enthusiasm to begin work in her new position. Even young Vincent, the only son of Ava and Col. Astor, seems pleased to have a young woman in the house. Julia is only two years older than Vincent, who just attained the age of eighteen last month. She feels quite grown up in his presence, however, especially being an "old married lady" as it were.

I don't think we are destined to become real friends, but perhaps friendly acquaintances will be more accurate, she surmises after meeting the young man on several occasions. Vincent never treats me like a servant, but not as an equal either.

"Julia," he often says with authority, "you are certainly the prettiest thing in this house, and one of the smartest too, I suspect."

"You flatter me Master Vincent," is her usual retort, and this provides the occasion of many lively interchanges between them.

"What is your opinion about the possibility of war in Europe," he inquires one day when they meet in the library. "And by the way, don't call me Master Vincent; just Vincent will be quite sufficient, thank you."

"My countrymen have been downtrodden for some time, Vincent, especially by the German Empire. I think one day they will rebel and try to throw off the yoke of German domination that is always a threat to Hungary."

"You may be right, Julia, if our country gets involved, I want to be a part of it. I don't want to just sit around playing with columns of figures like my father. I want to be in the thick of it and make my fortune in the war."

The mere fact that she is a woman and an employee of his father makes certain codes of behavior mandatory for Julia. She tries not to offer any strong opinions or criticism about controversial issues. She is very aware of her lack of education and sophistication, and knows she is quite ignorant on many subjects having to do with the ways of the world. Vincent is well versed in many subjects, and Julia hopes that these exchanges will help her to learn more about the world around her. She and Vincent do share some other common interests such as art and history, she discovers. This shared interest allows her to ask him questions now and then, and often results in an interesting conversation. They often meet in the Colonel's library where she is permitted to spend any free time she may have during the course of her day. Julia loves to browse through the many art and history books in the Colonel's collection. She cannot understand all the words, but she can enjoy many of the books filled with beautiful pictures of famous paintings and photographs of wonderful places all over the world. Vincent is flattered when she asks him for details about some of the paintings or photographs, and he is anxious to be of help in furthering her education. The library has become one of her favorite rooms in the mansion.

After only the first month of her employment, Mrs. Umber has entrusted Julia with the complete running of the kitchen.

"You have won my complete confidence," she assures Julia one day with a smile lighting up her entire face. "It appears that your culinary skills are already becoming legendary, and the Colonel is becoming more and more fond of your ethnic style of cooking. Just don't forget to take the garlic out of the spinach," Mrs. Umber reminds her whenever that vegetable is included in the dinner menu. The Colonel likes what it does to the taste, but he does not want to find it on his plate."

Col. Astor, it appears has noticed Julia's addition to his household with a little more than the usual interest.

"I believe he has taken an interest in more than your cooking," Mrs. Umber informs her one morning. "He requests your presence in his study this morning." She studies Julia's face for a reaction, and finding none, she smiles and quietly walks toward the door, leaving Julia to consider this latest revelation.

Julia enters his sanctum with some trepidation. Col. Astor stands as she enters the room and indicates a chair next to him. Julia straightens her shoulders, stands tall and walks across the room to where he is standing. He holds the back of the chair for her, as if she were a lady guest in his home, and the effect of this is rather disconcerting. She is very much aware of her rather dowdy appearance amidst all the fine wood and plush carpet. She pats her hair self-consciously with her hand and makes an effort to straighten her skirt. He seems to be aware of her slight discomfort, although she is convinced she does not show it. She waits with eyes cast down until her employer opens the conversation.

"Julia," he begins haltingly, "it is obvious to me that you are not only a woman of exceptional culinary skill but also one of unusual beauty." The Colonel seats himself in a chair across from her and studies Julia thoughtfully. "Your natural beauty is an addition to any room, my dear. This is why I have asked to speak with you today." Col. Astor rises to his feet now and begins to stride around the room. "As you know, I am presently a bachelor, and am therefore, in need of a hostess from time to time to assist me in caring for my house guests, especially when we are having a formal dinner party. He pauses in front of her and continues. "I am simply asking if you would consider joining me and my guests in the drawing room upon occasion after dinner. You would merely circulate among the guests to be sure that all their needs are being looked after. Mrs. Umber assures me that you have a quick wit and a pleasant manner; and with a few minor instructions from her, would be able to mingle quite successfully. I would provide you with a wardrobe for these occasions – gowns ordered originally for my former wife that I am certain would attire you admirably."

Julia hears everything Col. Astor is saying but is temporarily rendered mute. She is in a state of shock – a hostess at a Fifth Avenue gala – she, Julia Pedesch? This is unthinkable. She cannot believe she is hearing him correctly, but she manages to mutter an assent.

"I will be very careful with the gowns," is all she can muster.

"My dear Julia," the Colonel interjects, "I care nothing about the gowns unless you are wearing them. You would be doing me a great service to perform these extra duties from time to time, and I would expect nothing further from you except to be your usual gracious self. I only want my guests to feel at home. This house used to be a pantheon of society gatherings, and I hope it may be that again."

Col. Astor stands up now and walks across the room. He pulls the bell chord by the door that summons Mrs. Umber. "I honestly feel you will be an asset to me in this regard, Julia, and you might even get to enjoy the charade." Julia manages to smile and nod agreeably.

Mrs. Umber enters the study and surveys the situation before saying, "You called, Colonel?"

"Yes, Maude, I want you to bring down some of those gowns that were ordered for Ava last year. You know – the ones you have stored upstairs in the sewing room. Show them to Julia please, and if any alterations are required, you can arrange for that also." Turning to Julia now, he says gently, "I am so pleased that you will assist me in opening up the house again, Julia. It's been some time since music and laughter has resounded in these somber halls. Thank you and good morning."

Having been dismissed by Col. Astor in his most gracious manner, Julia walks down the hall behind Mrs. Umber.

"We'll go directly up to the sewing room, Julia, and I'll show you the gowns. Come with me girl; I think you're in for a bit of a surprise."

Julia follows the housekeeper up the stairs to a small room on the second floor. The room is more like a cubicle than a room and houses only a sewing machine, a small straight-backed chair, an ugly standing lamp, and an ironing board. There is a closet built into the wall on one side, and Maude Umber heads for that as soon as they enter the room. She throws open the doors and indicates the contents. One side is fitted with shelves, and holds nothing but sheets and blankets and what appear to be old curtains and bed coverings. The other side is fitted with a sturdy bar from which are hanging at least a dozen of the most beautiful gowns Julia has ever seen.

"Ta da," shouts Mrs. Umber, grinning like a mischievous child showing off her treasures. "Take a look at these, dearie."

Julia takes one look and almost faints from sheer pleasure. Never in all her life has she seen such materials. Accustomed as she is to sewing, her fingers have never encountered fabrics so exquisite. The first gown she selects is a sapphire blue, and the tulle skirt rustles as she removes it from its quilted hanger. She needs no urging from Mrs. Umber to try on this beautiful creation.

"You look like a princess, my dear," whispers Mrs. Umber with a look of awe on her halcyon face. The gown fit Julia almost perfectly because the former Mrs. Astor had been a woman of stature also. She had been a bit heavier than Julia, both above and below the waist; but with a tuck here and a dart there, Julia would be able to alter this gown to look as though it had been made just for her. She lay the gown across the chair and went to select another. Before she knew it, she had six gorgeous gowns tossed casually across the chair and the old sewing machine.

Each gown seemed more beautiful than the one before. She felt like a child at a costume ball. The colors of the fabrics, some with intricate beading, were breathtaking. Each gown was fashioned with exquisite detail – one off-white satin even had soft brown fur at the neck. Another had tiny gemstones sewed into the bodice and the sleeves. As she twirls and turns in these beautiful creations, they seem to give her courage and an aura she lacks when dressed in her own rather dowdy garments.

"I will certainly be able to charm Col. Astor's guests in these beautiful creations, Julia thinks to herself as she caresses the silky fabrics.

"You look so beautiful, Julia," Mrs. Umber repeats again. "I am so glad someone like you will get to wear these lovely gowns. You certainly do them justice, my dear."

Julia hangs the gowns up carefully and places them back in the closet. "I will begin altering them whenever I have a little free time in the morning, Mrs. Umber. I cannot take the dresses home to alter; George would never understand this latest development." She hums to herself as she glides down the stairs, glancing at herself in the huge hall mirror. "I will never forget this day," she vows silently.

# Chapter 13

It is the evening of Julia's first dinner party at the mansion on Fifth Avenue. She is so excited she can hardly breathe. Col. Astor has asked Julia to join him in the drawing room after the meal itself is over and mingle with the guests while they enjoy their cordials and after-dinner mints. The weather is getting warmer now, and the doors to the terrace are open to let in the gentle night air. There is even a moon and the entire patio adjacent to the drawing room is bathed in silvery moonlight. It is like an evening right out of a fairy tale, Julia murmurs to herself as she gazes out of an upstairs window at the scene enfolding below.

Julia has chosen the sapphire blue gown for the occasion and has wound her long blond hair into a French twist at the nape of her neck. Mrs. Umber comes to the upstairs sitting room to help her prepare.

"I suddenly realized this morning, Julia, that you probably don't own any jewelry, so I took the liberty of mentioning this to the Colonel. He gave me this to give to you." As she finished speaking, she proffered a small blue velvet box to Julia. As she opened the box, Julia's breath caught in her throat. Inside the box, nestled in the white satin lining, was a beautiful pearl necklace with a rhinestone clasp. Next to the necklace was a pair of earrings — each one a tiny pearl drop hanging from a small rhinestone cluster. Julia stared at Mrs. Umber in disbelief.

"For me? Are you sure? Col. Astor is so incredibly generous

and trusting," she mumbled. "Who do these beautiful jewels belong to, Mrs. Umber?"

"They were a graduation gift for the Colonel's daughter, Caroline," she answers. "Caroline died the year before the Colonel and Mrs. Astor were divorced. I guess he has kept them ever since."

"I will be so careful with them, Mrs. Umber. I will return them to the box as soon as my duties here are finished and I am ready to leave for home this evening. Shall I leave the box in the sitting room so you can return it to him in the morning?"

"That will be just fine, child, but meanwhile, please enjoy wearing them. They are the perfect compliment to that beautiful blue gown you have chosen for this evening.. You are a sight to behold, my dear, – a sight to behold! Now come with me, and I will show you to the drawing room. I'm sure the Colonel and his guests are already there."

As Julia approaches the drawing room she can hear the lilting strains of music coming from inside. Someone very accomplished is playing the grand piano, and the notes flow out into the corridor like a melodic breeze. As she opens the door to the drawing room, a pungent odor assails her nostrils – a mixture of cigar smoke and imported perfumes. She enters the drawing room rather cautiously. It is one of the most lavishly appointed rooms in the house. The walls are covered in cream colored damask with a pattern of tiny rosebuds and green vines. The drapes are a deep rose color but of light, airy fabric that allows the breeze to pass through from the garden into the room. The chandeliers are molded of gold and crystal, and the myriad of lights creates rainbows of color in every corner of the room.

Once inside the door, Julia glances around the room and realizes at once that no one has even noticed her entrance. She begins to relax a bit and takes in more of the beautiful surroundings, glancing first at the gorgeous gowns the women are wearing. As she does so, she smiles inwardly because her gown is no less beautiful than any that the female guests are wearing.

Julia straightens her shoulders and begins to circulate slowly around the room. As discreetly as possible, she questions a few of the guests as to their wishes.

"May I get you another crème de menthe or perhaps a small brandy?" she inquires in her sweetest voice. "There are some lovely white chocolate dinner mints, if you would care to try one."

Each time she encounters a small group of guests it becomes easier. The guests seem to take her presence for granted and even pay her an occasional compliment about her gown. Her response to these casual compliments is a simple, "Thank you very much."

The evening passes so quickly that before Julia is even aware, the last guest is being ushered out the door. Suddenly she realizes it is time for her to change out of her ball gown and prepare to return home. I must hurry, she thinks to herself. It would not do to miss the last streetcar uptown to Yorkville. She runs quickly up the stairs and into the sitting room where her fairy tale began. She removes the gown and hangs it carefully on the hanger Mrs. Umber has left there. She removes the beautiful pearl necklace and earrings as well and replaces them carefully in the velvet box. She hurriedly pulls on her street clothes and rushes for the back door.

"What an evening! I feel like Cinderella leaving the ball at the stroke of midnight, only there is no glass slipper and no handsome prince running after me down the stairs." She runs to the corner where the last streetcar is just pulling into the station.

"Good evening, Miss," the conductor greets her with a weary smile. "It's been a long day for you too I guess."

"Good evening Sir," she answers, and looking around, Julia realizes she is the only passenger on the streetcar. "Yes, it has been a long day, but a happy one nevertheless. I am tired though and anxious to get home to my husband and children." The conductor nods and moves the car away from the curb bringing her back to reality and the rewards of sleep.

One evening several weeks later, just before one of the Colonel's less formal dinner parties, Col. Astor once again requests

Julia's presence in the library. When she enters the warm, beautifully paneled room filled with the smell of leather and pipe tobacco, she feels at ease almost at once. Her eyes search the perimeter of the room for a glimpse of the Colonel. When her gaze finds him, she is stunned into silence, as she beholds the most beautiful man she has ever seen engaged in conversation with her employer. Tall and imposing in an off-white dinner jacket and highly polished boots, a rugged, tanned, blond gentleman is introduced to her as James McFadden, a "white hunter" from East Africa and an old and dear friend of the Colonel.

The gentleman turns toward her and proceeds to study her critically. Aha, so you are the mysterious hostess Jack has been telling me about. He certainly neglected to mention how breathtakingly beautiful you are."

Julia feels herself blush to the very roots of her hair, but she does manage to look up into the purest violet eyes she has ever seen and say, "it's very nice to meet you Mr. McFadden."

"Mr. McFadden," he roars, "how in God's green earth are we ever going to become soul mates if you insist on calling me Mr. McFadden?"

"But we've only just met, Sir," Julia stammers. "I didn't know we were to become soul mates, as you put it."

This remark causes James McFadden to laugh out loud. Julia surprises herself with her quick retort, but she has to regain her control at once or this man will have her groveling like a serving wench. She regains her composure long enough to accept the seat Col. Astor is offering her, and breathes a sigh of relief as she feels the solid cushion firmly under her legs. She is certain that if she had to stand unsupported one more moment in the presence of James McFadden, she would surely disgrace herself by fainting.

James continues to study her for a moment and then speaks again. "I know few people in New York these days, my dear Julia, other than my old friend Jack, of course; and I look forward to spending some time in his company. I have been on safari in East Africa for some eight months now and am badly in need of some charming female companionship," he announces without any hesitation or embarrassment.

Col. Astor stands up then and selects a pipe from the rack on the table next to his chair. He lights the pipe and walks over to the mantle where he fingers a photograph in a delicate silver frame. "This is my daughter Caroline," he says, addressing no one in particular. "She was a lovely young lady with her whole life ahead of her, cut down in her prime. You remind me of her in many ways, Julia," he adds thoughtfully. Julia wants to ask the Colonel more about Caroline, but before she can speak, he continues the conversation.

"I believe you will be a suitable choice to act as Mr. McFadden's companion this evening, Julia. I am exceedingly fond of my old friend whom I have not seen for some months, and I am enlisting your help to make his visit as pleasant as possible. I am hoping that you will provide a simple diversion and perhaps add a little female companionship to James's very rugged male existence, if only for a short time while he is visiting New York. I pray I am not asking too much of you, my dear," the Colonel concludes.

"Of course not, Col. Astor," Julia replies, "as long as Mr. McFadden remembers that I am a married woman with two children. I would not want him to anticipate that this association will result in anything more than a casual friendship, solely under the roof of your home." Julia hears her voice and it sounds so matter-of-fact and totally in control. The Colonel, Julia is sure, is unaware of her naïve innocence and total vulnerability to a man of such worldliness and charm. From the moment she set eyes on James McFadden she is completely and utterly beguiled by him; and the feeling appears to be mutual.

Julia circulates among the guests that evening, as is her usual custom, but at each turn around the room, she encounters James at her elbow. At one point in the festivities, he takes her hand and leads her out onto the dance floor to join him in a waltz. A few heads turn at this more obvious gesture, but Julia is too happy and excited to care. The Colonel does not seem disturbed by their dancing together, so the guests soon regard it as perfectly normal. The evening progresses without incident except that James invites Julia to dance on two more occasions. She is aware of the so-called rules of society – Mrs. Umber has furthered her education in that department.

"If a young lady dances more than three dances with the same young man, she has, as they say, been compromised." Julia can still see the serious expression on Mrs. Umber's round face as she makes this declaration.

"Of course, I am not subject to these societal rules, being a young woman in the employ of Col. Astor," Julia tells herself; "but I could feel the curious and jealous looks of some of the unmarried female guests as James whirled me around the room for the third time." James was aware of the stir they were causing, but was enjoying it to the utmost. Julia made every effort to avoid James McFadden after that third dance, and strangely, he seemed to honor her unspoken wishes, for which she was very grateful.

James has not seen a woman in many months, Julia reflects; and his appreciation of my modest attributes is overwhelming, as he never fails to remind me. One afternoon she encounters him strolling in the garden. He appears mesmerized by the Colonel's exquisite rose garden and walks there quite often. He looks up as she comes down the path toward the rose garden.

"Good afternoon my dear Julia. You are truly the loveliest creature I have ever seen, quite as lovely as Jack's roses."

"You flatter me as usual, James, but I thank you," is all Julia can manage as a response.

"Please join me for a walk in the garden, Julia. It is such a beautiful afternoon, and the weather here is so different from that in Africa. I had quite forgotten that there were so many beautiful flowers that bloom in the spring here in New York. Maybe you can help me identify some of them. I understand from Maude Umber that you are fond of flowers and are more than a little familiar with their names.

"That is true, James; I do love flowers. When I was a little girl in Budapest, our local priest had a garden filled with flowers. I would run up and down the rows of canna, peonies, and dahlias, chasing the elusive butterflies that are attracted to their blooms. He is the one who taught me the names of many of the flowers. He was always very kind to me and even let me pick some of the flowers from time to time. I have many fond memories of that garden."

They walk for a while in the garden, making small talk like two old friends. James takes Julia's arm as they walk, on the pretext of guiding her over the paths so she will not slip on a loose stone. Before they know it, the sun is beginning to drop toward the horizon and the afternoon is fast becoming evening. The sky has turned a vivid orange and soon the whole garden is bathed in a mysterious pink light. Julia inhales suddenly, overcome by the beautiful sight before her eyes. James turns toward her and before he can speak, she pulls her hand from his and hurries down the path.

Over his shoulder he hears, "Have a lovely evening James. I must get home now to my family. They are expecting me for dinner. I will see you tomorrow." Julia can feel his eyes following her down the path, but she does not stop or look back.

"He is what they call "a silver-tongued devil," Mrs. Umber cajoles as Julia enters the kitchen to get her wrap. "I'm very much afraid he is smitten with you, Julia, Maude Umber continues. "I can tell by the way he looks at you. Please be careful, Julia. Remember you are a wife and a mother, and a romance with this man can never come to anything.

"You're imagining things, Maude. He's just being attentive because I am the first woman he has seen in a long time. I'm sure he thinks of me as a daughter, just as the Colonel does. Stop making up fairy tales. I must get home now, but I'll be here early in the morning. Goodnight now." Julia gives Maude a peck on the cheek, grabs her sweater from the hook, and heads for the door.

Unfortunately, Julia is unable to heed Maude's words and almost at once the first real romance of her life sweeps over her, threatening to drown her in its intensity. She is totally unprepared to handle the deep feelings that are overwhelming her, and soon she is carried away by her own untested emotions. She keeps her strong feelings to herself, admitting them to no one; but sometimes she feels like anyone who looks at her can see how enamored she is with James McFadden. Julia finds it difficult to pray before she goes to bed at night because she is sure that God is angry with her for having these feelings. "I don't want to feel as I do," she prays, "but I don't know how to stop the yearning feeling inside me. I feel like a real woman when James looks at me with those beautiful violet eyes.

Julia never sees James outside of the Astor home, other than an occasional ride through the park or along the Hudson River when he begs her to accompany him. These outings are always encouraged by Col. Astor, so it is difficult for her to refuse, even if she wanted to. Gradually, they begin to spend more and more time together, and their relationship takes on an aura of intimacy between old and dear friends. Julia makes all sorts of excuses to Frieda and begs her to stay until dinnertime on several occasions so that Emma and Jerry will not be left unsupervised. George seems to be unaware of any change in Julia except that she may appear more distracted than usual in the evening.

On two occasions Julia stays at the mansion for the large parties that the Colonel gives to honor his houseguest and does not return home until long after George is asleep. The Colonel or James sees to it that she is returned home by hired car on these occasions, as the streetcar has long since stopped running. Julia has all she can to drag herself back home after these events, so caught up is she in the excitement of the party and this almost double life she seems to be leading. James and Julia dance more often now in full view of the guests, and Col. Astor seems to take a certain mysterious pleasure in seeing them dance together.

During one such evening James holds Julia closer than usual

and dances her out onto the balcony adjacent to the ballroom. They continue to waltz until the music ends, but he does not release her from his arms. Instead he tightens his hold around her waist and pulls her to him. Before she knows what is happening, his lips find hers and he is kissing her with a passion she has never experienced before. Instead of pulling away, she returns the kiss with all the ardor that has been pent-up inside her since they first met.

"I think I love you, Julia," are James' first words after their lips part. "I have never felt like this before about any woman. Please tell me you care for me too."

"Oh, James, I do care, you know I do, but I cannot love you. Your kiss took me by surprise. I did not think. . . . You forget I am a married woman with two small children that I love dearly. You are the most exciting man I have ever met, and I love to be in your company; but all we can ever be is friends. Please take me home now, James. I must go home right away."

James releases her at once and looks deep into her eyes where tears are beginning to form. She can feel the first drops sliding down her cheek.

"I will take you home at once, Julia," he says quietly. James brings Julia home in one of the Colonel's Model T's. As they approach the building where Julia lives, he pulls the car over to the curb.

"I hope I did not offend you, Julia, but I had to let you know how I feel about you. My heart soars when we are together, and I can think of nothing else but you and how very much I care for you."

Julia does not answer. James helps her out of the car and kisses her hand as he bids her goodnight. She walks up the steps to the front door without a backward glance. She pauses inside the hallway to catch her breath and listens for the sound of the engine as the car pulls away and moves down the street.

At first Julia is embarrassed for him to see where she lives, but then she realizes that this is the last thing on his mind. The fact that I have a husband and children waiting for me upstairs is of much more serious concern. Julia gathers her skirt and climbs the stairs.

# Chapter 14

In the days that follow, James and Julia try hard not to talk about the fact that she is married. They treat their liaison as if it were a friendship of the purest kind, although they both know in their hearts that this is not the case. Julia takes James' arm when it is appropriate to do so in public but keeps her distance in their more private moments. They continue this charade for another week and then the tension becomes intolerable for both of them.

Unbeknownst to Julia, James has received a telegram from his base camp in East Africa. He is advised that he must return to Africa in another month to lead a safari for a very wealthy businessman from London. He has convinced himself that somehow he is going to persuade Julia to accompany him. The decision comes all too soon.

James and Julia are enjoying a picnic on the patio at the rear of the mansion. It is Sunday, Julia's day off, and she is feeling more than a little guilty about spending it with James instead of being at home with her family.

"I know the children are in good hands with George," she muses, "and of course Frieda is next door if she is needed." Julia told George that her presence here today is at the special request of Col. Astor, which of course is not the truth, but she desperately wants this special time with James. They have so little private time together; today feels like a gift – a gift she cannot deny herself.

Col. Astor has gone out for the day, not by accident Julia is certain. Even Maude Umber has taken the afternoon off to visit a sick friend. So the two erstwhile lovers have the entire place to themselves. The afternoon takes on the aura of playing house, and Julia is enraptured with the idea of their being alone together in this beautiful, private place. Julia's thoughts turn entirely to James.

The sun is warm and there is a soft breeze in the air. The smell of the flowers fills her senses, and she is happier at that moment than she can ever remember.

"I don't think I've ever been this happy," she sighs.

James looks at her with unabashed affection and responds. "Neither have I my darling, but the time has come to talk seriously."

The look on James' face fills Julia with apprehension, but she smiles up at him and adds coquettishly, "you have my full attention, Mr. McFadden."

James takes her hand and leads her to the bench at the edge of the garden. "Please sit here with me, Julia. I have something important I want to say to you." He pauses briefly as Julia settles herself on the bench next to him.

"I have known for over a week now that I must return to Africa before the end of the month, Julia. A very important client is waiting impatiently for me to return to the continent to lead him and some of his prestigious friends on a safari into the Rift Valley. I refuse to consider the possibility of leaving the U. S. without you by my side, so I have taken some precautions to prevent this from happening."

James raises the beautiful crystal wine decanter and pours each of them a glass of ruby liquid while Julia sets out the fruit and cheese she has prepared onto tiny porcelain plates. When she turns back to look at him, James raises his glass and toasts her health with love in his eyes. He sets down his glass and takes both Julia's hands in his. She has never seen him look so serious.

As she gazes up into those deep violet eyes, she is not prepared for what happens next. James kisses the tips of her fingers and holding only her left hand in his, he places a diamond ring on the fourth finger of that hand. Julia is astonished. She would have bolted upright but she was totally captivated by the size and brilliance of the stone on her finger. Its perfection is unmistakable, even to Julia's unsophisticated eye. As if in response to her amazed look, James assures her immediately.

"It is a perfect blue white diamond of one and a half carats," James tells her matter-of-factly. "It belonged to my mother, and I have kept it with me for several years now in the hope that some day I would meet someone worthy of this special gem, and now I have. She would be so pleased to see someone as beautiful as you wearing her ring, Julia darling. It is a perfect fit too, I might add." James sat back then and waited for Julia to speak.

Julia is completely dazzled by its brilliance, made even brighter by the strong light of the noonday sun in the garden. She is rendered utterly speechless, an unusual condition for Julia. When she finds her tongue, she stands up and the words come out in a torrent of vibrant Hungarian – "*nemquel, nemquel, dragakishpofam.*" James is so startled by this outburst that he grabs her by the shoulder and forces her eyes to find his.

"Julia, my darling," he sputters, "speak English for God's sake! I can't tell if you're happy or angry."

His words seem to calm her, and she sits down again onto the bench with a thud.

"No, no my dearest James, what does this mean?" she stammers. "I am a married woman with two children. Have you forgotten?"

"No, of course not, dearest," James replies in a soft voice. "I only want you to know how very much I love you and want you to be with me always. If it cannot be right now, I understand; but certainly in a few weeks or a month at most. My life is still in Africa, as you must know; but I can return there alone now if I know that you will be joining me soon."

Julia turns ashen and can see the concern in his eyes. She is finding it extremely difficult to speak.

"But, James, I cannot leave George and the children. God would never condone that kind of behavior. He alone knows how much I love you, but my love cannot affect my duty to Emma and Jerry, and to George for that matter. It is true that I do not love George, as a wife should love her husband, but he has cared for me all my adult life when no one else would. If nothing else, he deserves my faithfulness. He has been a loyal and loving husband all these years. I could never leave him – never!"

Julia stopped to catch her breath and regain her composure, and then went on. "When must you leave for Africa, and why didn't you tell me sooner?"

"By the end of the month, Julia. I just got the telegram this week. You must have known I would have to return soon, and you certainly must know what my feelings are for you. Did you think I would just leave after all we have meant to each other? Did our time together mean nothing to you? You know that I love you, and I need you to be a permanent part of my life – not just here in New York, but wherever I am." He paused then, his voice beginning to break. Julia is caught completely off guard.

"I don't know what I expected, James. I guess I thought we would just go on caring for each other forever. I never allowed myself to think any further than tomorrow. And now tomorrow is here, and I don't know what to say much less how to say goodbye."

Julia stood up then, anxious to feel the hard ground under her feet. She walks over to James and takes his hands in hers. "You are the most exciting, wonderful thing that has ever happened to me, James, but I allowed my infatuation with you to blind me to reality. I am so very sorry, James. I really do care for you deeply, and I never meant to lead you on or cause you any unhappiness. I am so naïve and I am so ashamed."

Julia let go of his hands and raised herself up on tiptoe to place a kiss on his cheek. "I guess it's time we both return to reality and get on with the lives that are really ours. Make believe is over for both of us."

With these words trailing on her lips, she turns, gathers her skirts and races into the house, leaving James outside bewildered and miserable.

Julia runs the distance from Fifth Avenue to the streetcar station without ever looking back but with tears streaming down her cheeks. When she arrives at the apartment in Yorkville, she runs up the stairs to find Frieda and the children in the kitchen making a batch of *turos gumbotz*.

"Welcome home, Julia," Frieda greets her warmly.

Julia brushes away the remaining tears and tries to smile. "Hello Frieda," she answers, "and thank you for taking care of the children for me this afternoon. I hope they have been behaving for you."

"Good as gold," Frieda responds, "but they sure keep me busy"

Julia looks up then to see Jerry on the high kitchen stool trying to reach the canister with the confectionery sugar to sprinkle on the warm dumplings. These are his favorite treats, and he is not going to be deterred by the arrival of his mother. Clutching the canister to him, he climbs down, looks up at Julia and smiles. Then he notices that she has been crying. He throws himself into her arms.

"Don't cry *Mamushcam*, I didn't fall; I'm a good stool climber," he exclaims.

His look and the soft Hungarian endearment warm Julia's heart and bring a smile to her face. She wipes the few remaining tears from her cheek with the back of her hand. As she does so, the diamond, still on the fourth finger of her left hand, glints in the late afternoon sunlight streaming in the kitchen window. Immediately, she puts her hand behind her back and rushes from the room.

In her bedroom Julia slides the ring off her finger, puts it between the folds of a small embroidered linen handkerchief, and places it at the back of her dresser drawer.

"I will return this ring to you the first thing in the morning,

James McFadden, the very first thing," she says out loud to the empty room with conviction in her voice.

The next morning dawns gray and bleak, and Julia feels sick at heart. She dresses for work and, after feeding Emma and Jerry, getting them off to school, and preparing the tin pail with George's lunch; she leaves the apartment to make the trek to Fifth Avenue. As she rounds the corner at 840 Fifth Avenue, she sees an elegant touring car parked outside. A uniformed attendant is loading large leather valises on the back of the open car. As she peers around the corner, she sees a tall, solemn gentleman descend the steps, pause to look back briefly, and then enter the elegant car. Julia wants desperately to shout his name but the words stick painfully in her throat. She swallows hard, hears the driver start the engine of the car, and watches as it begins to move slowly away down Fifth Avenue. This is Julia's last view of James McFadden.

As the car pulls away she suddenly realizes that the ring is still in her pocket. Her hand goes instinctively to the pocket of her coat where the ring lays, wrapped carefully in the embroidered linen handkerchief.

"What am I to do? I cannot tell the colonel about this, but I must find some way to return the ring to James. I can't keep this expensive gift, this reminder of a love that was never meant to be." She pats the ring in her pocket and walks to the door to begin her day, her first day without the presence of James McFadden.

About a month later Julia receives a letter from James. It comes to her in care of Col. Astor, and he delivers it to her personally without asking any questions. Julia is very grateful for this and takes the letter from him without comment. She puts the letter in her pocket and goes upstairs to the small sitting room on the second floor. She often sits there in the afternoon to rest a bit and get away from the heat of the kitchen. She opens the letter with trembling hands. The handwriting is bold but rather small for such an imposing man. The letter is brief and to the point.

"I thought I knew your heart, Julia, but obviously I was mistaken. Despite our sad parting, you will always hold a special place in my heart. I hope this message brings you some comfort in times when you may feel alone. Please keep the ring and dispose of it any way that you want. I never wish to see it again. Your James."

Julia read the letter twice and then folded it in half and placed it with the ring in her pocket. "Tonight I will put it away in the little black box that I brought with me from Budapest and put the box in the back of my dresser drawer where it will be safe."

And so Julia places the ring, the letter, and a photo of James taken by Col. Astor one Sunday afternoon in a corner in the back of the dresser drawer. They will remain there in secret where she may gaze with awe on the sad words and the beautiful diamond solitaire, and remember James McFadden, the first and only real love of her life.

# Chapter 15

The autumn of 1910 is a period of impasse for Julia. She is still mourning James' leaving, but at the same time she is relieved to be released from the pressure of the intense emotions she has been experiencing, but still does not fully understand.

Julia considers her feelings." James and I were never intimate, at least not in the way that the maids and serving girls giggle about. I loved him intensely and completely with no thought to the future or the effect these feelings would have on both our lives. How naïve I was. I know now, more than ever, that I have a lot of growing up to do."

Even though Julia is a wife and a mother, she was never schooled in the sophisticated ways of the world. She knows nothing of the emotional or physical love between a man and a woman. She vows to read more on the subject and further her education in the matters of society.

"If only I had a female relative to talk to or even a close girl friend to confide in," she ponders, "perhaps I could gather my thoughts together and make some sense out of what has happened to me. I feel so totally ignorant about the ways of the world, especially regarding men and women." In the absence of either of these Julia turns her attention to her family and her duties at the Astor mansion.

Soon after James' departure, Col. Astor begins courting a young woman, two years younger than Julia, and there is talk of a possible wedding in the coming year. Col. Astor met Madeleine

Force earlier in the year on a cruise to Bar Harbor, Maine where she was traveling with her rather imposing mother, Frances. The Colonel laughingly refers to Madeleine's mother as "La Force Majeure." Madeleine begins spending more and more time at 840 Fifth Avenue, and inevitably she meets Julia and is drawn to her. Being so close in age, it does not take long for the two women to become friends. Col. Astor has no objection whatever to this liaison, as he looks on Julia now as part of the family.

Julia likes Madeleine almost at once. Not only are they close in age, but they have a great many things in common. In their talks together, they discover that they both love music and art, and more amazing than that, is the discovery that Madeleine likes to experiment in the kitchen.

"Desserts are my favorite," she informs her new friend, "but I barely know how to peel an apple. My mother never cooked a thing in her entire life, but I have always had this curiosity about how ingredients were put together to create the most wonderful flavors. It's the creative process that appeals to me I guess," she concludes with enthusiasm.

"How amazing," says Julia, "and I have always wanted to learn to appreciate art and classical music." I even dreamed of learning to play the piano one day, if that is possible. I've never even put my hands on a keyboard."

"Well, I am not exactly an accomplished pianist, Julia, but I would be happy to teach you a few simple tunes that I was forced to learn as a child. Would that please you?"

"Oh, yes, Madeleine. I would love to learn to play a few pieces on the piano. When can we start?"

"We can start this afternoon if you wish," says Madeleine with enthusiasm. "I will come and get you after lunch. Can you stay an extra hour today to get a lesson?"

"I'll be happy to stay, Madeleine, and tomorrow I'll pay you back by teaching you how to make crème brullet – Hungarian style."

They both laugh at this and Madeleine leaves the kitchen singing, "*crème brullet, crème brullet*, to be cooked another day."

Julia and Madeleine soon share many intimate moments together, like sisters. While Madeleine teaches Julia about real art and classical music, Julia instructs her in the art of dessert making. Julia feels so close to Madeleine that she soon begins to call her Maddie. She does not seem to mind; in fact, she encourages it on the grounds that she has never had a nickname.

"Julia, you are like the sister I never had," Maddie confides one day as they sit together in the big white kitchen. "Growing up as the only girl with three brothers was not much fun I can tell you. They picked on me unmercifully."

"I can't even imagine that, Maddie," Julia chides her friend. "I never had any brothers or sisters except in the foster home, and they treated me more like a servant than a family member. I feel like you are my long-lost sister, and I pray we will always be friends."

Madeleine leans over and hugs Julia with genuine affection. "That is all changed now that we have found each other, Julia. It must have been very lonely though, having no siblings to share things with. I never really appreciated my brothers when I was younger. Now that I am older, I enjoy their company very much. Maybe one day you can meet one of them. What about your husband? Can you share things with him?"

"I can't talk to George about the things you and I talk about, Maddie. He could not begin to understand the things that mean so much to me. He cares nothing for art or music, and truly, I think the only thing we share is our love for the children. George is so gentle and kind and protective. I know he loves me, but we have so little in common. It is so wonderful to have a real friend like you to confide in. I'm so grateful to have you in my life, Maddie. There is nothing I wouldn't do to be your friend forever."

Maddie returns these honest sentiments with a warm smile and another hug. "Friends forever," she says, and Julia knows that she means it sincerely.

The two women continue to get along like sisters, and each

day that passes seems to bring them closer. It is soon apparent that Col. Astor and Madeleine will wed in the spring of 1911.

"You will somehow be a part of the European trip we are planning for our honeymoon," Madeleine assures Julia.

Julia knows, of course, that she cannot leave George and the children for any extended period, but the thought of traveling to Europe with the Astors is a very exciting prospect. She cannot help but indulge her mind in a flight of fantasy. Just thinking about the possibility of traveling abroad in their company makes her head spin. All sorts of fairytale-type dreams begin running around in her brain. Perhaps I might even run into James McFadden again, she thinks to herself.

Julia has not consciously thought of James for some time now, but the talk of Europe and traveling has fired her imagination, and he has taken over her thoughts on a number of occasions.

"I will never completely get over my feelings for James if I live to be one hundred. He is truly the first man I ever loved. Loved and lost," she thinks to herself sadly, "but at least I know what it is to feel real love for a man. I only wish I could feel that for my husband, but it is not meant to be."

Julia returns home this evening in a buoyant mood, which seems to spill over onto Emma and Jerry. She scoops both children up in her arms as soon as she enters the apartment and kisses them soundly. Sensing her unspoken joy, the children begin to cavort around the kitchen table, singing and dancing and carrying on like two wild gypsies. Julia is in such a good humor, she cannot resist joining in and prancing around with them.

George looks up over his newspaper with his mouth agape and asks, "what in the world are you all doing? Have you lost your minds or is there something going on that your papa should know about? Did your mama find a hundred dollars on the street today or did she buy her own streetcar to take her to work?"

This last remark brings peals of laughter from the children. Even George begins to grin, a rare occurrence to be sure, and he stands up to join them. They all join hands and dance around the table like carefree gypsies from the old country. Julia has not felt joy like this in a very long time.

"It is so good to see you just having fun, my children. Even your papa is having fun," laughs Julia.

"Papa dances real good, doesn't he Mama," teases Jerry. "I want to see him dance with you Mama," Emma chimes in.

George surprises Julia then and comes toward her with his arms open wide. She steps into them easily, and they dance once more around the table. The children clap loudly and her heart soars to see them so happy.

One evening later in the week, George and Julia are alone having their coffee after dinner. Julia lowers her eyes to her cup and in a quiet voice says, "The Colonel is really going to marry Madeleine, George; and he plans to take her on a honeymoon to Egypt and Paris. They have invited me to sail with them to England after the wedding. Vincent is going to study at the University in London. Mrs. Umber will remain at the Fifth Avenue house, and Col. Astor would like me to look after Vincent in their townhouse in London. I would cook and keep house for him, and then return home with Madeleine and the Colonel when they get back from their trip to Paris."

George's face takes on a look of wrenching fear as he raises his eyes to meet Julia's across the table. She is terrified at what he will say next. Julia cannot believe the words she hears him saying.

"I know how much a trip like this would mean to you, *Juliashcam,*" he says in a quivering voice. "The children and I would miss you terribly, but I see no reason why you could not go for a month or two," he stammers.

Julia is so shocked she cannot speak. Never in her wildest dreams did she expect George to take her pronouncement so calmly. As she studies his face, she is aware that it is taking every ounce of strength he has to respond in this manner. She cannot help but think he must have suspected that something like this was coming, which gave him time to think about it and prepare his answer. George stands up now and begins to pace the floor nervously before he continues.

"My sister Flora is here now from Hungary, you know, and is living with our aunt in Long Island. I'm certain she would come here to Yorkville and stay with me and the children for that short time if I ask her to. I know how much a trip like this would mean to you, *Juliashcam*, and you know I cannot deny you anything if it is in my power to give it to you. I love you so much, and so do the children.

"Oh, George, thank you, thank you," Julia mumbles as the tears well up in her eyes. "You are the kindest, most thoughtful husband any woman could ask for. I can't tell you how much this means to me, George. Thank, thank you, thank you."

"Madeleine and the Colonel haven't set a date yet, but I think it may be soon – within the next month or so. I can't believe they are giving me this opportunity, George, and I thank you so much for letting me take it. You are such a good husband. I don't deserve you." She pauses to get her breath and compose herself.

"It's because I love you so, *Juliashcam*. I only want to make you happy. We'll be fine on our own," George continues with a shy grin as he places his big hand on her small one. "It will give Flora and me a chance to become reacquainted. Besides, Emma and Jerry have never met their aunt; so it will be a treat for them also."

George is really a very wise husband. He knows it is easier to acquiesce and make the decision easier for Julia by finding a solution to any of the problems that might stand in the way. She is so grateful to him for making the decision for her that she jumps up and gives him a big hug.

The children return to the kitchen just in time to see this. They immediately jump for joy in response to this unusual show of affection by their mother, and they proceed to hug their father too. George, unused to being the center of attention, blushes from head to toe, but Julia knows he is enjoying every moment of this spontaneous display of affection from his family. He stands up and begins to swing the children around – first Emma and then Jerry. The children, of course, do not even know why they are all hugging their papa. They only know that there is joy in the household this evening, and they are going to take full advantage of every aspect of it.

And so Julia begins dreaming of the possibility of a trip to Europe. The term Europe has previously meant nothing more to her than the horrible place she left almost eight years before. But being in the company of the Colonel and Vincent Astor and their friends and now Madeleine, has made her realize how glorious Europe could be if one knows something about the arts and classical music and history.

"I might even get a chance to practice my piano in London. I wonder if there will be a piano in the townhouse. Madeleine has told me about the art galleries and museums I can visit, and just walking around that great city will be exciting. I cannot believe this could really become a reality for me"

The days and weeks pass quite serenely until mid-November when Col. Astor announces his approaching marriage to Madeleine. Their engagement becomes official at a huge holiday gala during the first week in December at the famous Astor Hotel. The renowned Astor Hotel was the Colonel's pride and joy, having been built by him in 1897, adjoining the already famous Waldorf Astoria, previously built by his cousin, William Waldorf Astor.

Julia is almost as excited as the bride-to-be. Maddie rushes into the kitchen the day of the gala and informs Julia about what will transpire at the party. She looks radiant in a well-tailored tan suit and matching hat.

"He's going to announce our engagement, Julia. I can't believe it. I love him so much, and we will be so happy. Please be happy for me too, dear Julia," she begs. "I'm going shopping now for some things for my trousseau. It's all so exciting. I never knew I could be so happy."

"I am so happy for you, Maddie," Julia assures her. "You

deserve only the best, and I know the Colonel will do everything in his power to make you happy." Madeleine hugs her friend soundly and then runs from the kitchen like a school girl preparing for her first real party.

The fateful evening arrives. Julia, of course, can only read about it the next day in the *New York Times*. "Amidst a recreated garden of yellow and red roses and a full symphony-sized orchestra, Jack Astor announced, "I will marry this adorable creature in the spring with all our friends and family in attendance, and we will take up residence in the house on Fifth Avenue."

"This announcement gives us cause to chuckle," the newspaper columnist continued. "It is not enough that the bride-to-be is eighteen, barely a year younger than his son Vincent, but that Jack Astor also married his first wife, Ava, in the spring – on May 1st 1891 to be exact."

The *Tribune* and the *Sun* had an even bigger field day with this announcement in their efforts to make up for being excluded from the first earth-shattering Astor event – the divorce of Jack and Ava Astor. This event had occurred just a year ago in 1909, thirteen months after the death of their only daughter Caroline. Mrs. Umber described for Julia how the divorce was carried out in a very secretive manner apparently, in a small town across the river in Rockland County, New York. She told Julia how Henry Taft, brother of the then President, had been the lawyer representing Ava, and how he had arranged to have the final papers recorded and sealed very quickly.

"The press was furious with the Colonel," Mrs. Umber said, "for cheating them out of what they considered to be the best society story of the decade."

Col. Astor, by all accounts, didn't give a damn what anyone thought, least of all the press, and proceeded with his plans to marry the beautiful young Madeleine Force, as the press like to label her.

# Chapter 16

Julia is totally engrossed in the plans for the up-coming wedding. Before she even realizes it, she is functioning not just as a cook/housekeeper, but also as a wedding planner, sister and friend to the excited bride-to-be.

"I simply cannot manage without you, Julia," Madeleine reminds her almost daily. "Since my mother took ill a few months ago and is not available to assist me with my wedding plans, you have become indispensable. I just don't know what I would do without you, my dear friend."

Julia is not displeased by her friend's need for her. Madeleine leans on her for everything, and she almost feels like she really is her sister. They talk over everything and then make Madeleine's decisions together.

"Will you come with me to order the invitations, Julia? I want to be sure they are in perfect taste and that I select just the right color and type. How long do you think the train should be on my wedding gown? I don't want it to remind anyone of the first Mrs. Astor."

"I am very much out of my element, my dear Maddie. Remember that there were no invitations to my wedding. And as for a train, I never even had a wedding dress, so you cannot rely on my judgement. Just go with what your heart tells you, and you will be the most beautiful bride in the world. Col. Astor already thinks you are the most beautiful woman in the world, so you can hardly make a mistake in his eyes."

"Col. Astor is handling this entire affair with his usual flair and societal aplomb," Julia announces one morning as they are discussing the flowers for the church. Maddie breaks out in laughter. She taught Julia this rather uppity phrase and she giggles every time she hears Julia say it; it is so completely out of character.

"Don't I sound like a society matron?" Julia responds to Madeleine's laughter.

"Of course you do, Julia dear, and it's the one thing that can make me laugh out loud," Madeleine answers. "But please remember, I love you just the way you are. All you ever have to be with me is just my friend. You're a breath of fresh air, Julia, compared to my society friends."

"Thank you for saying that Maddie. I am so happy that I can give you the love and emotional support you need at this important time in your life. I want to be like a sister to you in every way possible. I am so happy for you and the Colonel that I can hardly contain myself. I'll never be a society matron, but I don't care as long as I have you in my life."

Later in the day when Julia is sitting alone in an upstairs room, she cannot help but be aware of the big difference between Madeleine's pending ceremony and her own, just a few short years ago. There is absolutely no resemblance whatsoever. "It's amazing, though," Julia thinks to herself, "my ceremony is just as binding as Madeleine's will be. They are really all the same in the sight of God."

Because of the negative response of the Press and a similar feeling in society in general, the wedding plans are being kept rather low key. Only the closest friends and relatives will be invited to attend. It is definitely not to be the social event of the year by any standards, but the bridal couple seem not to care and appear completely happy.

And so it comes to pass that Jack Astor marries Madeleine Force on June 3, 1911. Julia does not attend the ceremony, of course, but Madeleine regales her and Mrs. Umber with all the details of the big event. Much to Julia's delight, the newlyweds immediately settle down to a life of domesticity at 840 Fifth Avenue. It is wonderful for Julia to have Madeleine there every day, and they manage to spend a lot of quality time together. Julia's music lessons, for example, continue now in earnest.

"You are my very best pupil. Julia," Madeleine praises her. They both laugh at this, because of course, Julia is her only pupil.

The Colonel has many pressing business meetings to attend during the day, but spends most of his evenings at home with his young wife. They attend the theater quite often and are patrons of the opera as well. Madeleine and the Colonel appear to be very happy together, despite the difference in their ages. Even Vincent seems to be adjusting to the changes in the household. He will never think of Madeleine as his stepmother, of course, but more like a sibling cousin. All is peace and tranquility at 840 Fifth Avenue except for the constant badgering by the local press.

The celebrated newspaper columnists continue to haunt the newlyweds and cause public opinion to be divided concerning the respectability of the Colonel's actions. Annoyed and somewhat pressured by this, Madeleine and the Colonel decide to call a halt to this constant harassment and spend the winter of 1912 abroad in order to let the gossip die down at home. This then is to be their long-awaited honeymoon trip to Egypt and Paris.

Although Vincent is still less than thrilled with the match, it does further his desired course of action; and so he does not complain or offer resistance. More than anything he wants to spend time studying in London before continuing his financial education in the United States. To placate his son, the Colonel agrees to this request. It is decided that while the bride and groom are traveling through Egypt and France, Julia will act as housekeeper for Vincent for the first month or two of his stay in London, until more permanent arrangements can be made. Then, if all goes well, when the Astors conclude their travels; Julia will join them, and they will all return to the U. S. together.

When Madeleine and the Colonel leave for Egypt in November of 1911, Julia is dreadfully lonely. She misses her dear friend more than she could have imagined. The house on Fifth Avenue is to be closed from the end of the month until January 15th, when Vincent returns home from boarding school to begin preparing for his term in London. At present he and Julia have first-class tickets on *The France*, leaving New York on March 2nd and arriving in Southampton on the 14th. The Colonel purchased these tickets before he and Madeleine left on their honeymoon. He also arranged for hotel reservations for Vincent and Julia in Southampton. They will stay there for a few days and then go on to the townhouse in London, which Col. Astor leased for them prior to his leaving.

"You shall have the entire month of December and January to spend with your husband and children, Julia," Col. Astor informs her a week before they leave for Europe. "I hope you will have a wonderful Christmas and New Year and are all rested before you and Vincent prepare to leave on *The France*. I very much appreciate your returning to the house on February 1st to assist Mrs. Umber and help Vincent prepare for the journey. You will of course, be fully compensated for the months you are off. Consider this our Christmas gift to you and your family," Col. Astor concludes.

"Thank you very much, Col. Astor," Julia responds with genuine gratitude in her voice. "You have been so kind to me and more than generous while I have been in your service. I hope you know how grateful I am. I wish you and Madeleine, er uh, I mean Mrs. Astor, a wonderful trip abroad, and a blessed Christmas as well."

"Thank you Julia, and please know that I am aware that you and my wife are on a first-name basis, and I find that charming. You need not worry about calling Mrs. Astor, Madeleine, in my presence, Julia. I have come to look upon you as one of the family," he adds and places a kiss on her cheek.

The anticipation of the trip is almost more than Julia can

bear. She is trying to be calm and give George and the children her undivided attention, but it is a struggle. They spend a good deal of time together preparing for the holidays. George has promised that they can have a real Christmas tree this year, so Emma and Jerry are busily engaged in making ornaments with which to trim it. Julia has purchased colored paper and has given each of them a pair of scissors.

"Can I make two kinds of chains, Mama?" asks Jerry. "Emma learned how in school and she is teaching me."

"He's doing real good too, Mama," high praise from his sister. "I want to start stringing the cranberries soon," continues Emma, "if you will give me a needle, Mama."

"I guess you are old enough now to handle a needle without poking a hole in your finger, Emma; but please be careful. We don't want blood on your Christmas decorations." Jerry laughs at this and adds, "I'll be careful too, Mama. I won't let the scissors slip while I am making the chains."

"You are both so talented and so grown up now," Julia says as she encircles both children in her arms. "It is truly a joy to have this time to spend together to prepare for the Christmas holiday."

"It is very good to have you home with us, *Juliashcam*," George chimes in. "I will even have a week off myself between Christmas and the New Year. The supervisor has promised my whole crew this time off for the holiday. Next year the other crew will get it, but this year it is our turn. I'm especially glad because you will be leaving us soon."

This is the first time George has mentioned Julia's leaving since he agreed she could go. She has almost forgotten herself, for a little while; so caught up is she in the holiday preparations.

"We'll take care of you, Papa, don't worry," says Emma with finality.

"I'll help too, I will," Jerry chimes in. "I won't get into any mischief, I promise. I'll be so good for Auntie Flora and you'll all be proud of me, honest!" They all smile at this and exchange hugs all around.

Emma is growing by leaps and bounds and seems to be everywhere at once. She is fast becoming a beauty too. Julia can see it already as the golden curls frame the round six year-old face, always wreathed in smiles. She is truly a joy to behold. Jerry, now barely four, looks up to his sister as though she were a queen. He adores her and no one can do or say anything against her when he is around. He fancies himself Emma's little protector – her guardian angel. Next to Julia and his Aunt Flora, Emma is his favorite person in the whole world.

"I like my *Florinanny*," he says, "but I love my Emmy."

Christmas Eve arrives before they know it. "We're ready, Papa, we're ready," shout both children.

"Then let us go now and pick out our Christmas tree," George shouts back.

Julia bundles the children up warmly and promises to have hot chocolate and *polacinta* waiting for them when they come back. An hour later they return dragging the scrawniest pine tree Julia has ever seen up the stairs.

"We should have gone yesterday," George whispers to Julia. "There were almost no trees left at the lot on the corner. I will know better next year, but for now, Julia, tell them it is beautiful, I beg of you."

"Of course, George," Julia whispers gently; and with that, the tree comes careening through the door.

"Whew," says Jerry, "that was a tough job, Mama. Isn't it the best tree ever?"

"It's really not, Mama," Emma interjects resolutely, "but it looked so lonely on the corner, we had to pick this one."

"It is absolutely beautiful and special, my dears; and the best thing of all is that it is ours. It will be the best Christmas tree ever when you get all your homemade decorations on it." Both children grin from ear to ear and run to give her kisses.

"Come now children," says George, "let's get some of Mama's hot chocolate and that *polacinta* she promised." With that, both children race for the kitchen table and begin loading their plates with the oversized crepes. Jerry grabs the currant jelly, but Emma holds out for the strawberry. After filling the center with dollops of the sweet confection of their choice, they roll up the crepes and begin stuffing huge bites into their mouths.

"Didn't you two ever hear of forks?" George asks watching this display.

"Oh, yes Papa, but we're too hungry," is the answering chorus from overstuffed mouths. George and Julia look at their children and then at each other and begin to laugh.

"You'd think you hadn't eaten for a week," says Julia. "I'm glad Flora isn't here to see this. She'd think your mama doesn't feed you any more."

Both children began to laugh now too, between mouthfuls. George and Julia dig into the pile and they all have a feast on this wonderful Christmas Eve.

As the day of Julia's leaving comes closer, she is overwhelmed with concern about what and how much she should pack. "Will I have the right sort of clothes, will my manners be acceptable, and will Vincent and I get along together?"

Reflecting on the latter, she realizes that, except for their occasional encounters in the library, she and Vincent have not said more than a perfunctory hello and goodbye to each other in the last year. Julia knows instinctively that he does not dislike her because he is always respectful and polite, but that is all she knows. Though they are contemporaries, they have never considered each other more than acquaintances. They developed no real relationship as she and Madeleine had.

"Perhaps we will find a common interest to talk about after a time. It seems to me that all Vincent cares about is money and things financial – things I am totally ignorant about. Obviously, he is preparing to take over his father's empire one day. I am determined to give it no further thought just now, and so I will relax and let nature take its course. Vincent, I am certain, will be too busy studying to worry about me anyway except in the matter of what's for dinner. He does like my cooking I know, and that's got to be a bond of sorts."

The day finally arrives when Vincent and Julia are to depart for England. As excited and happy as she is to be going to Europe, she is very sad to leave Emma and Jerry. Julia feels a bit guilty for not being too sad to leave George. He is such a kind and good man and a loving husband, she has to keep reminding herself.

"I am lucky to have him I know, but after meeting James, I will never again be content with just good and kind. I miss the passion and deep emotion of that brief encounter; and although George loves me, I know he is incapable of showing it in any tangible way that even borders on passion. I thought I had resigned myself to this long ago, but sometimes, like today, I miss what I might have had with James." Julia shrugs her shoulders, pats her hair into place and turns her full attention to her children.

She hugs the children to her and bids them farewell with promises of a quick return and presents that will be brought back for both of them. George kisses her tenderly on the forehead, and she returns this caress with a kiss on his cheek.. He then announces that the taxi is waiting outside to take her to the pier and the huge floating hotel that will carry her back to Europe for the first time since they left Hungary.

So many conflicting thoughts fill her head as Julia turns from her family and walks toward the door where she will embark on this grand adventure. She looks back over her shoulder and sees the smiling faces of her family, overflowing with love and pride in their mama.

"I am truly blessed," she thinks to herself as she descends the stairs. George follows behind carrying her valises to the waiting taxi.

## Chapter 17

The townhouse is perfect for their needs. It has two sunny bedrooms and a small but elegant den, which serves as a library as well. The highlight of the den, in Julia's estimation, is the inclusion of a small spinet piano in the corner. It is made of highly polished mahogany, and the ivory keys seem to gleam in the sunlight. Someone has lovingly draped a fringed silk shawl over one corner, and there is a tiny silver frame in the other corner containing a miniature country scene. There are heavy mauve-colored drapes (portieres the English call them) on the windows, which can be drawn to keep out the cold. There is no central heating in most London homes, including this one, and Julia soon learns that only a very few government buildings are equipped with any kind of heating device. Because of this fact, there is a fireplace in every room, and some of the andirons are quite unique – goblins and dragons bear the weight of the logs in several of the rooms. The andirons in Julia's bedroom are cranes with their long necks bent and whose beaks hold the logs in place. They are really quite charming, Julia notes and she polishes them often so that their long necks and crested heads maintain a sheen despite the almost constant fire in the grate. Vincent has hired an old man to bring them wood every other day, so there is never a lack of heat in the townhouse.

The living room is large and airy and captures what sunlight is available in this rather dismal winter environment. The furnishings are a bit severe and stodgy for Julia's taste, but she vows to brighten them up with some of her excellent crocheted antimacassars. The rugs in the townhouse are all oriental and woven with beautifully vivid colors. Julia cannot help but imagine what beautiful fabrics some of these designs would make, and she envisions magnificent ball gowns worn by beautiful women at some elegant royal occasion in English society.

The townhouse is also blessed with beautifully ornate gas lamps, some with beaded shades that give off enough light to read by even in the evening. Brass candlesticks adorn every mantle, and small oil lamps made of pewter are placed conveniently throughout the rooms. These, Julia assumes, are used mostly at night after they are all tucked into their beds. They would be used to light their way from one room to another, especially to the water closets which are at both ends of the upstairs hall.

There is a small kitchen and dining area where meals may be taken looking out of a bay window onto beautiful Hyde Park. Julia examines the kitchen thoroughly, as this will be her special domain. It is all white and appears very sterile at first glance.

"I can't wait to add a few womanly touches like a bowl of fruit on the table, flowers in a ceramic pot on the windowsill and perhaps a copper pot or two to hang above the big porcelain stove," Julia informs the empty white room.

"It seems that most of the essentials are here," she comments to Vincent one evening shortly after they are settled in. "There are a few items missing, however, that I really consider essential to a well-equipped kitchen. For example," she continues thoughtfully, "there is no large wooden board where I can roll out the dough for the *rugelach* you like so much or a ricer to shred the potatoes for your favorite pot pie."

"Father has given you a substantial allowance, Julia, to run this household here in London, so go and purchase whatever you want to complete the kitchen," Vincent responds dryly.

This is Vincent's only comment on the state of the kitchen,

but he does take some time during our first week of residence to help me learn my way around the city however, He even brings home a large-scale map of the City of London and spreads it out on the kitchen table. He then proceeds to mark where we live and where certain points of interest are located.

"Now pay attention, Julia, he says with authority. "This is where we live and this is where you can get the bus or catch a taxi." He marks each spot with a colored pencil as he explains it to me. "I will show you how far our townhouse is from the best green grocer in the Hyde Park section of London, and I will direct you as to the most efficient route to get there."

"Thank you so much, Vincent," Julia replies with sincerity. Your explanations are very clear, and I know I will be able to find my way around quite easily now. It was very thoughtful of you to take the time to do this for me."

"It was no trouble at all, Julia. I know Father would want you to enjoy your stay here in London, and making you feel at home in the city is a good start to accomplishing this I think," he concludes with a pleased look on his youthful but stern countenance. "If you encounter any problems in finding your way around," Vincent goes on, "do not hesitate to come to me for clarification."

Julia grinned at this last remark. Vincent was beginning to sound more and more like his father every day. Julia felt that they both enjoyed this exercise, and with Vincent's map and subsequent tutoring, she was soon scurrying around the neighborhood making purchases like a native. With this wondrous map, Julia is also able to find out where the museums, galleries, and other public places are located, as well as the best routes to get there. She is really enjoying this adventure and plans studiously to make the most of her time in this wonderful city.

The walls in the small but cozy den are paneled, and the carpet on the floor is of a deep wine color. All the furniture is upholstered except for a curved mahogany desk in the corner which has a magnificent tooled leather top. All in all it is a most pleasant setting, conducive to Vincent's study habits and glorious by Julia's standards.

Vincent's school is within walking distance, only a few blocks away; and he seems to enjoy this daily stroll in the fresh air even if it is sometimes shrouded in the all-too-common fog of the city. So much of his time is spent indoors that this is often the only exercise he gets during the week. On weekends he plays cricket with some of his school chums and sometimes participates in a polo match. A friend of his has a stable of horses he tells Julia, and is instructing him in the art of this sport of kings, as he calls it.

Julia gets most of her fresh air and exercise walking to and from the market each day. She loves to buy the fresh herbs and vegetables that are available there and to use them to make their meals varied and interesting. She also loves to walk in Hyde Park. It is filled with trees and plants of all kinds and there are always people coming and going – business people en route to luncheon engagements, nannies pushing perambulators, and young lovers holding hands. Julia misses her sweet children when she sees young ones skipping rope or playing hide and seek among the bushes that line the paths in the park. She tries not to linger on the lovers; it always tears at her heart and reminds her of James.

Julia has her own room for the first time in her life. It is decorated in pink silk and has cabbage roses in the wallpaper. It has become her oasis – a fairyland where she can think and do whatever she wants in complete privacy. The view from the window is wonderful too and includes a view of the lower end of the park. She can walk in the park and meander in and out of the lovely shops and boutiques in the surrounding neighborhood.

During the late afternoon while Vincent is still in school, she often searches out the warmth and comfort of the den where she can sit down at the spinet and play. Unbeknownst to the Colonel or Vincent, Madeleine has taught Julia to play a few simple melodies, and she revels in her newfound talent. She checks the English newspapers every day searching for concerts in the area that she can attend. She has also learned where the art galleries and museums are and takes full advantage of her daytime hours to visit many of them. She is absorbing the art like a sponge and finding special delight in the mixture of color and design she finds all around her.

Vincent comes home for dinner most week nights, but on the weekends he often has plans with his friends, so Julia has more time to herself and can enjoy the theatre and other cultural distractions on these evenings as well. During the week she prepares simple meals and then retires to her bedroom to read or to write letters home. The den is Vincent's domain in the evening from Monday to Friday. He does his studying at the big mahogany desk, and she seldom sees him at all after dinner on these evenings.

And so the time passes amicably between them. Julia is seldom bored as she still loves to cook, and Vincent always appreciates her culinary efforts. She enjoys her free time to indulge herself in whatever strikes her fancy. She does miss not having anyone to discuss these new pursuits with, but she is certain that she and Madeleine will make up for lost time when they are all together again in the big house on Fifth Avenue.

Meanwhile Julia shares some of her adventures with Emma and Jerry in her letters home. She tells them about the street musicians she sees in the Park, and how the gardens are like sculptured paintings even when they are not in bloom and only green. She describes the wonders of the green grocer and some of the unusual herbs and spices she is able to purchase there. Best of all, she tells them about the plays she has seen and the concerts she has attended and how much she looks forward to taking them to events like this when she returns home. Emma especially would enjoy the ballet, and Julia promises to take her when she gets back to New York. Vincent describes the cricket matches so she can tell Jerry about them. Julia is sure Jerry thinks that cricket is a silly name for a man's game, but she assures him that it is a national pastime here in England.

"Perhaps it will raise his enthusiasm for our national pastime – baseball," she says to Vincent one evening when he comes upon her writing to her son. "At any rate, these sojourns of mine give me plenty to write about to the children, and these letters have become a sort of journal of my experiences here in London."

Julia thinks of Madeleine often and wonders where she and the Colonel are and what wondrous sights they are seeing in Egypt. Madeleine had promised to write to Julia, but only one brief postcard has found its way to London thus far.

"Dearest Julia," it begins. Egypt is more exciting than I could have dreamed possible. I am keeping a journal of the trip so I can share our adventures with you when I return. Much love, Maddie."

After all, Julia reasons, she is a newlywed and I am not family, only a friend. We will have lots of time later when we are all back in New York for her to tell me about their adventures. Julia consoles herself with these thoughts but continues to wonder where and how her dear friends are. After all this time, she now thinks of the Colonel as a friend also, although she would never presume to call him anything but Col. Astor.

Suddenly in the first week of April, a wire arrives from Col. Astor that changes the course of all their lives.

"Madeleine," he announces, "is with child. We will all be returning home on the maiden voyage of the newest vessel in the White Star Line, the *Titanic*, on April 10th from Southampton."

Julia can hardly contain her joy at this turn of events. However, when she advises Vincent of this change in plans, he becomes furious.

"How can they do this to me?" he shouts. Julia explains again that Madeleine is going to have a baby, but this only incenses him further. "My father is too old to be a father again," he rails. "He is ready to be a grandfather, not a father. What can he be thinking of?"

Julia says nothing and waits for the harangue to be over. Vincent finally calms down and announces, "I will not return to the United States now under any circumstances – baby be damned! I am going to finish my University term here in London, and that is that," he roars defiantly. "Father will just have to understand and find a way for me to stay on."

As it turns out, the Colonel does understand and gives Vincent permission to complete the year. He arranges for him to stay with some very old and dear friends of the Astors living in London for the remainder of the term. The Colonel's acquiescence eventually appeases Vincent's rage, and he settles down to resume his life as an academic. The Colonel's friends, it seems, have a son only a year older than Vincent who attends the same school. This will provide him with the opportunity for some additional companionship outside of the friends he has already acquired.

The following week the Colonel sends his second cable which advises that he has made some rather special arrangements. He and Madeleine and their entourage will be permitted to board the *Titanic* at Cherbourg, during a brief stop before it continues on to its main point of embarkation at Southampton. He further advises that Julia's cabin will be in the same first class corridor as the suite reserved for the family, so they will all be in proximity to one another.

Julia receives the news with mixed feelings. Part of her hates leaving the elegant environment she has learned to enjoy here in London and the feeling of being on her own as the lady of the manor, so to speak. The other part of her is filled with joy at the thought of seeing her precious children again and also her dear Madeleine. She has missed her friend and the intimacies they shared more than she thought possible. Julia is sure that Madeleine will need to rely on her more than ever now that she is to become a mother herself. What joy we will have sharing the wonder of this new experience in her life, Julia reflects.

She turns her thoughts to the business of packing and the preparations for leaving the townhouse and then hurries to her bedroom to write home to George and the children and tell them that she will soon be returning home.

# Chapter 18

The gilt-framed calendar stares at Julia from the sideboard. April 8th it seems to scream at her. She swallows hard and returns to her packing. She has been shopping for the past two days, making sure that Vincent has all the provisions he will need to sustain him until he moves across town to stay with the friends of the Astors at the end of the month. Julia has already arranged to hire a temporary cook/housekeeper to come in for a few hours each day to prepare Vincent's meals and keep the townhouse clean and orderly prior to his departure. She doesn't want Vincent to feel neglected in any way as a result of her leaving. She knows he would not blame her directly for this inconvenience to his life, but it is her intention to help maintain peace between Vincent and his father in any way that she is able. In truth, her motivation is also colored by her loyalty to her friend Madeleine. Julia doesn't want Vincent to blame Maddie in any way for this change in plans.

Although Julia is excited about traveling on the *Titanic*, which is being touted not only as extremely elegant but also as the first unsinkable ship ever to cross the Atlantic, she is apprehensive as well. She has read much of the publicity about this elegant vessel, and is well aware of the stature and importance of many of the celebrated first-class passengers who are scheduled to make this maiden voyage. Many immigrants like herself will also be making the trip in steerage, or third class as it is now called. This knowledge evokes all sorts of dark memories from the past.

Visions of narrow bunks, slop buckets overflowing on the floor, and the stench of sweaty bodies assails her memory. She silently prays that she will never, ever have to travel that way again as long as she lives.

Col. Astor informs Julia by another wire that he and Madeleine will be accompanied on the trip by his manservant, Mr. Victor Robbins, Madeleine's maid, Miss Rosalie Bidois and also Miss Caroline Louise Endres, Madeleine's newly hired nurse. Also in the entourage will be Kitty, the Astor's pet Airedale.

"As she reads the wire Julia wonders, "will I be relegated to socializing only with the so-called help. Even though my cabin will be in the first class section, will I even be permitted to talk to Maddie, my dearest friend." These and other questions plague Julia's mind and distract her from the business at hand. Finally she forces herself to stop this conjecturing and places her full attention on her packing. "After all," she reminds herself, "in two days I will be on board the *Titanic* with the Mr. and Mrs. John Jacob Astor sailing for New York City and my husband and children. Nothing else is more important than this one fact of life.

She closes her suitcase with finality. It is finally done. All her belongings and mementos of London are packed into these valises and are ready to be taken with her to the coach that takes them to the pier.

Julia says her good-byes to Vincent that evening, and he wishes her a pleasant voyage. As a parting gesture he even arranges for a large, elegant carriage to come and collect her the next day and take her to the ship. They part amicably and Vincent thanks her for taking such good care of him these past weeks.

"I hope that we will met again at the house on Fifth Avenue," he says, smiling down at her. Julia even feels as though he means it sincerely. She brushes his cheek with her lips in a sisterly manner and they both retire for the evening.

Julia awakes early and realizes that is really time to leave. Her heart is racing. She dresses quickly, makes a cup of tea to go with her usual breakfast scone and gathers her suitcases about her. She hears the coach pull up outside and waits breathlessly for the coachman to come to the door to fetch her bags and load them onto his huge conveyance. Horse-drawn coaches are still popular in London, especially in the areas down by the docks where cobblestone streets are not easily traversed by motor vehicles. She jumps when the doorknocker clangs against the heavy wooden door but manages to open it in her most ladylike manner. A rather rotund coachman is standing before her with his hat in his hand.

"Are you ready, Miss?" the coachman inquires in his best cockney. "I'll load your bags on the back of the carriage and strap them down good before we leave for the pier."

"I'm quite ready, sir," Julia replies in her most gentile voice, and prances down the steps of the brownstone and into the carriage as though it were an every-day occurrence. She knows she cuts a fine figure in her mauve silk gown with the pale pink rosebuds on the bonnet. A glance at herself in the front window of the brownstone as she passes, assures her that she looks every inch a lady. Her spunk and courage return as though by magic. Julia steps up into the coach with the aid of the coachman and settles herself for the ride to the pier. She feels like a real lady and determines to act like one from now on.

"The trip shouldn't take more than half an hour, Miss, unless there is more traffic than we planned on. There is so much excitement at the docks over the sailing of this new ship. I ain't seen the likes of it for some time in these parts. The newspapers ain't had nothin' else on the front page for these past two days," he continues. "They say that more 'n a hundred people will come just to see the sailing. Such a hullabaloo over a ship." He shakes his head in consternation – "all dang foolishness if you ask me."

Julia looks out the window of the carriage and sees that the horses appear restless, which gives her cause for some concern. The coachman looks up from where he is strapping the valises onto the rear of the coach and notices the worried look on Julia's face as she watches the horses pawing the cobblestones. He stands up and walks over to the window where she is peering out. He tries to cheer her up.

"Don't worry, Miss," the Coachman says reassuringly. "It's just that there are so many people and carriages out and about who want to see the great new ship, the *Titanic*. The horses will calm down once we get on our way. Never fear, you'll be safe with me," he adds confidently.

Julia tries to relax and settles back in her seat. She folds her hands in her lap in an effort to convince herself that she is totally calm. She looks back at the brownstone that has been her home for the past weeks with some sadness and then turns her eyes forward to the road ahead. The Coachman is in his seat now and the horses appear calm and ready to go. Once again she is embarking on a new journey and she doesn't want to miss a moment of it.

After about three blocks it is apparent that this trip to the pier is going to be more difficult and take a bit longer than the coachman supposed. Julia can feel the tension from the driver and his horses as they try to force their way through the crowds of people and other carriages. Everyone seems intent on only one thing – getting to the pier to catch a glimpse of this glorious new ship, the *Titanic*. It seems to Julia that an hour has passed already. She knows this cannot be so, but she is very much aware that time is slipping away all too rapidly. Horses begin rearing up and carriages in front of them are coming to a standstill. Suddenly from the right comes an especially large carriage drawn by four horses instead of the usual one or two. It comes careening down the street at break-neck speed. The coachman is trying desperately to slow the animals down and his desperate cries of "whoa, whoa" can be heard above the din of the traffic.

"Hang on Miss," Julia's driver shouts above the racket, and with that, he turns the coach out of the path of the oncoming horses. His response is too late however. The two coaches collide and two of the horses go down onto the cobblestones. Valises and boxes are tossed everywhere, and the street is totally blocked with crazed animals and injured passengers. Julia is thrown clear of the debris, but one of the steamer trunks breaks loose and lands on her ankle, pinning her to the ground. The crowd hems them in until suddenly a voice belonging to a blue uniform arrives on the scene and begins to take charge of the chaotic situation. The tallest English Bobby Julia has ever seen takes charge of the mishap and has soon conscripted several strong men to assist him in righting the carriages and giving aid to the terrified horses. He then turns his attention to Julia and the passengers of the opposing carriage. By this time a Red Cross Lorry arrives on the scene, and soon the occupants of the other carriage and Julia are loaded onto stretchers and placed inside the Lorry to be transported to the nearest hospital.

By the time they arrive at the hospital, Julia's ankle is throbbing and her head is pounding. She knows now that there are two other people involved in the collision, as both of them are in the Lorry with her. They are taken off first and rushed inside the hospital. Julia senses that their condition is quite serious. Then it is her turn. Two white-coated attendants lift her out of the Lorry and onto a set of wheels that can roll her onto the stretcher inside the hospital. Before she can utter a word, she is placed on a bed in a sterile white room, and a young doctor is staring down at her.

"How do you feel, Miss?" the doctor inquires gently. Julia looks up into the largest pair of deep brown eyes she has ever seen. A little gasp escapes her lips.

"I'm a bit shaken," she mumbles, "but the only thing that really hurts, besides my head, is my ankle." The brown eyes scrutinize the swollen red ankle with the big bruise where the trunk struck it.

"It appears that you have a badly bruised and sprained ankle, Miss, but we have to be sure it's not broken before we proceed any further." After a few pushes, pulls and probings, to which Julia responds with the appropriate grunts and groans, it is determined that the ankle is indeed only severely bruised and sprained, but not broken.

"I will tape it up for you," says the doctor matter-of-factly, "but I must insist that you stay off it for several days until the swelling goes down. That is a mean bruise you have there, and it will take some time for it to begin to heal as well. As for your headache, I think a bit of medication and a glass of cold water will take care of that in short order."

The brown eyes fixed themselves on Julia's ankle and then traveled up to her face. "You seem a bit preoccupied, Miss, have you heard a word I said?"

"Oh yes, doctor; forgive me but my mind was on another matter entirely. I am sailing on the *Titanic* today," she exclaimed rather louder than she intended.

"Oh, I am sorry, Miss, but that ship sailed twenty five minutes ago and is already out in the Atlantic. I'm afraid you've missed that voyage for sure," he adds.

The brown eyes survey Julia, and the realization of her plight suddenly becomes apparent. The doctor speaks more gently. "Please keep calm and don't get too upset. After all there will be another ship leaving Southampton in a week or two, and you can board her as soon as you can stand comfortably. I will even help you exchange your ticket and arrange for your baggage to be sent to the pier at the proper time. It's not the end of the world you know, and maybe God had a reason for you to miss the ship." He grinned to himself at his foolish attempt to assuage her unhappiness, but actually he did make Julia feel a bit better about her dilemma. "At least you are safe and sound with only a bruised ankle and a slight headache to show for your trouble," he adds ruefully.

Julia is touched by his kindness and manages a smile by way of a thank you.

"My name is Julia Pedesch," she says suddenly, "and I can't thank you enough for helping me and being so kind. I need to ask another favor of you though," she continues. "I was to meet

Col. John Jacob Astor and his wife on the *Titanic* and sail home with them. I am their housekeeper in New York and was staying in London with their son until the *Titanic* sailed for home. I must get word to them that I missed the ship. Can you help me do that?"

The doctor looks down at Julia and smiles warmly. "Well now, my name is Frank, Dr. Francis Kallan actually," he responds, "and of course I will help you. You look awfully young to be a housekeeper if you don't mind my saying so. I usually think of them as the older, more motherly type. He pauses. Julia does not respond, so he goes on. "The hospital has a wireless, and we can send a message to the ship for you. Please don't worry; I'll take care of it right away. You just write down your message on this piece of paper, and I will send it off for you within the hour. Col. Astor will be relieved to know what has happened to you, I am sure."

Julia could feel her face glowing with relief and gratitude. "Thank you, Dr. Kallan. Once more you have rescued me."

"That's Frank, Julia, and it is my pleasure. It's not every day I get to save a damsel in distress in more than a medical way. Now get some rest, and I will take care of sending your message. I'll stop in to see you later on."

With these parting words, Dr. Francis Kallan strides from the room, and Julia sinks down into her pillows, which are cool and soothing under her throbbing head. Within minutes her eyes close and she is peacefully asleep.

When she finally wakes up, it is to a room flooded with light. A nurse is pulling back the curtains with rather loud gestures and a tray of food is staring at her from the bedside table.

"Time to wake up and get some nourishment," the figure in the starched gray uniform declares with authority.

Julia sits up in bed and surveys her surroundings with a bit more care. Her situation has not changed. She is in a hospital and the *Titanic* has really sailed without her.

"I had hoped it was merely a dream," she whispers.

"What did you say my dear?" the nurse inquires moving closer to the bed.

"Oh nothing, nurse, I was just thinking out loud. Thank you for the breakfast."

"You're quite welcome, my dear. Just ring when you are finished. I will have someone come in to pick up the tray and then a nurse will give you a lovely sponge bath. That will surely make you feel more comfortable. Then Dr. Kallan will be in to check on you."

"Will I be able to leave the hospital tomorrow, nurse?"

"I really can't say," she replies with the hint of a grin, "only the doctor in charge can make that determination." With that said, she leaves the room, closing the door behind her. Julia turns her attention to the breakfast tray in front of her. Suddenly the smells emanating from under the stainless steel dome reach her consciousness and she feels a ferocious hunger envelop her.

"I'm starving," Julia blurts out loud. "Whatever that is smells divine." She proceeds to scoop the metal dome off the plate with a flourish and surveys the contents underneath. "Mm pancakes, my favorite," she shouts gleefully to no one in particular.

The nurse returns and surveys her sternly. She places the napkin on Julia's chest, plumps the pillows behind her, and once again leaves the room. Julia wastes no more time, but attacks the food as if she has not eaten for days. Just as she is wiping up the last vestiges of syrup, a voice can be heard in the doorway.

"Good morning, Miss Julia. You certainly seem to be enjoying your breakfast."

"Oh I am, she grins as Dr. Kallan comes over to the side of her bed. "I haven't enjoyed a meal this much in a very long time, and more so because I didn't even have to prepare it myself."

Dr. Kallan grins back at her and comes closer, studying her as she wipes her chin with a corner of the napkin. "That last bit of syrup missed my mouth," she giggles. He returns her smile and then becomes suddenly serious.

"Julia, you can leave here in another day or two," Dr. Kallen says. "The swelling is almost gone in the ankle, and if you don't plan to do any mountain climbing or hiking in the immediate future, I can release you on your own recognizance. You will have to keep the wrapping on for another few days until the sprain heals, but with the extra support, you can put some weight on that foot and get around a little. By the way, where do you plan to stay now that you have missed the *Titanic*?" he continues.

"Why I hadn't given that any thought as yet," Julia responds. "When I got into that coach yesterday, I certainly did not expect to end up in a hospital with a bruised and sprained ankle. I can't return to the townhouse where Vincent and I were living because he has probably already left there to move in with some friends of his father's in London. Besides, I'd just as soon he didn't even know I missed the boat. I'm embarrassed enough as it is. Maybe I can find a modest rooming house where I can stay for a short time until my ankle is strong enough for me to return home. I also have to get a sailing schedule and book myself passage from England back to America. I have so much to do; it's overwhelming," she adds with a deep sigh.

Julia stops her ramblings abruptly and looks up to see Frank Kallan grinning at her. "What is so funny, Dr. Kallan?" she demands.

"You are," he answers back. "You've been prattling on here for so long about all the things you must do, you've worked yourself into a state. Calm down now, Julia, you are among friends. We will all be glad to help you get settled and solve some of your immediate concerns. Nurse Davis has a friend who owns a fine rooming house just down the street a few blocks. I'm sure she would be glad to check with her and see if there is a room available for a week or two. Meanwhile, I will personally locate a vessel schedule for you and deliver it here in person so you can begin planning your return trip. When you decide which vessel you want to sail on, I will make the booking for you and have the ticket delivered to you at the rooming house. Now then, does that not put your busy female mind to rest? All will be taken care of,

Julia; we are your friends too after all," he concludes with a gentle smile.

Julia cannot help but return the smile. "What a fine man you are, and what a good friend you have been," she tells him and means it most sincerely. "I will never be able to thank you enough for all you have done for a veritable stranger."

"And now, my dear Julia, we are strangers no longer, but good friends. Perhaps one day we will meet again in New York City, and who knows, maybe I will need to come to you for help. At any rate, it is my pleasure to be of assistance. It is not often I get to aid a beautiful damsel in distress." He chuckles at his own words, and Julia leans across the bed and gently places a kiss on his forehead.

"Thank you, doctor – uh, I mean Frank. I hope with all my heart that we will somehow meet again one day." She tries to stifle a yawn, but the observant physician catches it out of the corner of his eye.

"Enough talking now, my beautiful patient. It is time for you to get some rest. I will check in with you this afternoon and perhaps I will have the vessel schedule with me already." With that, Dr. Francis Kallan strides from the room, signaling the nurse to follow him, He pulls the door gently toward him, but before it shuts, Julia's eyes begin closing, and before it closes completely she is sound asleep.

# Chapter 19

The soft afternoon light is casting shadows across the bed when Julia awakes. There is a great deal of noise and commotion coming from the hallway outside her room. What is going on out there; another accident, she wonders. Suddenly the door flies open and Dr. Kallan enters the room.

"Julia, I have some terrible news," he stammers. "It just came over the radio that the *Titanic* sank last night in the North Atlantic after striking an iceberg. They say that fifteen hundred people may have been lost at sea." Frank Kallan pauses to get his breath.

"But how can that be?" Julia hears herself shouting. "The *Titanic* is unsinkable. Everyone said so – unsinkable! How could it sink and take fifteen hundred people with it? I don't understand, Frank. I don't understand."

"I'm not sure, Julia," Frank Kallan responds. "They are saying that there were not enough lifeboats for all the passengers. The iceberg was so large below the water line," he went on; "it broke right through the hull and the ship filled with water so quickly that it went right to the bottom. Anyone who jumped or fell into the water died of exposure because the water in the North Atlantic is so very cold. Only about seven hundred people made it to the lifeboats, the paper says." When he finishes speaking Frank Kallan sits down with a thud, and Julia sees that he is weeping.

"Dear God, did Col. Astor and Madeleine survive this terrible disaster?" Julia begins to sob convulsively. "No, no it can't be true," is all she can manage to say.

Frank Kallan sits down on the edge of Julia's bed, gathers her into his arms and holds her close. Her sobbing continues and when the nurse enters the room, drawn by the sound of weeping, the doctor asks her to bring him a mild sedative.

"You need something to calm you down, Julia," he says quietly and releases her, laying her gently onto the pillows and tucking the sheet around her shoulders. The nurse returns almost at once with the sedative, and Dr. Kallan takes a glass from the bedside table, fills it with water, and then pours some grains of powder into it. He raises Julia up off the pillows for a moment and says softly, "drink this down, Julia; it will help you relax and make you feel better."

Like a robot Julia obeys the doctor and then falls back against his shoulder. Frank Kallan rests his chin on the top of her head and begins rocking her gently as he would a child. Within a few minutes her sobbing begins to subside and Julia feels her body relax against him. He holds her tightly for an instant, unwilling it seems to break from this embrace. Then he slowly lowers Julia onto the pillows. Frank Kallen gently places a kiss on Julia's forehead and then rises to his feet.

"Sleep well now, dear Julia. It's obvious to me that God arranged for you to miss the *Titanic* for a reason. It was not your time, Julia. He has things for you to accomplish in your life, and that is why he spared you. Things will look better tomorrow, I promise; and I will be here to help you," he adds in a whisper.

When Julia awakes the next morning, her head aches and she has trouble connecting to reality. What a nightmare I had, she thinks to herself. Just then, the nurse comes in to open the curtains and raise the window to allow fresh air and sunshine into the room. Suddenly the voice of a newsboy rises from the din of the street sounds.

"Read all about it: *Titanic* sinks at sea," the voice shouts. "Col. John Jacob Astor confirmed as missing."

Involuntarily Julia sits up in bed, slides her feet to the floor and hobbles to the window. The voice rises up once again, and she gasps in disbelief.

"It's true, it's really true," she stammers. "My poor Maddie and the baby and Col. Astor and all those poor helpless people. How could it happen? It was unsinkable; everyone said so." Suddenly she found herself staggering, overcome by the pain in her ankle, and she felt herself sinking to the floor. The nurse rushes to her side, grabs her under the arms and lays her across the bed. Then she rushes from the room to find Dr. Kallen.

She meets him in the hall already en route to Julia's room. He is standing over the bed almost before Julia knows what has happened. She hears the nurse excitedly explaining to the doctor what has just transpired. Frank Kallan looks down at Julia and knows immediately by the look on her face that she is in pain. He attempts a smile but is met by her tears.

"It wasn't a dream, was it Frank?" Julia whimpers, the words catching in her throat.

"No, Julia, I'm afraid not. It really happened; the *Titanic* really did sink to the bottom of the North Atlantic. I was listening to the radio just before Nurse Davis came to fetch me. The reporter said that many of the names of the missing are confirmed already, but there are others we will not know about for weeks, or perhaps months. Some of the survivors were picked up by a freighter named *Carpathia*, but exactly who and how many is still to be determined. There is still a chance that Col. Astor's wife was a survivor, Julia, but you must be prepared for the worst.

Frank Kallen sinks down on the edge of Julia's bed, and when she looks up at him, she can see that he too is overcome with emotion. She wants to comfort him the way he has tried to comfort her, but she is hurting too much to even move. Her ankle is throbbing now, along with her head, and a feeling of complete desolation comes over her. Madeleine's face keeps swimming before her eyes, filling Julia with fear and trepidation. My dearest friend, I cannot bear the thought that I may never see her sweet face again. Julia makes an effort to pat Frank Kallan's hand in a gesture of comfort, and then closes her eyes, willing it to all go away, even if just for a little while.

She awakes bright and early the next morning feeling more like her old self again, physically at any rate. She has been sleeping since the trauma of yesterday afternoon through the entire night without waking once, and the rest seems to have benefited her swollen ankle considerably. Her first thoughts are again of the terrible news of the day before, and she suddenly realizes the grim reality of what has happened. As she basks in the sun streaming in the hospital window, Julia chokes back the tears that are threatening to slide down from behind her swollen eyelids. She takes a long, deep breath, murmurs her morning prayers, and vows that she will accept the truth and get on with her life the best way she can. I will have plenty of time to sort out all my feelings and questions during my trip home to George and the children, she reminds herself.

Just then Frank Kallan enters the room. "Good morning, my dear," he declares. "You look much better today and rather like a woman with a purpose I might add."

"I am feeling better, thank you Frank, and I'm sorry if I behaved badly yesterday. It was just such a shock hearing about the *Titanic* and the loss of Col. Astor and possibly his wife Madeleine, who was such a dear friend to me. To make matters worse, Frank, Madeleine was pregnant with their first child, so two lives may have been lost instead of just one. I will not rest easy until I know that she and her baby are safe. I pray to God that they are, but meanwhile, I know I must pull myself together and get on with my plans to return home."

As if he knew what she was about to say next, Frank Kallan put out his hand and shoved a thin piece of paper at her.

"Here, my dear, is your sailing schedule, just as you requested." He bows low in an effort to inject a bit of humor into the presentation.

"Oh, Frank, how very kind of you to indulge me like this. I can't wait to see when the next ship will be sailing from

Southampton." She spread the sheet out on the bed and began scanning the pages. "It appears that there is not a ship sailing until week after next, Julia notes rather sadly, "but the *France* is scheduled to leave on the 28th. Can you help me obtain a ticket on the *France*, Dr. Kallan?"

"Not if you persist in calling me Dr. Kallan," the doctor retorts.

"I'm sorry Frank," Julia answers quickly. "I forget now and then. You see, I was always taught to respect men like you – doctors, ministers, barristers and so on."

"You can respect me all you want, Julia, and still call me Frank," the determined doctor insists. Julia smiles up at him, nodding in agreement.

"Well, Frank, now that we have that settled, will you send someone to the pier office for me to see about getting me a ticket on the *France*?" Julia can hardly keep the excitement from her voice. "I am really anxious to return to America and my family. I feel like I have been away from them forever. As soon as I have my ticket, I would like to send a wire home also, to let them know I am really on my way. Emma and Jerry will be so excited."

"Is that your daughter and your husband?" asks the doctor.

"Oh no," Julia answers. "Emma is my daughter and Jerry is my son. My husband's name is George, but of course he will be pleased to learn that his wife is returning home also. It has been such a long time since we were all together in New York and I miss my children so much."

There must have been something in the tone of Julia's voice or the look on her face as she spoke that denoted sadness, because Frank Kallan looked at her with a concerned expression on his handsome face.

"Are you sure you feel well enough to make this trip alone, Julia? It is a long way for a young woman to travel by herself, and I cannot help but be a little worried about you."

"Please don't worry, Dr. Kal . . . I mean Frank. I assure you I will be just fine. I am quite used to being on my own and besides, I know the *France* quite well. That was the ship that brought me to England in the first place so I will feel right at home."

"I suppose I will have to take your word for it my dear. I will dispatch someone to the pier office immediately, madam," he continues in a teasing tone, "and your wish will be granted as soon as he returns."

"Frank, you are truly a friend, and I will be grateful to you for the rest of my life," Julia adds with absolute sincerity in her voice. She stands on tiptoe, balancing on her one good foot to place a kiss on the doctor's forehead. He hugs her as he helps her sit back down and is beaming like a schoolboy.

The afternoon passes quietly enough and just after the dinner trays are brought in, Dr. Kallan enters Julia's room. In his outstretched hand is her ticket on the *France*.

"Your servant, madam," he teases again and hands her the envelope containing the ticket and boarding pass. "You're all set now, and I will be able to discharge you tomorrow morning and have both you and your luggage delivered to Mrs. Thomsen's rooming house where you will be most comfortable until your ship sails on the 28th. Frank Kallan bows low again to give more emphasis to the statement. Julia returns his mock bow with a deep curtsey of her own, wavering a little as her ankle fails her for a moment. She catches herself quickly and looking up, hugs the envelope to her. Frank Kallan smiles at her obvious pleasure and strides from the room.

Julia sits on the edge of the bed and is lost in thought. Mama will be home soon, my children, and will not be leaving you again. Of this I am certain; my place is with you and your papa. The adventure is at an end and about time too. She falls asleep that night dreaming of Emma and Jerry and how good it will be to be with them again. She sleeps soundly and peacefully for the first time in several days.

Many days pass before Julia gets any answers to her many questions, and even then the news is sketchy and inaccurate. Col. Astor's body is not reported found until April 22nd, and by the time she sails on the *France* no word of Madeleine has yet been reported.

"It is assumed," says one newspaper, "that Mrs. Astor has met her fate in the North Atlantic along with her husband."

This news or lack there of, leaves Julia devastated, and she spends the major portion of her voyage in her room or out on the deck staring at the horizon. This cannot be happening, she keeps thinking. It is like a nightmare from which I cannot awaken.

One day follows the next, an interminable parade of grief. Eventually her thoughts turn to Vincent. He must have been told of course, but how did he take it, she wonders. He is now head of the vast Astor empire whether he is ready for that responsibility or not. He is very much alone in the world right now with no one to guide him or help him endure his grief or shoulder any of his new responsibilities. Vincent will certainly return to New York now, Julia reasons. He will have to arrange for his father's funeral. She pauses in her thinking, realizing suddenly that there might have to be a second funeral as well – for Madeleine and her unborn child.

After further reflection, it occurs to Julia that, although she and Vincent were only a year apart in age, they were many years apart in experience. Vincent has led a rather sheltered life up to now, protected by his father from the everyday trials and tribulations of life. The heir to the Astor fortune is going to have to grow up in a hurry. Perhaps Madeleine will be able to help, if she is still alive. Thinking about Madeleine once again brings tears to Julia's eyes. She lowers herself into a deck chair and closes her eyes.

When Julia opens her eyes again it is dark on deck. A huge yellow moon is shining down on her from the star-studded sky. She looks around her and realizes that she is quite alone at this end of the deck. It must be dinner time already she thinks to herself. I have taken most of my meals in my cabin this trip, but perhaps I will dine in the salon tonight. Maybe it will lift my spirits. She rises from the deck chair and turns toward the companionway which leads to her cabin. I will have to freshen up a little before I can go to the dining room, she determines patting her slightly windswept hair.

Before she can pull the door handle, it opens in front of her and a tall elegantly dressed man steps through the narrow opening. Julia steps back in surprise, looks up and a gasp escapes her lips. She grabs the edge of the door for support.

"James?" is all she can muster.

"Julia, is it really you? I cannot believe my eyes." Without another word, James McFadden enfolds the stunned Julia in his arms and they stand silent for a moment with only the moonlight marring the blackness of the deck. James regains his composure and with his hands firmly on her shoulders, he holds her away from him.

"Let me look at you, my dearest girl," he murmurs in disbelief. "My God but you are more beautiful than ever, if that is possible. What brought you to Europe and what are you doing on the *France?* He crushes her to him again and begins kissing her hair. It takes all Julia's strength to free herself from his embrace.

"James, James, let me breathe," she gasps. "I will tell you everything, but let me catch my breath. I cannot believe it is really you, I think I must be dreaming.

"You are not dreaming, my dear. I am really here and I cannot wait to hear what you have to tell me. May we please go into the lounge where we can talk together. It will be quite empty right now as most everyone will be at dinner. The last seating is already in progress. If you are hungry, we can order a bite to eat in there. Please, Julia, please let us have some time together."

"Dear James, of course we will talk. There is so much I have to tell you."

James takes her hand and leads her through the door and down the companionway to the elevator leading to the lounge.

# Chapter 20

Julia looks around the elegant lounge. It is rather quiet at
the moment as most of its usual patrons are now enjoying their
dinner in the main salon two decks down. James leads them to a
small table in a far corner of the room where he can be assured of
privacy and quiet should any diners from the earlier sitting decide
to return. He pulls out the large upholstered chair closest to the
wall and waits for Julia to be seated. He then takes another chair
at her right and pulls it up closer. Some light from the beautiful
full moon outside is coming through the window, illuminating
Julia's face. James studies her for a moment – a beautiful face
with fine bones whittled sharp with pain. He runs his finger down
her cheek, pausing at her chin in a slight caress and begins to
speak.

"What has happened to you, dear Julia? Your face betrays
you. I can see clearly that you are very disturbed. Please tell
me what is wrong so that I may help you." James takes both
Julia's hands in his and leans forward waiting intently for her
to answer.

"James," she says in almost a whisper, "I don't know where
to begin. This past month has changed my life more than I can
tell you."

"Just begin at the beginning, my dear. I have all the time in
the world to listen.

Julia hesitates at first and then the words tumble out in a
torrent. She tells James everything that has transpired almost

since the day they had parted in New York. She explains about the wedding of Madeleine and Col. Astor and of how her friendship with the new Mrs. Astor had blossomed. She told him of the Colonel's request that she accompany Vincent to England while they were on their honeymoon, and of their abrupt decision to return to New York when they learned of Madeleine's pregnancy.

James, of course, had learned of the sinking of the *Titanic* just before he boarded the *France* at Cherbourg but was unaware that Julia had been living in England with Vincent. He was also unaware of the deep friendship that had developed between Julia and Madeleine or the fact that Madeleine was pregnant. James had been unable to return to New York for the Astor wedding so had not had an opportunity to meet the new Mrs. Astor. He had been on safari in East Africa almost continually since he had left Julia in New York. He listened to Julia's every word, giving her his rapt attention.

When Julia finally pauses and seems to be exhausted from her long monologue, she puts her head in her hands and the tears begin to fall. "Oh, James," she sobs, "it is such a relief to get it all out. I haven't had anyone to talk to about the Astors except the very kind doctor who took such good care of me in the hospital after the accident. You were such a good friend to the Colonel; I know you must understand how devastated I am over his death and possibly that of his wife and child."

James leans forward and takes Julia's face in one large tanned hand. With his free hand he takes a large linen handkerchief out of his pocket and begins to gently wipe the tears that are still trickling down her cheeks.

"Of course I understand, dear heart, and I too am deeply sorry about the Colonel's death. Jack and I have been close friends for many years now. He was almost like an uncle to me after my father died many years ago. Jack was not old enough to be my father, nor young enough to be my brother, so I often referred to him as my good uncle. We enjoyed many of the same interests when I was younger and I had the pleasure of leading him and some of his friends on several successful safaris. I will miss him very much."

"I know you will, James. It is so good to have someone to talk to who really understands. In a way our shared knowledge of the Colonel allows us to be a comfort to each other, and that is a blessing." Julia takes a deep breath and relaxes back into her seat. A weight seems to have been lifted from her shoulders and an aura of peace comes over her. James takes the opportunity to change the subject somewhat.

"How about a bite to eat, my dear? We are both somewhat emotionally exhausted, and I think a pick-me-up would be in order. Do you agree?"

Julia smiles up at James. "I think you are right, James. Actually, I do feel a bit hungry for the first time since I boarded this ship. May we order something here though? I don't feel up to the main dining room just now, especially with this tear stained face of mine."

"Of course, my dear. I'll go over to the bar and see if I can find a menu. I'll be right back." James rises to his feet and heads across the room in the direction of the bar. Julia follows the tall man with her eyes and then takes the opportunity to glance at her reflection in the window behind her chair. Her hair is still a bit disheveled from the windy deck, but except for the few tear stains on her cheeks, she is not too upset with her image. She pats a few renegade hairs into place and pinches both her cheeks to give her a little color and turns back to the room.

James is already heading back to their table. Julia studies the tall man intently. She had forgotten how very handsome he was. As she considers this fact, she can feel her cheeks flaming on their own. Memories of their last evening together assail her. She can still see James' car pulling away from the curb on Fifth Avenue the next morning and memories of the beautiful diamond ring still tucked into her dresser drawer at home make her lower her head.

As James reaches the table, he is aware of her mood change almost at once and determines to change it.

"You look more beautiful than ever," he says in an effort to bring a smile to her beautiful face. Julia does not smile but turns to James McFadden with tears once again in her beautiful green eyes. "Thank you, James," she responds softly. "You always did know the right thing so say. I still feel so badly about the way I treated you. I never meant to hurt you; you know that, don't you James?"

"Of course I do, Julia. I wanted so much for you to be mine that I did not allow myself to even consider any other possibility. I was so arrogant to think you would leave your husband and children for an old man like me. I hope you have forgiven me for my disgraceful behavior. I loved you from the moment we met, Julia, and I still love you, but I would never again force myself on you as I did at the Astor mansion."

Julia interrupts him. "You never forced yourself on me, James. Without meaning to, I encouraged you. I was so naïve, James, and you were truly the first man I ever loved." As soon as these words leave her lips, Julia blushes and turns away. She had not meant to say that. It had just slipped out and now she was desperately embarrassed.

James feels her discomfort and rises to his feet. "We both were carried away by the moment, Julia dear. I never felt love before either, even at my ripe old age. But now, we both know our love for each other can be nothing more than the love of good and caring friends. You will always be uppermost in my heart and I sincerely hope that at some time in the future we will meet again. But for now there need be no embarrassment between us. We are but two friends who love and care about each other and are fortunate to have met again on this vast ocean. And now we shall enjoy a meal together." With that said, James puts down the menu in front of Julia and says, "Madame, *Avez vous faim*? I recommend the *poisonne roulette* and the *salade de jardin*." Julia smiles up at him now, and in her best French, learned from Madeleine, she answers, "*Tres bien, monsier, je suis faim!*"

# BOOK II

# Chapter 21

As the *France* is led into the harbor by a team of tugboats, Julia stands at the rail and begins to reevaluate her circumstances. The last time she entered this harbor she was a passenger on the *Catalonia*. She was a child then, barely thirteen years old, and a married woman besides. So much has happened to her since that first arrival into New York harbor that it seems like a lifetime ago. And now here she is arriving for the second time; but this time it is a returning – a homecoming. The city in the distance now seems familiar and welcoming, and she knows she is returning home.

No matter how hard she may wish it, however, she is no longer the same Julia Pedesch who left New York several months ago. She not only looks different, turned out in her stylish English silks, but she feels different. A terrible tragedy has touched her life, unlike any she has ever known before, and she is powerless to alter it. For the first time since Julia left Hungary, she is experiencing a mixture of deep sadness mixed with fear – sadness over the death of her dear friends and fear over what will become of her now. Her employment by the Astors has been terminated by fate. Where will she go from here? What path will her life follow now that she is back in the bosom of her family. She is no longer the ignorant peasant girl she once was. She is now a pseudo-lady, educated and altered forever by the beneficence of the powerful John Jacob Astor. She still has much to learn she knows, but she is well on her way to becoming an independent

American lady with a mind and will of her own. Even James has added to her store of knowledge – unwittingly teaching her about adult love. Madeleine gave her the gift of friendship as a sister might and opened up the world of music and art to her. The Colonel himself saw the lady in her and trusted her to become his hostess, allowing her to mingle with his guests and enjoy his hospitality. Even Vincent has added to her education – schooling her in the elements of politics and world affairs. How fortunate she was to have had these people in her life.

Julia closes her eyes and thinks back over her previous life. "I suffered untold hardships as a child in Hungary," she reminds herself. "I did without basic necessities while following George across the country from mining camp to mining camp. I suffered the death of several of my own children, but nothing prepared me for the tragedy of the *Titanic*. Losing Madeleine and Col. Astor was terrible enough, but all those innocent men, women and children who died through no fault of their own has left me with a sad and hopeless feeling that knows no bounds. Even seeing James again has not raised my spirits. This terrible disaster has shaken my strong faith in God right to the very core of my being."

How could her merciful God allow such a tragedy to happen? This question haunted Julia. If God is love, why did he abandon so many of his flock? The answer came to her suddenly that morning as she gazed out over the gray waters of New York harbor. She could still hear dear Father Bergard's voice in her head as if it were yesterday and feel the deep-set gray eyes concentrating on her face. How could she have forgotten his words.

"Remember this, my dear Julia, when something really bad happens that you do not understand. God gave men free will to make their decisions in this world, and those decisions can ultimately affect not only those making them but hundreds of other lives as well."

How powerful those words were, and as always, they made Julia aware of the truth. The answer was clear to her now. The misuse of that awesome power was the cause of the *Titanic's* demise. The arrogance of the builders, the foolish desire for speed, the shortage of sufficient lifeboats, the lack of due diligence on the part of some members of the crew all contributed to the horrendous disaster. Simple God-fearing men making the wrong decisions or no decisions at all had actually changed the course of history. There was a lesson here after all, something to take away from this terrible reality of devastation. Julia resolved to remember this lesson and to build her world around it.

"I will never allow myself to make decisions affecting other people in my life unless I am absolutely certain of the consequences," she said out loud into the wind. She prayed silently that with God's help she would be able to give her children the strength and insight to make the right decisions in their lives. She vowed that she would never allow circumstances beyond her control and other people's choices to rule her life so ruthlessly. Even her dear friend Madeleine had taught her a great lesson before she married Jack Astor, and that was to value her own judgement and above all to her own self be true.

"If your heart tells you it is right, Julia; then follow your heart," she could still hear Maddie saying. "But if your heart is in doubt, reevaluate your decision. Remember, God works from the inside out. This is how I determined to marry Jack Astor, and I know in my heart I made the right decision," Madeleine had concluded. Julia remembered her words when she bid farewell to James McFadden for the second time.

Father Bergard would have liked Madeleine, Julia thinks to herself. She certainly did follow her heart by marrying Col. Astor, despite the negative opinions of her society friends and the members of the press. God seems to have a counter plan for her though, and only he knows what the final result of that will be.

As she looks out over the City of New York, Julia's voice rises into the wind and she vows she will never be insecure or afraid again.

"I will teach my children the self-reliance they will need to succeed in this world. They will become whatever they desire to be and will not be afraid to take a chance in order to make a better life for themselves. Most importantly, they will learn to be true to themselves and to trust in their God."

The ship's horn suddenly sounds the All Clear and the Purser's voice comes over the loudspeaker.

"All passengers proceed to their embarkation stations, please. Have your passports ready and prepare for arrival in New York."

Julia faces the stairs ahead of her, squares her shoulders and proceeds to the embarkation station. She and James have already said their farewells. He is scheduled to board a train from New York to Chicago that same evening where an important client is waiting for him. They decided not to meet again and to leave the ship separately. James asked if he could write to Julia occasionally and she had acquiesced. They had parted as dear friends, both aware that there was much more between them than friendship.

As she walks carefully down the gangway Julia knows she will be alright. She will put this ordeal behind her and concentrate all her energies on her son and daughter. The thought of seeing Emma and Jerry again suddenly works its magic.

She fairly flies down the stairs with all the anticipation of a school girl returning home from her first semester at boarding school. Life is going to be good!

As soon as her feet touch the sidewalk, Julia begins scanning the street for a taxi. She spies a car coming in her direction and steps out into the street to hail the driver. To her complete surprise there in the front seat next to the driver is George with Jerry on his lap grinning from ear to ear.

"Mama, Mama," he yells, "it's me, Jerry, I came to bring you home."

"Oh my dearest," is all Julia can say. "Come here and give your Mama a kiss." Jerry flies out of the taxi and into her arms, almost knocking her down in the process. "How I have missed you," Julia whispers into his soft blond hair, "but where is your sister? Didn't she come to meet me too?"

"No, Mama," mutters Jerry with a mischievous look in his green eyes, "she is too busy." Seeing her crestfallen face, Jerry continues quickly. "She's busy at home with Florinanny getting the welcome home party ready." She wanted to come, Mama, but Florinanny really needed her to help. Please don't be mad at her, she couldn't help it, honest!"

Jerry looks up at his mother with a pleading look on his cherubic face. She hugs him soundly and assures him that she will forgive his sister for not coming to meet her. Then Julia turns to George who is beaming at her like a schoolboy.

"I have missed you *Juliashcam*," he says gently., "It is so good to have you home again. You look so elegant and are so very beautiful. I feel like I am greeting a princess." He lowers his head, suddenly embarrassed at his own words. Julia takes his big hand in her small one and kisses the leathery, work-worn fingers.

"It's been such a difficult time, George; there is so much I have to tell you. But for now, let's just go home. All I want at this moment is to be with my family."

With these words still on her lips, she climbs into the taxi and snuggles herself next to her son. Jerry has abandoned his father's lap and jumps into the back seat ahead of her. George is directing the taxi driver where to put the luggage and then settles back in the front seat next to the driver.

"I love you Mama," Jerry whispers in her ear. "I'm so glad you're home with us again."

"I love you too, Jerry," Julia answers hugging him to her. "I'm very glad to be home again with you and Emma and Papa." Jerry grins and snuggles closer to his mother.

As the taxi rounds the corner of York Avenue, Julia looks up at the brownstone building ahead of them. She spots Emma's face in the window with her nose pressed against the glass.

"Mama, Mama," she cries as she rushes down the front steps

of the brownstone. "I thought I would never see you again. Please don't leave us again, please." Tears of joy are streaming down her chubby cheeks and the sight of her is enough to break Julia's heart.

"Oh my darling Emma, you have grown so much in the past few months. You are already a beautiful young lady. I promise you I will not leave you again. Mama is truly home to stay, and I mean it from the bottom of my heart."

Julia gathers up her skirts and follows Emma up the stairs and into the house. George and Jerry follow behind carrying her valises and the shopping bag full of gifts she has brought for the children. As soon as she crosses the threshold and is standing in her small but neat living room, Julia is greeted by her sister-in-law Flora and several of her neighbors who have turned out to welcome her home. Her nose wrinkles with pleasure as she detects the familiar smells of Hungarian food. A huge pot of stuffed cabbage is simmering on the stove next to a pot of sesame noodles and a caldron of liver dumpling soup. Never has a homecoming smelled so good. Julia had forgotten how much she missed the food of the old country, and her peasant appetite comes racing to the fore.

"You have all gone to so much trouble for me," Julia tells them, "and I want you to know that I love you and missed you all. How wonderful to come home to so many caring friends. I haven't smelled food like this since I left New York to go to London, and the smells are making me so very hungry. Now, please let's eat, and then I'll tell you all about my trip."

Flora and her neighbors – Mrs. Ludkin the landlady, her sister Helen Dumbrowski and Julia's dear friend Kate Ryan from the old neighborhood all jump into action and begin scurrying around the kitchen. They empty the pots filled with Hungarian delights into huge bowls and place them ceremoniously on the kitchen table. The aroma of the cabbage fills the kitchen and Julia's mouth immediately begins to water. George brings out several huge loaves of bread he has purchased down the street and begins cutting great slabs onto a plate. Flora sets down a bowl of real Hungarian sweet butter next to the bread. There are jars of shiny red and green peppers and a bowl filled to the brim with cucumber and onion salad dripping with real sour cream. Plates are passed all around and the feast is underway. Julia will never forget this homecoming. She glances around at her dear friends and drinks in the faces of her children – smiling with full mouths; and she silently thanks God for her many blessings. This will be a good year she thinks to herself. He and I together will see to that.

When they are all so full of food they can hardly breathe, they gather in the small front room. The children beg to hear about the *Titanic* and how their mother missed boarding the doomed ship, thus bringing her back to them safe and sound. They had heard the terrible news of the *Titanic* from the newsboys hawking the headlines on a daily basis, but the depth of the loss was still not a reality for them. They are also unaware that Col. Astor and perhaps Madeleine have been lost at sea as a result of the disaster. Although the children had never actually met the Colonel or Madeleine, they knew all about them from their mother. Julia would always tell them about the parties at the mansion and the grand people who would come to visit the Colonel and his new wife.

Flora and the neighbors were interested too, of course, but mainly because Julia had worked for these New York celebrities. She had become somewhat of a celebrity herself, if only by association. Most of her neighbors have never been as far away from home as Fifth Avenue. They all worry and care about each other here in Yorkville, so what impacts one of them has importance for all. They share each other's joys as well as their sorrows. They can sense that Julia is very upset by the death of Col. Astor, who was always so kind and generous to her, and they endeavor to share that sorrow with her.

When the neighbors and the children heard about the accident with the carriage and how Julia ended up in the hospital, the oohs and aahs fill the room. They knew from Flora that she had missed the ship, but had not heard the details of what prevented her from sailing on the ill fated *Titanic*. Julia has to assure them repeatedly that she is feeling just fine and that her ankle is as good as new, thanks to the wonderful care of Dr. Frank Kallan.

After what seems like hours, with all the stories told and many memories shared, Julia bids farewell to her neighbors. She gives a special hug to her dear friend, Kate Ryan, for making the trip here to Yorkville from the old neighborhood. Julia reminds her that without her help she would not have been able to move to this apartment. Kate hugs her and assures her that they will always be friends and begs her to come back to the old neighborhood soon to visit. As Julia walks her friend to the door, she sees the tears in her eyes and knows her happiness for her friend is genuine.

"You are the best friend I have ever had since arriving in America," Julia tells her and reiterates how much their friendship means to her. Julia hugs Kate once more and agrees to a visit the following week.

Julia glances over at Emma and Jerry, who is almost asleep in his sister's lap, and with a sign to George, rises from her chair. She gathers Jerry into her arms and George scoops up the weary Emma. Her blond curls fall across her eyes, giving her the appearance of an angel with her halo slightly ajar. Julia and George slip them into their beds without a word and then with a look of silent agreement, head for their own bedroom.

# Chapter 22

Julia's first day back in New York dawns sunny and uneventful. She prepares breakfast for the family and sees Emma off to school. She fixes George's lunch, places it in the small tin pail and puts it aside to deliver to him later. She grabs her mop and broom from behind the door and proceeds to straighten up the apartment, removing all traces of the party that took place the night before.

Julia cannot help but compare these rather mundane routine duties to those that filled her days in London. Unlike this apartment, the townhouse floors were covered with lush carpeting, designed to keep out the cold and to give the entire interior a feeling of warmth and gentle opulence. Julia's cleaning weapon of choice was an elegant carpet sweeper that removed every thread and crumb with expert care. She used an elaborate feather duster to make the decorative knick-knacks sparkle and a soft specially-made polishing cloth to give the furniture an imperious shine. The townhouse also came equipped with a very special mop designed to gently keep crumbs from sticking to the colorful ceramic tile floor in the kitchen and pantry – a far cry from the worn linoleum that served them here in their New York apartment.

Julia finishes her household chores and turns her attention to unpacking her valises. She notes the change in quantity and quality from her worn valise that originally accompanied her to America. I have come a long way she whispers to herself. Flora stands by watching her quizzically and then speaks.

"Your clothes are very beautiful, sister-in-law; the Astors were very generous to you I see. How are you going to adjust to being just plain Julia, wife and mother, after the life you have been leading with the Astors? We all know you were an employee, of course, but a very special one if those clothes tell the tale. What will you do now, Julia, now that you are back to being just Julia Pedesch?"

Her very direct question catches Julia quite off guard. She turns to look at Flora, but after searching her face, she can find no hint of malice there, only genuine concern.

"I don't know, Flora, but you are right to suppose that I can no longer settle for just being Julia Pedesch. There must be more for me in life than that. I care for George and I love my children more than life itself, but I need to be something more – something special. I want to learn and improve myself and find my special talents. I need to do this, Flora; I need to do it for me and for the children. Will you help me?"

Flora studies her beautiful sister-in-law for another moment and then answers without further hesitation. "Of course I will, Julia. I'll stay as long as you need me, and maybe some of your courage will rub off on me," she answers. "I have always admired you and am glad to have you as a friend as well as a sister-in-law. If it weren't for you and George, I would not have had the courage to come to America, and for this I will always be grateful to you both."

Julia embraces Flora and assures her that they will always be friends and that she will continue to do whatever it takes to help her sister-in-law to realize her dreams as well. Flora, she suspects, has no real dreams. She is so happy to live in a country where she can be free to be herself and have the time to enjoy her brother and her niece and nephew. Flora is still of the Old World, and it takes very little to make her happy. I envy her this trait, Julia thinks to herself, as I, myself, want so much more.

Julia spends the balance of the morning getting acclimated

to her new surroundings. Home still feels a bit strange to her after London and a prolonged hospital stay. At midmorning she takes Jerry by the hand, and together they deliver George's lunch pail to him at the work site. George beams with pride as Julia approaches his station, looking more like an elegant uptown lady than a Yorkville housewife. The other men in his crew stare in disbelief as she approaches her husband, gives him a hug and hands him the small tin pail. Jerry lets go of her hand and rushes up to his father. He stands tall and shakes his father's hand like the little man that he is. Then with a sly glance toward his mother, Jerry gives his father a hug and says, "see you tonight, Papa." This is truly the bright spot in Julia's first day back at home.

On their way back to the apartment, mother and son pass the large Byzantine Catholic Church. St. Constantine's façade looms ahead like an imperious general bidding them enter. Julia takes Jerry's hand and guides him up the steep flight of stairs leading to the massive front door.

"It's not Sunday, Mama," Jerry blurts out, "why are we going to visit God?"

The look on his mother's face must have provided a partial answer because Jerry lowers his eyes and assumes the role of a contrite little boy almost at once.

"Why, Jerry, his mother answers at once, "we visit God every day – maybe not always here in church, but wherever we happen to be. Don't you remember me telling you that God is everywhere? We thank him for each new day in our morning prayers and for each meal we eat, and we thank him and say goodnight at the end of each day before we go to sleep. I just want to pay him a special visit today to make sure he knows I am home from England and back again with my wonderful family."

"Okay, Mama, Jerry agrees, "let's make sure he knows you are home."

They enter the huge edifice hand in hand and kneel down in the last pew."

"Good morning, God," Jerry begins. "Mama's home and we

came to let you know. She is never going to leave us again – never – she promised."

Tears well in Julia's eyes as she silently thanks God for her son and for all the blessings he has seen fit to bestow upon her since her arrival in this wondrous country. It truly is the land of opportunity she thinks to herself.

"Where else in the world could a peasant girl from Budapest become part of the household of a man like John Jacob Astor? Even his wife, Madeleine, treats me like a sister and the bond between us is strong and true."

As she thinks of Madeleine, the tears come again, and she wonders if she will ever see or hear from her again. Her reverie is suddenly broken by Jerry's voice.

"Don't cry, Mama, I'll never leave you either," whispers Jerry. "We will always be together – you and me and Papa and Emma – always."

Julia hugs her son to her and leads him out into the aisle. They bless themselves and leave the church as they entered, by the big front door. As they round the corner to their apartment building, Julia sees that a newsstand has been set up on the corner just outside the grocer's shop. She hesitates and then steers Jerry over to the stand.

"Ask the man for today's paper, Jerry, and I will send you back out with the money to pay for it," Julia directs her son.

A headline about the *Titanic* catches her eye, but she also wants to check out the Help Wanted Section as finding a job is her next order of business. As she scans the front page, she is amazed to see Madeleine's name emerge.

"Mrs. John Jacob Astor found safe after all, picked up with several other survivors by the crew of the freighter *Carpathia*. She remains in seclusion in a hospital in Zurich where she is awaiting the birth of her child and mourning the death of her husband."

The article provides very little information other than these few basic facts.

"God bless you Maddie," Julia says aloud, wondering as she does so if she will ever set eyes on her dear friend again.

As soon as she reaches the front steps, Julia rushes into the front room clutching the newspaper. She spreads out the pages on the small round dining table and begins reading the rest of the article about the *Titanic*. All the horror of that disaster comes flooding back and she wipes her tears with the back of her hand.

"I cannot wallow in the past," she says to herself and begins rifling through the paper anew to find the section containing the Want Ads. She soon finds the section she is searching for and she proceeds to scan the columns under Employment Opportunities. There are several advertisements for an experienced seamstress with references required. There are two positions for a governess to small children, a housekeeper for a large family which prefers live-in arrangements, and one ad for an artist's model – six mornings a week from 8:00 a.m. to 1:00 p.m. Julia blushes just thinking about being an artist's model, but then reconsiders as she looks again at the hours required.

If I work in the morning while Emma is in school, I can still do sewing projects at home in the afternoon. This will allow me to hold down two jobs and still have quality time with the children and take care of my home. Flora will still be with us, so if the work gets too much, she can help out. Maybe now we can finally put some money away toward a home of our own..

Julia determines to go and see about this job the first thing in the morning. For now though, she puts all thoughts of work out of her head and concentrates on her children and the husband who will soon be returning home, hungry for his supper.

Julia is still trying to make it up to George for the months she was away from home, and he never fails to appreciate her efforts.

"He is such a good man, she thinks to herself. "If only I could feel even one little bit for George what I felt for James McFadden."

As thoughts of James begin to flood back into her mind, she

rises and walks into the bedroom. She suddenly finds herself scouring the dresser drawer for the black velvet box containing the beautiful diamond James had given her. As she turns the jewel over in her palm, the pain of her loss comes back to overwhelm her once again.

I know I will never love like that again, and I will treasure this precious memory forever. It will have to sustain me as I spend my life being Mrs. George Pedesch.

Julia puts the tiny box lovingly back into the drawer, takes a deep breath and glancing in the mirror, brushes the tears from her cheeks. She pats her hair into place and heads for the kitchen. George is just coming through the door, and before he can utter a word of greeting, Emma and Jerry are upon him.

"Papa, Papa," Jerry shrieks, "we went to church today to visit God, and it wasn't even Sunday."

"I got a drawing prize at school today," Emma interjects proudly, holding up a piece of blue ribbon attached to a crayon masterpiece. George laughs out loud and hugs his two obstreperous children to him in a bear hug that sends Emma into peals of make-believe anguish.

"You're too strong, Papa; you hug me so tight I think I will break."

"Nonsense," growls George. "I am your very own protector bear, and I will never hurt you. Let anyone else try, and I will squeeze the breath of life out of them," he continues, growling for effect.

"I bet you could too," Jerry joins in the fun. "You're the strongest man I know, Papa," he adds, the pride evident in his voice.

George glows with pleasure at the praise heaped upon him by his adoring children. They are truly the pride and joy of his life, and he adores them unashamedly. To punctuate his role as protector, he hoists Jerry up on his back and begins to crawl around the floor swaying from side to side and growling for all he is worth. Jerry whoops with joy and Emma runs beside the pair.

"My turn, Papa, my turn now. Jerry has been riding long enough. Please, Papa, please give me a turn to ride the bear."

George roars again and rolls Jerry off onto the rug. He then sits back on his haunches and grabs for his daughter as if to eat her alive. She squeals with delight and runs behind him, waiting for him to scoop her up on his back for her turn around the room. Peals of laughter and bear-like roars fill the apartment, and Julia cannot help but laugh too at these wild goings-on. She surveys these antics from the kitchen sink and suddenly knows that her family is more important to her than all the passionate love affairs of a lifetime.

"I am married to a kind, decent, God-fearing man who loves me and his children with equal abandon," she says to no one in particular. She vows on the spot,. "Dear God, I will be the best wife and mother I can possibly be from this day forward. I will never let my family down, and I will always make sure that they know how much they are loved. As God is my witness, I will do everything in my power to see that all our dreams come true."

# Chapter 23

As soon as George leaves for work and Emma is out the door on her way to school, Julia rushes into the kitchen and begins studying the Want Ads again. Flora has gone out for a walk and taken Jerry with her to get some fresh air, so Julia is quite alone. She looks again at the advertisements that she circled the night before, trying to decide where to begin. The housekeeper job does not seem suitable because they want a live-in, and she needs to return home each evening. Julia knows she can handle the seamstress jobs but decides to put them aside for last. Next comes the governess position and the opening for an artist's model. She studies the latter warily, as though it will taint her just by the mere reading of it. She sits back in the chair and studies the ad.

"Why not, she says to herself in her boldest voice. All my life men have said I was pretty. Why not capitalize on my more obvious talents for a change. What harm can it do? It certainly pays well, and the hours are made to order for me. It might even be fun." She smiles to herself as she envisions what she thinks an artist's model really is. Pictures of seductive women scantily clad pass through her mind's eye. Julia gets up from the chair, straightens up to her full height and walks to the hall where she studies herself in the long mirror there.

"I am tall by today's standards, being almost five feet seven inches in my good walking shoes. I have good posture, wavy blond hair, and hazel eyes, which sometimes change color, depending upon my mood and what I am wearing. I remember

Anna telling me I was evil because I had eyes like a cat. Sometimes they actually turned yellow or deep green. My skin is fair, but I usually have a natural blush on my rather high cheekbones. James called me beautiful, but I think I am at least satisfactory. I am not thin by any means, but have the gentle curves that may be of benefit to an artist's model."

As she studies her reflection intently, the image in the mirror smiles back at her, and she knows almost at once what her course of action will be. She washes her face, combs her hair, and puts on her third best dress. Julia surveys the result in the mirror once more, smiles at the image, and leaves the house to wend her way downtown..

The address in the ad is only five or six blocks away on a side street where garrets and lofts are popular as places of residence for struggling artists. The advertisement says fourth floor right, and Julia proceeds to the location indicated. It is the top floor of the building and she can see that a huge skylight dominates almost the entire section of the roof. The tiny brass sign outside the door at number 4A says: Pierre Manot, Artist in Residence. The nondescript wooden front door is open, and there is only a screen door between the inside and the outside of the flat; and even it is slightly ajar. Geraniums grow in two large pots beside the door, and it gives Julia the quaint feeling of being back in Europe.

She knocks gently on the screen, peering into the inner rooms as she waits for someone to respond. No sound comes from within except for the squawking of what must be a rather large bird. Julia taps again on the screen, and is about to call out when a young man appears at the door, seemingly out of nowhere. He studies Julia from top to bottom as if she is a statue in a museum.

"Turn around," he says with authority, "toss your head back and let me hear you laugh." Julia is jolted into action by the mere force of his voice, and so does as he bids her.

"Very nice, and dutiful too," he adds. "I think you will do very nicely."

"But sir, she stammers, you don't even know why I am here."

"But of course I do," he answers quickly, "you are my new model. You were sent from Heaven to pose for me, and I never reject anything sent to me by the Almighty."

Julia looks at him in complete astonishment and then begins to laugh.

"You are the most preposterous man I have ever met," she blurts out.

He grins at her with a boyish grin that would melt the heart of any mother and comes toward her with his arms spread wide. Before Julia knows what is happening, she is enfolded by two strong well-muscled arms and then just as abruptly, held away by those same arms. The strange little man studies her intently from all angles and pronounces her hired at once.

Julia gasps at this pronouncement and all she can manage to say is, "My name is Julia, and I assume you are Monsieur Manot, Sir." Pierre Manot looks back at her, and a broad smile envelopes his face.

"Julia is certainly a beautiful name, my dear, but I prefer to call you angel, my little angel. You will start today, and we will get the benefit of the early morning light. Please come inside and sit down on the dais. I am anxious to get back to work. You will call me Pierre and I will expect you here in my flat every morning by eight o'clock. I do paintings by commission, which is why I can afford to pay rather more than most of the artists in our colony. I assume the sum mentioned in the ad meets with your approval or you would not have come. I am also a sculptor and I may ask you to pose for me in that medium from time to time. I like to utilize my God-given talents in both mediums, but at the moment my painting is taking up all of my time."

After this rather long monologue, all Julia can mange to say to Monsieur Pierre Manot is, "Yes, I will be here by eight o'clock each morning, and I expect to be paid at the end of each week," she adds. The latter statement takes Pierre by surprise, but he does not take exception to her statement. "A woman who knows her own mind," he mutters to himself, "and isn't shy about saying what she thinks either. She may be somewhat of a challenge, but I like her already and she certainly looks like an angel." He turns to Julia and points to the dais.

Julia steps up on the dais where he indicates a bench and seats herself facing him. As she looks around from this vantage point, her eyes fall upon a huge canvas on a large wooden easel. The canvas depicts a beautiful garden full of trees and flowers. In the midst of the garden is an old wooden bench, but there is no one seated on the bench. Pierre's eyes follow her gaze.

"This is where you come in," he says pointing to the empty bench in the canvas. "In a few days you will be a part of that canvas. My beautiful angel will be sitting on that bench under the trees, amidst the flowers looking as beautiful and innocent as you do now. I cannot wait to begin," Pierre sighs. I think I must have been waiting for you to knock on my door, my angel, and now here you are, just as I am ready to complete the most important part of the painting. Now let us begin."

Pierre asks Julia to go behind the screen in the corner of the room and don the peasant-type costume she will find there. She does as he bids and then comes out and seats herself once again on the bench. Pierre spreads her long hair over her shoulders and arranges her skirt to suit the pose. They work for the next few hours until the sun finally reaches its zenith overhead. Julia does exactly as Pierre directs her – she turns where he indicates, looks in the direction he requests, and generally follows all his directions as he feverishly daubs paint onto the canvas in front of him.

Suddenly he stops daubing and puts down the brush. He looks up from the canvas and their eyes meet. "You are truly my angel," Pierre says softly. "The gentleman who commissioned this painting will be awestruck when he sees it. Thank you, Julia, for coming through my door this day."

Julia is so pleased by his reaction that she cannot wait to

inspect the canvas. She jumps down from the dais and confronts the canvas. Her breath catches in her throat.

"Can that beautiful creature in the painting be me?"

"Oh, Pierre," she gasps, "I am beautiful; you have made me beautiful. I cannot believe it is me." She sits down speechless and waits for him to respond.

"It is you, my angel. I have been able to capture the beauty inside you as well as outside, and that is what the world will see in this canvas. Go home now and come back to me tomorrow. This is only the beginning. We have much work to do."

Julia rises from the chair where she is sitting trying to compose herself and fairly floats toward the door. "Goodbye, Pierre. I will be here promptly at eight o'clock tomorrow," she assures him.

That night at dinner Julia cannot wait to tell George about her good fortune. Not only has she found a job, but she is to be the subject of a magnificent painting already commissioned by some important member of society. Pierre has not revealed the name of his customer, and Julia for one, does not really care. All she knows is that she will be part of a painting destined to hang in someone's private gallery, and she will be paid for this privilege.

She tries to be very business-like in her explanation to George, but the words just come tumbling out, carried by her natural enthusiasm.

"A model, you say?" George remarks with a quirk of his head. "How did this happen, *Juliashcam?* You are a seamstress, a cook, and an accomplished housekeeper, but a model? What do you know about posing for a painter?"

"It was a big surprise to me too, George, but when I went to meet the artist he said I was perfect. If you could see the painting he is doing, you would be as pleased as I am. It is really a work of art; it is so beautiful, and he made me beautiful too. The work is not difficult, George, and the pay is more than fair; and best of all, I can be home in the early afternoon to be with the children when Emma returns home from school. I plan to get another job as a seamstress as well, so even more money will be coming in.

We can save and have a home of our own before we know it. Please, George, don't be upset with me. It's like a sign from God – a way to secure our dream even sooner than we hoped. Please be happy for us."

George listens intently to her explanation and his face begins to soften. Julia knows instinctively that he cannot bear up under her onslaught for very long and is bound to weaken. He does not disappoint her, and takes her hand in his, kissing her fingers as he does so.

"You know I can never refuse you, *Juliashcam*," he whispers. "If this is what you really want to do, then I will not stand in your way. Perhaps one day you will be recognized as the subject of a famous painting by a well-known artist. Will that make you happy?"

Julia smiles up at her husband with obvious and sincere gratitude and places a kiss gently on his cheek. George blushes and shouts to Jerry, "come now son let us finish the sign we have been making for your mama."

"What sign?" Julia questions immediately, glancing at their son.

"Papa and I are making you a sign to put outside our door," Jerry answers. "It says: Seamstress – Inquire Within, he announces proudly.

"Then when you are home with the children in the afternoons, you will also be open for business, in a manner of speaking," suggests George. "We thought you might want to take up sewing again, so we planned this as a surprise. Today certainly seems like the best time to tell you of our surprise," George continues with a secret smile directed at his son.

"What a wonderful idea!" Julia shouts. "My two men have launched me into business and without my even having to ask." She gathers them both into her arms and hugs each in turn.

"Let's celebrate," says Jerry with enthusiasm. Mama is going into business!"

Just then, Emma appears in the doorway. She has been next

door doing homework with her friend Anna and has heard the commotion through the thin walls of the apartment.

"What is going on, Jerry? Is something wrong with Mama or Papa?" she asks anxiously.

"Nothing's wrong, Emmy," Jerry answers. Mama is just telling us about her new job. Then Papa and I surprised her with a sign for the door that says 'Seamstress' and she got all excited."

Emma looks up at her mother with complete confusion on her pretty face. Julia hastens to explain the day's happenings as best she can.

"So you see, Emma," she says proudly, "your Mama not only has a job outside of home every day, but her own business at home as well. I think we are well on our way to making our dreams come true. Between what your Papa makes and what I will be earning, we will have our own home before you know it."

"That is wonderful news, Mama. I can see now why you are all in the mood to celebrate. I can help too," Emma continues. "I can tell all my friends at school that my mama has her own sewing business right out of our house. You'll have more business than you know what to do with, Mama."

"God bless all of you," Julia says with deep conviction, realizing again how lucky she is to have a family that is so supportive. She vows to herself that she will make them proud of her and justify this unabashed support. They all retire into the front room and George brings out the bottle of wine they have hoarded since Christmas. There is still about a cupful in the bottle, and he doles it out so each of them has a sip to toast their good fortune with.

"When we have our own house some day," George remarks looking at the now-empty bottle, "I will grow grapes on a trellis over the driveway and make my own wine in the cellar. We will never have to dole out the wine when that day comes. There will always be enough for every celebration."

Julia will have cause to remember that statement in the years to come, but right now even the tiniest glass holds promise for their future.

The next day is Sunday, and they dress very carefully in preparation for mass at St. Constantine's. All of them seem to know instinctively how very much they have to be thankful for this Sunday morning. The sky is deep blue, the sun is shining, and all is right in the Pedesch world. George is beaming as he offers Julia his arm before going up the long steps of the church. Even Emma takes the arm of her brother and makes her entrance like a perfect little lady. Jerry is bursting with pride, and they make quite a picture as they enter the hallowed halls of the splendid parish church of St. Constantine.

At the offertory the congregation comes up to the altar single file with their offerings —fresh baked bread, fruits, vegetables, small lengths of cloth and even a basket of cakes. Very few members of this mostly peasant congregation have hard money to give to the church, but each family provides some sort of sustenance for the Priest and the Sisters who live in the rectory at St. Constantine's.

Today is special for the Pedesch family though, and to celebrate the occasion and show their deep gratitude to God for all his blessings, George places a small silver coin in the collection plate. Heads turn in disbelief as the tinkling sound of the coin in the plate echoes down the pews; even the Priest takes a second look. They are all so proud, Julia is sure her heart will burst.

Jerry, especially, can hardly contain himself, and he shouts out, "my Mama is a business and we're saying thank you to God."

A few snickers can be heard in the crowd, but they make their way back to their seats without further incident. George does not even have the heart to reprimand Jerry for his exuberance. They all kneel down and say the prayers, following along with the Priest who speaks only in his native Hungarian.

After mass, they return home and Julia prepares a huge breakfast of *polacinta, suluna*, fruit and strong black coffee. They take a long walk after breakfast ending in the nearby park. George and Julia sit on a bench while Emma and Jerry mount the swings and the makeshift merry-go-round.

"Tomorrow I will hang out my sign, George, and when I return from Pierre's I will officially be in business – my very own seamstress business."

George smiles back at his wife and raises her hand to his lips, as if in tribute.

# *Chapter 24*

Monday morning dawns clear and crisp. Julia sees almost at once that George has hung out the sign he and Jerry made for her even before he left the house to go to work. She had prepared his lunch pail the night before so he could take it with him. She proceeds to get Emma ready for school and Jerry dressed to go next door to their neighbor's where he will remain until noon.

Flora returned to Long Island on Saturday. Her cousin Mary is ill and she is needed to help care for her and the children until she is well again. Julia's neighbor, Mrs. Ober, is delighted to watch over Jerry in the morning, as she has a little boy the same age. The two boys keep each other company, freeing Mrs. Ober to do some cooking ahead and keep up with her laundry and cleaning chores. In the afternoon when Julia returns home, she often returns the favor and watches over her son, John. Again, the boys get on well together so it gives Julia time to do her sewing and housework as well. She often reads to them too, when they feel inclined to listen. Emma brings home simple books from the school library that she thinks Jerry might like. Julia enjoys the reading as much if not more than the boys do. It increases her vocabulary and helps her improve her English. George sometimes listens to these stories when she reads to Jerry in the evening, but he still makes no attempt to master the words himself.

Julia completes her chores and leaves the house in time to get to Pierre Manot's promptly at eight o'clock as he requests.

Before she even knocks on the door, Pierre is there and ushering her into the studio.

"The light is just right, my angel," he says. "Sit down at once. I don't want to waste another minute."

Julia scurries up onto the dais and spreads her skirts as he had directed the day before. Pierre studies her for a moment and then signals her to tilt her head in the direction of the light streaming in from the side window. She obeys without hesitation, and he begins to paint feverishly. They do not speak for some time and then suddenly Pierre throws down his brush. Splatters of paint hit the floor below the canvas, leaving a rainbow of color across the bare floorboards. Startled, Julia looks up to see Pierre staring first at her and then at the painting.

"May I look?" she asks anxiously.

"Why of course," answers Pierre, "but be prepared for a shock."

Julia steps down from her perch on the dais and walks over to the canvas. She gasps at what she sees. It is just like looking in a mirror. Pierre's painting is not a mere likeness of Julia; it is Julia. She can hardly believe her eyes, and says so.

"Sit down, Julia," Pierre directs. "I have something I want to say to you. This painting is like a miracle for me. I have never been able to paint a likeness so perfectly as I have on this canvas. My brush seems to know every curve of your features before I do and guides my hand in the painting. I am truly inspired and would like your permission to do an entire series of paintings with you as the centerpiece. The gentleman who commissioned this painting is an old and dear friend of my father's from our days in Paris. I am certain that when he sees this finished work, he will want to buy others that I create. If I am correct, will you pose for me, at least until that series is complete?"

Julia is so taken aback she can hardly find her tongue. Finally she stammers out an ascent, and Pierre breaks out in a grin from ear to ear.

"I would like you to meet the gentleman who commissioned

this painting, Julia. He is a wealthy importer of French fabrics and has his own fabric house here in Manhattan. The series I have in mind would depict a number of famous women in French history clad in gowns made of beautiful French fabric. These paintings will be hung in the gallery of his salon. *Monsieur* would provide the fabrics that I would drape over you and paint you wearing them. What do you think of the idea?" Pierre adds excitedly.

"I will be pleased to be your model, Pierre," replied Julia, "but perhaps you had better ask *Monsieur* first before we make any further plans."

"How can you be so calm, my angel?" Pierre shouts. "You could well become the mystery woman of Chatelaine Fabriques, and I, Pierre Manot, would be your creator. What a lucky day for both of us when you walked through my door looking for work."

"I guess this is all happening just a bit too fast for me, Pierre," Julia stammers. "I think I would like to go home now, if you don't mind."

"Of course you may go, my angel, but please come back here tomorrow, and with a little luck I will have *Monsieur* Chatelaine here to meet you. You are my good luck charm, dear angel, and before you go, let me give you a small advance on your first weeks wages. With that Pierre presses two dollar bills into her hand, kisses her fingers gallantly and says, "there is lots more where that came from, my dear Julia. *Au revoir ma Cheri.*"

Julia is still in a fog as she leaves the studio and heads for home, but the feel of the crisp dollar bills in her hand brings her back to reality. She decides to stop off at the dry goods store on her way home and purchase a small amount of cloth and thread and maybe even a pattern to begin her seamstress business. Then if anyone does come to place an order, she will at least have one dress pattern on hand to offer them.

Inspired by the idea of her very own business, Julia puts all thoughts of Chatelaine Fabriques out of her head and walks toward the neighborhood dry goods shop. Mrs. Berger opens the door for her as she approaches the shop and greets her warmly.

"How nice to see you this morning, Julia, and what can I do for you today?"

"Well, Julia answers hesitantly, "I've decided to open up my own seamstress shop in my house, Mrs. Berger, and I want to get a few basic supplies to start me off."

"You couldn't have picked a better time, Julia. We've just gotten in a new shipment of supplies. What can I put aside for you today?"

"Do you have any remnants, Mrs. Berger – enough to make a child's dress or a lady's skirt perhaps?"

"Why I think so, Julia. I just folded some remnants this morning and stacked them in the corner over there. Take a look through the pile and let me know if you see anything you like. By the way, do you need any patterns to start your business? I was just putting some discontinued styles into a box that might interest you. The women around here would never know the difference and besides, from what I've seen, you could make an apron look like a ballgown anyway. You are so talented with a needle, my dear."

"Why thank you for those kind words, Mrs. Berger. I'm certainly going to do my best to make our neighbors a little more fashion conscious, I assure you." Julia heads for the remnants and makes a few selections. Next she goes through the pattern box and finds about a half dozen patterns that will be quite suitable for either expansion or minimizing. Her last stop is the thread tray where she selects not only the necessary black, white, navy and brown, but a spool of heavier weight scarlet and one of beautiful lavender that she can use for decorative touches. Pleased with her purchases, she goes to the cash register with the two dollar bills still clutched in her hand.

"Will this be enough to cover all my purchases, Mrs. Berger?" she inquires.

"More than enough, Julia," Ms. Berger responds, and with

that puts three small silver coins back in her hand. "I threw in a few pieces of left-over ribbon too," she adds, "They are too small for me to sell but might serve as a trimming for something you are making."

"Thank you so much, Mrs. Berger, and please pass the word along that I am officially in business now."

"I will be happy to do that for you, Julia," Mrs. Berger replies smiling. "You'll have more customers than you know what to do with pretty soon. Good day and come back and see me soon." Julia gathers up her packages and hurries home to the apartment.

As she rounds the corner, the sunlight catches the sign hanging outside their front door and makes it glitter in the swaying breeze. The realization of her new status in life suddenly manifests itself. "I, Julia Pedesch, am a business woman in New York City." Now I must look and act like a successful one, she thinks to herself. No sooner have these thoughts formed in her mind, than she is aware that she really does not know what that entails. She thinks of the few business women she knows – shopkeepers really, and much older than she is. She wants to look successful, especially if she is going to make her customers more fashion conscious. She decides to ask Pierre tomorrow morning when she goes to the studio to meet *Monsieur* Chatelaine. Surely, he will know how to help her. She races up the steps, her head brimming with thoughts and ideas for making fashionable dresses. She runs head long into Emma who is just returning from school. She sees how excited her mama is and wants to share the feeling with her. Emma flings her tiny arms around Julia and covers her face with kisses.

"I love you Mama, and I hope some day I will be as beautiful as you are." She beams up at Julia waiting for some kind of a response.

"I love you too, Emma, and you are already beautiful. Come now and help me set up my threads and fabrics in case I get a customer this afternoon. I want to use this part of the front room for my business. I will set up the sewing machine in the corner near the window to get as much light as possible, and I will store the threads and fabrics in that small cabinet we used to use to store groceries. Papa will have to make me a screen too so that customers will have a private place to go and change when I am doing a fitting. I want it all to be very professional, you see," Julia concludes almost out of breath in her enthusiasm.

Emma helps her mama for awhile but soon gets bored with all this talk of business and returns to the kitchen for a piece of fruit and a place to spread out her beloved paper dolls. Julia stands back to survey her handiwork and then follows her daughter into the kitchen.

Perhaps one day soon I will have a real customer arrive at my door, Julia thinks to herself. Until then, however, I am content to wait. She turns to her eager daughter and they begins the business of dressing her dolls in earnest.

Julia rushes through her morning chores and arrives breathless at Pierre's door a few minutes before eight the next morning. He greets her with open arms and ushers her into the studio. As she walks across the familiar room, she notices a figure sitting in the corner with his back to them. He is studying the canvas on the easel in front of him and is unaware of Julia's arrival at the studio. He does not even turn as she makes her way across the floor to stand next to him. After what seems an interminable moment, he stands up and turns to face her. Julia gasps at the sight of him. He is tall and imposing and would be extremely handsome except for the jagged red scar that mars his otherwise perfect cheek.

Pierre rushes forward and attempts an introduction. "Julia, my angel, I would like to present to you, *Monsieur* Louis Chatelaine."

"Louis, this is Julia, the model I told you about."

Louis Chatelaine steps toward Julia and bows low over her hand, which he kisses gallantly.

"I have never before seen a painting come to life before my eyes, *Mademoiselle*," he says matter-of-factly. "Pierre has certainly caught your essence in this magnificent painting," he continues. "When you are in the room with the painting, it is like being in the presence of identical twins – a mirror image. I am rendered speechless, my dear, and that is a rare occurrence for me, I assure you."

Julia manages to mutter, "Thank you, *Monsieur*," and takes her place next to Pierre.

"Louis has agreed to commission the series of paintings I described to you, Julia. There will be eight in all, and each one will feature you draped in one of Louis's finest French fabrics. Your face and form will come to represent the finest fabric house in Paris, which now has an annex here in New York City. Come now, have you nothing to say to *Monsieur*?" he continues.

"Oh, of course, Pierre. I feel so honored to be a part of this series and to be associated with such a prestigious fabric house. It is your amazing talent as a painter, dear Pierre, that has given me this opportunity, and I will always be grateful," Julia concludes lowering her head demurely.

Louis Chatelaine stands up abruptly. "It is settled then," he says. "Pierre, you will contact me as each painting in the series is complete. I will have the first four fabric samples delivered to you by the end of the week. As for the settings in which you display *Mademoiselle* Julia draped in my fabrics, I will leave those to your discretion as the artist. I know you will select a setting appropriate to the fabric and the beauty of the model. I must go now, but I will be looking forward to seeing the first painting in the series. It was a great pleasure to meet you, *Mademoiselle* Julia, and I look forward to the next time." With those words, Louis Chatelaine strides from the room and down the stairs and into his waiting limousine.

Julia sits down with a thud. "I cannot believe this is happening to me, Pierre. How ever did you meet such a rich and powerful man?"

"His father and my father were friends in Paris many years ago, Julia, when Louis and I were boys. Both men were starving artists until Louis's father gave it up and went into the fabric business with Louis's uncle. My father continued to paint, and with his friend as a patron, finally succeeded in making somewhat of a name for himself in Paris. I, on the other hand, could not rest until I could make my way to America. And so, Julia, here I am in this garret struggling to make a name for myself as an artist. After I was here for about a year, I got word from Louis that he was coming to America too and would be following in the footsteps of his father and uncle. Thus, we have remained friends, and like his father before him, Louis has helped me to succeed also. Our lives seem destined to be linked to one another, and I look upon him as I would a brother."

"That's quite a story, Pierre, and believe me, I am very happy for you. I will consider it a privilege to be your model for this new series. But now tell me, Pierre, how did Louis get that dreadful scar on his face, and does he have any family here in America?"

"The scar is rather a long story, Julia, but I can tell you that he got it defending his mother's honor. She was an exceptional beauty and sought after by many of the eligible and not-so-eligible gentlemen of the French aristocracy. Louis's father was not a coward, but he had become too ill with a lung disease to be able to defend his wife's honor in the traditional manner. Men still settled their disagreements by dueling in those days, even though it was forbidden by the French government. And so Louis defended his mother's honor against a particular villain, a long-time enemy of his father, and received the scar as his reward. His opponent, I might mention, died in the effort to kill Louis and that, my dear Julia, is why Louis came to America."

"It's like a fairy tale gone awry," Julia says out loud. "Did Louis never marry since coming here?"

Pierre shook his head. "He almost married, Julia, but unfortunately she died of diphtheria before the wedding could take place

"I see," Julia said quietly, suddenly remembering the death of her daughter Mary from this dread disease, shortly after their return to New York. She rises from her chair then, gives Pierre a hug, and starts for the door. "I'll be here in the morning, Pierre, ready to go to work."

"Au revoir, my angel," Pierre responds. "I will look forward to our new adventure. Meanwhile, have a wonderful afternoon with your family."

# Chapter 25

As she approaches the apartment, Julia notices two women standing outside talking animatedly.

"I was here first," the taller woman insists.

"No you weren't," the other woman counters, "we both came around the corner at the same time but from different directions."

"Well, the seamstress doesn't seem to be at home anyway, so I guess it really doesn't make any difference who was here first," the first lady says with obvious frustration.

Both women look up as Julia approaches.

"Good morning, ladies. Are you waiting for me?" Julia inquires in her most polite tone. "I am Julia Pedesch, the seamstress in residence here, happy to be of service" she continues.

The two ladies look up at the same time and walk toward Julia.

"I'm Annabel Taylor," the tall one announces. "You were recommended to me by Mrs. Berger at the dry goods shop."

"Your daughter and mine are in the same class at school," interrupts the smaller of the two. "She told me her friend's mother was a seamstress, and so here I am. I'm Edna Phillips. Helen Phillips is my daughter." She paused to let this information take affect.

"Well, I am delighted to meet both of you," Julia responds with her most elegant smile. "Please come into the house and we can discuss what I can do for each of you. The women exchange pleased glances and follow Julia up the stairs and into the apartment.

Julia is so excited she feels like singing. It takes all her strength to keep her exuberance under control. She ushers both ladies into the front room and after they are all seated, she proceeds to make them feel as comfortable as possible. She addresses the tall one first.

"Would you care to tell me what I may do for you, Miss Taylor," she begins in her most solicitous voice.

"Oh my yes, Mrs. Pedesch. I have a lovely piece of velvet, a gift from my mother, and I would like to have a skirt made from it."

"Please call me Julia, Miss Taylor, and did you bring the fabric with you?"

"Why yes I did, Julia. Here it is."

Annabel Taylor produces the small package she has been carrying and slowly and lovingly removes from inside the brown paper parcel the loveliest piece of deep purple velvet. Julia examines the fabric and rubs it between her fingers with obvious pleasure.

"This fabric certainly is beautiful. It will make a magnificent skirt, Miss Taylor. Let me see if I have a pattern that is worthy of it and that will please you."

Julia stands up and goes over to the cabinet where she keeps her newly acquired patterns. She selects one and brings it over to show the young woman. Annabel Taylor studies the pattern for a minute and then turns to Julia.

"This is just what I had hoped for, Julia," Annabel says enthusiastically. I cannot wait to see the finished product, and please call me Annabel. You know my taste so well, I feel like we are friends already."

Julia smiles and then is suddenly aware that her first business transaction is about to take place. It also occurs to her that she has absolutely no idea of what to charge for her services. Prices must certainly have increased since her days of sewing in the mining camps. Besides, this was real fashion now, not simple mending projects or the remaking of children's pinafores.

Julia takes a deep breath, looks Annabel Taylor squarely in the eyes and announces, "it will take at least two fittings and a week to complete, and the cost will be $5.00, Annabel."

To Julia's utter surprise, Annabel does not bat an eye, but only wants to know when she may come for her first fitting.

"If you do not mind waiting a few minutes while I help Mrs. Phillips, we can have your preliminary fitting this afternoon, Annabel.

"Oh Julia, that would be just fine. I'll be happy to wait. I am so excited. I can't thank you enough."

"Best save your thanks for the finished product," Julia warns with a smile and turns her attention to her other customer.

She addresses the fragile looking woman seated opposite her. "You have been more than patient, Mrs. Phillips. Please tell me what I may do for you."

"Please call me Edna, Julia; after all, our daughters are classmates," she begins. "I would like a party dress for my daughter, but I would like it to be a surprise. Is that possible?"

"If you have another dress that fits her well that I can use as a basic pattern for size, I think it can be managed," Julia answers. "Will we be using your fabric or do you wish me to purchase what I think would be appropriate?"

"Helen just adores pale green, Julia, and that is the color of the dress I would like you to make for her. I would prefer something in a lighter fabric, something cool for the summer months. That is when her birthday is you see, July 17th to be exact. My husband and I are planning to give her a special party to mark the occasion and invite her closest friends from school for games and ice-cream and cake.

"I think I know the kind of dress you would like, Edna. I'll select a few fabric samples for you to choose from next time you come and perhaps a sketch or two of what it might look like, and we'll go on from there. You must bring me a dress of Helen's first to use as a pattern. We'll talk about the cost next time after you make your fabric selection. Give me a day or two to get the samples and then come back with Helen's dress. Let's say Thursday; I should have some samples and a sketch or two by then."

"Thank you so much, Julia. I'll be back on Thursday and thank you for agreeing to make Helen's special dress. It's such a load off my mind. She will be so pleased, I am sure."

"My pleasure, Edna; see you on Thursday." Julia rises and ushers Edna Phillips to the door. She turns back to Annabel Taylor and is immediately aware of a strange look on the young woman's face.

"I can't believe this, Julia, but it just so happens that I am a first year student at the new Parsons School of Design up on the East Side. I would love to help you create a few designs for Helen's party dress. It would be a work-study project for me and hopefully would provide you with some ready-made ideas. Then all you have to do is select some fabrics and let Mrs. Phillips make her decision. You would be doing me a favor, and maybe I would be doing you one as well," she concludes.

Julia can feel the grin spreading across her face. She clasps both of Annabel's hands in hers and in her best American style, she announces, "let's shake on it."

And so Julia's first day in business has been a good one. After Annabel Taylor leaves the apartment, she goes into her bedroom and gets down on her knees.

"Thank you, dear God, for all the blessings of this day, but especially for starting my new business off so well. I know this is all your doing, and I will do my best to continue on the path you have set for me."

As she blesses herself and rises to her feet, Emma comes bounding through the door. Julia had forgotten she was next door at Mrs. Ober's — she was so busy attending to her first customers.

"Did she come, Mama, did she, did she?" gasps Emma.

"If you mean Helen Phillips' mother, she certainly did, Emma, and I understand I have you to thank, my darling daughter."

"I just told Helen what a good sewer you are, Mama, and to be sure to tell her mama," Emma went on.

"Well from now on, Emma, you will be my official advertising manager."

"OK, but what is ad-ver-tising, Mama?"

"That means telling people about the business you are in," Julia answers laughing, "and you do that pretty well, I must say."

"Oh great, Mama; wait till I tell the kids in school that I am a manager already. I'll get you lots of business. I promise I will."

"Of that I have no doubt, my dear, but right now let me get started on the business I already have before I have to start thinking about dinner for this family. Julia turns to examine the piece of velvet against the skirt pattern and hums softly to herself.

# Chapter 26

Her business increases daily until Julia does indeed have more than she can handle, just as Emma had predicted. Everything she touches seems to flower under her needle.

"God is certainly with me, guiding my hand these days, Julia affirms to herself. If business continues like this, I will have to consider moving my business out of our apartment and into a storefront of my own. Jerry is going to start school this fall too, and expenses are already on the rise. He seems to grow out of every pair of pants within a month, and his shoes are barely worn before he needs another pair in a larger size."

Julia brings the subject up to George the next night at the dinner table, and he surprises her by agreeing with her right away.

"If you can find a storefront close to the apartment," he says thoughtfully, "the children could check in with you on their way home from school and you would not have far to travel to come home in the evening. Have you also considered leaving Pierre and running your business full time, *Juliashcam?*"

"Yes, George, I have, but I promised Pierre I would stay until the series is complete. I gave him my word. We are on number six right now, so it will take just a bit longer until the series for *Monsieur* Chatelaine is complete. I think I should mention it to him though, so he knows what my intentions are for the future.

"You can tell him tomorrow, *Juliashcam*, but now let us spend the remainder of the evening with Emma and Julius."

George still insists on calling his only son by his given name, and Julius does not correct him. His father is the only person afforded this privilege by their son, and although he grimaces every time George uses it, he always responds as if it were the most normal thing in the world. Julia is very proud to be raising such a sensitive and considerate son, and tells him so as often as the situation calls for it.

For some reason, George never did object to them changing Irma's name to Emma. Perhaps because Julia explained to him that Emma was in fact the direct translation of Irma into English. He accepted that explanation without recourse which made Emma very happy.

As she enters Pierre's studio the next morning, Julia realizes he is not alone. Louis Chatelaine is also there and they are in a huddle discussing the recently completed canvas. Both men look up as she enters.

"Ah Venus walking," says Louis as he comes toward her, arms open wide. "You are even more beautiful in person, *ma cheri,* than you are on the canvas, if that is possible.

"And you, *Monsieur* Chatelaine, are a born flatterer," Julia counters.

"We were just discussing the theme of the sixth canvas," says Pierre. "Louis wants to show off his new collection of velvets so we thought a winter hunting scene might be appropriate. What do you think, my angel?"

"How about a velvet riding habit with a long flowing cape," Julia suggests, "something in a deep burgundy color to contrast with the dark green foliage of the forest. But then, perhaps a spectacular ball gown celebrating the hunt would be a better choice. After all, not all your customers are accomplished horsewomen; but they all love to attend full dress balls, do they not?"

"Hmm," mutters Louis thoughtfully, "a valid point, my dear, but I do rather like your idea of the riding habit with the cape. It lends such drama to the scene. After all, a velvet ball gown is not exactly new, and I want this series to represent new thinking in fashion. A woman might be inspired to learn to ride just to wear a riding habit from the house of Louis Chatelaine."

"It is amazing, Louis, how you have gone from strictly a fabric house to a total couture salon in a matter of months. You have really taken New York by storm, and every society woman wants to own at least one Louis Chatelaine ensemble. You make what I do for a living seem more than a bit humbling," Julia says with genuine praise in her voice.

"Now, now, my dear Julia, what you do serves quite a different clientele, one that could not afford the price of a Chatelaine original. You do very much what I do only in a lower echelon of the societal structure." Louis stands back and grins at her, confident that he has chosen the right words to make Julia understand.

"Well, if you two will stop complimenting each other and let me get on with my painting, I will be very grateful," says Pierre with mock chagrin. "I only enjoy the benefit of my model's presence for a few hours each morning, and so I must make the most of them. What shall it be then – a riding habit or a ball gown?"

"The riding habit," Louis answers, "but have her standing and walking her horse through the *bois* rather than astride. This will allow you to show off the ensemble to its best advantage and emphasize the beauty of the velvet fabric as well, to say nothing of its model," he adds gallantly.

Louis bows low and strides toward the door. Julia takes her place on the dais. Pierre brings out a beautiful piece of wine-colored velvet and lays it across her lap. He drapes a section of it over her one shoulder and then stands back to survey the effect.

"You are right, Julia, burgundy will be the perfect color for this habit. Do you think you might sketch it out for me so I have some idea of what you have in mind?"

"Why of course, Pierre. I am no artist, as you well know, but

I can show you a rough design of the riding habit I envision in my head."

While Julia works on the sketch, Pierre begins adding paint to the canvas. By the time she completes her simple little design, he has created the *bois* that Louis requested. The deep green of the leaves and the undergrowth in the forest appear so real. One can almost hear the leaves crackle underfoot as the lady in the painting walks her horse through the lush green foliage. Julia shows Pierre her sketch and reclaims her place on the dais.

"May I talk to you seriously when we take our break?" Julia inquires as she relaxes into the pose Pierre has requested.

"*Certainement* my angel, just give me a few minutes to outline the riding habit as you have sketched it. Putting you in it is the easy part, but getting the design jut right takes a bit of concentration. After all, *ma cher*, Louis is my paying customer, and his fabrics are what we are trying to sell here."

Julia sits quietly watching him work, in awe as usual of the quality and speed of his skill. With only a few strokes of his brush Pierre can make a scene come alive.

"More amazing even than this," she thinks to herself, "is how he can put me in the scene so magically that sometimes I am not sure which is me – the lady posing on the dais or the lady in the painting. Pierre is a true genius and capable of so much more than painting for a house of couture. The society that buys Louis' fabrics would also pay huge sums, I am sure, for family portraits executed by Pierre Manot."

"*Tres bien*, we can break now," says Pierre as he surveys the painting from all angles. "What is this serious business you wish to discuss with me, my angel?"

"Come here and sit beside me," Julia suggests. "I will make us a cup of tea while we talk. I have recently become aware, my dear Pierre, that my seamstress business has grown to the point where I can no longer contain it at home in our apartment. I have more work than I can handle and not enough room to work on what I do have. I think it is time for me to concentrate on my business full time, and that would mean that I would have to stop modeling for you. I promise I will stay until the series for Louis is complete, but after that I will have to stop. Please don't be angry with me, Pierre. You have been so kind to me and I have loved every minute of our association, but you should be thinking of bigger and better things also. You could do portraits of high society people, like Louis' clients and command huge sums for them. You would be rich and famous before you know it. Please think about what I am saying and look toward your own future as you are always advising me to do. I love you like a brother, Pierre, and I only want the world to know what a wonderful and talented artist you are. The time has come for both of us to begin a new phase of our lives. Please say you understand and that you agree."

Pierre looks at Julia and the tears begin to roll down his boyish cheeks.

"I have wanted to try my hand at portraits, my angel, but until now have not had enough faith in my own talent. With you and Louis both encouraging me, I think I am ready to try. Louis has already told me he would send a few of his customers my way to get me started. After that, it is simply word of mouth and my talent that will sustain me. As for you leaving me, my angel, it will be the saddest day of my life, but I do understand that you must concentrate on your future too. As long as I know we will always be friends, and that I may see you from time to time, I will be able to persevere."

They hug each other soundly and finish their tea. Julia returns to the dais and Pierre continues painting for another hour and a half. He seems more pensive than usual when he finally puts down his brushes.

"I will have Louis bring over the burgundy fabric this afternoon so we will be all ready for tomorrow's sitting, my angel. I know he will love the design, but I want him to actually see it before I go any further. It has been a wonderfully productive day, my dear. Please go home and attend to your business now, and I will see you bright and early tomorrow." Pierre kisses Julia tenderly on both cheeks and lead her to the front door.

When she arrives at the studio the next day. Pierre is grinning like an imbecile. Instead of rushing her up onto the dais so he can begin work and benefit from the early morning light, as is his custom, he puts his hands on her shoulders and pushes her down into the only comfortable chair in the room.

"Julia, my angel, wait until you hear. Louis is on his way over here right now, but I cannot wait. I must tell you the news before I burst."

"Tell me at once Pierre before you make me crazy. What in heaven's name is going on?"

"I showed Louis your design for the riding habit and about your plan to expand your business, my angel, and he wants to make you a partner in his instead."

"A what?" Julia exclaims.

Before Pierre can respond, the door of the studio opens and in strides Louis. He is beaming from ear to ear and walks directly toward Julia who is across the room, removing his hat and his white gloves as he does so.

"Julia, *ma cheri*, come and sit down. I believe we have some serious business to discuss."

Julia follows his lead in silence and joins him on the tiny loveseat in the corner near the parrot's cage. The bird eyes them speculatively and begins to squawk, "Louis, Louis, friend or foe."

Louis grins at the huge bird and responds, "Ask Pierre, for I don't know."

The bird, known as Henri, squawks again in the closest thing to a human laugh Julia has ever heard.

"Pierre has succeeded in training his feathered friend with a sense of humor," chuckles Louis. "Do you not enjoy our bit of repartee, my dear Julia?"

"Hush now Henri," interrupts Pierre, who joins them in a cross-legged position on the floor. "This is serious business, so calm down now and go take a nap."

The bird seems to sense the seriousness of the situation in the tone of his master's voice, for he shuffles to the rear of the cage, puts his head down on his red chest and appears to go to sleep immediately.

"What amazing control you have over this bird," Louis says admiringly, "but now let's get down to business." He turns to Julia.

"Pierre tells me that you want to expand your seamstress business, Julia. Before you do that however, I would like you to consider a proposition I have for you. Please let me explain before you attempt to interrupt. For over a year now I have considered taking in a partner at Chatelaine Fabriques – someone to handle the design element, oversee the production and assist me with the occasional fashion shows we are planning. I admire your flair for design, and you certainly have shown that you know how to put fabrics together to their best advantage , so production should come naturally to you. You are a beautiful woman, as you must be well aware of by now, so you would be an asset to me by your mere physical presence. This beauty would also give you an edge, I believe, in working with some of our prima donna-type models. In my years of working with women I have learned that beautiful women have more respect for other women who are as beautiful or more beautiful than they are. They will not compromise you either, as I or another male associate might. I will offer you one third of the profits to start and of course expect you to develop a following. Well, my dear, what do you say?"

Louis sits back then and studies Julia cautiously. She is still in shock from his proposal and words do not come easily to her lips.

"You would trust me with such responsibility, Louis?" she manages to say, "and you would pay me such an exorbitant amount to manage this portion of your business. After all, I am totally inexperienced in the world of couture fashion."

"We would be partners, *ma cheri*, and I would teach you all you need to know about international business. Experience in couture is not an issue for me. I am still rather new at the game myself. Remember, fabrics were all I knew until very recently. With your natural expertise in design and the actual production of an ensemble, plus my contacts in the fabric business as well as New York society, we cannot help but succeed. I have long wanted to be more than just a fabric house, albeit a successful one. Now with you as my partner I know we can become one of the finest fashion houses in New York and attract the cream of New York society as our customers. Soon all of New York will love you as much as Pierre and I do, and you will be able to live wherever you want and send your children to private schools if that is your desire. You will truly come into your own and be the Contessa you should have been at birth."

"Thank you, Louis, for that lovely compliment, but being a Contessa, as you put it, is not part of my dream. I am very happy just being Julia Pedesch, and all I ever wanted was to succeed on my own merits and some day to own my own home in America. A home of my own is central to my dream, along with the happiness of my two children and a husband who has treated me like royalty since the day we were married. Your faith in me and the friendship you have shown me is all I need to make my decision. I would be a fool to do otherwise. Of course I will consider your offer, but please understand, Louis, I cannot make this decision alone. I must consult my husband before I give you my final answer. I owe him that courtesy. May we talk again tomorrow here at the studio? I promise I will give you my answer then."

"Of course, Julia. I will be here in the morning and anxious for your answer. Sleep well tonight and more importantly, *ma cheri*, do be kind to your husband and keep him in a good mood so he will be prone to agree with your decision, which I feel in my heart is to join me. I will go now and let you and Pierre get back to work, but I will look forward to tomorrow. *Bon jour mes amis*, until tomorrow."

As Louis hurries from the room, Pierre turns toward Julia. He picks her up off the floor and begins twirling her around the room.

"Pierre, Pierre," she cries. "Put me down; I am getting dizzy."

"Dizzy, dizzy," repeats Henri in the corner. Pierre and Julia both burst out laughing and collapse in a heap on the floor.

"Sorry, my angel. It's just that I am so happy for both of us. I see a wonderful future ahead, and I just cannot contain myself. But, you are right, let's get back to work. Louis will be as anxious as we are to have the series completed now."

Julia rises then and goes straight to the dais. She drapes the piece of burgundy velvet across her shoulders and cocks her head in the manner that Pierre designates. He works feverishly for about another hour and a half and then announces that the painting is finished. He stands back to admire his work and Julia joins him in front of the canvas.

"Oh, Pierre, it is so beautiful," she exclaims. "Louis will love it. By the way, what is to be the subject of the last piece in the series," she inquires.

"A coronation gown," Pierre responds. "A ball gown to end all ball gowns – one you might wear if you really were a Contessa."

"Do you think he will want me to design this gown, Pierre, or does he already have one in mind?"

"Oh no, my angel, Louis has already selected this most important gown. It is to be a copy of a real coronation gown worn by Queen Isabella of Spain, scaled down of course, but what Louis like to refer to as elegantly simple. It will be done in cream satin under black lace, and on you it will be no less than stunning."

"Oh I can't wait to see it, Pierre. Will you work from an historical sketch or will someone draw one based on an old restored painting? And another thing, Pierre, surely Louis isn't going to the expense of making up such a gown unless he has a customer lined up to purchase it, is he?"

"Your business acumen is showing already, my angel. No, Louis will provide me with an actual color drawing done many years ago by an artist of the day. It has been in one of the museums and he has arranged to take it out on loan for me to use for a day or two. I will paint the gown into a gala ballroom setting and paint you into it, ma cher. And as for the customer, I don't know who it is, but you can be sure our Louis has a client waiting in the wings for this one-of-a-kind gown."

"Well, posing won't be as much fun as being there, but I'll settle for this for now," quips Julia. "Goodbye, Pierre. Wish me luck when I talk to George about Louis' offer. He seldom refuses me anything, but still I want him to be happy for me and not just give in because he loves me. This partnership could secure our future, and that's the only thing to consider here. George is not highly educated, but he is very wise in his own way. I am certain he will want what is best for us and for the children. At any rate, I will do my best to convince him and will give you the verdict tomorrow when we begin the last of the paintings in the series. Until tomorrow, Pierre."

# Chapter 27

As Julia walks home she is already planning in her mind how she will explain this amazing happening to George. If she becomes Louis' partner, George can quit his job as a street cleaner and look for something better. Perhaps that iron works they saw out in Hunts Point near the park last month would hire him. The work would be hard, but he would not have to be outside in all kinds of weather as he is now. It is near the end of the streetcar line too, so he could ride to and from work instead of making that long walk downtown every day. Riding back and forth on the streetcar would give him some time to think and listen to the conversation around him in English. George seems finally to be trying to improve his English a bit. Jerry has been bringing home books from the school library, and George is making a concerted effort to listen to his son read. He is trying to speak more in English at home too, for the sake of the children. He does not want them to be ashamed of him when they bring their friends home and are forced to speak only Hungarian to their papa. Julia loves him for the supreme effort he is making on their behalf, but she still harbors a deep-seated resentment for all the years he wasted refusing to embrace this new language. As she rounds the corner her thoughts return to the situation immediately at hand.

As she enters the house, Emma is in the kitchen doing schoolwork with her friend, Anna, from next door. They have their heads buried in a huge geography book and are talking very animatedly about a map that takes up two whole pages.

"This is where my mama and papa came from," Julia hears Emma say.

"What a funny place to come from – Hungry," giggles Ann.

"Not Hungry – Hun-ga-ry," insists Emma, rather put out at her friend's attitude. "It's near the Baltic Sea and not too far from Germany our teacher says."

"Oh," says Anna apologetically. "I'm sorry, but I just couldn't help it. It sounded so much like Hungry when you said it in class."

"That's okay," says Emma as she puts her arm around her friend's shoulder. "I know you didn't mean to hurt my feelings. Where did your mama and papa come from, Anna?"

"Rumania," is the response. "Is that anywhere near Hungary?" Anna continues.

"Why I think so," says Emma, "But let's look at the map in our book to be sure."

As Julia enters the room, both girls look up and smile.

"We're learning about geography, Mama," her daughter informs her with authority. "Anna's mama and papa came from a place called Rumania, and it looks like it is close to Hungary where you and Papa come from when we look on our map. Maybe you knew them when you were our age," she adds questioningly.

Julia smiles at the two girls. "I doubt that, Emma. Hungary is rather a long way from Rumania, although it looks quite close when you see it on a map. It would take several days to walk from my village to where Anna's parents lived, I am sure. But compared to how far away we all are now here in America, it was pretty close at that. Remember that it took Papa and I three whole weeks to come to America by boat from England and another two weeks just to get to England from our village in Hungary on a smaller boat. Travel in Europe was not easy then like it is now here in New York. I'm glad you are learning about where we came from though, because I would never want you to forget your European heritage even though this is our home now."

As she looks at her lovely daughter, now age nine, the realization that she is fast becoming a young woman suddenly hits home to Julia. Emma is the pride of her life – sweet and gentle like her father but infused with a rare beauty and a gift for learning. In the latter, she certainly takes after her mother whose thirst for knowledge is never satisfied. Julia thinks back and recalls how she never could seem to get enough learning. The more she learned, the more she wanted to learn. This new opportunity Louis was offering her would surely help Emma to get the education she needs and expose her to the best that New York has to offer. She will meet boys from the best families, and eventually, God willing, will make a good match for herself. Julia prays silently that George will agree and allow her to accept Louis' offer without any feelings of guilt. Julia did not intentionally plan to become the main breadwinner of their family, but if that is God's plan for her, so be it. She knows she will make the best of it and have fun doing it too.

George would be happier working at the iron works. Julia is sure of that. She allows herself to daydream. If things work out, maybe he could eventually leave the iron works and just stay at home and take care of a house and garden and grow his grapes the way he always talks of doing. Julia waits anxiously for his footsteps on the stairs so she can bring this dilemma to a conclusion, one that will benefit not just her, but all the members of their family. Suddenly she hears the downstairs door slam, and she begins to count George's steps till he comes through their front door.

As George arrives at the top step Julia is the first thing in his line of vision. She assumes that he must know at once that she has something she wants to talk to him about. Her heart is pounding so loud she is sure he will hear it.

"Hello my *Juliashcam*," George greets her with his usual warm smile and walks directly toward her.

Emma has gone to Anna's house to finish her studying, and Jerry is playing with Mrs. Ober's son, John, next door so they are quite alone for a change. Julia rises to meet her husband and deposits a kiss on his cheek. George takes her hand and leads her to the couch where he lowers himself down carefully.

"Are you all right, George," she asks, concern apparent in her voice.

"Yes, of course, *Juliashcam*," he answers between clenched teeth. "I only pulled my back out a little on the job today. They gave us new pushcarts, and they are much heavier than the old ones. Since they let so many of the men go, we all have to cover twice as big an area as we did before. I did not realize the new cart was so heavy when I went around the corner, and even though I am pretty strong, I must have pushed it wrong and pulled something in my back. I'm sure after a hot bath and some of your famous liniment, I will be a new man by tomorrow."

"Oh George, I am so sorry you are hurting, and I will run a hot bath for you before we have our dinner; but could we talk for just a few minutes though before I do that?" Julia pushes a big pillow behind her husband and proceeds to remove his boots in an attempt to make him more comfortable. He allows her to cater to him a little which is most unusual, so she knows he must really be hurting. She pauses after she removes his boots and begins very slowly.

"George, I have been given the most wonderful opportunity – one that will benefit you and the children as well. It could make our dreams come true – what we have hoped and prayed for so long. Julia takes a deep breath and begins again. "Louis Chatelaine, Pierre's friend that he is painting the series for, has offered me a partnership in his company, Chatelaine Fabriques. He is expanding the business to include haute couture – high fashion clothes, George, and he wants me to head up the design and production departments. He says I have a flair for fashion and my knowledge of sewing allows me to oversee the production of the clothes as well. I will also organize and participate in fashion shows to display our line to our society customers. He will pay me one third of the profits to start, and I will cultivate my own following. Isn't it exciting, George? I still can't believe my good fortune."

George relaxes back against the pillow and studies her thoughtfully.

Is this what you really want to do, Julia? You were just thinking of renting a storefront to expand your own business and now you are talking of giving up your business altogether for a partnership in someone else's."

The use of her given name by her husband did not bode well, Julia thought to herself. She paused to regroup her thoughts and then launched forth again.

Oh, yes George, if you had only met Louis and could see Chatelaine Fabriques, you would understand. His customers are the kind of people I used to see at the Astor's when I worked there for the Colonel. They are cultured and elegant and have lots of money to spend on beautiful clothes. Louis himself is somewhat of a nobleman in his native France and has many important contacts all over the world. It is truly the opportunity of a lifetime, George, and I want to take advantage of it more than anything else I have ever done. I am twenty-four years old and am already a business woman in my own right. Please let me do this, dear George. I know I can make you and the children proud of me. And best of all, with the kind of money I will be earning, you can quit that miserable job of yours and get something where you can be inside instead of outside in all kinds of weather, and where you won't have to worry about throwing your back out."

Julia took another deep breath and began again. "Remember that iron works that we saw in Hunts Point where they make railings and fire place screens and so on? I'll bet they would be anxious to hire a man like you there. You have always worked well with tools and besides, you could ride to work on the streetcar each day like a gentleman. With both of us working hard, before long we will have that house in the suburbs we have dreamed of for so long – the one with the grape arbor over the driveway so you can make your wonderful Hungarian wine. We can have a garden and a place for the children to play away from the busy streets of Manhattan. Oh just think of it, George; it is the answer to our prayers. Please say you agree with me and wish me well in this exciting new opportunity."

Julia pauses again, takes a deep breath and looks deep into her husband's eyes, trying desperately to read his decision there. George leans forward a bit and settles into the pillow once more. He looks straight at Julia and begins to speak.

"If it means that much to you, Julia, and Louis is everything you say he is, how can I refuse you? You have painted a picture of a wonderful future for us and our children. I had hoped that somehow God would see fit to allow me to give you our dream, but it seems he has other ideas. You have all the talent and charm to succeed, and I would not want to stand in your way." George pauses to consider his words before going on.

"I must confess, *Juliashcam*, I will not mind quitting the street-cleaner job. As a matter of fact, I think it is only a matter of time before they discontinue the whole system and let everyone go. Garbage collection with trucks is becoming the way of the future in New York City, so, being unable to drive, I would have to look for work elsewhere anyway. Your suggestion is a good one. I will go out to Hunts Point tomorrow and see if there is a job for me at the iron works. All I ever wanted in life was to be with you and the children and to somehow be responsible for your safety and your happiness. Seeing you and the children safe and happy is all I need to be happy too. I love you, *Juliashcam,* and am proud to be married to such a beautiful and talented woman."

"Oh, George, I love you too," Julia answers, and at this moment she means it with all her heart. "I can't wait to tell Louis the good news tomorrow when I meet him at Pierre's studio. I will make you and the children so proud of me. I promise. Now, let's get you into that hot tub to soak while I work on getting our dinner ready. I think we should have something special tonight to celebrate this occasion, so I will just run down to the corner and pick up a little wine to go with our chicken *paprikash*."

Julia helps George up from the couch and leads him slowly and carefully to the bathroom. His stubborn Hungarian pride will not allow him to let her help him to undress, but he does permit her to run the hot water and to add a little Epsom salts to aid his aching bones.

"I'll be back to help you when dinner is almost ready," Julia adds gaily and leaves the room to go downstairs and walk to the wine shop on the corner.

When she returns from the store with the bottle of wine, Emma and Jerry have both returned to the apartment. They look up as Julia enters and in a chorus ask, "is Papa alright, Mama? He's been in the bathroom an awfully long time."

"He hurt his back at work today and is in the tub soaking to make it feel better," Julia tells them. "Jerry, to go the door and tell Papa I'm home and dinner will be ready in about twenty minutes. Ask him to call me if he needs help getting out of the tub." Jerry heads for the bathroom and dutifully gives his father the message.

"What can I do, Mama," Emma asks, looking up at her mama with a worried expression.

"You, my darling daughter, can set the table and toss the salad with that special dressing your papa likes. Don't look so worried, Emma. Papa will be fine, and besides we have some wonderful news to share with you." Julia turns back to the stove and continues her preparations for their dinner.

"Tell your Papa dinner is ready," Julia calls to her son who is engrossed in his toy cars on the floor of the living room.

"Okay, Mama," he answers as he heads for the bathroom door, and realizing it is open, goes on to his parents' bedroom. "Papa come to the table; dinner is ready now." George ambles to the doorway and follows his son into the kitchen where the women in the family are waiting."

"Sit down, here, and you can pour the wine while I dish up

the *paprikash,*" Julia offers. George pours wine for his wife and himself and then pours half glasses for both of the children.

"Wow," shrieks Jerry. "This must be a really special occasion if Emma and I are getting wine too."

"It is a very special occasion," Julia assures him. George, do you want to do the honors or shall I?"

George begins speaking almost at once. "Your Mama has had an offer to work with Mr. Louis Chatelaine as a partner in his fashion company and so will not be working out of our apartment any more. As a matter of fact," George continues, "she will not be working as a seamstress at all any more, but as a lady of high fashion, designing beautiful clothes that other people will cut and sew together." He sits back, enjoying the impact his words have wrought on the children.

"Is this really true, Mama?" Emma asks. "I can't wait to tell my friends you will be a real lady of fashion."

"Yes, Emma, it is really true; and if all goes as I expect, we will soon be able to move into a house of our own. Papa will be able to tend to the house and the garden and grow the grapes he has always wanted to nurture."

"Until then," George interrupts, "I will quit being a street cleaner and try to get a job at the iron works out in Hunts Point."

"Is that the place near the park where we visited on Sunday?" Jerry inquires.

"Yes, my son, it is," replies George, and I will be able to go there and back every day on the streetcar, just like a real gentleman," he adds.

"Wow," is all Jerry can muster. "We're really getting up in the world, huh Papa?"

"It appears so, Julius. Your mama always seems to know what to do to bring this family closer and closer to realizing our dream."

"Three cheers for Mama," shouts Jerry. "Three cheers for all of us," Emma chimes in, and her face is alight with happiness and pride.

"Thank you, Lord, for all our good fortune," Julia adds. "And now let's eat."

Jerry dives for the bowl of spicy chicken paprikash and begins to fill his plate. They all raise their glasses and toast one another. Another adventure has begun.

# Chapter 28

When Julia arrives at Pierre's studio next morning, Louis is already there. The two friends are engrossed in conversation when she enters the room, but look up immediately when they realize she is there.

"Come here at once, Julia, and give me your answer or I shall lose my mind," says Louis laughingly.

"The answer is yes, Louis – yes, yes, a thousand times yes," she responds dancing gaily around the room to emphasize her joy.

Louis grabs her hand, Pierre leaps forward to grab the other, and they twirl around the room together like three wild and crazy children.

"There are no words to tell you how very pleased I am, Julia. When can we begin?"

"Give me a week or two, Louis. I need a little time to finish the few orders I have for my own customers and to be sure that George can get at job a the iron works on Hunts Point."

"Has he quit his other job, Julia?" Louis asks with obvious interest.

"He is doing that today, Louis, and then he will go out to the Point by streetcar to see about a new job. I pray that he gets one because George will not be happy unless he is at least the partial breadwinner in our family. He would stay home with the children in a minute if I ask him, but he is a strong and proud man and needs desperately to be the support of his wife and children. I could never live with myself if my joining Chatelaine Fabriques injured his self respect in any way. As a man, I'm sure you can understand that, Louis, so please be patient with me."

"Do not worry on that score, my dear Julia. We will be ready for you whenever you are ready to begin. By the way, Julia, have you given an thought to learning to drive a car? I could teach you and help you get your license, and the company would provide a car for you to use to get back and forth to the salon from your home and also to visit customers when necessary. What do you say?"

"Why Louis, I hadn't even thought about learning to drive. Well actually, that isn't quite true. I used to daydream about being one of the first women in our neighborhood to drive a car, and what freedom it would give me. I knew we could never afford to own a car, so I put the idea right out of my mind. But if you say the company would allow me to use a car for business, I would be foolish not to want to learn. It would be so exciting, and you would really teach me?"

"Of course, my dear, and we can get started whenever it is convenient for you. You are a quick study, and I wager we'll have you driving in no time."

Julia could not believe her good fortune – "Me, Julia Pedesch, driving a car in Manhattan. Emma and Jerry will be so exited I know, but George may not be quite so pleased." She keeps these thoughts to herself, however, and thanks Louis for all the wonderful opportunities he is giving her.

Suddenly Pierre breaks into the conversation. "Have you two forgotten we still have the last painting in the series to finish." Come, my angel, up on the dais. I have painted in the ballgown from the museum sketch, but now I must put you in it."

"Of course, Maestro," Julia teases. "I am ready to go back to work at once."

"*Adieu* you two," Louis shouts from the doorway. "I will see you both when Pierre tells me that the final painting is complete. Julia, *ma cher*, you have made me a very happy man."

Pierre waves to Louis and then turns his attention to the canvas in front of him. He paints without pausing for almost an hour, and then turns to Julia with his brush poised in mid air.

"It is *fini*," he states with feeling, and calls Julia over to look at the finished canvas. She looks with awe at the lady in the painting bedecked with jewels and dressed in a magnificent ballgown and blushes to the roots of her hair.

"It is me; no matter how unfamiliar the gown and the surroundings appear to me, Pierre, you have captured my likeness once again to perfection. It is always a humbling experience to view myself through your eyes. You make me feel so beautiful and so secure within myself. I cannot thank you enough for that gift."

"Painting you has been one of the joys of my life, my angel. I only hope that this will not be the last time I am able to transfer your beauty onto a canvas. And now I must send you home to finish your other work so you will have no dissatisfied customers. I will inform Louis that we have completed the last painting, and he can come pick it up tomorrow. Could the three of us have dinner together one evening next week to celebrate the end of our collaboration and the beginning of your new one at Chatelaine Fabriques?"

"Why of course, Pierre, I would be honored," is Julia's reply. "Do you think I could ask George to join us? He probably won't want to go to a restaurant; he's not much on eating out, but I'd like to invite him to be a part of our celebration anyhow."

"Of course you may ask you husband, my angel; I've always wanted to meet the lucky man who captured your beautiful heart."

A retort rises to Julia's lips, but she catches herself and answers only, "thanks Pierre, I'll ask him tonight and let you know."

At dinner that night, Julia invites George to have dinner with Pierre, Louis, and herself as a way of celebrating their new partnership. She is disappointed but not surprised by his answer.

"I would not feel comfortable, *Juliashcam*. You know my English is still not very good, and I would not want to be an embarrassment to you or your friends. I will remain at home with the children and cook them something special so that they will feel a part of the celebration too. Please don't insist that I go with you. This is your big moment and I want you to cherish it. Go and enjoy and make the children and me proud of you, as if we weren't already."

Julia pats her husband's cheek and assures him that she does understand. She arises earlier than usual the next day, anxious to complete several of the orders she has not yet finished for her customers. The wool serge suit for Edna Phillips still needs a good deal of work. Each seam has to be pressed before the next one can be stitched. Edna is one of her original customers, the one whose daughter is still in Emma's class, so Julia wants to take particular care with this order. She takes out the suit, heats up the iron, and begins stitching the seams in the skirt. This suit will bring in $15.00 and she is very proud of the workmanship. The other orders are for much simpler items, which she can complete in less time. She looks at the pile of unfinished items and selects a cotton shirtwaist for another old customer, Annabel Taylor. This piece requires only a few buttons and buttonholes, so Julia decides to complete it before continuing with the serge suit. As she works, she thinks about Annabel, the would-be designer. She recalls how creative she was in designing the party dress for Edna Phillips' daughter, Helen. Her talent will stand her in good stead after she graduates, Julia determines.

As she works, Julia hopes that these ladies will understand when she tells them she will no longer be operating as a seamstress. "I am sure they will be pleased for me but will miss my skill with the needle as well as my reasonable prices. None of them can afford to shop at Chatelaine Fabriques, so I probably will not see much of them in future. I'm sure they will find someone else in the neighborhood to sew for them, but in a way, I will miss being that someone."

Emma enters the room and breaks through Julia's daydreaming at once.

"There is a lady coming up the steps, Mama. I guess she must be a new customer. I don't remember seeing her here before."

"Thank you, Emma. I'll have to explain to her that I am no longer in business as a seamstress."

"I guess Papa will have to take the sign down when he comes home, Mama, so people will stop coming with their sewing for you to do."

"You can remind him for me, Emma. Now please answer the door for me."

Emma runs to the door and ushers in an elegant lady, dressed in the height of fashion.

"May I help you?" Julia inquires, smiling as she opens the door wide.

"May I come in?" is the rather cool response.

"Please do," Julia answers, "but I must tell you that I am no longer doing sewing from my home."

"I am not looking for a seamstress I assure you," is the curt reply. "I am Jacqueline Convers, and I just want to get a look at Louis' new partner. I am one of his models at the salon and a very special friend as well." The last statement was given special significance and with a look of complete authority. "I'm here to tell you that if you have any designs on Louis, you can put them out of your head right now. Louis and I have a very special relationship, if you get my meaning, and I do not want any interference from any new partner."

"You have nothing to fear from me, Miss Convers," Julia answers without hesitation. I am a happily married woman with two children and have no designs on Louis, I assure you. We are merely good friends and soon-to-be business partners, and nothing more. Now, may I show you out?"

Jacqueline Convers flushes at this and proceeds toward the door. "I'm sorry if I have spoken out of turn, Mrs. Pedesch. I assure you it will not happen again."

With these words trailing over her shoulder, Jacqueline Convers passes through the door and down the stairs without a backward glance.

"Who was that woman, Mama?" Emma wants to know.

"Just an employee from Mr. Chatelaine's salon, Emma dear. No one for you to be concerned about."

Julia returns to her sewing, realizing for the first time that there is more to being in business, especially the fashion business, than just being creative and a good seamstress. She smiles to herself. "You have a lot to learn, Julia my dear, but you will learn; I promise you that."

George arrives home that evening and Emma attacks him as soon as he begins to climb the front steps.

"You must take down Mama's sign, Papa, now that she is not going to be sewing here any more."

"All right, Emma," George answers wearily, "but how about giving your papa a chance to come in the door first. A hello and a hug would be nice too," he adds shaking his head.

"I'm sorry, Papa. I was just afraid I would forget to tell you about the sign. Did you have a good day at work today?"

"Yes, I did, Emma dearest, because I quit my old job and went to Hunts Point and got a new job at the iron works there. Call your Mama; I want to tell her the good news."

"Oh George, I heard what you just said to Emma. I was in the front room sewing when you came in, and I heard you talking to her. I am so happy for you. Did you go out there by yourself to apply for the job? How did you know where to get the streetcar?" When do you start?"

"Whoa, *Juliashcam*," George responds with a grin. "So many questions you ask. Give me a moment to get my thoughts together, and I will tell you everything. I may not speak very good English, my dear, but I know enough to ask a few questions and get directions to where I want to go. I will start work on Monday, and I can take the streetcar right on our corner and get to Hunts Point in less than half an hour with only one change in between.

Hunts Point is where the streetcar line ends. There is nothing else on the Point except fields, woods, and the brick house that the owner built right next to the iron works. They make some interesting wrought iron pieces, *Juliashcam*, and the work does not appear to be too difficult. I watched the men working out on the floor for a short while. You just heat the metal over the furnace, then bend and twist it into the shape of whatever you are making. I think I am going to like making railings, fireplace tools, and small light poles. I feel good about it already. It will be so good to create something for a change, instead of just pushing a cart around and collecting worthless material. My only concern is the children – who will look after them until I get home from work? My hours will be from seven in the morning until three in the afternoon, but it will take me a half hour to get back home."

"Don't worry about that, George, Julia interrupts. I have already alerted Mrs. Ober next door to watch for the children when they come home from school. She will keep an eye on them until you are back at home. She is happy to help us out. Jerry plays with her son John almost every day after school anyway, so nothing will really be different. Emma is already a pretty responsible young lady, and knows to begin her homework as soon as she arrives home; so I think it will work out just fine. Come sit down and relax now. Dinner will be ready in about an hour. I cannot tell you how very proud of you I am, George. Our dreams will be coming true in no time. I just know it."

Julia gives her husband a big hug and a kiss to show him her true gratitude. Emma and Jerry, watching from the doorway, begin to giggle at this unusual show of affection between their parents and Julia swipes at them in a playful gesture.

"Can't I hug my own husband without sending you two into gales of laughter?" she chides. "Papa has made a big contribution to our dream today, and I want him to know how very proud of him I am," she adds.

"We're proud too," both children chime in together. "And we

like it when you hug Papa. Is dinner going to be ready soon? We're starving," says Jerry.

"I'll go take the sign down first, George says, "so my daughter will not be upset with me." He grins and heads for the front door while Julia returns to the kitchen to begin preparing the evening meal.

After Emma and Julia clear away the supper dishes, Julia returns to her sewing. By the time bedtime comes around, she has completed most of the items needing her attention. Only two skirts and the serge suit remain unfinished, and she is certain that she can finish them by the end of the week. Julia is more than a little anxious to begin work with Louis and embark on the next phase of her career.

As Julia climbs into bed that night next to her husband, an overwhelming feeling of love and gratitude comes over her. Observing his peaceful countenance and listening to his even breathing, she silently thanks God for giving her such a man for a husband. Passion is certainly very exciting. She learned that from James McFadden. But the kindness, compassion, and caring that she receives from this man who is her husband is worth more than all the passion in the world.

"I must somehow let him know how very much I appreciate him and care for him," Julia whispers to herself. She leans down and places a gentle kiss on his forehead and then closes her eyes.

## Chapter 29

As Julia steps down from the streetcar two blocks from Chatelaine Fabriques on her first official day of work, her hands are icy cold and her breath is coming in short gasps. Her nerves are jumping as if they have a life of their own. She takes a deep breath, straightens her shoulders and strides up the walk that ends at an imperious front door. She stops just short of the entrance and then decides to detour and go into the tiny coffee shop on the corner and soothe herself with a cup of coffee and a cigarette. Louis is the only one, besides Pierre, who has witnessed her new habit, but he does not seem to mind. He himself is a devotee of cigars. The cigarette has a calming effect on Julia, and the coffee warms both her insides and her cold hands as she grasps the cup in both of them. As the hot coffee penetrates her insides, she begins to feel better almost at once.

"It's just nerves," she tells herself. "I should be thrilled. This is the beginning of a new life for me — a whole new life." She stands up and automatically squares her shoulders. Holding her head high, she walks slowly to the cashier to pay her bill before leaving the shop. She walks outside in the sunlight and her confidence returns.

As she enters the door of Chatelaine Fabriques, she is greeted by a tall liveried man who directs her inside.

"We have been expecting you, Madame," he says with the trace of a French accent and ushers her into the inside lobby. "Monsieur Chatelaine is waiting for you in his office. Please go right in." He points to a mahogany door at the right side of the lobby with the name of Louis Chatelaine emblazoned in gold letters on it. Julia heads for the door, but before she can knock, Louis bursts through and gathers her into his arms.

"Julia, ma cher, you are finally here. Welcome to your new home away from home."

Several people turn to look at them and suddenly people are clapping and wishing her welcome. Julia is so overwhelmed she can feel tears begin to sting her eyes. Louis, sensing her discomfort, bows to the group on her behalf, puts his arm around her waist and leads her inside his office.

"I am overwhelmed, Louis," she stammers. "These people do not even know me; how can they be so friendly?"

"You had better get used to it, Julia. I have given you quite a buildup, you see; and besides, they recognize that you are the lady in the paintings. That alone has provided you with a certain notoriety, so to speak. At any rate, when they really get to know you, they will love you and admire you as much as I do."

"There is one employee who already does not admire me, Louis," Julia responds. "I had a visit from your friend, Jacqueline, a few days ago. She made it quite clear that she was not all happy about me becoming your partner."

"Pay no attention to Jacqueline, ma cher. She is an old flame that I have been unable to put out – a woman scorned – you know the scenario. I am sure you explained that we are merely good friends and nothing more, so she will give you no more trouble. And now, let us get to work. I want to show you around and introduce you to some of our employees."

Julia spends the remainder of the day meeting people and trying to remember their names. She plays a game with herself linking their names to something unusual about their appearance. The chief cutter is a middle-aged man named Eduard, who has rather long pure white hair. He reminds her of one of the Shakespearean actors Madeleine used to point out to her in one of the illustrated books on classical plays they used to enjoy sharing in the Astor library. The actor's name was also Eduard. Louis' private secretary was a pretty, diminutive redhead with a high pitched voice like that of a child. Her name is Trudy, and the name fits her totally. She cannot be even five feet tall, and in Julia's mind she will always think of her as Tiny Trudy. And so it goes this day, meeting face after face and trying desperately to remember each one.

When the noon hour approaches, Louis suggests that they go around the corner to one of the local cafes and have some lunch. Before leaving the building, however, he leads Julia into another office toward the rear of the main part of the salon. He opens the door and waves her inside. The room is not overly large but has two huge windows on one wall draped in mauve silk. There is a leather-topped mahogany desk in the center of the room, and in the corner in front of one of the windows stands what Louis describes as a professional drafting table. On the other side of the room is a small settee covered in the same silk as the drapes and a small table elegantly set with a lovely silver tea service. Julia looks at Louis, waiting for an explanation.

"This is your office, Julia. I hope you like it, but if there is anything you wish to have changed, you have only to ask me."

"My office?" Julia manages to say. "I never dreamed of anything so beautiful, Louis. I assumed I would work at a table in the cutting room, near a window perhaps to take advantage of the light. I never in my wildest dreams expected anything like this. What have I ever done to deserve such treatment?"

I have complete faith in your abilities, Julia, and I know that you will be an asset to Chatelaine Fabriques. I want you to be comfortable and happy working here. I am a good businessman, you know, and am aware that happy employees make productive ones. The more productive you are, the more money we will make for our salon. And that, my dear Julia, is what we are in business to achieve, *n'est pas?*"

"Oh thank you, thank you, dear Louis. I will do my very best to make you proud of me." Louis takes her arm and leads her from the room and out the front door into the sunlight. They have a tasty lunch in a cozy café that seems to be overflowing with animated, well-dressed people. Louis notices Julia's admiration for the people around them and informs her that most of them are in some way involved in the business of haute couture. Julia admits to Louis that she has not seen such beautiful people since her days at the Astor mansion.

"Well, Julia, they are not in the same financial class as your former employer, but they aspire to get there. Many of them are exceedingly talented and will soon make New York City the fashion capital of America, and perhaps one day, the world."

"I'm sure you are right, Louis, and you must know how excited I am to be a part of all this. I will work very hard to make Chatelaine the finest salon in New York City."

Louis smiles at her enthusiasm and raises his water glass in a mock toast – "To us, Julia, and to the House of Chatelaine, success and nothing less." Julia raises her glass to meet his and they toast each other.

The next few months fly by in a joyous parade of events. Louis announces the launching of their new couture line and some of New York's wealthiest socialites are literally standing in line to have a dress designed just for them from the House of Chatelaine, as they are now known. Julia feels like she is caught up in a whirlwind of good fortune, and everything she touches seems to succeed. Louis has given Julia her own label to design. They call it the Contessa Line, which of course is Louis' idea; and it is an instant success.

Their major competition still comes mainly from the few established fashion houses of Paris. Balenciaga is still the king of huge evening coats and has recently introduced fitted suits and the chemise. Chanel is the toast of Paris and has recently broken a fashion taboo by introducing trousers for women. Paris is all agog, but New York is still making up its mind. One of Julia's personal favorites is Edith Head who designs mostly for the film industry. Talking pictures are all the rage now and her popularity is soaring. It is the element of daring in her designs that fascinate Julia so much. Edith Head is not afraid to try something new. As a matter of fact, intrigued by Chanel's trousers, she designed the first pair of these formerly masculine creations for Katharine Hepburn, and from then on, every fashionable woman in New York wanted a pair of them.

Louis' old friend from Paris, Paul Poiret, has dominated Paris fashion since 1909, but closed his house last year because of illness. His styles were influenced by Art Nouveau and Asian designs; and Louis wanted to carry on his memory in New York in a special line to be designed by Chatelaine. Julia agrees to take on the challenge and begins working on a line of coat and dress ensembles similar to those that had made Paul famous. She includes some creative touches of her own and then adds a few suits tailored with light corseting and some long sweaters that could be worn with them. The line features fabrics that are a departure from their normal stock in trade, and include some braiding and metallic touches that have an Asian flavor.

Louis features these designs for a month or two, but they both soon realize that Paul's day is over, and trying to revive his particular style is a mistake. At Louis' request, Julia concentrates on the more elegant creations they were used to featuring, made with the velvets, satins and silks they are so well known for. They even do a "signature line" patterned after the outfits in the portrait series Julia did with Pierre so many months ago. The new line is an immediate hit and orders begin to pour in. Their best seller is the green velvet riding habit that Julia had suggested, and they both laugh at this turn of events.

One day over lunch Louis looks at Julia very seriously across the table and then begins to speak in earnest.

"Julia, *ma cher*, don't you think it's time you thought about moving uptown and out of that dinky little apartment you are living in. After all, it is 1915 and you are a successful businesswoman. Orders are pouring in, and business has never been better. It's time to leave the old neighborhood and give yourself and your family something better."

"I know you are right, Louis, but I am not sure how George will feel about moving. We always dreamed of having our own home one day with a yard for the children, a garden for me and a grape arbor for George. Neither of us want to live in the city any more. If you were really serious about teaching me to drive, perhaps now is the time. Then we can think about moving to the suburbs and I could drive to work each day. I might even be able to drop the children at school on my way. What do you think, Louis?"

"You take care of convincing George, and I will take care of the driving lessons, *ma cher,*" was his immediate response.

When Julia arrives home this evening George is already there. He is sitting on the front steps, but instead of his head being buried in his newspaper, he is just staring off into space.

"You are home early, George. Is anything wrong?" Julia asks anxiously.

"Mr. Estok is closing down the iron works, *Juliashcam.* His health has suddenly taken a turn for the worse, and he wants to retire while he still has time to enjoy what is left of his life. I will only be working there for three more weeks while we finish the orders we still have in the house. He is even selling his house next to the works and moving himself and his family down south away from the cold New York winters."

"I am sorry to hear that he is ailing, George, but did I hear you correctly? Did you say Mr. Estok is selling that brick house with the grape arbor over the driveway?"

"Yes, *Juliashcam.* He told me about selling the house just this morning."

"George, do you know what this means? W could buy that house and you would have the grape arbor you have always dreamed of. There is plenty of room for a garden, and nothing but woods and fields for the children to play in. And now Louis is teaching me to drive, and I will have a license soon and a car to use so I can drive back and forth to work. Oh, George, our prayers have been answered – a home of our own, at last."

George is looking at Julia as though she has totally lost her mind. "How can we afford a big house like that, Juliashcam?"

"Believe me, George, we can; we can. I have been putting money away for some time now. My seamstress business did rather well before I closed up. Since then I have been saving most of what I earn at Chatelaine. Your salary has been paying the rent and putting most of the food on the table. I pay for the children's clothes because I have no time to make them any longer and of course, my own as well. There has been quite a lot left over, George, and I have been putting it in a bank near the salon. You will be so happy when you see how much we have in our account. Do you remember, George, it was not too many years ago that I used to keep our money in an old sock of yours. As a matter of fact, I still have that old sock in the back of my dresser drawer as a reminder of how far we have come since those days in the mining camps."

George is saying nothing. He is just staring at his wife in disbelief. Julia takes this opportunity to press on and make her point so that George will understand how this turn of events has potentially changed their lives. She takes a deep breath and continues her monologue.

"I know we can afford to buy this house, and Louis will explain to me how to do the financing. She pauses for a minute and runs into the bedroom and gets the bankbook from her dresser drawer. "Look George, look at the amount. Surely it is enough to put down on a house of our own."

George takes the bankbook from his wife's hand and turns the pages one by one. He says nothing for several minutes and then turns to Julia in utter disbelief.

"How in the world did you manage to save so much money, *Juliashcam*? Is Louis so generous to all his employees?"

"George, you forget, I am not just an employee. I am Louis' partner, and business has been very, very good. How do you think Louis can afford to live uptown where he does? The House of Chatelaine is a New York landmark already. We are even featured in the new *Vogue Magazine*. We are not rich, George, but we can certainly afford a home of our own, and this house is just what we have always dreamed of. Please say you agree, and we can buy the house from Mr. Estok."

George begins to smile, and soon the smile envelopes his entire countenance. Julia cannot remember ever seeing her husband smile like that. It was wondrous to behold. George comes toward her with his arms open wide and takes her into them in one of those bear hugs that almost takes her breath away.

"My darling *Juliashcam*," he whispers into her hair. "You have done it again. You have made our dreams come true. I will talk to Mr. Estok tomorrow, and let him know that we want to buy his house before he sells it to anyone else."

"Oh thank you, George. You have made me so happy, but let's not tell Emma and Jerry until we know that the house will be ours. I don't want to get their hopes up until we are sure it will be ours. Now I really have a good reason to learn to drive, and I am determined to have my license before we move. I cannot wait to tell Louis the good news tomorrow."

Julia hugs her husband again and places a big kiss on his cheek. Humming happily under her breath, she walks to the top of the stairs and through the door, leaving her husband on the steps still grinning from ear to ear.

"I'll call you when dinner is ready, George." Julia tosses the words happily over her shoulder as she heads upstairs to the apartment. "Thank you again, God," she whispers to the air as she makes her way to the kitchen to start their evening meal.

## Chapter 30

"Louis, Louis, let me tell you the most exciting news," Julia fairly shouts as she enters his office. "The house in Hunts Point is for sale, and George has agreed we can buy it. Isn't that the best news? I am so excited I can hardly stand it. Now I must get my driver's license, and as quickly as possible. When can I go and take the test?"

"Whoa, *Cherie*, take a breath," Louis interrupts with laughter and surprise in his voice. "I have never seen you like this. You are behaving more like Emma than her mother, and even she does not get that animated very often. Of course I am happy for you. Your dream is finally going to come true. Congratulations! Now, as for the driver's license, you are almost ready, but we will have one more final lesson to make absolutely certain. After that, I will call and make an appointment for you. One person is allowed to accompany the perspective driver, and that will be me, I assure you. You have certainly come a long way, *ma cher*, since we first met. That God you are always thanking certainly does look out for you in a very special way. Maybe you could put in a good word for me now and then."

"I pray for you every day, Louis, not that you need it of course, but I do ask my God to take special care of my very dear friend and partner. You are a big part of my success, as you well know. If I were not working for you, my dream would still be a long way off in my future. I thank God every night that you and dear Pierre came into my life. I do have one favor to ask though, Louis. Will you please explain to me what is involved in buying this house and how I should proceed. Home ownership is rather a new experience for me, and I don't know where to begin. Will you also agree to be a financial reference for George and I?"

"Yes to all your questions, Julia. As a matter of fact, I will introduce you to my attorney who will handle all the legal work for you. If all goes well, we should have you in your new home by early next month."

"Oh, Louis, I knew I could count on you. Thank you again for your help and support. I wonder how the children will react to the news. They both loved Hunts Point when we took them there one Sunday for a picnic, but living there may be a bit different. Emma and Jerry are both doing well in school, and I don't think they will object to changing to another school, but I won't be sure until I tell them. They are both so outgoing and make friends easily. There is a large elementary school only a few blocks from the streetcar station in Hunts Point, so getting back and forth will be an easy task. It's hard to believe that Emma is in fifth grade already and Jerry is close behind her in third. They are growing up so fast, Louis. It seems like yesterday that they were only babies."

"I don't think you have anything to worry about *ma cherie*; the children will love it just because you and George love it. You Pedeschs always stick together. I really envy you. It must be wonderful to have so much love in a family. I cannot even imagine it, but then I have been away from home for such a long time now."

Louis changed the subject abruptly then, and Julia could sense a sadness in him she had not seen before. He paused and then turned, giving her his full attention.

"When will you know if the house is truly yours, Julia?"

"George promised to speak to Mr. Estok today, so hopefully he will have an answer when he comes home from work this evening. When can I have my last driving lesson, Louis? I want to have my license before we move in so I can concentrate on the move Being able to drive the car back and forth will be such a help to us while we are moving. Sometimes, Louis, I feel like I am dreaming and will wake up any minute and find out that all this good fortune is just a dream."

"You are definitely not dreaming, *ma cher*. Let's plan to set up your driving test for this coming Saturday. We can go down to Hunts Point and practice on some of those roads that you will hopefully be using in the near future. What do you say about that?"

"That would be perfect, Louis, and now I guess we both better get back to work. I have a meeting with Eduard in the cutting room in half an hour to prepare for the new line of riding clothes we are planning. I'll see you before I leave for the day, so you can wish me luck."

The rest of the day seems to drag by. Although her meeting with Eduard goes well and she is excited about the new line of riding clothes, Julia is finding it harder and harder to concentrate on the business at hand. Eduard is a pleasure to deal with, and he seems almost as excited as Julia is about the new line. They are the only fashion house in New York that produces this special kind of sports clothing. The line of riding habits has made an instant hit with the young society maidens, now that many of the wealthiest families in New York were also establishing sprawling new homes in the more northern suburbs of Westchester and Duchess Counties. Even the Vanderbilts, who are building a new home along the Hudson River in Hyde Park, are customers of Chatelaine, and are the first to place an order for their beautiful riding habits. It seems now that every society woman in New York City wants to learn to ride and to be dressed in the height of fashion while doing it.

Eventually the day comes to an end, and Julia rushes home to the apartment to confront George and find out about their new home. George is sitting on the steps as usual when Julia comes around the corner, with Emma on one side and Jerry on the other. They are all grinning like the Cheshire Cat from Alice in

Wonderland. The minute they see their mama, the children jump up and race to meet her.

"Is it true, Mama; it is really true?" shouts Jerry. "Are we going to live in the park and have picnics every day?"

"Oh Jerry, don't be so silly," Emma breaks in. "We're not moving to live in a real park. It just looks like one because there are lots of trees and no other houses there."

"My daughter, the realist," says Julia to no one in particular. "She always tells it like it is even when she is excited. Jerry, on the other hand, is prone to exaggeration and never seems to be calm when anything new is going on. What a contrast these two are, and how I love them both."

"I gather your papa has spilled the beans," Julia says smiling at them both. "Can I assume, George, that Mr. Estok agreed to sell us the house?"

"Yes, my dear *Juliashcam*," was his immediate reply. "The house is ours if we want it, and he would like to complete the sale as soon as possible.

What wonderful news, George. No wonder you could not wait to tell the children. When you go to work tomorrow, you can tell Mr. Estok we definitely want the house. I mentioned the price to Louis, and he agrees it is a fair one. He even offered to have his lawyer do all the paper work for us, and will serve as a financial reference if Mr. Estok requires one. I am so excited, George. I cannot believe we are finally going to see our dream come true."

"Louis is giving me my final driving lesson this week and will take me to the driving test on Saturday. Soon I will be able to drive back and forth to work. If things continue to go well at the salon, George, we may be able to buy a car of our own before long. But now," says Julia in a more somber tone, "I think we should all go to St. Constantine's together and say a special thank you to God for being so very generous to us. After we go to mass there on Sunday, we can go down to Hunts Point and admire our lovely new home and have another picnic like we did the first time we saw it. Don't you agree, George?"

"Of course, *Juliashcam,* that is a wonderful idea, and I'm sure Emma and Julius will think so too. We've come a long way since Budapest, and I thank the good Lord every day for giving me such a beautiful and clever wife. Without your charm and determination, we would never have come so far so fast. I pray our children take after their Mama too. They will be sure to succeed in America if they do."

George looks at his wife with such love and pride in his eyes, she has to go to him and kiss him tenderly on the cheek. He turns her face in his strong hands and proceeds to kiss her back, right on the mouth. Julia is so surprised, she gasps, but she catches herself and returns the kiss with all the ardor she can muster.

"You have always been there for me, George, watching out for me and taking care of me through all the trials and the bad times. I always feel safe with you, and you have given me two beautiful children as well. I am very proud of our family and will continue to do whatever it takes to keep us together and insure our future."

Emma and Jerry are staring up at their parents with big grins on their faces. They are not used to seeing such open affection between them.

"It is a good thing," Julia thinks to herself, "for them to know that honest affection does not have to be hidden from our children. No matter what I feel in the deepest part of my heart, I am proud to be George's wife and will always be loyal to him. I want my children to feel secure and know that their parents not only love them but each other as well."

The days and weeks that follow are somewhat of a blur. Julia never realized how many papers there would be to sign in order to purchase a house. Louis' lawyer, Mr. Burke, is a Godsend, but she still has to leave work on several occasions to complete the procedures necessary for closing. George wants the house in Julia's name only, but she insists it be in both their names, so he has to sign many of the papers as well, even though he cannot read many of the words. Julia can see the pride in his eyes each time he completes his signature in his strong Hungarian hand.

Finally the day arrives when it is all theirs. Julia holds the deed in her hand and caresses it as though it were alive. She thanks Mr. Burke for all his help, and taking George by the hand, ushers him toward the sidewalk. Mr. Burke's office is very near the House of Chatelaine. George and Julia traveled there by streetcar, but while they are inside, Louis has driven the car he has given Julia to use and parked it at the curb right outside the lawyer's office. Julia sees the car as soon as she steps out into the light and smiles to herself.

"You are in for quite a surprise," she whispers to her husband. "Your wife is about to drive you to your new home for the first time."

Julia leads George over to the curb and tells him to get into the car. He looks at her with fear and trepidation. George has never set foot in a car in his entire life, and obviously is not anxious to alter that fact. Julia smiles at him reassuringly and enters through the driver's door. George follows her lead and seats himself on the passenger side. His hands are clenched in his lap and his face is a frozen mask. Julia says nothing, but starts the engine of the Ford and proceeds to steer them into the line of traffic on Madison Avenue.

"It's all right, George," Julia assures him and pats his hand.

"Please keep both your hands on the wheel, *Juliashcam*," is his only reply.

Julia grins and immediately places both her hands securely on the wheel in full view of her terrified passenger. Not another word passes between them until they cross the streetcar tracks and enter the narrow paved road leading to Hunts Point and their new home.

"We're here, George," Julia announces proudly, "and safe and sound I might add."

George says nothing but opens the passenger door and raises himself out of the car with as much dignity as he can muster.

Julia alights from the car, feeling like a queen, and immediately reaches in her purse for a cigarette. She is more nervous than she thought. She inhales the smoke deep into her lungs and then exhales with such relief that George looks up questioningly.

"Yes, *Juliashcam*, safe and sound," he repeats. "You are a brave woman and will never cease to amaze me. Just when I think I understand you completely, you do something so extraordinary that I am completely surprised. Thank you for being the woman you are and putting up with a simple man like me. All I ever really had to give you was my love and devotion, and that you will always have until I take my last breath."

"That, my dear husband, is more than I can ever expect, and I love you for it. Now, let's go and inspect our new home so we can go back to the apartment and prepare for the move."

They walk through the grounds in companionable silence until they come to the grape arbor. George's eyes begin to mist, and Julia is sure she can see a tear slide down the rugged check, but she says nothing.

George stares up at the arbor like a man bewitched and then murmurs softly, "I will make the best wine in New York City, maybe in the State even."

"And I will grow the most beautiful flowers," Julia chimes in. "I want to plant the red cannas I remember from our homeland. They are the one happy memory I still carry with me. Do you think they will grow here, George?"

"If we turn the soil over well and add lots of fertilizer, *Juliashcam*, I think you will be able to grow anything you want," he assures her.

After they complete the tour of their land, as Julia loves to call it, they walk up the steps and approach the front door. Mr. Burke has given Julia the key. They know that the Estok family moved out the week before, so they do not hesitate any longer. Julia hands George the key and waits. His hand is shaking slightly as he puts the key into the lock. The door opens immediately, and they enter the long front hall.

Julia has been inside the house twice before, but it is like seeing it for the first time now that it actually belongs to them. The hall leads into the dining room and across from that is the biggest kitchen she has ever seen, except of course in the Astor mansion. There are three big windows filling the room with sunlight. In one corner is a huge wooden table which the former owners left behind because it was too big to move.

"I can roll out enough dough on that table to make bread or noodles for an army," Julia announces. Look at the huge sink and the stove that works with gas, George. It is the most beautiful room I have ever seen. Anna Frye should see me now. Thank you dear God for reminding me that there is truly justice in the world. I will work very hard to be worthy of all the blessings you have seen fit to bestow on me."

George leaves the kitchen and passes through the dining room on his way to the living room with Julia close behind him. This is the room that used to be called a parlor many years ago, but now is much larger and is intended to accommodate a whole family and their leisure pursuits. There is room for a big couch and two chairs at least. A bookcase would be a nice addition to one corner, Julia notes; and of course, a small table where Emma and Julius could play games and even do their homework.

"I will add a tall standing lamp with one of those big beaded shades that are so popular now and a new radio," Julia assures the large room. "The one we have in our apartment now is so small and the sound is not very clear. The children really love listening to the stories and even the music is a welcome addition to their homework sessions now that they are growing up."

George is heading toward the back of the house, and Julia follows right behind him. There is a small laundry room at the rear of the first floor together with a tiny bathroom complete with sink. There is even a small metal sink and counter across the back wall that must have been used for potting plants and carrying out other garden tasks. The more they see, the more Julia knows this house was made for them.

"Let's go upstairs now, George," Julia says as she stands poised at the bottom of the stairs. He follows behind her up the staircase that begins just inside the front door.

A small oval window at the first landing illuminates the stairway and the additional few steps to the second floor. There is one large master bedroom with its own small bath attached and two smaller bedrooms with a bathroom between them which the children can share. It is hard to believe that when they first came to America twelve years before, they had not even seen inside plumbing. Julia is thrilled with the house, and George shares her enthusiasm.

They cannot leave, however, until George takes Julia on a tour of the cellar. They return to the kitchen and there find a door and the stairway leading down to the lower reaches of the house. This area would become George's special domain where he planned to produce the wine from his own grapes growing now on the precious grape arbor. There is, Julia notes with surprise, a huge barrel-like structure already installed at one end of the cellar. Apparently, the former owner had considered setting up an operation to produce wine but never found the time to complete the project. George was in his glory!

"Half the work has been done for me Julia," he remarks triumphantly. "I will have this barrel in full working order in no time. I still remember the skills of the monks in the seminary outside of Budapest. I used to watch them by the hour preparing the grapes after the harvest and making the mash into their wonderful wine. I cannot wait to begin. We will never be without wine again in our house, *Juliashcam*," he concludes with pride evident in his voice.

Julia assures him that she cannot wait to taste his first batch of wine, and on that note they return to the first floor and leave the house through their very own front door. George gets in the car without hesitation or comment this time. He is totally preoccupied with his thoughts of the house and the wine-making that will take place there. Julia starts the engine and steers the Ford in the direction of home.

# Chapter 31

They arrive at the apartment to find the children waiting excitedly. "Is it is ours now, Mama?" Emma asks with all the reserve of a bouncing ball.

"Is it, is it?" echoes Jerry, jumping up and down.

"Yes, my dears, it is ours," answers Julia, "and now we must get busy packing up our belongings in preparation for moving. Each of you must go to your room, collect all your treasures as well as your clothes, and put them in a neat pile on the floor. Papa will go downstairs to the grocer's and ask him for boxes that we can use to pack things into. When he brings them upstairs, we can begin filling them with our belongings. Uncle Pierre has a friend with a truck who will help us move all our things to the new house. He will be here first thing tomorrow morning so we only have today to get ready."

Julia barely finishes her sentence when she hears a knock at the door. There is dear Pierre with his sleeves rolled up and a huge grin on his face.

"Mover Pierre at your service, *Madamoiselle.*"

Julia rushes to give him a hug and thank him for coming to help them. Both children attack him with hugs and a babble of words about the new house and the move now in progress.

"*Sacre Bleu*," shouts Pierre in his rich French accent. "Such excitement in the Pedesch household today. If I did not know better, I would think you were moving," he adds with a chuckle. Emma and Jerry laugh too and lead him into their room begging for help in sorting out their treasures.

"Isn't it wonderful to have such good friends, George? If it were not for Pierre and Louis, we would never have been able to make our dream come true. There is nothing I would not do for either of them."

"You are absolutely right, my dear, and I will always be in their debt as well. Perhaps some day we will find a way to truly repay them for all their kindness to this family." George turns away thoughtfully and walks toward the door. "I will go now and get the boxes from the grocer," he says matter-of-factly and disappears down the stairs.

Pierre has the children well in hand, so Julia heads for the kitchen to gather their dishes, eating utensils, and pots and pans. She cannot leave any of these old friends behind. She has collected them from the time of their first home at the immigrant shelter, and all hold memories she will cherish forever. Her big cast iron pot with the dents all on one side has cooked so many stews, soups, and noodles before it ever graduated to *toltott kapszta* (stuffed cabbage) and *esirke prprikas* (chicken paprika). That old pot was a hand-me-down from Bertha, her first real friend at the mining camp in Pennsylvania. She even has a big slotted spoon that she brought all the way from Hungary, a gift from Maria, Fr. Bergard's housekeeper. She fingers the spoon lovingly. It is her only reminder of how far away from the old country she really is and of the few people who ever cared for her there. The children's voices suddenly break through her reverie and she begins to clear out the cabinets with a vengeance.

"We are all ready to go, Mama," shouts Jerry. "Can we leave now?"

"Slow down my son," Julia answers. "Remember what I said. The moving man will not be here until tomorrow morning. Your Papa will be bringing up the boxes in a minute and then you and Uncle Pierre can begin filling them with the things you and Emma will be taking to our new home."

"Oh, I'm sorry, Mama, I forgot. It's just that I am so anxious to move to the park. No one else in my class lives in a park. I am the only one, and that makes me special."

"I give up," Julia says to Pierre. "Maybe you can make him understand that Hunts Point is not a park. Meanwhile, here comes Papa up the stairs with the boxes, so let's all get to work."

By early evening they have packed up all their belongings into the boxes and as much of their clothes as their two old valises will hold. The few pieces of furniture will be loaded into the truck next morning by George and Pierre and his friend, the moving man. Pierre insists on taking them all out to dinner to celebrate their hard work and even succeeds in convincing George. They go around the corner to the local Italian family-style restaurant and feast on bowls of spaghetti and loaves of fresh Italian bread. George and Pierre both have a glass of deep red Chianti, and they are a merry group to be sure.

The children fall asleep as soon as their heads hit the pillows. They are exhausted from the hard work and the excitement of this day. Julia and George allow them to sleep in the clothes they are wearing, as they have packed all their other clothes as well as the linens, in preparation for the early morning move. Pierre sleeps on the couch so he will be ready bright and early to help George move the furniture.

The moving man arrives right on time and parks his truck at the curb. Most of their neighbors are outside too, offering their help and wishing them well. George and Pierre are hard at work carrying the furniture down to the curb where Pierre's friend, Max, is almost single-handedly loading it onto his truck. His young son is with him, and he guides the furniture into place. Max, who is built like Paul Bunyan from Jerry's storybook, is doing most of the heavy lifting and apparently with ease. Julia always thought George was strong, but she has never seen such strength in any one man before. Jerry is almost speechless as he watches Max perform his physical miracles.

Before long, everything is loaded and secured, and they are

ready to leave. George and Julia say their good-byes and depart from their friends and neighbors with hugs and tears all around. They assure their old friends that they will return to visit and that they are welcome in their new home at any time. Fanny Ober is crying quietly on the stoop, and Julia goes to comfort her and thank her again for all her kindness. Jerry shakes hands with her son, John, who has been his best friend as long as they have lived there.

Emma, however, appears the saddest of all. She looks with longing at the windows of their old apartment and the ones next door where she can see her friend Anna with her nose pressed against the glass. Anna has been quite ill this past week and is still not allowed to go outside. Emma waves to her, and Julia sees the tears creeping down from under the lashes. She goes to her and puts her arms around her in an effort to provide comfort. Emma hugs her mother tight and allows the tears to fall.

"You will see your friend again, Emma, I promise. I will even drive her over to our new house on a weekend to spend time with you. Don't be sad. Remember this is a wonderful new beginning for our family, not an ending." Emma smiles up at her mother then, and with a final wave to Anna, straightens up and walks to the car without another backward glance.

Julia drives the car to Hunts Point with George, Pierre, and the children inside. Max follows behind in his truck, and they arrive in a short time without incident. Now that the realization of their new surroundings is upon them, Emma and Jerry are ecstatic. This will be the first time that they will have their own rooms and be able to play outside without worrying about the ball going out into the road where a car might hit it or them. Cars are everywhere now in the City so playing in the street has become more than a challenge. Mothers are constantly running outside each time a screech of brakes rents the air. At least here in Hunts Point, this will not be a consideration. After all, as the children keep reminding her, they are living in a park.

The weeks and months that follow their move are filled with

excitement and wonder as they adapt to their new home and their new-found space. The sturdy brick house is like a castle to Julia, and she loves nothing more than to just sit in her big sunny kitchen and look around her. She has planted seeds in her garden and George has brought her some canna plants from the local nursery, along with the fertilizer he knows is needed to keep the plants healthy. Julia spends most of her weekend outside cultivating and watering and just watching the myriad butterflies swarming from flower to flower in the bright afternoon sun.

Emma and Jerry have adapted to their new school with no trouble whatever, and both enjoy taking the streetcar back and forth to school whenever Julia is unable to drive them. George has lost his fear of the car now and even agrees that they can buy a car of their own as soon as they can afford it. He will never consider driving, of course, but owning one that his wife can drive is all right with him, he tells everyone.

Meanwhile, business is never better at Chatelaine, and Louis is more than a little pleased with their success. The Contessa Line has become a signature line, and they are often featured in the fashion magazines. One of the older magazines that began in 1903, the year Julia came to America, chose to feature them twice. *Woman's World* has the largest circulation of all the women's magazines, and although it is not so highbrow as *Vogue*, it is very popular in New York City households. Julia can even remember pouring through old issues when they lived on Delancey Street. George would sometimes find them in the street bins when he was a street cleaner, and bring them home to her. This magazine helped her form her prices too when she was working as a seamstress. She would scour their ads for the prices of skirts, blouses and dresses, and set hers accordingly. Julia managed to keep up with this magazine over the years and was truly delighted when they did a spread on Chatelaine.

Julia asks Louis if they can consider designing a mid-priced line that perhaps some of the *Woman's World* readers could afford. At first he is against it, thinking it will lower their image among the society patrons, but then he reconsiders.

"Why not, Julia; this could be an innovation of the future, *n'est pas?* We would be the first salon to feature a line of ensembles for the middle class housewife and young working woman. Why not make our wonderful clothes available to a whole new group in our society? You are a genius, Julia. Start working on this new line at once. Now we must come up with a name for this new line"

"How about American Chic," Julia offers. We won't stress any French or European influence, but concentrate on the pure American flavor of the line. I will design clothes that can go to the office and, with a small change or addition, can continue on to a restaurant and the theatre in the evening."

"That is a superb idea, *ma cherie.* I like it; I like it very much You will begin today."

And so the new line of American Chic is born and puts the House of Chatelaine on the fashion map of the world once again. Louis is overjoyed, and Julia is thrilled that the women of New York have so readily accepted her new idea. The line is already being requested by some of the more prestigious stores of the mid west, and is fast becoming a household word among middle-class suburban housewives and the new legion of working women in America.

Julia continues to work long hours during the week but manages to get home most evenings in time to cook dinner for her family and even help Emma and Jerry with their increasing amounts of homework. The weekends are another story. Julia refuses to leave the house on weekends except in cases of extreme emergency. Louis has already learned that planning any event including Julia on the weekend is next to impossible. Occasionally, she acquiesces if a special fashion show is held over for a new or prestigious customer, but these occasions are few and far between.

Julia's garden takes a good deal of her time on the weekends, especially now that her cannas are ready to bloom. She has started cooking again too, on a grander scale, including some of her old specialties that she previously did not have time for. George even prepared a special plot in the garden where she can grow the herbs that add so much to their traditional Hungarian dishes. Basil, rosemary and parsley proliferate together with garlic and coriander, giving a sultry aroma to this corner of the garden.

Julia is convinced she has the best of both worlds and is supremely happy in her new surroundings. Emma and Jerry are thriving too, and George is more relaxed and happy than she can ever remember. He spends a good deal of time in the cellar perfecting his wine-making equipment, but comes up for air more often now that the weather is getting warmer. He spends long hours cultivating his vines and securing the arbor over the driveway so that the grapes will get the maximum amount of sun. He is even sporting a healthy tan, and Julia is sure he has never been happier since they left the old country.

George, Julia discovers, has acquired some new friends. Several Hungarian men who live on the edge of Hunts Point in an apartment building adjacent to the property spend a lot of their time on the Point, taking walks, rabbit hunting and running Hungarian picnics. George has met them walking past the house or in the woods, which he sometimes explores on his own. They all speak Hungarian, and so George is in his glory. She even caught them singing some old Hungarian folk songs the other day in the wooded area across the road from their house.

George suggested to Julia, on more than one occasion, that they join with these men one weekend and have an old-fashioned Hungarian picnic.

"Two of the men have wives and children," he explained, "and it would be a real treat for Emma and Julius, who know nothing of the old world customs. The men will build a huge fire in a pit in the woods and they will cook *szalonnaval* (Hungarian bacon) and *kolbasz* (sausage) over the fire as we did when I was a boy."

Julia remembers Anna Frye and her family having a picnic like that once, but she was not included in the festivities until it was time to clean up. She searched her memory and soon the smells of the food cooking came to the fore and tickled her taste buds. How she had wanted to taste the roasting meat and join in the revelry, but this privilege was denied her. She would not deny her children the chance to learn about their Hungarian heritage.

As she listened to George describe the plans for a picnic, Julia knew she would enjoy sharing this old custom with her family and some new friends. There was no doubt that she loved the elegance of her position at Chatelaine, but there is still a part of her – the peasant part – that enjoys remembering her roots.

"I want the children to revere their heritage too, George, and this is a wonderful way to celebrate that."

She looks up at her husband and smiles. She can see immediately how important this is to him. Unlike Julia, George needs the companionship of men like himself, secure in the bond of their language and similar beginnings in Hungary. Julia would enjoy meeting the wives, of course, but she knows in her heart that they will have little in common with each other at this stage of her life. She promises herself that she will try to fit in and tells George that she will be pleased to take part in a picnic. He is overjoyed and only a few days later he informs her that the first picnic will be in two weeks on a Saturday. Emma and Jerry talk of little else once their father gives them this news. Julia mentions it to Louis at the salon next day, and he raises an eyebrow and looks more than mildly surprised.

"Going back to your roots, my gypsy princess?" he jokes. "Perhaps you will invite me as an interested bystander and personal friend of the family."

"I would love to have you and Pierre join us," Julia counters, "but you had better learn to dress down a bit if you come or George's friends will mistake you for an impoverished Count from the old country."

They both laugh at this last remark and return to their respective offices.

"I will call Pierre this afternoon," Julia declares. "He at least will probably enjoy this kind of festivity." She hums an old gypsy tune as she enters the cutting room.

# Chapter 32

The day of the picnic arrives sunny and warm , and the children are so excited you would think it was Christmas. George has gone into the woods early in the morning where he and the men are preparing the pit for the fire they will build to cook the meat. Besides all the Hungarian delicacies planned for this picnic feast, the star attraction is an entire hog donated by one of the men whose brother owns a pig farm. This pig will be cooked in the pit all day covered with cornhusks and the leaves of some local plants that will protect it from burning.

"It will take all day to cook thoroughly," Julia explains to Emma and Jerry, "which is why it has to be started so early in the morning."

They beg to go and help with the preparations, so Julia sends them off with a strict warning to stay clear of the pit and not to get in the way.

Julia is preparing the *toltott kapszta* and cucumber salad with sour cream. The other women are providing the *szalonnaval* and *kolbasz*, long loaves of bread, ears of corn and pots of noodles smothered in potcheese. One of the women is in charge of desserts, and she has been baking pastries and other Hungarian delicacies for more than a week. George volunteered to provide the wine of course, and he will be bringing it to the picnic site in a large keg he has fashioned for that purpose.

Julia is beginning to get excited herself now. This is such a departure from their normal routine, and the preparations are evoking strange feelings within her. Although she has few happy memories of her youth in Hungary, she does recall watching these picnic rituals from the sidelines wishing she were part of the fun and excitement. She even remembers how good the food smelled, especially the *szalonnaval,* skewered on sticks and held over the fire. Hungarian children are not allowed to eat the meat until they attain the age of twelve, because it is so hard to digest. Instead they put large slabs of coarse bread on the ends of their sticks and hold the sticks under the skewered meat held by the grownups in order to catch the drippings on their bread. The drippings are almost as good as the succulent meat, and Julia remembers well when one of Anna's sons gave her a small taste on one occasion when a picnic was in progress. He was the only one in their family who ever showed her any kindness. It tasted so good and Julia had thanked him most sincerely. She never forgot that wonderful tangy taste and how the grease dripped from her chin in her excitement to get it into her mouth. She was looking forward to enjoying it again today at their picnic.

By three o'clock the party is in full swing. There are about twenty people present and at least half a dozen of them are children. The grownups are enjoying George's wine, and the children are filling up on apple cider and jugs of fresh buttermilk. The pig has been removed from the fire pit and is cooling on a huge wooden slab nearby where it will soon be carved by one of the men. The skewers of *szalonnaval* can be heard crackling over the flames, and a table next to the pit is laden with the other items on the menu that need to be kept warm. Next to that is another table filled with breads of all kinds, bowls of salad and fresh vegetables – some steamed and some raw. The steamed ones send their own special fragrance into the air to mingle with the scent of the roasting meat. Julia can feel her stomach growl in anticipation of the forthcoming feast.

She can see Emma and Jerry playing with several of the other children. They are racing around the circle of fire with their sticks in an effort to catch the drippings from the roasting *szalonnaval.*

Suddenly without hesitation, Julia rushes over to join them with her stick in her hand.

"Come on Mama, we'll help you get some juice," Jerry shouts as he moves his mother closer to the circle. Julia feels like a child herself and abandons herself to the joy of the game.

By six o'clock the fire has all but disappeared, as has most of the food. The table is moved back from the fire now and is covered with what is left of the multitude of desserts that were there earlier. There are still a few *pitesz* (pastries) remaining, but none of the revelers is able to eat another bite, not even the children. At this point in time, the children are all lying down under the big oak tree across the road, and the youngest ones are almost asleep in the laps of their siblings. The men, full of wine by now, are beginning to nod off in various corners of the clearing, and the women are busy wrapping up leftover food and cleaning up the picnic area. One of the older men is playing a sweet gypsy tune on the concertina. One of the older girls is swirling her skirt around her ankles in an attempt to dance like a gypsy. Everywhere people are content, filled with good food and the joy of comradeship. Julia goes in search of Emma and Jerry and finds them with three of the older children sitting in a group playing marbles.

"Time to go in, my dears," she declares and points toward the house. "The picnic is over now and everyone is heading for home before it gets dark."

"Okay, Mama," says Jerry, collecting his marbles and putting them in the canvas bag he always carries them in. "I'm ready too."

Good-natured shouts of goodnight and thank you fill the air as all the families gather up their leftovers and prepare to leave. Julia notices Pierre is still by the pit busily engaged in conversation with a lovely young woman she has not had the pleasure of meeting.

"Goodnight, Pierre," she shouts across the road, but he acknowledges her with nothing more than a casual wave, and she continues on into the house. Louis never did show up Julia realizes, but she is not surprised. He really has nothing in common with these people anyway and would only have come to please her. She looks back briefly as she reaches the door and sees Pierre usher the young lady into his car. She smiles to herself and enters the house tired but happy.

Julia arrives at the office a bit later than usual the next day. The excitement of the picnic took more of a toll on her than she realized apparently. She smiles to herself as she recalls the sights and smells of the recent event.

"And what are you smiling about so early in the morning?" a voice calls from the doorway. Julia looks up to see Louis leering at her.

"I was just thinking about the picnic yesterday," she answers. "You missed a good party and some really wonderful food," she adds. Louis's mood changes abruptly and Julia notices dark circles around his eyes.

"I am deeply sorry that I missed it *ma cherie*, but I have a genuine excuse. I received a cable yesterday morning that my father is very ill in Paris, and I must leave for France in the morning. I hope I won't have to be away too long, but while I am gone, I must ask you to look after the business for us. Alan Burke, our lawyer, will help you if anything out of the ordinary arises. Please forgive me for doing this to you at such short notice, but as you can well imagine, I have no choice. I spent yesterday securing passage and packing my bag."

"Do not give the House of Chatelaine another thought, Louis. I assure you I will take care of everything. Fortunately, this is not our busiest season, and since we have just finished developing our spring line for American Chic, I will have more time to devote to the Contessa Line. Your only concern must be for your father. God speed on your journey."

Julia went to him then and gave him a hug and a kiss on both cheeks. He returns this show of affection and strides from the room.

It becomes increasingly apparent after Louis has been gone only a week that the workload is growing too big for Julia to handle alone. Some changes arise in the American Chic line requiring her undivided attention. More importantly, they are experiencing serious problems obtaining certain fabrics from Europe because of the onset of war there. These fabrics are what make the Contessa Line so popular, so Julia must spend a good deal of her time locating other sources. It appears that they may have to depend more and more on domestic sources. More orders than usual are pouring in for both lines, and Julia is suddenly inundated with paper work.

Tiny Trudy, Louis's loyal secretary, tries to help Julia, but she really knows how to do nothing except care for Louis and his personal affairs. Julia realizes that she must make a decision, and rather quickly at that. She places an ad in the situations wanted column of the local newspaper that afternoon requesting the services of a secretary who is familiar with the workings of the fashion industry. She receives the first response to her ad the very next day. Julia invites the young woman to come in for an interview. Her name is Rene Charles, and she can perform secretarial duties, she informs Julia, but is also a recent graduate of the Parsons School of Design. Julia smiles to herself remembering Annabel Taylor, one of her first customers when she was a seamstress, who had also attended that prestigious institution. Rene is tall and attractive with a pleasing manner, and Julia hires her on the spot.

"Your Parsons training is a bonus, Rene, and should stand you in good stead here at Chatelaine," Julia assures her.

She briefly explains the problems they are incurring and asks if Rene can begin work at once. The young woman happily agrees and together they set her up in a corner of Julia's office. While examining the room where she will be working, Rene notices the rather large drafting table in the far corner, and her eyes brighten immediately.

"May I use this sometimes, on my own time of course?" she asks Julia.

"Of course," Julia answers. "I would love to see some of your work as soon as we get through this jumble of orders that are bogging us down right now. Our main concern at present is to get this business running smoothly again. You will devote your time to locating new fabrics for the Contessa Line and processing as many orders as possible. I will concentrate on the problems with American Chic, and together we will get the House of Chatelaine back on track before Louis returns. Do you think you can survive the pressure, Rene?"

"I will do my best, Mrs. Pedesch," answers Rene with a confident smile. "I always loved a challenge and I guess this will fit into that category nicely," she adds.

"I believe you have a grasp on the situation, Rene," comments Julia, "and please call me Julia. We do not stand on formality here at Chatelaine."

Rene and Julia work long and hard but do not quite reach their goal when Louis returns from France without any warning. You can imagine his surprise when he walks into Julia's office and sees the lovely Rene working intently in the corner. After giving Louis the welcome home he deserves, Julia turns to introduce him to Rene. She is standing now and Louis is staring at her with more than a little interest.

"Louis, may I introduce Rene Charles. She is my new secretary and would-be designer. Rene just graduated from the Parsons School and is anxious to become part of the fashion world. Business problems escalated after you left, and I desperately needed help, so I took it upon myself to hire her. I hope you don't mind that I made this decision on my own, but I really had no choice. Several problems arose that required my full attention and". . . her voice trailed off as she realized Louis was not really listening. He was still staring at Rene, and she, in turn, could not seem to take her eyes off Louis.

"Of course I don't mind, *Cherie;* after all, we are partners, *n'est pas?*"

"I am so relieved, Louis," Julia answers. "I am so glad that you are back," she continues. "How is your father?"

"He has made a miraculous recovery, Julia. Even his doctors are amazed at his constitution. We did take the precaution of moving him out of Paris and into Province because of the dangers of the war. He is staying with a great aunt of mine in a chateau out in the country where he will get nothing but fresh air and good nourishing peasant food. I expect he will be with us for another few years at least. But now, let me hear more about this lovely creature you have hired. Please come into my office, *Mademoiselle* Charles, so we may become better acquainted. You can fill me in on all the tawdry business details over lunch, Julia. I shall be back for you in an hour or two." With that remark on his lips and Rene on his arm, Louis walks purposefully out of the office.

In the weeks that follow, the House of Chatelaine gradually returns almost to normal. With Louis back and taking the reins once again, together with the additional help provided by the very competent Rene, they are well on their way to returning to business as usual. Rene has indeed been worth her weight in gold and has succeeded in locating several excellent domestic fabric sources, thus lessening their dependence on European sources. Louis is very pleased with the results of her research and they are all getting along famously.

Rene has even found time to work up a few designs of her own. Julia discovers this one morning when she arrives at the office to find Rene hard at work at the drafting table.

"May I look?" Julia inquires.

"Oh of course, Julia, I am most anxious for your opinion," answers Rene.

"These are quite a departure from our usual gowns," Julia observes. "They are a bit like the ones I've seen by that new designer, Emilio Pucci. I am not sure how Louis will react, but if he has no objections, I would like to 'give you your head,' as they say, and see where it leads you. We could use some new ideas at

Chatelaine, and I hope he will agree. Let's bring a few sketches in to him now and see what his reaction will be. What do you say, Rene?"

"Maybe it is too soon, Julia. I have only been here a few months," is her reply.

"With Louis it is always better to invoke the element of surprise, my dear Rene, so let's do just that and take these sketches to his office right now."

They knock on Louis' door and are admitted almost at once by Tiny Trudy.

"He will be glad to see you, Madame Julia," she chirps. "Please go right in."

Louis stands as the two women enter and bounds across the room. He gives Julia her perfunctory kiss and hug and then turns to Rene.

"How lovely to see you, *Mademoiselle*," he croons. "Please sit down, both of you, here on the settee. Trudy, please get coffee for the ladies," he orders, and turns to face them.

"Rene has done some sketches, Louis, which I want you to see. They are a bit different than we are used to, but I find them a refreshing change. If you think they are too radical for the Contessa Line, perhaps we could do some modifications and use them in the American Chic line. What do you think?"

Julia places Rene's sketches on the table in front of Louis and waits for his reaction. Rene draws in her breath and seems to be holding it as she waits for Louis to speak. He studies the sketches critically and then places them back on the table.

"They certainly are a departure from what I am used to," he says at last rubbing his chin thoughtfully, "but they have a certain excitement about them that I have not seen before. Is Emilio Pucci a favorite of yours, my dear? You seem to be quite fond of the geometric patterns, but you use them in the design motif itself rather than in the fabric layout as he does. I am really quite impressed. Whatever inspired you to cut off one shoulder of the gown and add that deep slit on the opposite side of the skirt? It is very innovative and most provocative. I think that one could be a best seller."

Rene is speechless, and Julia is overjoyed at his words.

"I knew you would see the possibilities, Louis. Do I have your permission to proceed then?"

"Not only my permission, ma Cherie, but my insistence," he states with finality. With that he takes Rene by the shoulders and raises her to her feet. He kisses her on both cheeks in the usual French manner and says, "Welcome to the House of Chatelaine, *ma cher* Rene. You are now officially a contributing member of the team and our first full-fledged professional designer."

Rene has still not spoken a word, but at this juncture appears to be overcome with emotion. "Oh, *Monsieur* Chatelaine," she stammers through a mist of tears, "thank you so much for giving me this opportunity. I will make you proud of me, I promise."

And so their new relationship begins, and the House of Chatelaine makes its entrance into the year 1917 with hope for an even better future. The United States has thus far remained out of the War in Europe, although by the end of January, Germany declares unrestricted submarine warfare in a zone even larger than the one it proclaimed in 1915. On February 3rd, President Wilson retaliates by breaking off diplomatic relations with Germany. Later that same month Congress passes a bill permitting U. S. merchant vessels to arm. After some new depredations by German submarines against neutral shipping, and the discovery of a plan by Germany to unite itself with Mexico and Japan against the U.S. if it enters the war, President Wilson on April 2, 1917 requests Congress to officially declare war. On April 6th Congress passes a resolution declaring a state of war with Germany.

# Chapter 33

The people of the United States learn that their country has entered the war when President Wilson makes the sad announcement on the radio. By April 1918, the U. S. Air Service has three squadrons at the front, most of them equipped with French aircraft. The war continues in Europe devastating most of the countries around the Mediterranean until Germany finally signs the Treaty of Versailles in June of 1919 bringing the hostilities to an end.

Young Jerry is more angry than pleased when he hears that the war is over. He has prayed it would last long enough for him to join up, but since he is now only fifteen, his dream is not to be realized. Julia, on the other hand, thanks God every night that her son will not serve in the army of his country, at least not yet.

Their dear friend, Pierre, is becoming more famous as the years pass. Since the onset of World War I, he digressed from painting portraits of society family members and began a series of paintings depicting the faces of war. He went abroad for several months with special permission from the U. S. Government, armed with only a camera, and took hundreds of photographs of the men in arms. Pierre went right to the front lines whenever he could and photographed the horror and degradation he found there. His focus, however, was on the faces of the young men, and he concentrated on them, not on the horrors of the war. He knew he wanted to convert these photos into paintings, but as a memorial to the bravery and faith he encountered at the front, not as a testimony to the horror he had witnessed.

He visits Julia and her family when he returns from Europe, and he looks more tired and worn than Julia has ever seen him. He shows them many of the photographs he has taken, and even young Jerry winces when confronted with the realities of war. Pierre decides to rent a small house in upstate New York on the banks of the Hudson River and begins the arduous task of converting his photographs into a series of paintings. George and Julia make the trip to Duchess County to visit him on at least two occasions. Julia is concerned because he appears so thin and worn. Pierre is consumed with his work and seems to almost resent their presence as an intrusion. This project of his has become an obsession and nothing and no one can deter him from his purpose. They come away saddened from these visits, but love their dear friend none the less.

Pierre remains in the little house on the Hudson for over two years. Although he completes more than a dozen paintings, he never completes the full scope of his work. He dies of pneumonia in the fall of 1921, alone in his little house with no one there to comfort him. Louis arranges to bring the body of his dear friend back to New York City, and they all attend his funeral at a small Protestant Chapel in the neighborhood where he has maintained his studio for so many years. Julia weeps bitterly for her dear friend and is inconsolable for several days. Only she knows how much she will miss this man, who was her only true friend and confidante all these years. Pierre was like the brother she never had, and she loved him and would miss him as if he were. Julia remembers back to the good times, like the first picnic at Hunts Point. She wonders whatever happened to the lovely young girl Pierre seemed so enamored with that day. He never mentioned a woman in his life and Julia never saw the young woman again. Pierre seemed destined to live out his life alone with only his beloved parrot to keep him company. Julia smiled to herself remembering her first meeting with the absurd pet who literally ruled the roost in Pierre's studio. The parrot died, conveniently, she recalls, the year Pierre left for Europe.

Julia feels a deep affection for Louis too, of course, but she never loved anyone the way she loved Pierre. No one would ever call her My Angel again as long as she lived. Louis and Julia both mourn Pierre's passing, but in such different ways. They cannot really help each other emotionally. George tries his best to comfort her and the children who also miss their Uncle Pierre. Without any of them realizing it, Pierre had become an important member of their family.

Time heals all wounds, and so Julia's life goes on. In the spring of 1922, Louis goes to Paris again, and this time he takes Rene with him. His goal, he tells Julia, is to search out new fabric sources, since many of their original ones have been lost to the war. He also wants to visit the few fashion houses that have survived this critical period in our history. Julia does not question his choice of companion, and is pleased that he thinks Rene is talented enough to be included in this trip. After all, she was Julia's discovery.

A few weeks after Louis and Rene arrive in Europe, Julia receives a cable from Louis that inevitably changes the course of her life. He surprises them all by marrying Rene. At first Julia is hurt that she was excluded from this important event, but then she realizes that it probably was not planned, but just sort of happened spontaneously. She had suspected for some time now that Rene was beginning to return the affection that Louis demonstrated from the beginning. Despite the difference in their ages, Julia thinks Louis was smitten from the day he first set eyes on the young design student. At any rate, she takes it as a sign that perhaps her days at Chatelaine are coming to an end.

Louis and Rene do not return to New York until the end of the year. They spend Christmas with Louis' father in Province as well as extend their honeymoon from Paris on into Madrid. Business is still thriving at Chatelaine, but Julia's enthusiasm is waning. She vows she will talk to Louis as soon as he returns about buying out the American Chic line and opening her own small salon in a less expensive part of town.

"I will hire competent help and continue to make an adequate living," she says to herself. I will miss working with Eduard of course, but I am confident that I can find another talented cutter who will be up to the task. Being on my own again after so many years will be a challenge I know. If I handle it right though, I will be able to spend more time with the children, who are rapidly becoming young adults right before my eyes."

Jerry, at fifteen (almost sixteen he keeps reminding his mother), remains full of exuberant energy, but still talks of nothing but joining the Army after he graduates from high school. Although the terrible war in Europe is now over, our soldiers are providing occupation forces in all corners of the world. He sees himself in places like Paris, reliving the tales he remembers hearing about from Uncle Pierre. Julia says very little when this subject comes up; but she fears she will lose her son if he goes too far away from his family.

Emma is a young lady now of seventeen, and much to Julia's dismay, is already being sought after by a tall handsome would-be engineer from the fashionable section of the city known as Morningside Heights. Charles, who is five years her senior and attending Columbia University, comes from a wealthy family and tends to be what Julia refers to as arrogant. She is not happy with the match and has made her feelings known to Emma. She feels certain that she should make herself more available to her naive daughter at this critical stage of her development. Emma is totally enamored with Charles already, and Julia is certain she is incapable of thinking clearly about the future of this relationship.

The first time Charles and Julia meet, he is picking Emma up on a Saturday afternoon to take her to a local movie, or so he says. He calls Julia "Mom" and informs her that he intends to marry her daughter when the time is right. From that day on Charles and Julia are engaged in their own private war with Emma as the prize. When Julia looks into her daughter's eyes she knows in her heart that she is ultimately going to lose this battle, but she will never give up the fight. Even Charles eventually will be forced to admit that she is a worthy adversary.

And so it happens that when Louis and his bride return to New York, Julia convinces him that they should part company in their business. Louis emphatically disagrees with her at first, but then, encouraged by Rene who is full of a newfound ambition, he finally agrees to the arrangement Julia proposes. She will buy out his interest in American Chic, and they will part friends and go their own ways. The process is over before they know it. Their lawyers handle all the legal arrangements, and Julia takes ownership of her shop on Seventh Avenue just outside the garment district three months later.

Julia had spent considerable time canvassing the area for a possible location for her new shop while Louis was away, and found the one she finally chose on her second time out. The proprietor was eager to rent the space and it has many of the amenities she requires. Best of all, the rent he is charging is within her carefully executed budget. One thing she has learned from Louis is how to budget for success, and now that knowledge is paying off. Julia is able to pick up display cases and clothing racks quite reasonably from a nearby supply house. George and Jerry provide the labor force to paint the main showroom as well as the small office and storage area in the rear of the building. They even have a small lavatory next to the office to complete the ambiance.

After interviewing about a dozen young women, Julia chooses one to work full time and another to come in only on the weekends. The latter is tall and thin and can double as a model if a customer wants to see how a garment looks on the runway before she buys. Emma helps out on Saturdays until she graduates from high school and demonstrates her ability to do bookkeeping as well as be a teenage clothes horse. Unfortunately, Charles is still very much in the picture, so he often comes by on Saturdays to pick her up for a date after she finishes work for the day. Julia is finding it more and more difficult to be civil to this cocky young man who threatens to marry her daughter.

Emma will graduate from high school in the spring, and George is so excited he can hardly bear it.

"A high school graduate in the family," George keeps repeating. "I am so proud of Emma and what she has accomplished. Did you ever dream, *Juliashcam*, that we would have a daughter graduate from high school?"

"Why of course I did, George, but I too am very proud of our daughter. Now, if we can only discourage that arrogant Charles Carney from hanging around, I will be the happiest mother in New York City."

"Oh he's not so bad, *Juliashcam*," George counters. "I think he really loves our Emma, and his family is rich so he will be able to take good care of her. She'll be a lot better off than you and I were when we were starting out. You can be sure of that, he concluded with a nod of his head."

"Money isn't everything, George," Julia answers with a slight edge to her tone. "I'm more concerned about Emma being happy than how rich she may become. Neither of our children will ever have it as hard as we did, but I pray they will both find happiness and live to see their dreams come true. Emma and Jerry are the most important things in my life. I will do whatever it takes to keep them safe and happy, even if it includes punching a six foot tall engineer in the face to keep him away from my daughter."

George shrugs and turns away. "You are impossible when it comes to Charles," he says as he walks away, "and I think you are wasting your breath. That young man is on a mission when it comes to Emma. I can see it in his eyes. I will speak to him myself, *Juliashcam*, and let him know that we are concerned. After all, I am her father. I have a right to speak my mind. He is so used to hearing you shout at him like a crazy person, he may listen to the quiet pleadings of a concerned father. Please, Mama, calm down and let me try."

George rarely refers to Julia as Mama, unless he is very serious.

This word together with the earnest tone of his voice provides Julia with some momentary comfort. She is convinced, however, that George's interference will do no good either but she refrains from arguing with him. After all, as he says, he is her father and should make his wishes known to this determined young man. At this point in their relationship, Emma has stars in her eyes and will not listen to either of her parents.

"Please God," Julia prays silently, "make her see that we only want what is best for her. We just want her to be happy because we love her so much. I never realized until recently how strong-willed my daughter is. She is so sweet and genuinely kind, and everyone she meets instantly adores her."

Charles' parents are apparently no exception, and fall under Emma's spell as soon as they meet her. She spends more and more time at the brownstone in Morningside Heights, much to the consternation of her mother.

"Mr. and Mrs. Carney make me feel so special, Mama," she tells Julia each time she returns from visiting Charles' parents.

She especially enjoys having meals there, served by a uniformed maid — an experience heretofore unknown to their teenager daughter. As the days pass, Julia's concern grows, but neither of her parents can convince her to see other boys. Charles Carney has become the center of Emma's world, and she wants no other.

Meanwhile, Julia has so much to do and to think about with running her new business, she has little time to spend arguing with her daughter. They do get to spend some time together, as Emma continues to help her mother out at the shop. She seems to enjoy just being around beautiful new clothes, and likes nothing better than to try on new pieces that arrive weekly. Mother and daughter seem to share a love of fashion, and this at least is a strong bond between them.

And so, the days pass in a flurry of buying, selling and the business of running a salon. In between the business decisions and the many long hours, Julia manages to find time to plan a graduation party for Emma. It will be on a Saturday evening they decide and all her closest high school friends together with a few of Julia's close business associates will be invited. Even Louis and Rene will be included in the invitation list, although Julia is quite sure they will find an excuse not to attend. Julia and Emma plan the menu together and even agree on the decorations. Julia does not mention Charles during the preparations but concentrates on the party planning. She does not want this special time with her daughter to be marred by any discord if she can help it. George does not take part in any of the party decisions, but spends his time in the wine cellar making certain there will be no shortage of wine for the adult guests at least.

# Chapter 34

Saturday arrives before they know it. The graduation party is a big success, by Julia's standards at least. George is a bit overwhelmed by it all but manages to survive by keeping busy. His main concern is keeping the wine carafes filled for the grownups until the end of the evening, as well as the punch bowl for the young people. He also has strict orders from Julia to keep the two liquid refreshments very separate from one another.

Emma spends most of her time with Charles so does not circulate as much as Julia would like, but everyone seems to have a good time. By the time the last guest leaves and Emma says goodnight to Charles, Julia is exhausted but happy. Another milestone in the lives of the Pedesch family has come and gone.

Emma continues her modeling career after graduation just as she planned and loves every minute of it. She finds a job almost at once in a fur warehouse off of Seventh Avenue. Emma is thrilled at the prospect of showing off luxurious coats of mink and sable. The warehouse caters to the fur merchants who stock all the well-known department stores in New York City, as well as the local private salons that cater to the wealthy uptown crowd.

She has made friends with one of the other models at the warehouse, and she and Ginger spend a good deal of time together. Ginger is tall and slender and has long wavy red hair. She has boundless energy and loves to dance more than anything else. She has been teaching Emma some of the latest steps – the

Charleston and the infamous Black Bottom. The latter is a bit shameless for Julia's taste, but seems to be very popular with the youth right now. When Ginger comes to the house, she and Emma put records on the old victrola and start dancing. If Charles happens to be here with one of his college friends, they join in too. It's like having a dance studio in the living room observes Julia. George usually hides in the cellar, but Julia sometimes takes a chair and becomes the enthusiastic audience.

"Now that Charles' father is back at home and they have hired a live-in nurse to help Mrs. Carney, Charles and I will be able to spend time together again," Emma announces one morning. "So to celebrate, Ginger and I are going to double date this weekend, Mama," she adds. "Ginger has a real nice beau, and I'm sure he and Charles will get along famously. He's studying to be a lawyer at Fordham and is real smart."

Ginger, Julia knows, is not a fan of Charles' so it has caused some friction between the two girls. Julia secretly applauds Ginger's taste in young men, and tells her so the next time she comes to the house for dinner. The date takes place as scheduled, but for some strange reason, Emma never mentions the idea of double dating again, at least not with Ginger. Julia hesitates to question Emma about this, and she offers no further information, so Julia leaves the subject alone.

The days pass uneventfully for Emma and Ginger until Emma is offered a job by an old friend of Pierre's who is a fashion photographer. Jacque wants to expand Emma's career into photographic modeling. Emma is very pretty but built like a boy, which is all the rage now in this age of the so-called flapper. Some girls are going to extremes to acquire that boyish look by binding their breasts and wearing bras one size too small. Jacque uses his contacts in the industry and very soon has Emma starring in fashion layouts for magazines like Vogue and Mademoiselle. Under Jacque's tutelage, Emma's career is on the rise, and before long, she is making substantial money on her own.

"A chip off the old block," Jacque teases Julia. "Pierre would be very pleased and proud. He was so fond of Emma and thought of her as the daughter he would never have."

Ginger, however, is not built like Emma and cannot do justice to the fashions of the day with her lusty, robust figure. She continues modeling the fur coats because her figure is not so important underneath yards of mink or silver fox. Eventually, Ginger is discovered by a talent scout and is whisked off to Hollywood to make a screen test. Emma is devastated at losing her best friend. Many tears are shed before Ginger's parting, and even Charles, easily impressed by Hollywood types, seems saddened by this turn of events.

Julia cooks a huge farewell dinner for Emma's best friend, complete with all Ginger's favorite Hungarian dishes. Ginger promises to write and to come and visit when she is a star. This promise does not occur for several years however.. The closest any of them ever get to Ginger in the next year or two is in a movie theatre watching her dance with the likes of Dan Dailey. Ginger, now a honey blond, does manage to send Emma a signed photograph of herself which Emma displays proudly in her bedroom. They correspond for a while, but soon Emma receives only an occasional post card from Hollywood or some exotic location around the world where Ginger is busy shooting a new movie.

The loss of old friendships seem to be commonplace in Julia's family of late. Julia receives a call from Rene a few months after she and Louis are married, telling Julia that she is expecting their first child. Julia is very happy for both of them and tells her so. Rene assures Julia that she will call as soon as the baby arrives, but Julia never hears from her again. She learns later on from a mutual friend that Rene lost the baby in her seventh month. Julia's heart goes out to her and to Louis, and she sends a note of condolence as soon as she hears the news. Rene never favors Julia with an acknowledgement. Julia tries to reach Louis at the salon on several occasions, but is never able to reach him. She leaves messages with Tiny Trudy who is still very polite and kind when she calls, but Louis never responds. Julia hears later on from other mutual friends that he and Rene went on an extended trip abroad. Louis left another close friend, Philippe Renot, to run the House of Chatelaine in his absence. Julia thinks of them often and prays that God will ease the pain of their loss. She remembers well how terrible it is to lose a child, even one that has not even entered this world yet.

Julia is still mourning the loss of her friendship with Louis when she receives a surprise telegram from England. Dr. Francis Kallen is enroute to New York to attend a medical convention and wishes to pay her a visit. As she reads his name on the telegram, all the horror of the sinking of the *Titanic* comes back to her in a rush. She has not thought about her days in the Southampton Hospital for some time now. How good it would be to see her old friend again. Julia hastens to send a return telegram to the ship, letting Dr. Kallen know how very pleased and happy she will be to see him. The second telegram announces that he will be in New York two weeks hence and will come out to Hunts Point as soon as he is settled in his hotel.

"I will call you when I arrive at the hotel," he adds. "I am so looking forward to seeing you after all these years."

George does not seem terribly pleased when Julia tells him about Frank's forthcoming visit. He is still uncomfortable around most people except his Hungarian cronies, mainly because his command of English is still at a minimum. Julia assures him that Dr. Kallen does not stand on ceremony, and that they will get on well together.

"After all," she reminds George, "I might not be here as good as new if it weren't for Dr. Francis Kallen. He was so very kind to me in the hospital and he repaired not only my body, but my mind as well. I was sickened and devastated by the loss of lives on the *Titanic*, George, especially those of the Colonel and Madeleine. Dr. Kallen helped me to cope with my loss. He also helped me book passage to come home to you and the children as quickly as possible. I would never have survived that tragedy without him."

"I understand completely, *Juliashcam*," George answers. "I guess I always felt a little jealous of the good doctor because you held him in such high regard. Please forgive me. I will make him feel like one of the family; I promise you that. Now, when is he coming?"

"He should be in New York in two weeks, George, and will call us when he gets settled in his hotel. May I invite him to come out to the house and perhaps stay overnight once before his convention begins?"

"Why of course, *Juliashcam;* I know you must have a lot to talk about. I will be proud to have him as a guest under our roof. I'll also make sure we have a very special batch of wine for the occasion."

"Thank you, George," Julia answers, "I was sure you would help me make Dr. Kallen feel welcome. I am really looking forward to his visit. I will start preparing some special foods this week, so there will be plenty in case things get really busy at the salon before Frank arrives."

Jerry is also excited at the prospect of meeting Dr. Kallen, who is coming to New York all the way from England. Julia is certain that he will have a million questions to ask him. Emma is taking the news in her stride. She is pleased for her mother, but more interested in her career and her beau than anything else right now.

The two weeks pass quickly, and then the phone rings one warm Sunday afternoon. Frank Kallen's voice is at the other end of the line.

"Julia, is that you; is that really you? It's Frank, Frank Kallen. I'm in New York, and I cannot wait to see you. When may I come?"

"Oh Frank," Julia answers. "It's me, and it's so good to hear your voice. Come out tomorrow if you can. I can't wait to see you either. And plan to stay over, Frank. We have a guest room now, and you are more than welcome. George says so too," she adds hastily.

"That will be perfect, Julia. I'll be there first thing in the morning." Frank hesitates then and adds, "What about your work, Julia? Won't I be interfering with your work?"

"No, Frank, of course not," Julia responds immediately. "The salon can do without me for a day or two. I am not indispensable, you know, even though I am the boss," she adds with a shy giggle. "We are all looking forward to your visit, but me most of all. I will be looking forward to tomorrow. Do you need directions, Frank?"

"No Julia. The concierge at the hotel will provide them. I will take a taxi out to your house, so the driver will certainly know how to get to Hunts Point. Since you told me you are the only house there, I don't foresee any problem. Until tomorrow, my dear Julia."

Julia returns the phone to its cradle and sits down. She can feel herself still smiling at the sound of Frank Kallen's good-humored voice. What a wonderful visit this will be. She stands up and without thinking, glances in the mirror. I am older – much older than the young girl Frank Kallen remembers. Will he still think me pretty, she wonders. Will I recognize him? It has been so many years since we have seen each other. She begins to feel a little panic and rushes upstairs to scan the clothes in her closet. The choice of dress becomes paramount in her mind. There is so much to do before Frank arrives in the morning.

Inevitably the morning comes. Julia prepares breakfast for George and Jerry and gets her son off to school. Emma has an early shoot she reminds her mother, so she grabs her piece of toast from the kitchen table as she scrambles for the door.

"Please try to be on time for dinner, Emma," Julia reminds her. "Dr. Kallen will be here today, and I would like us all to be together at dinner tonight."

"I'll be here, Mama. I promise," says Emma. "I wouldn't disappoint you for the world. I know how much Dr. Kallen's visit means to you. Bye now, I've got to run, but I will see you this evening – in plenty of time for dinner," she adds again.

Frank Kallen arrives at Julia's door about ten o'clock that

morning with a bouquet of flowers in his outstretched hand. When Julia opens the door, they fall into each other's arms like long lost relatives. Time seems to disappear, they are both so genuinely glad to see one another. Frank still has all his hair, but it is sprinkled now with gray, and very becoming Julia thinks to herself.

"You look wonderful, Frank," she says as she holds him away from her. She pretends to peruse him with a serious eye, not unlike that of a doctor.

"Not nearly as wonderful as you look, my dear Julia," he responds, grinning from ear to ear. "You haven't changed a bit except a little rosier in the cheeks than the last time I saw you. New York certainly does agree with you," he concludes.

"Come inside, Frank," Julia insists. "We have so much to catch up on."

She ushers him into the living room and places the small overnight bag he is carrying on the stair landing. Frank places his hands on Julia's shoulders and turns her around. His admiring glance takes in the entire surroundings and comes back to rest on her.

"It appears you have made your dream come true, Julia. You have the wonderful home you always wanted complete with a husband and two fine children, to say nothing of a successful business of your own. God has certainly watched over you just as you always said he would."

"I have been very lucky, Frank, and am so grateful. My only sadness comes when I think of the death of Col. Astor and my dear friend Madeleine. Col. Astor's death was confirmed in all the newspapers, but I have never seen or heard anything more about Madeleine or the baby she was carrying the night the *Titanic* sank. I did read that Madeleine was picked up by the *Carpathia* and transported to Europe, but I have never heard another word since then." Julia pauses and lowers her head as she feels the tears start to come.

"Well now, my dear Julia, I can fill in a few blanks for you that will make you happier I'm sure," interrupts Frank Kallen. Julia raises her head to look him full in the face.

"Madeleine's baby survived, Julia," Frank begins. "She gave birth to a son in August of 1912, and named him John Jacob Astor V. It was in the London papers, and I am surprised that you did not read about it here in New York. The fact is that as long as she did not remarry, Madeleine inherited from the Colonel the income from a five million-dollar trust fund and the use of his Fifth Avenue and Newport homes. During the First World War she relinquished all claim to the Astor fortune to marry William K. Dick. They have two sons, I believe, but are separated at the moment, or so the London scandal sheets would have us believe. Her name has recently been linked with a prize fighter – Enzo Fiermonte, but I have heard nothing more about your old friend recently," Frank concludes.

"I don't know what to say, Frank" Julia stutters in amazement. "I had absolutely no idea about any of this. I must have been so busy with my business and my children that I just didn't keep up with the news. I am so relieved to know that Maddie is alive and that the baby she was carrying survived. I doubt if our paths shall ever cross again, but it is such a relief to know that she survived that dreadful disaster. Thank you so much for filling me in on all the details, Frank. Knowing that Maddie is alive at least has put my mind at rest, and I can stop wondering about her fate from now on. As for the rest of the story, we are so far removed from one another now, Madeleine will be relegated to the memories of my earlier years in this country – a part of my life that is gone forever."

"Now, Frank, let's get on to more pleasant things, beginning with you. I want to know all about you and what has happened in your life since we were last together in England."

"There is really not much to tell, Julia. I'm still a bachelor and affiliated with the Southampton Hospital just as I was when we first met. I've been very involved in research these past few years and have made a few worthwhile discoveries in the field of respiratory disease."

"Then the first thing you are going to lecture me on is the

evils of smoking I'm sure, Dr. Kallen sir," Julia quips with a laugh. "I am still a victim of that evil weed as you used to call it."

"Not to worry, Julia," Frank answers with a smile. "I packed no lectures in my bag when I came to visit you. Part of my reason for being in New York has to do with that evil weed though," Frank admits. "I am to present a paper to the Asthma Foundation on some of my findings. I must admit I am rather proud of my work and the strides we are making to lessen the effects of that dread disease that affects so many children every year. Smoking certainly does not help, my dear, but then you already know that I'm sure. Anyway, enough about me. Tell me all about you and your family."

Julia fills Frank in as much as possible about all the goings-on within the Pedesch family, beginning with her working with Pierre, and later on with Louis, and ending with the purchase of their home and her new fashion salon. She also brings him up to date on Emma and Jerry and Emma's new career as a photographer's model. Julia mentions Charles only briefly in relation to her daughter, but somehow she thinks Frank can read between the lines.

Their visit is an altogether wonderful one, full of nostalgia and good feelings. Emma does indeed make it home on time for dinner, and Jerry does ply Frank with innumerable questions about England. George keeps the wine flowing as promised, and they all spend a wonderful evening together like old friends. Emma seems to be drawn to Frank Kallen and appears most comfortable in his presence. Julia is so pleased because Frank always had that same effect on her as well. Emma show Frank to the guest room, and we all say goodnight.

The whole Pedesch family has breakfast together next morning with Frank Kallen as the guest of honor. Julia prepares a huge breakfast and even Emma sits down and polishes off a plate of bacon, eggs and toast. She is quite animated throughout the meal and really appears sad to say farewell to their guest when it is finally time for her to leave for work. They exchange hugs and

Emma rushes out the door. Jerry shakes Dr. Kallen's hand and hastily follows his sister out the door on his way to school. George stands up then and puts out his hand to Frank Kallen.

"It has been a pleasure to have you in our home," George says most sincerely.

"The pleasure, George, has been mine," responds Frank gallantly. "I have enjoyed every minute I have spent with you and your family, and I will be sorry to leave. Thank you again for letting me be part of your family even for a little while."

With that Frank excuses himself and leaves the table, heading for the guest room. He returns a few minutes later with his overnight bag in one hand and his hat in the other.

"Goodbye, dear Julia, and thank you so much for giving me this wonderful time. I will call you after the conference and before I leave to return to England."

Julia rushes to Frank's side and throws her arms around his neck and plants a kiss on his forehead. "I will miss you, Frank. Let's keep in touch from now on and perhaps we will have an opportunity to see each other again when you attend another conference."

"I sincerely hope so, Julia" Frank Kallen says with a bit of a tear in his eye, "but I will keep in touch, I promise. God bless you all and thank you again."

Julia offers to drive Frank into the city but he insists on taking a taxi. When it arrives she opens the door for him and gives him one more hug. As she closes the door behind her dear old friend, she cannot but wonder if she will ever see Dr. Frank Kallen again. So many of her old and dear friends have become as memories in her life. She realizes, on further reflection, that this is what life is all about though, and she is grateful for the fond memories and looks forward now to the new memories that will be made.

# Chapter 35

More and more Julia's life seems to be slowing down and becoming not only less complicated but more serene. George is content at home now and her business could not be better.

"I am so glad I had the good sense to hire my dear friend and former customer, Annabel Taylor, after she graduated from Parsons," Julia tells George one morning at the breakfast table. "She has become my right hand now, and is very well able to stand in for me when I want to take a day or two off to stay at home and work in the garden or just be by myself. I still love my work, and Annabel and I have been able to expand the original American Chic line far beyond my wildest expectations. She is very talented indeed, George, and she has added a new career line to supplement our original one. This one is directed to young married and working women, with an emphasis on the latter."

"It sounds like she has become indispensable to you, *Juliashcam*," George comments. I am so pleased that her abilities allow you to have a bit more time at home with me and the children. You worked so hard to get us this home, and now you should take time to enjoy it. If Annabel can help make this happen, I am all for it."

Jerry, in the meantime, is realizing his dream of joining the Army. He joins up the day after he graduates from high school. Julia and George have to give their consent because he is only a few months shy of turning eighteen. George and Julia discuss it and finally agree that there is nothing to be served by holding him back. He will only resent them for doing it and may not want to come home even to visit if they disappoint him. And so, with a mixture of fear and love, they give in and Julia signs the military consent form. Jerry is stationed in Texas but still has hopes of going abroad to France. He writes quite often and promises to come home for a visit on his first leave. It is very lonely without him, but at least Emma is still with them, although time spent with her family is less and less these days.

Julia is convinced that she should have seen this calm interlude as an omen of things to come, but until the day Emma bursts into the shop sporting a large diamond solitaire, she was oblivious to what lay ahead.

"Charles has proposed, Mama, and I have accepted," Emma announces excitedly. "We plan to marry in the spring of 1929 when Charles will be fully established with that communications giant he calls AT&T. Charles wants to be sure we have economic security before we set up housekeeping," Emma continues, feeling very important and full of herself.

"Charles has definitely had an effect on her thinking," Julia muses. "Economic security indeed? What young lady of nineteen is worried about economic security?" she rants.

It is apparent to Julia that Charles is influenced by his father who has had a tough time these past few years in an unsteady market. Julia is aware that the attitude of the well-do-do living in Morningside Heights is quite different from families like theirs from the lower Bronx and Hunts Point in particular.

Emma will be twenty in March, and they plan to marry in April. Julia knows that George will be happy for her. All he cares about now, or has ever cared about, is that his beautiful little girl is getting all she wants out of life, including the man of her dreams. He does not seem to be aware that Emma is no longer his innocent little girl, but has become a grown woman now, and with a mind of her own. George, Julia fears, is getting old before his time and very set in his ways. He leaves the entire running of the house and their lives to her. With Jerry gone and Emma seldom at home anymore, Julia feels like she is living alone. She desperately misses Pierre who was her only real confidante, and she still misses Louis and the talks they used to have. Julia has never had time to make women friends, and she regrets that now, but of course, it is too late. She is not yet forty yeas old, and yet she feels like her life is over. She sees other women having lunch together in tiny cafes on Sixth Avenue, and she yearns to join them. Their conversations appear animated, and she wonders what they find to talk about so happily.

Julia looks forward to the rare letters from Jerry and wishes he would come home for a visit. Even Jerry has found time away from the Army to meet a young lady, and his letters are filled now with news of their dates, as well as his military exploits. Julia realizes she cannot spend any more time feeling sorry for herself, and so turns her attention to the demands of running a successful fashion house – American Chic.

In an attempt to add some culture to her life, she begins to frequent museums and galleries on the weekend, as she used to do in London, when living there with Vincent Astor so many years ago. Annabel does not object to being left in charge of the salon on Saturdays and of course, on Sunday the salon is closed. Julia sometimes wishes she had someone to wander the city and visit these places with, but even that is unimportant when she begins to rediscover all the beauty and knowledge in the world around her. She has forgotten how accessible this beauty is in this wondrous City of New York.

Today is Sunday, and while wandering through one of the newest entrants on the museum scene – the Museum of Fashion and Industry, she is shocked to find on exhibition the series of paintings done by Pierre so many years ago on commission from Louis Chatelaine. Julia's face smiles down on her from the huge canvasses, and she finds herself looking self-consciously around the room to see if anyone notices the resemblance. There is no one else in the room just then except one tall gentleman standing in the corner. His back is to her, and he seems to be studying one of the canvasses. She walks a little closer, curious to see which canvass has captured the man's attention. It is the last one in the series – the one of the rider in the *bois,* dressed in the green velvet riding habit. It was always one of her favorites, and it pleases her to see that someone else admires it too. The man turns suddenly, and they stare at each other in total disbelief. Julia thinks she is seeing a ghost, and for a moment, she is afraid she will faint right there in the gallery.

James McFadden is older now but just as handsome as the day they said goodbye on the deck of the *France* enroute to New York. His thick, luxuriant hair is heavily streaked with white and he has a small neat mustache on his tan, rugged face.

"My God, Julia, is it really you?"

James stares at her, incredulous, taking in every detail of her being with his deep violet eyes. She is struck dumb. She cannot manage to speak a word.

James continues. "I only just arrived in New York and had a few hours to kill before a meeting with a client, and so I wandered into the museum. This museum was not here when I last visited the City, so my curiosity motivated me to come in and take a look. The special exhibit was on fashion," he continued, his eyes still locked on the beautiful woman in front of him. "I entered this gallery and there you were looking down at me from some of the most exquisite paintings I have ever seen. I wasn't entirely sure it was you, Julia. But now that I have seen you once again in the flesh, there is no doubt in my mind. It is you, Julia; it truly is."

James pauses to take a breath and then stares at Julia, waiting for some sign of recognition. Julia pulls herself together and turns toward him.

"Yes, James, it is me. This series was commissioned for the House of Chatelaine and painted by a dear, old friend and talented artist, Pierre Manot. I was his model for some time after I returned from England and keeping house for Vincent Astor. So much has happened since, then, James.

But then of course, you know that the Colonel died when the *Titanic* sank in 1912."

Julia realized suddenly that she was babbling like an idiot, trying desperately to keep her wits about her. James, sensing her shock and discomfort, suggests that they sit down on one of the benches at the rear of the gallery. They sit down on a low marble bench. James McFadden takes her hands in his, and once again, as he did so many years before, kisses the tips of her fingers – one by one. Julia inadvertently draws in her breath and pulls her hands away.

"Forgive me, Julia," James says softly. "I didn't mean to offend you. Seeing you here looking so lovely suddenly made all the years just slip away. I have never stopped loving you, dear Julia, and so I got caught up in the moment. Please, please forgive me."

"I do forgive you, James. I really do. It's just that it has been such a shock seeing you again after all these years. I simply was not prepared to ever see you again. I was also shocked to see the paintings because I have not seen them either since I parted company with the House of Chatelaine several years ago. The scene in the *bois* – the one you were studying so intently – was the last one in the series and was Pierre's favorite painting of me. Seeing it again brought back some wonderful memories of my dear, dear friend, Pierre."

"May we go somewhere together and have a coffee or a cup of tea?" asks James. "We have so much to catch up on."

"I guess there's no harm in that James," Julia answers. "There must be a cafe right here in the museum where we can get some refreshment and talk for a bit."

As she answers, Julia heads toward the doorway leading out of the gallery. James follows close behind, and they head down the stairs to the first floor. In the lobby is a sign indicating a café on the premises. Together they walk to where the sign indicates and find a small charming restaurant in a garden at the side of the museum building. James follows Julia in and asks the hostess to give them a table in the corner where they can have a bit of privacy.

"We're old friends meeting after many years," he explains, "so we would appreciate a quiet corner if you please."

The hostess smiles knowingly and leads them to a tiny intimate table in one corner where an apple tree is growing right out over the table. It forms a small bower of its own, and is the perfect place for lovers to meet undetected. James thanks the hostess and they sit down opposite one another. No one speaks for a few minutes and then a waitress arrives to break the silence.

"What would you be wanting?" she queries in a charming Irish accent.

"Sure and I don't know just yet, me girl. We're after looking at the bill of fare a moment if it's all the same to you," James responds.

A wide grin covers the girls face as she studies James.

"Are you after makin' fun of me, Sir, or are you from Galway same as me?"

"No my dear, Galway is not my home, but I have visited there many times and I love the lilt of a real Irish brogue. It is infectious for me – so when I hear it so sweet and pure, it just colors my speech to match your own. Please don't take offence. We'll be after orderin' tea and two wee scones, if you have them," James concludes, grinning all the while with a boyish innocence Julia never perceived in him before.

"It will be my pleasure, sir," the waitress responds, "and no offense taken from yourself in the bargain," she adds and disappears around the corner with her order book in hand.

"You have not changed a bit, James McFadden," Julia ventures. "You're still as charming as ever, especially where the young ladies are concerned."

"The only young lady I ever really wanted to charm was you, Julia," James answers with a strange smile on his handsome face. "I didn't fare too well the last time we were together, so I would like to make up for it now. So, tell me

Julia, what has been going on in your life since we last saw each other on shipboard?"

And so Julia brought James up to date on all the aspects of her life since they said goodbye so many years ago on the *France*. She described her short career as an artist's model and her deep friendship with the artist, Pierre Manot, including his untimely death. Julia explains about Pierre's friend, Louis Chatelaine, and how he encouraged her and ultimately was responsible for her having her own fashion salon. She described Emma and Jerry and the home they had in Hunts Pointe. When she finished, James looked at her with tears in his eyes.

"You have made such a success of your life, Julia. You are to be congratulated. I, on the other hand, have continued on alone. I still take clients out on safari as I did years ago, but I am getting older now, and this very physical activity will have to come to an end soon. My reflexes are not what they once were, and I am beginning to feel the strain of this lifestyle. Unfortunately, if and when I do retire, I will be alone. I never married so I have no family to share my old age with. If only things had been different for us."

His voice trails off, and the wistful look in those still beautiful violet eyes brings a lump to Julia's throat.

"Where will you live if you do retire, James?" she asks in an effort to keep the conversation from becoming maudlin. You must have some family members or close friends you could align yourself with."

"I'm afraid not, Julia. I am an only child and entirely without family at this point in my life. Jack Astor was one of my few close friends, and when he died, I seldom came back to the United States. This is my first trip to New York in almost ten years. With a job like mine, there is little time for making lasting friendships. Don't misunderstand, Julia, I am not sorry about the career choice I made. I have loved every minute of it – the excitement of the hunt, being out of doors all the time, and of course the money. I met many interesting and influential people during my career, and all of them exerted an influence on my life. None of these influential people ever affected me as much as meeting you, Julia my love. You were and still are the love of my life, and I thank the good Lord you take such stock in, for bringing us together once again."

Julia can feel the blush rising to her cheeks, and her heart is pounding in her chest.

"It is truly wonderful to see you again too, James, but you should not say such things to me. I am still a married woman, and with two grown children now as well. I wish with all my heart that we could remain good friends. I do care for you James, truly I do; but more than friends we can never be." Julia cast her eyes down and waits for James to respond.

"We will always be friends, dear heart. Please know that you have nothing to fear from me. It's just that I cannot be around you on an intimate basis, as friends often are, because I love you much more than as a friend. I cannot help it, Julia, you are the only woman I will ever love, and I am not ashamed to tell you that. I will return to Africa shortly. I have a small villa there on the coast where I raise some sugar cane and a little tobacco. That is where I will eventually spend my days, but make no mistake; you will always be in my heart."

Julia flushes again and is determined to change the course of the conversation.

"I think it is time for me to return home to Hunts Point now, James. It has been lovely to see you again. Will you write to me from time to time and let me know how you are doing? You are often in my thoughts, and I would feel so much better knowing that you are well and happy. God bless you, James McFadden, and keep you safe all the days of your life."

Julia stands up, walks toward him slowly and putting her hands on his shoulders, she places a kiss on his forehead. James cannot contain himself. He covers her small hands with his large ones and pulls her close to him. He then releases her one hand and cups her chin gently with the other. Leaning down, he finds her mouth and before she can resist, James McFadden covers her mouth with his and kisses her with all the passion that has been pent up in him all these years. When he finally releases her mouth, he holds her away from him, gripping her shoulders and studies her face long and hard. Julia is breathless and unable to speak. Her body is trembling and she gropes for the chair behind her. James releases his grip on her shoulders and eases her gently into the chair.

"Oh my dear Julia, please, please forgive me," James begs, almost beside himself with passion and remorse. I could not help myself, dearest. I have loved you for so long and love you still, God help me."

Julia looks up at the stricken face of the only man she has ever loved and tears begin to make rivulets on her cheeks.

"I have loved you too, James. Please do not ever forget that. If things were different I would not be leaving you now, but as it is, I have no choice. I am a wife and a mother and must return now to the responsibilities my God has seen fit to give me. At least I will go to my grave knowing what it is to really love a man with all my heart and soul, and this will keep me going. God bless and keep you, James McFadden, wherever you are in the world."

And with those words still on her lips, Julia stands up, turns and goes through the door and down the stairs and out of the museum into the busy street. She does not look back. She is afraid if she does, she will run back into his arms like a schoolgirl and never want to leave them again. It is true – James McFadden is still the love of her life, and now he knows it as well. No man before or since they met ever touched her heart the way James has. Julia is shaking and the tears are streaming down her face as she turns the corner and walks up Madison Avenue to her car.

When she returns home, she goes straight to the bedroom. She opens the top drawer and slides her hand to the back of the drawer. Her fingers find the tiny black box, hidden there for so many years. She takes out the box and sits down on the edge of the double bed. She pulls the silken chord to open it. The contents of the box fall out onto the coverlet, and there in the late afternoon light is the diamond ring – still sparkling the way it did when James first presented it to her in the garden of the Astor mansion. Julia puts the ring on her finger, admiring the brilliance of the stone and falls back on the bed weeping.

"Thank God George is in the cellar and cannot hear me," she whispers to herself. "He would never understand, and I would not hurt him for the world."

The tears finally subside and she sits up on the bed. She takes the beautiful ring from her finger and returns it to the black box. Julia places the box in its hiding place at the back of the dresser drawer, closes the drawer and scans her image in the mirror in front of her. Her eyes are red from crying and her hair is falling out of its neat bun.

"You look a wreck," she says out loud, as if expecting the image to answer.

She hurries into the bathroom to find some face powder and a comb. She doesn't want George to see her looking like this. After a few necessary ablutions, she checks her image again and finds it satisfactory. Julia goes downstairs and into the kitchen to prepare the evening meal for herself and her husband as she has done so many times before.

"Life does go on," she thinks to herself. "I am glad that at least I know what true love really is, and this knowledge will have to sustain me for the rest of my life. I can only pray that both my children will fare better than I and will marry for love. Their happiness is the most important thing to me now."

# Chapter 36

Emma's planned marriage to Charles in the spring of 1929 does not take place. The stock market crashes this year disrupting thousands of lives and rendering many formerly wealthy families destitute. The Carneys do not escape the wrath of this dread economic downturn. Charles' father loses everything when his chemical company becomes a worthless entity, and within weeks of the crash he suffers another stroke and dies. The death of Lawrence Carney leaves Charles not only with some very heavy debts but also with the burden of a spoiled, useless mother who he will have to care for during the remainder of her life. Without Lawrence, Maude Carney has the persona of a lost and lonely child who is incapable of taking care of her affairs or making a decision of any kind. Used to only the best that life has to offer, Maude becomes despondent and unruly when faced with the reality of having to move from her extravagant brownstone environment in Morningside Heights to a much less fashionable neighborhood on the upper East Side.

"She is the consummate prima donna, Mama, but she is Charles' mother after all," Emma declares to Julia one day in a fit of utter frustration. "The woman is impossible. She wants to be the only woman in Charles' life. She does not seem to realize that we will soon be man and wife, and she will have to get along with me. After all, we will be living in a home where I am in charge, not her," Emma adds defiantly.

"Hush, Emma, that is no way to talk about your fiancée's

mother, even if it is the truth," Julia reprimands her. "If you truly love Charles, you will have to learn to accept his mother and show a little tolerance and compassion. After all, Emma, the woman is a widow now and has never in her life had to make do. She is totally unprepared for her new circumstances. Be gentle with her, Emma. It will stand you in good stead with your husband and with your God," Julia concludes.

A country-wide depression ensues that is the direct result of the stock market crash. The "great depression," as it comes to be called, has little effect on their family, for which Julia thanks God. The fashion business is in a slump, to be sure, but enough families survived the crash to be able to continue to support this industry. American Chic fares better than most because their lines are priced much more reasonably than those of the high fashion houses such as Chatelaine. To cut costs to the bone and enable them to survive, Julia is forced to let go a few of her employees – cutters and sewers mainly. Julia herself, together with Annabel and even Emma one day or two a week, man the cutting boards and sewing machines themselves in an effort to continue production. Eduard, who opted to work for Julia when she left Chatelaine, even offers to work for half pay. Customers are few and business is lean, but they manage to remain open.

Julia reads in the newspaper that Louis has closed his salon and moved his family to France. He will live in his father's villa in Province, Julia imagines, and will retire there with his wife and child. Rene did finally produce another child – a daughter, and so they were a real family after all. Julia says a silent prayer for her old friend and wishes them well in their adopted country.

Emma is, of course, upset that her marriage has to be postponed, but rallies nicely when Charles advises that they will be married in April of 1930, as soon as he has his father's debts under control. The rents in New York City are still quite high for a struggling young engineer, but conversely, the depression has driven down the cost of homes in the suburbs. Banks have foreclosed on many homes in areas just outside the city such as

Riverdale and areas of Long Island, and they are currently for sale at less than half their original value. Charles, having a good head for business, decides that they will take advantage of this opportunity and buy a home in Riverdale, which is in the upper Bronx close to the fabled Westchester County where the few remaining millionaires have taken up residence. The decision to buy a home, rather than set up housekeeping in an apartment like most newlyweds, is of course predicated on the fact that Maude Carney will be living with the couple after they are married. It is much easier to find a house with three bedrooms than an apartment with similar accommodations. Charles and Emma agree that they want to have children as soon as possible, so under the circumstances, they must have at least three bedrooms, since his mother will be with them for the foreseeable future. All this having been decided, the wedding is officially set for April 12, 1930.

Emma and Charles have decided to keep the wedding small. Julia and George have no relatives here in America other than Flora, George's sister, and of course, their dear Jerry, who they hope can get leave to be the best man. Julia has already sent word to Flora in Long Island, and she is thrilled at the prospect of Emma's upcoming marriage to 'such a fine young man,' as she likes to call him.

There are only two relatives on Charles' side, and these are the Campbells – his Aunt Molly and Uncle Peter. Molly is Maude's sister and Peter is her husband. They live in a small town in New Jersey called Oradell, just over the George Washington Bridge and have no children. Molly, Emma tells Julia, is very ill with a disease they call Parkinson's and so does not travel very much. Their presence at the wedding will depend on her health at the time it seems. Emma and Charles do have friends they will want to invite, but the number of guests will still be rather small. Julia will contact Mary Ryan from the old neighborhood and Harriet Ober and her family will be anxious to attend as well. Louis, of course, will be absent, but Pierre, Julia knows, will be looking down on them from Heaven on that day. Julia plans to give Annabel Taylor the day off to join in the festivities, and may even close the salon for the day in honor of the occasion.

The wedding will take place at St. Constantine's, although Maude would have preferred a more modern church in her old uptown neighborhood. Julia silently thanks God that the bride's family gets to make these important decisions. Since the wedding will be small, Emma has agreed to have the reception in the small church hall in the basement of St. Constantine. The women of the church will provide the catering, and George will take care of the wine. Emma and Julia plan the menu together and agree to feature all the Hungarian delicacies for which their ancestors are famous. Much to Julia's amazement, Charles, for some reason, seems to be agreeable to anything they want. And so the date is set and the arrangements are made.

Jerry calls from Texas to assure his parents that he can get leave and will be proud to be Charles' best man. The one detail remaining is who will stand up for Emma as her maid of honor. Emma puts in several calls to California in an effort to contact her old friend Ginger, but is unable to reach her thus far. Her disappointment is evident.

"How about asking Anna to be your maid of honor," Julia suggests one morning at breakfast, trying to be as tactful as possible. "She was your best friend all through elementary school, and I am certain she would be thrilled if you ask her."

"I have given that some thought, Mama," Emma assures Julia. "It's just that Ginger and I were so close, and we kind of made a bargain to be there for each other's weddings. I will call again this week, and if I can't reach her by Friday, I will ask Anna to stand up for me."

"That sounds reasonable to me, Emma," Julia agrees. "I hope you can reach her, but if not, Anna will make a beautiful Maid of Honor, and will be thrilled to be asked in the bargain."

As it turns out, Emma is unable to reach Ginger, who apparently is out of town on location shooting a movie. She manages to put aside her obvious disappointment and calls Anna, who is overjoyed at the prospect, just as Julia predicted.

The wedding dress is the next order of business. Emma is adamant. She does not want a long formal gown but rather a white street-length creation that she will be able to wear again if the occasion arises. She asks Julia if they can design the dress together and it can then be created at American Chic. Needless to say, Julia is thrilled with the idea, and they begin to put their heads together at once. Emma and Julia have experienced several differences in their natures over the years, but designing this special dress is not one of them. Julia makes a preliminary sketch and Emma adds and subtracts a few touches. Within a few days they have the perfect design. They are both so excited and pleased by their successful collaboration, and it is the first of many adult bonds to be forged between them.

Julia brings their final design to Eduard who still works for her. They select the fabric and he begins work on the cutting almost immediately. Within a week they have the dress ready for Emma to try on. The final fitting and alterations will take another week, and then all that is left is the veil. On this subject Emma and Julia cannot seem to agree. Julia wants a more traditional type veil, and Emma is determined to wear only a little white hat covered with miniature lilies. In the end Emma wins and even Julia has to admit when Annabel finishes the creation, that it is the perfect compliment to her dress.

And so the fabled wedding takes place on April 12th as planned. Julia wears a long, pale blue chiffon mother-of-the-bride dress that she designed herself and feels quite grand, reminiscent of the old days when she played hostess for John Jacob Astor. George is decked out in his first tuxedo. Jerry had to verbally beat his father into submission to get him to agree to wear it. It is more than a little apparent to all who know George, that he is miserable in his 'monkey suit' as he calls it. Jerry, of course, is elegant in his dress uniform, and looking more proud and happy than Julia has ever seen him. Anna looks lovely in a soft, flowing pink dress that comes just mid calf on her long shapely legs. Jerry can be seen casting sidewise glances at this delightful young beauty. Even Emma is a bit surprised at how her young friend has turned out – a real beauty now at age twenty.

The mother of the groom arrives in a long cream colored lace dress adorned with pearls, better suited to a woman half her age. She is covered in stone martin skins slung carelessly around her rather broad shoulders even though the temperature that April day is in the mid fifties. Her son Charles does not seem to notice the rather elaborate ensemble his mother has chosen. He has eyes only for Emma.

A few minutes before Emma walks down the aisle of St. Constantine, a large black limo pulls up to the church with brakes screeching. A liveried chauffeur gets out and opens the door permitting a stunning redhead, radiant in a green silk dress, to alight. Ginger has made it to the wedding, and what an entrance. Emma looks out the door of the church and sees her dear friend hurrying up the steps. She turns and meets her at the top step, and they hug each other like long lost friends.

"Now everything is perfect," says Emma to her friend. "My best friend is here to see me get married, and I couldn't be more pleased."

"I wouldn't have missed it for the world," says Ginger, wiping the tears that have started to trickle down her well made-up cheeks. "Remember we promised, Em; we would be there for each other's weddings, and here I am. I only got your message a few days ago, but managed to get a flight in time to make the big event. I didn't take the time to call 'cause I thought it would be more fun to surprise you."

"Well, now that you're here, Ginger, we can get this show on the road," laughs Emma. "Get a seat you gorgeous thing, and be sure it's on the bride's side," she adds, "because here comes the bride."

Emma grabs her father's arm and the wedding proceeds as planned. George escorts his daughter down the aisle with tears in his eyes, but his head held high. Emma is taller than her father now, but it makes no difference to George. He stands tall and is the proudest man in the church that day. The priest says the Mass in English, but adds a special blessing for the bride and groom in Hungarian.

The small reception is held in the basement of the church, and the smells emanating from the kitchen are astounding. Every Hungarian delicacy you can think of is being prepared, plus the most amazing wedding cake Julia has ever seen. It is seven layers high and topped with a tiny bride and groom fashioned from confectionery sugar and caramel syrup.

They even have five musicians to entertain the guests and provide music for dancing. This was Louis' surprise gift to Emma. He was so pleased when he received her invitation to the wedding that he offered this gift by way of apology for his lack of attentiveness lately. He flew in from Paris alone to attend the wedding, explaining that Rene was at home recuperating from an illness. Julia does not question him further, but has a feeling that she is recovering from the loss of yet another child. It was such a pleasure to see her old friend again, and she did not hesitate to tell him so, as well as to thank him profusely for his generous and thoughtful gift.

"A wedding must have music, Julia, and it is my extreme pleasure to provide it. Let us dance together, *ma cherie,* for old times sake," says Louis, and for an instant the years they spent apart seem to drop away. They waltz gaily and both of them agree that Pierre is there with them, if only in spirit.

The wedding reception continues until early evening when the last piece of wedding cake is distributed and the bride finally throws her bouquet. Ginger is the lucky recipient and actually blushes at her good fortune. She blows a kiss to the bride and groom as they leave on their short honeymoon to the shores of South Carolina. Maude, meanwhile, is relegated to the care of the Campbells and will remain in New Jersey until the honeymooners return home to Riverdale one week hence.

The young couple set up housekeeping as soon as they return. At the end of the first week Charles drives to New Jersey to bring his mother home. Emma seldom complains now, so the fact that her mother-in-law is living with them never elicits another unkind word from Julia's even-tempered daughter. Maude is a nice enough woman Julia decides, but she is still living in the past – before the crash – and continues to think that she and her son have an inexhaustible supply of money just as they always had when Lawrence was alive. She and Julia get along all right when they have to be in each other's company, which, thank God, is not too often. Julia makes every effort to be pleasant and to overlook her constant complaining and sulking. In many ways Julia realizes Maude is like an overgrown child and is lost without her husband, Lawrence, who doted on her every whim.

"He used to call me his Princess," Maude loves to remind anyone who will listen. Unfortunately, that was how he treated her and she soon came to expect it. Maude came from a rather poor Irish family, but when she married Lawrence Carney when she was twenty and he was forty, all that changed. She was afraid of everything – being alone, thunder and lightening, dark places and germs, among other things. The latter was such a fetish with her that when Charles was a young boy and they spent summers in the Catskills, she would have the milk shipped up there from New York City especially for him. She simply didn't trust the 'country milk' as she called it, and was sure he would be poisoned if he drank it.

Emma confided in Julia later on that Maude has also instilled her fear of thunder and lightening in her son. Whenever a severe storm arises, Charles excuses himself and leaves the room at once, even if he is at the dinner table, and goes to the basement to hide from the storm. Maude can usually be found there with him.

How sad Julia thinks to herself. We are all a product of our own upbringing, and we can only hope and pray that this behavior will have no effect on Emma and any children they bring into the world.

George feels the absence of his children very much and spends each evening now with the wine jug at his feet, drinking himself into a stupor. There seems to be nothing Julia can do to dissuade him from this nightly pursuit, which only changes when either of his children come to visit. Unfortunately, these visits are few and far between these days with Jerry back in Texas and Emma in Riverdale already pregnant with their first child. Despite all Julia's efforts to go to Riverdale and care for her, Emma loses the baby in the sixth month. She is despondent over this loss but manages to pull herself together, ready to try again.

"Our daughter is made of strong stuff, like her mother," Julia reminds George when his concern overwhelms him. "Charles, I am happy to report, is very supportive and puts his grief aside in favor of his wife's resolve," she continues. "I am still not his greatest fan, but I do feel a measure of compassion for this young man, saddled with a dependent mother and now suffering the loss of their first child. We can certainly relate to that experience, George, having lost so many of our own dear babies."

George nods in agreement and is temporarily consumed with mourning the loss of this first grandchild, but soon forgets and reverts to his old habits. He works in the garden a little these days, but spends most of his time in the wine cellar reading his Hungarian newspapers and drinking himself to sleep. Julia keeps busy at work and at home and is content for the most part. She lives mainly for visits from Emma and her new granddaughter.

Joan, born in the spring of 1932, is her pride and joy. The birth, so soon after the miscarriage, is a difficult one for Emma, and the doctor advises her not to plan on any more children. The danger to her is very real, and Julia silently prays that she and Charles will heed this warning.

Emma's recuperation from the birth takes almost a year, but when she is finally able to bring Joan to Hunts Point to visit, George seems to come alive again. Joan is just beginning to stand up and attempt to walk. He takes her tiny hand in his and they walk up and down the driveway until Julia must physically interfere.

"George," she shouts from the kitchen window, "pick her up. Her tiny legs cannot go another step. You will wear out your granddaughter before she is two years old."

George laughs but obeys Julia instantly. He picks Joan up in his strong arms and walks with her into the garden. The little girl coos with delight as her grandfather points out butterflies and the tiny ladybugs that adorn the huge canna and the many other flowers blooming in the garden. They converse in their own special language that none of the rest of the family seem to be able to understand, but it is a joy to behold. In her little baby voice, Joan calls George, Poppy, and he responds with the biggest grin Julia has ever seen. Their new granddaughter has changed George forever, and Julia thanks God for it. Each time Emma brings Joan to visit, she calls George before she gets to the top step.

"Come Poppy, come and chase *bubberflies* with me," she shouts at the top of her tiny voice. This chubby three-year old is the only one who can dislodge George from his basement hideaway now. When he hears her tiny voice call his name, he forgets about the Hungarian newspapers and his winemaking and bounds up the cellar stairs like a young man rushing to meet his sweetheart. Even Emma cannot elicit this kind of reaction from her father these days. Little *Jonushcam* has become his reason for living.

A new tradition has begun of late. Whenever Emma and Joan come now, George always initiates a picnic in their honor. These are not the huge gatherings they used to have when Emma was little, but perhaps a half dozen of his cronies with their wives, children and grandchildren. George manages to gather them all together and convinces them to provide all the Hungarian foods that they enjoy so much. George, of course, agrees to provide the homemade wine, dig the pit, build the fire and generally supervise the cooking that will take place. He urges Julia to make several of their favorite desserts, and she complies without hesitation.

Emma helps Julia in this preparation, and it is a good way for her to learn some of their cooking traditions. The how-tos of Hungarian cooking are all in Julia's head so Emma has to learn by watching and taking part in the effort.

George is determined to give their granddaughter as much of the old-country heritage as he can. He personally skewers Joan's chunk of bread and helps her catch the drippings from the savory roasting *szalonnaval* being cooked by the grownups. Joan gallops around the circle of adults with her stick waving in her hand.

"Me some, me some," shouts the tiny child gleefully.

Joan adores her grandpa from the first time she sets her big hazel eyes on him, and it is obvious that the feeling is mutual. Not since Emma was a very little girl can Julia remember seeing George as happy as he is when his granddaughter is with him. It is as if she has given him a new reason to live.

Without mentioning it to Emma, Julia is teaching her granddaughter to speak Hungarian. By the time Joan is approaching five, she already takes to the strange-sounding words very easily. Emma leaves Joan with her grandmother for a week or two each summer now, and Julia treasures this precious time like no other. She takes time off from the salon and devotes herself totally to her granddaughter. Joan seems to enjoy the learning – like a game of identifying the various items in the kitchen and around the house. Julia spends hours telling her stories of the old days too, as she sits in rapt attention on her grandmother's lap in the big rocking chair in the kitchen. As Joan gets older, Julia speaks to her of the way it was when her grandpa and she first came to this country. Eventually, as she get older and Julia thinks she will understand, she vows she will tell her about Hungary and how she met and married her grandfather.

Emma accuses Julia of trying to make a gypsy out of this beautiful blond cherub. Her answer is always the same. "We have a special bond, Joan and I, and when I hear that baby voice call out *'edeal Grandmama,'* I know my life has had a purpose."

# Chapter 37

Life continues in a comparatively peaceful pattern for the next few years until early November, 1936 when Emma becomes pregnant again. Charles is upset with her and does not hesitate to say so. The doctor made it quite clear after Joan's birth that Emma should put thoughts of another baby out of her mind. Emma, it appears, had other ideas.

"I don't want Joan to be an only child," Emma insists. "If God did not want me to become pregnant, Mama, he wouldn't have allowed it. You're always telling me that He knows best, so why should I question him now?"

"All right, Emma, there is no point in arguing about it now. You must promise me though that you will take it very easy and will not overtire yourself," Julia tells her daughter. Charles is already frantic about the prospect of your harming yourself. Please, please say that you will take it very easy until the baby is born. You can spend more time with Joan — reading to her and playing quiet games. Rest assured, I will be watching you like a hawk and will be in Riverdale to help you as often as I can."

"Enough lecturing, Mama," Emma retorts. "Do you and Charles really think I would do anything to endanger myself or the baby. I will be very careful, I promise. Besides, Maude is here to help me too. I think you all discount her and the help she can provide. She loves Joan too, you know, and will be happy, I know, to amuse her from time to time so that I can get some extra rest."

Julia refrains from further comment, knowing she will have to trust her daughter's own good judgment. And so the next six and a half months come and go with Julia suffering only mildly from motherly angst. Emma does indeed take it easy, and Maude actually is a help, just as Emma predicted she would be. Julia silently thanks the Lord for getting them through these first six months of Emma's pregnancy without any major problems. This, however, was to be the calm before the storm.

At the beginning of her seventh month, Emma gets a little anxious about having enough room for the new baby in the room which she and Charles share. She begins setting up the bassinet she had used for Joan and laundering all the baby clothes and blankets that had been so lovingly put away. Emma does not bother to voice her intentions to her mother or her mother-in-law, but proceeds to do all this work on her own. By the time Julia is aware of what Emma is doing, it is too late. Emma collapses after dragging the bassinet from the living room where Charles had left it, after bringing it down from the attic the day before. Emma's impatience is almost her undoing. Fortunately, Maude had presence of mind enough to call the doctor who sent for an ambulance and then to call Julia at the salon.

Julia leaves Annabel in charge and drives straight to the hospital just in time to see the ambulance arrive with Emma. They rush her inside and straight up to the maternity wing. Julia sees Dr. Kramer running down the hall as they put the stretcher into the elevator.

"Don't worry, Julia, I'm sure Emma will be fine. The baby just seems to be in a hurry to be born. I'll come get you as soon as I know what's happening. Please wait in the lounge, and I'll come for you there."

Dr. Kramer dashes for the elevator, and Julia remains staring at the closed door, feeling the tears starting to trickle down her cheeks. It seems like hours later when the elevator finally disgorges Dr. Kramer. He comes into the lounge and heads straight

for where Julia is sitting. His brow is covered with sweat, and he
is still in his scrubs.

"It's a boy, Julia," is his first statement. He pauses and then
adds, "he's very tiny – only three pounds, but with a lot of care,
I think he'll make it. Emma is very weak, but she survived the
Caesarian quite well, all things considered. She'll need a lot of
help for several months, and it will take some time to get her
strength back. She's pretty anemic right now, Julia, so we will
have to help her build up her blood. But she's basically strong,
and has a great attitude. She will overcome this; I am certain of
that," says Dr. Kramer confidently. "I have told her already that
this must be the last baby," Dr. Kramer adds. "She could never
survive another pregnancy, and I thinks she believes that now."

Tears of relief come then and Julia is unable to stop them.
Martin Kramer takes her gently into his strong arms and lets her
sob until there are no tears left.

"I am so relieved, Martin," Julia is finally able to say. "I was
so frightened that we might lose her and the baby. By the way,
has she given him a name yet?"

"They are calling him Charles," Dr. Kramer answers.
"Apparently there was no question about that if it was a boy.
Emma and her husband made that very clear when we first
determined she was pregnant. I guess he'll be a junior after his
father." Dr. Kramer flashes Julia a knowing smile. "I have to go
back upstairs now, Julia, but please don't worry. You can see
Emma first thing in the morning. She will be in recovery for the
next several hours and cannot have visitors while she is still in
intensive care. Emma and the baby will remain here for at least a
week, and then I believe Emma can go home. We'll have to wait
and see about Junior," he adds and heads for the elevator once
more. "See you in the morning, Julia, and congratulations on
your new grandson."

Julia hurries to the phone to call Maude who is at home with
Joan waiting anxiously to hear from her. "It's a boy, Maude, and
both Emma and the baby are doing well. I will come to your

house from the hospital as soon as I have talked to George. See you in awhile."

Julia hangs up the phone and dials George at home. The phone rings four or five times before George's slurred voice answers.

"Hullo," Julia hears him say.

She can tell he has been drinking. "George, it's me. Emma has had a baby boy, and they are both alright. I'm still at the hospital but am on my way to Emma's house to talk to little Joan and Maude. I will be home in an hour or so. Don't worry, everyone is fine," she adds.

"A boy?" comes the voice from the other end. "We have a grandson, *Juliashcam*. I am so happy. Are you sure Emma is all right? I was so afraid when Annabel called to tell me you had gone to the hospital. Please tell me Emma will be all right, please *Juliashcam*, please," he pleads.

"Don't worry, George. I promise you, Emma is fine and she will be home in about a week. I will take you to see her tomorrow. I must go now. Joan and Maude are waiting, but I will be home soon." Julia hangs up the phone and hurries to her car.

The next few weeks are a nightmare. Emma has to stay in the hospital a bit longer than Dr. Kramer anticipated, but she does finally come home at the end of two weeks. Charles, Jr. remains at the hospital in intensive care for the first full month of his life. At the end of that time, Martin Kramer announces that the hospital cannot care for this tiny baby as well as his parents can, and he suggests that Emma and Charles bring the baby home to care for him themselves. The decision to do this involves many qualifications. The room where the baby will reside has to be kept at ninety-three degrees all the time. This precludes Emma and Charles from keeping him in the same room with them, as Emma originally planned to do. No one but Emma and Charles and the doctor will be permitted to go in or out for several months until it is pronounced safe by Dr. Kramer. The danger from respiratory infection is still very great.

Poor little Joan, barely five years old, does not believe she has a brother, because she is not allowed to see him until he is almost seven months old. Even Julia, his maternal grandmother, cannot visit her grandson. All she can do is pray and make her daughter's work load as easy as possible so that all her energies can go toward taking care of her son. Maude, too, is not permitted entrance to the baby's room. She resents this bitterly until she realizes that Julia is also barred from Charles, Jr.'s room. She spends her time knitting little garments and playing games with Joan. She even takes Joan to the playground occasionally when the weather gets a bit cooler. Joan is starting school this year and is very excited about the prospect of going to Kindergarten.

"I can take my brother to school for 'show and tell,'" she announces excitedly one morning.

Julia does not bother to explain why this is an impossibility. Joan begins school in mid September, and Charles Jr.'s inner sanctum is finally opened to the public – or at least his immediate family – on October 1st. Joan is beside herself with joy at the prospect of being able to finally see her own little brother.

"I really do have a brother, I do, I do," she shouts on the first day she is permitted to enter the sacred room. "I knew he wouldn't hide from me forever, I just knew it," she shrieks with childish glee. "oh Mommy, he's so tiny and wonderful. Can I hold him, can I, can I?"

"All right, Joan, but you must sit down in the chair and be very still while I put him in your arms," says Emma gently. "No sudden moves, dear, you don't want to frighten him," Emma warns as she places the tiny infant in the arms of her small daughter.

The tiny infant opens his eyes wide and inspects his sister with open curiosity. Joan grins down at him, and he responds in kind. The little face lights up with a grin from ear to ear and a little baby giggle emanates from the tiny rosebud mouth. Joan is entranced and from then on she designates herself as her brother's special guardian angel. It is love at first sight between the two young siblings, and Emma is more than a little pleased. She did not know what to expect at this first meeting – jealousy, resentment, apathy? Anything was possible considering the length of time these two little beings had been kept apart. It was instantly apparent, however, that Charles had won his sister's heart with one tiny giggle. From that day on, Joan stood guard over her tiny brother. His crib is her first stop each day when she arrives home from school.

"Joan sits herself down next to his crib and tells Charles all about her day, Mama. It is a joy to behold," Emma tells Julia on the phone. "I have never seen such devotion between brother and sister. I loved my brother, Jerry, but we never had a relationship like these two. It's really special, Mama."

The bond between her grandchildren grows by leaps and bounds, and the sight of this childlike devotion is a constant joy to Julia. Before long young Charles is released from his confinement and joins Emma in her room which they will share for the next few years. Charles is never as happy as when his sister returns from school each day and resumes her position as his guardian and favorite playmate. And so the days pass in peaceful contentment once again. Emma is resigned to not having any more children and is gaining back her strength a little each day. Charles is gaining stature at AT&T, and even Maude has settled in somewhat to her new and less extravagant existence. The Carney household seems to be in a state of well-deserved peace.

Emma continues to send Joan to Hunts Point for a week or two each summer, and Julia cherishes these special times with her granddaughter. She is so full of questions about the 'old country.' Eventually as she gets older, Julia is able to tell her more and more of the details of her early life and how she came to meet and marry her grandfather and come to the United States.

Even at a young age, it is evident that Joan is interested in her grandmother's past, and Julia keeps reminding her to listen carefully and always to remember. Perhaps one day, Julia muses, she will be telling my story to her children. Meanwhile, Emma comes often to visit her parents in Hunts Point and brings the baby with her. George delights in his grandson and is already talking about the day when he can attend his first Hungarian picnic. Emma laughs out loud when she hears this.

"That time will be here before we know it, Papa," she says lovingly. "I want both our children to experience the special joys that only you and Mama can provide. Jerry and I have such wonderful childhood memories, and I want my children to have them too."

George beams at his daughter and opens his arms to give her one of his famous bear hugs. They hug each other soundly, and for a moment Julia forgets that Emma is a grown woman with two children of her own. She sees only the beautiful little girl with the blond curls caught in the embrace of her doting father. A knock on the door brings Julia abruptly back to reality.

"Well it looks like the gangs all here," shouts the tall, handsome soldier standing in the open doorway.

"Oh, Jerry, is it really you?" Julia rushes to hug her son, and he gathers her up in his embrace and lifts her right off the floor.

"Yes, Mama, it's really me," he answers as he sets his mother back on her feet while grinning from ear to ear. "And I've brought someone to meet you, Mama," he adds with a more serious note in his voice. "Come here, Rose, and meet your new mother-in-law."

A tall, thin, olive skinned girl with long black wavy hair enters the room. She walks in slowly, her eyes furtively glancing around the room from one person to the next. She stops next to Jerry and grabs his arm, as if for support.

"Mama, I would like you to meet Rose, my wife. We were married yesterday in Austin and took the first plane to New York so we could tell you the good news. I had no idea that Emma and the kids would be here too, but it makes it all that much better," Jerry goes on. He covers Rose's hand with his own big one and turns toward his father who is standing silent and appears stunned.

"Papa, this is Rose," Jerry says. "This is your new daughter-in-law. We are married, Papa, and I brought my wife home to meet the family. What do you have to say about that?" Jerry takes a step back and waits for his father to speak.

"Hello, Rose," is all George can muster at the moment. He just stands there in a complete state of shock.

Emma rushes over to her brother and proceeds to hug him and then turns to her new sister-in-law and says, "welcome to the family, Rose."

Her greeting is so warm and genuine that it suddenly makes everything all right, and before they know what is happening, everyone is hugging everyone else and they are all laughing and crying at the same time. Rose is officially indoctrinated into the Pedesch family.

"I knew you would all love each other; I just knew it," Jerry says with real emotion in his voice. "It's so good to be home with all of you. I never realized how much I missed you all. And the kids – why Joan has grown so much since I saw her last, and now I have a nephew as well as a niece. Boy, am I getting up in the world. I guess Rose and I will have to get busy and provide these kids with some cousins to play with, huh, Emma?"

"Whoa there brother; give your new bride a break, will you," quips Emma with a smile. Rose, meanwhile, is flushed with embarrassment, and Emma rushes over to her and gives her a reassuring hug.

"Don't mind this big lug, Rose. He never did have much tact, and I guess the Army wasn't able to teach him any either." Rose looks at Emma gratefully and lowers her eyes to the floor.

"Come on everyone, let's sit down and have something to eat," Julia interjects and strides into the kitchen. Everyone follows her into the big country kitchen and they all take chairs and settle around the big oak table. Julia opens the refrigerator door and starts emptying its contents onto the adjacent counter.

"Now I really know I am home, Rose," Jerry declares. "Mama is getting ready to feed us in style. Boy, I sure have missed your cooking, Mama. The Army food gets real pitiful real fast, especially when you're used to good ole Hungarian goulash and stuff like that. No one could ever cook as good as you, Mama," and then realizing how this sounds, he turns to Rose. "But you do make the best spaghetti and meatballs, Rose. I swear you do."

Rose looks up at her new husband and smiles. "You don't have to say that Jerry. I know what a great cook your mother is. I hope maybe she will teach me how to cook the things you like so much."

"I most certainly will, Rose, and it's so nice that you want me to. Now tell me how long will you be here in New York, and will you be staying with us?"

"We only have a few days for a honeymoon, Mama, and then I have to be back at the base to start a new training program. I booked us a hotel room in the City so I can show Rose something of New York. She's never been here before and I want her to see a show and go to a dance hall before we go back to Texas. We'll come see you again the day before we leave, and maybe you'll make me some of your famous stuffed cabbage. I sure do miss your cooking, Mama."

"That's a date son," Julia answers. "Meanwhile let's get you all fed now, and then we can have some of your father's wine, and you can tell us all about what you're doing in the Army and how you met Rose."

The evening is a great success and when Jerry and Rose finally leave to go into the City, Julia is suddenly aware that another era has begun in their lives. Emma left much earlier because she had the two little ones to bed down at home, but it was evident that she was thrilled to see her baby brother again after so long an absence. She seemed pleased about the marriage to, and Julia hopes that she and Rose will eventually become friends as well as sisters-in-law.

Things are changing so rapidly in their family, and Julia is beginning to think more and more about giving up her work at the salon. Maybe when Jerry gets out of the Army, he and Rose may want to live with us until they find a home of their own, she thinks to herself. We would have to move, of course, The house in Hunts Point could never contain two families, even for a short while. And suppose Rose gets pregnant, Julia wonders. That would make it even more difficult. They would just have to move. But what about George? Even suggesting such a move to George seems out of the question right now. Oh well, thinks Julia, I am jumping ahead of myself to be sure, but it never hurts to plan ahead.

As Julia gets down on her knees at the side of the bed this night, she asks God to help her sort this all out and to guide her in doing what will be best for all concerned. She cannot imagine not working at all. She has worked all her life. What would she do with herself all day? There are so many questions to be answered, so many decisions to be made. Julia tries to turn her mind off and pushes her head further into the pillow, but it takes awhile for sleep to come to her. All will be resolved in God's good time is the last thought in her mind as she drifts off into oblivion.

# Epilogue

The year is now 1963, a memorable one for many reasons. The Pedesch family is now living in a modest two-family house in a small suburb of New Jersey.

Jerry and Rose came to live with them when Jerry gave up his career in the Army and retired in the spring of 1940. They had their first son that year which helped Jerry make this decision. He determined that it would be better for them to say goodbye to the Army and settle down on the East Coast.

"I've seen enough of those Army brats," Julia can recall him saying. "I don't want my son to be one of them, Mama," he concluded, and Julia did not disagree. And so, Rose and Jerry and their young son, George, came to live with Julia and George in New Jersey. Jerry and Julia went house hunting, and were successful in finding what they considered to be the perfect house for two families. They all moved in together in 1941 and Jerry found a job almost immediately working for the local New Jersey utility company. In 1943 their second son, Eugene, was born. The new house was filling up rapidly.

Julia makes the decision to sell American Chic before they make the move to another state. She offers it to her dear friend and assistant, Annabel Taylor, who accepts the offer immediately. Julia knows that Annabel is well equipped to take over for her and that American Chic will continue to thrive under her tutelage. Julia promises to keep in touch and the deal is consummated.

Time passes more or less uneventfully for the next few years.

Julia sometimes misses the excitement of the business world and her involvement with the fashions of the day, but she is learning to be content with her home and her garden as her main focus now. She still keeps her hand in, sewing tiny outfits for her four grandchildren.

"I confess I am beginning to feel my seventy years," she admits to her granddaughter, Joan, one afternoon during a visit. "My lungs are beginning to give out, and I do not even enjoy my cigarettes any more. I feel very much alone right now, Joan, and somewhat abandoned, even by my God." Tears form and begin to run down the elderly face, thinner but still beautiful, her granddaughter notes with sadness.

"Jerry died eight months ago – killed in a freak automobile accident. My beautiful Emma is gone too, taken away two months ago by that dread killer of women, breast cancer."

Joan sits quietly at her grandmother's bedside while Julia's monologue continues.

"George still drinks his wine each night, and provides little company for me. Rose is still with us, and we manage to provide a bit of company for each other. Her sons have moved away now, but keep in touch with us on an irregular basis."

"I look forward to visits from you, Joan, and occasionally your brother, Charles, but the days pass slowly. I spend most of my time lost in reverie about the past. Sometimes I think back to the Astors and to my dear James. I wonder how Madeleine is and if her life was a rewarding one. I think often of Louis and dear, dear Pierre, and I wonder where it all went. My memories are so precious to me, and I hold onto them with more tenacity each passing year."

Joan is a married woman herself now with four beautiful children. She comes to visit as often as she can, but it is a long ride from Westchester County in New York to New Jersey. Her children are young and close in age. The last one, her only boy, is just an infant. Brett was born while Emma lay dying in the hospital, so she never got to see her only grandson. Charles, Jr.

is still single and living in Emma's old house with his father. The situation there is rather grim, Joan tells her grandmother, as the two men do not get along very well without Emma there to referee.

Joan is thoughtful like her mother and calls often. Increasingly when they speak, Julia finds herself drifting back into thoughts of the old days when she was a youngster herself. Though her visits now are few and far between, Joan and Julia make the most of each one. That special bond still exists between the two women which makes Emma's death somewhat easier to bear for both of them. No one sees Joan's suffering as her grandmother does. She loved her mother more than anyone else in her life.

Joan arrives before lunch one morning, and Julia asks George to leave them alone for a little while. He is disappointed but shuffles off back to his newspapers in the basement. Julia tells Joan that she knows that God will be calling her soon, and Joan seems to understand.

"I have a request to make of you, my dear granddaughter," Julia murmurs softly. "I want you to write the story of my life after I am gone. You have a way with words – you always did even as a child. I want my story to live on, Joan, if only to prove a woman can do anything she really wants to do in this wonderful country. Promise me that you will do this for me, please."

"I will do my very best, Grandma," Joan answers, a bit taken aback, "but I am not sure I am up to the task. It may take me some time to complete this labor of love, with four children to care for, but rest assured that eventually it will be done. This much I can promise you."

Joan kisses Julia tenderly and they hug each other close as if to seal the bargain

"It is like having my dear Emma back with me for a few moments," Julia whispers. "Thank you for your promise, Joan, and now I want to give you something. Go into my top dresser drawer. In the back is a small black box. Bring it to me, please."

Joan retrieves the velvet box, secluded there so long ago. Julia opens it and takes out the beautiful diamond ring nestled in its satin folds. Joan's eyes open wide as they rest on the shiny object in her grandmother's hand. A gasp comes from her mouth, and she looks at Julia with great anticipation.

"Oh Grandma, did Grandpa give you that ring after you were married? Joan asks. "I have never seen you wear it. It is so beautiful. Why did you hide it away all these years?"

Julia returns the ring to its box and turns to her granddaughter.

"This ring, my dear Joan, is the key to the one story I never told you. It was given to me by the only man I ever truly loved and has spent its entire life in this little black box hidden away in the recesses of this old dresser drawer."

Joan starts to interrupt, but Julia continues.

"Over the years I have admitted to you many times that, although I love your grandfather, I was never 'in love' with him. I am not sure if you ever believed me, my dear, but now I think perhaps you will. I want to tell you the story of this ring, and then I want you to take it with you. Keep it in a safe place and some day give it to your new son when he finds the girl of his dreams."

Joan joins her grandmother on the bed, She curls up at the foot as she has done so often as a young girl. Julia leans back against her pillows and proceeds to tell Joan about James McFadden. When she finishes there is a companionable silence between them. Then Joan leans toward Julia and smiles. She takes her hands in hers.

"What a beautiful story, Grandma. I'm so glad you shared it with me. Now I know that you were able to experience real, true love in your life. So many women do not, and I often wonder if I ever will."

Before Julia can ask her granddaughter what she means by that, Joan continues.

"Your story reminds me of a line from a favorite poem I read a long time ago, Grandma."

*"One can find women who have*
*never had one love affair,*
*but it is rare to find*
*any who have had only one."*

. . . . . Francois Duc de La Rochefoucauld (1613-80),
a French writer and moralist

# Fini